Knight of Rome Part I

By

Malcolm Davies

Chapter 1

Mid-morning on the twenty-eighth day of September in the fourteenth year of the reign of the Emperor Augustus, former centurion Justus Cordius strode alongside the second of the train of four wagons he commanded. Each wagon was loaded with goods to trade in the city of Augusta Treverorum on the Mosel River close to its junction with the Rhine. In its short existence, the city had become a bustling centre of commerce where the peoples of both sides of the brooding border rivers came together in an uneasy peace to make money. Justus was fifty years old, the same age as his Emperor. He was a wide-shouldered man of average height for a Roman with a full head of black hair showing no sign of going grey. Upright and active, he still had enough teeth left to chew his way through a slice of dry smoked meat.

There were fifteen companions with him, all veterans of the legions. Thirteen of them had completed their full service and received their reward in the form of land grants in Gallia Lugdunensis, to the south. With the land came a cash payment to help every man to begin his new civilian life. The remaining two had been less fortunate. Both had been discharged early as unfit to serve. One had lost the fingers of his left hand to an axe blow and could no longer hold his shield in the ranks. The other had been hit in the side of the head with a lance which destroyed both his right eye and his hearing on that side. They had gravitated towards Justus when they learned of his retirement and he had willingly taken them in; a man has a duty to help old comrades who have fallen on hard times.

Justus Cordius had led the fifth century of his legion. He had not been a distinguished soldier who acquired great wealth but he had been solid, reliable and unflinching in battle; the sort of officer who was generally said to be "the backbone of the army".

He had one characteristic in common with all his companions; he loathed farming. Their home had been the army and their trade had been war for the best part of their lives. Outside of a framework of rank and discipline, alone in a ploughed field hoping that the crop they had planted in badly ploughed furrows of unequal depth would amount to anything, they were lost and miserable. Their district boasted only one tavern on the Roman road that cut through it, and there they had gravitated to drown their sorrows. The idea of setting up a trading company had developed out of their shared complaint about their lot in life; that nothing could be worse than being a farmer. It was now four years since they had clubbed together for their first ramshackle cart with its two high wheels and pair of ancient mules. They had prospered. Now their lands were rented out or run by slaves and each year they made six profitable journeys to Gallia Narbonensis, even further south than their homes, where they bought knives, scissors, axe-heads and saws together with wine and luxuries. They then hauled their stock to the borderlands to sell as far north and east as Raetia, beyond even Upper Germany.

Justus sniffed the air. It carried a faint hint of the wet decay of the coming autumn. Beneath his boots the track was still firm but bore a light scattering of early fallen leaves and pine needles. This would have to be their last trip of the year. Soon the hours of daylight would dwindle and heavy winter rains followed by snow borne on bitter east winds would make it impossible to travel using wheeled transport. Those despised farmsteads they called their homes would be welcome enough then. But today the weather was mild. Although the leaves of the broad birch and oak were more yellow than green now, the air was pleasantly warmed by the sun that shone through a faint haze of high cloud. It was often like this in late September where the Belgic lands met Upper Germany. As if summer was unwilling to leave, it gave ten or so days of its July heat as a last blessing before the seasons finally turned.

They had used this route several times before. The going was not the best but the track was fairly straight, giving a good view ahead and the forest had been cleared back twenty paces on either side. The first wagon drew level with a place where two trees had fallen in a winter gale some years ago. They were rotten now; their broken and tangled branches overgrown with alder and brambles. Somewhere a cuckoo called. The sound was grating in Justus' mind. He had a sudden intuition that something was wrong. Without hesitation he pulled a bone whistle on a thong from the neck of his tunic, put it to his lips and gave one shrill blast. With rapid but sure movements he reached under the wagon bed beside him and withdrew a shield and a short sword from the carrying rack. Only when his shield was on his left arm and the sword held firmly in his right hand did he look about. All his men were leaping from their positions high on top of the wagons or striding closer alongside arming themselves with practised ease.

Two bearded men, one with flaming red hair, had leapt over the fallen trees and up onto the lead wagon where one of them clubbed at the driver's shining bald head while the other thrust with a spear. The three Romans who had been with him ran back without a second glance at their assailed comrade; they could do nothing for him. Two were holding shields and swords. The third scrambled past Justus and dragged a bow and quiver of arrows from under the now vacant driving bench of the second wagon and shot at the triumphant attackers who were dragging the corpse of their victim to the ground. Two knots of warriors were running towards them from both sides. They were heading for the gap between the back of the second wagon and the mules hauling the third.

It was a well-planned ambush. The tactic had clearly been to immobilise the column and then divide it in two, allowing them to slaughter the shocked defenders who would undoubtedly be panicked at the sudden onrush. They had done their reconnaissance well enough. Although they would be taking on a large party, it was composed of middle-aged men. Some were balding, some carried too much belly;

one of them lacked an eye and the other a hand. It should have been easy.

Justus looked left and right. He understood their intentions instantly. He gave two repeated short blasts on the whistle clenched between his teeth. The Romans responded. They formed two ranks facing each other across the narrow gap. The impetus of the raiders' wild charge was too strong for them to be able to stop and reassess the situation. The first of them were forced into space dividing the Roman shield walls by the pressure of the warriors running behind them. Short swords began to flicker out from between the Roman shields stabbing at whatever part of an opponent was in reach. The one-eyed man had turned his bow on their stragglers and even the man with the missing hand was using the crook of his left elbow and forearm as a support while he lunged at them with a spear clenched in his good right hand.

The raiders forgot the chance of plunder and fought desperately for their lives. One of them thrust a lance at Justus, lowering the point of aim at the very last moment to strike at his unprotected knee but the ex-centurion had expected the move. He pulled his leg back and smashed downwards with his shield snapping off the lance blade. Then, confident he would be protected by his comrades on either side; he took half a step forward and slashed at the wooden shaft. More by good luck than judgement he sliced through his opponent's leading fist. The man howled and dropped the weapon. He held up his arm, staring in amazement at the ruin that had been his hand, now a stump with a flapping thumb gouting blood. He half turned as if to show it to his companion who was distracted at the sight and took a sword deep into the belly.

They began to back off, still facing the Romans and threatening them with spear points and axes as they retreated into the trees. One was quicker witted than the others. He sprinted to the head of the column, leaped up and whipped the lead mules off down the track. They broke into a canter, glad to be dashing away from the howling men and the smell of blood. As quickly as it had begun, the skirmish was over.

The defenders relaxed and watched philosophically as one quarter of their stock vanished along the track. They had learned the hard way to divide their goods evenly between the available wagons to make sure each load was more or less of equal value. Justus did not have to order them not to run after it. They knew better than to try.

"Fucking Germans," one of them spat out.

His comrade sighed.

"You always say that. How do you know they were Germans? Could be Belgae, could be Nervii, could be all sorts of savages out here."

"Look at the size of 'em," the first one said, "fucking Germans."

Apart from their own man who had been dragged to the ground and butchered, there were three corpses lying on the bloody trackside and one man coughing and spluttering gouts of blood with a gaping hole through his ribs. Justus stamped on his throat. The snapping bones crunched crisply and he was still.

"See what they've got on them," he said.

They had all been big men, taller than the Romans by a full head in some cases. They were dressed in a mixture of dressed animal skins and coarse wool, unarmoured and poorly equipped. Their axe heads and spear points were small and the best weapon they possessed was a pugio; an old legionary dagger. One of them had a bronze helmet and two silver arm bracelets. Another's face was tattooed with writhing serpents.

Neither Justus nor his men were triumphant. This had been one more fight in the many they had survived, either in full-scale battle or attempted robberies on the road. They had lost a comrade, which was to be regretted but other than that, it was something to shrug off as all part of the day's work. They squatted in a loose ring a little away from the blood-slicked ground and took their midday break early. A wineskin was passed around. They tore at hunks of coarse bread they had baked that morning with slices of cold bacon. Some had to pour a little wine over their crusts to soften them before they mashed them up in their almost toothless mouths and cut their bacon into small pieces to be able to swallow their food. After ten minutes, Justus spoke.

"The thing is lads, I don't fancy keeping on this track. There may be more of them up ahead and that might make 'em start feeling brave enough to have another go …"

"Maybe they're part of a big force that's crossed the river to plunder the whole area," one of his men interrupted.

By the "river" he meant the Rhine. It was the Rhine that preoccupied them all; that watery barrier beyond which the giant, screaming warriors of their secret nightmares plotted the downfall of civilization.

"In which case, we ought to warn someone," another suggested.

As always, they looked to Justus Cordius for a decision.

"Right then, this is what we do. There's a legion headquarters about two days west of us. We'll make for it and report to the commanding officer. If it's all kicking off round here again, he'll need to know. Collect poor old Curly's body and wrap it up. Whatever happens he comes with us. We'll take the bracelets and the bronze helmet along to show. Someone might know which tribe they're from. Oh, take the head of that tattooed one. The patterns might be a clue."

"Could just take skin off his face," a voice suggested.

"Yeah, so you could tan it and sell it for a souvenir. We all know your games…"

"Head," said Justus firmly to end the discussion.

Curly's blood-stained body was wrapped in a blanket and tied up tightly. They laid it on the floor of a wagon with a reverent gentleness which might not have been expected from such hardened men by anyone who did not know them.

It took over an hour to turn the wagons around. The good ground at the side of the track was not wide enough to risk using the mules to simply swing them around. If a wheel became bogged in a deep rut, they would have to unload everything to get it out, before reloading it again on a harder surface. They unhitched the mules and manually heaved and hauled the wagons to face back the way they had come. Justus allowed only eight men, himself included, to get the job done. The others were spread out hidden in the trees as lookouts in case the raiders returned.

They sweated and swore, used branches as levers and eventually brought up the mule teams and harnessed them once more, ready to move off back the way they had come. Justus blew a shrill blast on his whistle and counted in the rest who emerged from the dark skirts of the forest. They were all there. No-one had got lost or had his throat cut by a silent, revenge-fuelled enemy. He gave the command to move off.

The sun was barely past its zenith when the trees to the west of them thinned into a narrow glade which appeared to lead to a distant track on the rising ground ahead. It wound around the base of a splintered rock that towered above the forest canopy.

"Looks like this is our road, lads," Justus said and they turned off and plodded onwards, three wagons, fifteen live men and one dead one.

They made a cold camp that night, no fire and six pickets spread around for protection. The moon was bright and the sky a blaze of stars. It would be cold before dawn and everything, including the men and animals would be covered in a silver coat of dew.

As he was falling asleep, Justus Cordius realized what had unsettled him before the raiders struck. It was the call of the cuckoo. One of them must have used it as a signal but it was too late in the year; cuckoos were silent in autumn and winter. No-one knew why.

"Blessings on you Lady Fortuna," he thought. "If they had imitated a jay, we could all be dead."

Chapter 2

Far to the north and west over the Rhine in the unconquered lands, on the same day that Justus Cordius and his convoy were attacked, Badurad of the Suevi was leading his clan into their winter quarters. He rode bareback on a tall bay horse at an easy walk. He was at his physical peak at thirty-six years of age, dressed in trousers and a jerkin of ochre dyed wool over which he wore his armour; a leather shirt sewn with dozens of over-lapping, fish-scale metal plates. Half of his head was shaven but he wore the pale blond hair on the other side in a long braid which could be twisted up into the Suevian Knot by which all men could know his ancestry. He carried an oval shield and, to the amazement of strangers in that metal-hungry country, he wore a long sword at his side. The sword was the ultimate symbol of his power and status. Only a warrior of enormous fame and prestige might own so fine a blade. Badurad was such a man; a renowned chieftain amongst his people, an adviser to a tribal king.

His name meant "war counsel" and that was his special ability. Not only was he skilled and fearless in the fight, he possessed a shrewd sense of tactics. His overlord had recognised this and always listened carefully to Badurad's advice. Battles against the odds had been won as a result. Honours were heaped on the "war counsel", including the almost priceless gift of the sword but it was reputation he valued above all. No costly weapon or fine horse could match the pride of being a man who was known for deeds that were turned into songs by the bards and recited when men drank together.

Badurad's clan numbered one hundred and sixty people. Among them were eleven warriors who owned a helmet, some body armour or both. A further twelve men carried shield and spear, all good men in a fight. The remainder were wives, children and slaves. They moved through the forest with their small horse herd, their cattle and three teams of oxen pulling high-sided carts loaded up with food-stores, tools and equipment.

They were travelling towards four small, open valleys linked together like beads on a necklace by a brook which ran down to the great river a full two days march away. A family of slaves had been left there over the summer to scythe down the long grass and turn it into hay. They would also have cut poles to support hut roofs, chopped firewood and woven fish traps to be set in the deep pools. Soon there would be berries, nuts and mushrooms for the women and children to gather and the men would hunt boar and deer. The people had been free of disease throughout the year. Many calves and foals had been born. The grain harvest had been plentiful. No-one should go hungry over the coming months when the snow imprisoned them in their valleys, the brook froze over and wolves howled in the night. Badurad stood on the pinnacle of his wealth and fame where he could expect to remain for several years unless fate decreed otherwise.

He should have been contented but he was not. He rode with his head held high, his shoulders squared and a serene expression on his face but inwardly he was in turmoil. He had suffered a severe setback that he could not understand and it had unnerved him. It had begun the night of the last new moon when he had been feasting with the king.

Huge fires blazed and roared in the circular clearing cut in a grove of trees on top of a low hill. From time to time, an ember would fall inwards and spill a column of golden sparks that exploded into the night sky. Thirty important men, clan chieftains or champion fighters, sat facing inwards on crude log benches, their faces and clothes lit in flickering yellow and orange by the flames. On a higher seat, the king was resplendent in a Roman breastplate that scattered reflected light each time he moved. He had plundered it from a legion officer he had cut down with his own hands. That exploit had given him his kingship.

Slaves scurried out of the gloom behind them fetching hunks of smoking meat, slabs of bread and pitchers of ale so that no man's hands were ever empty of food or drink which would have been dishonourable to their kingly host. From time to time, a warrior would leap to his feet, ale-horn sloshing over in his hand, and recount a funny story to gales of laughter; another would praise one among the company which made the assembly drain their drink in response and shout for more.

At last the king stood up and raised his arms for silence. He looked around to make sure he had everyone's full attention before he spoke.

"Nobles of the Suevi, my friends and battle brothers, welcome to this gathering where I see among you the fiercest, the wisest and the most cunning of my loyal followers. Your fame goes before you and all men know of your deeds, what more can a man ask?"

A great roar of approval surged over him. The king lifted one hand and continued.

"Well, if we can seek no higher honour in this world, what of that realm of mysteries known only to the initiated, can we look for glory there?"

He paused, seeing unease pass across the faces turned to him. Matters of shades, of spirits and of gods were best left alone. Men they could fight. Beasts they could master or bring down in the hunt. But the other worlds above and below filled them with dread.

"A priest came to me," the king said, "a holy and learned priest. He asked me to name a man who is worthy to perform a great duty. He asked me to name a man who is a fit person to journey to the grove of the white horses that we all know of but never enter and there assist in the mysteries. Did I know of such a man, someone whose name stands in such spotless regard that he could accept this sign of highest esteem among all the Suevi? I told him that I did. I told him that Badurad is courageous and wise and noble. I told him that Badurad is the man. Stand up my battle counsel and tell us if you will undertake this task?"

Badurad stood up slowly and pulled himself to his full height. He raised both his arms out to the sides.

"For the good of my people and my king, I humbly accept."

The king beamed. The warriors shouted acclaim. Badurad sat down again, folded his arms and contemplated the dancing firelight.

The king raised his ale horn and saluted Badurad.

"Travel well to the grove, my friend. You are expected in four night's time."

When Badurad arrived back at his clan's summer village, he slid down from his horse and tossed the reins to a waiting slave. Then, ducking his head low he entered his hut. For all his wealth and standing, it was a humble dwelling, simply furnished. The free peoples across the Rhine frowned on luxury. Excessive comfort led to weakness and too many possessions either made a man selfish or others envious. A warrior needed nothing but his courage and his weapons. They would earn him all he required; a wife to share his life and give him children, horses, cattle and slaves to work the fields.

Badurad's wife, Odila and their daughter, Saxa squatted by the hearth laying out pieces of doeskin before sewing them together into a simple shift. The little girl jumped to her feet and ran over to him, wrapping her arms round one of his legs and beaming up at her beloved father. He bent over and lovingly stroked her head. His wife smiled at the sight.

"I have news," he said. "I am chosen to attend the sacred horses."

Her eyes went wide. She rose and walked over to him, hugging him to her. She was almost as tall as her husband, broad-shouldered and wide-hipped. He felt the strength of her firm arms squeezing his ribs.

"Our name is honoured," she told him.

Suevi women were not owned by or subservient to their men, nor were they sold in marriage by their families. Young men and women came together as equals and the bride's gift to her new mate was always the same thing; a spear and a shield. It was a way of saying, "Your duty is to fight and hunt, leave the rest to me. United we are strong." So Badurad's glory was also reflected on his wife, his family and his clan.

The next day he pushed a pole through the arms of his battle-shirt and hung it spread out between two trees. He stood on one side with a patch of soft leather coated with wet sand from the bucket at his feet and polished each fish-scale plate. His son, Otto, stood on the other side patiently working at the same task.

Otto was nearly sixteen, all gangly arms and legs and elbows and knees, already a fraction taller than Badurad. In two or three years he would begin to fill out and become as powerful as his father, or his mother. The boy's long side-lock hung to his waist, it had never been cut and his eyes were so palely blue they seemed almost colourless in bright daylight. He was whistling through his teeth as he sanded the metal plates until they gleamed.

"I know you want to come with me," his father told him. "And you know you can't. You've been man enough not to plead with me so here is your reward. The next time I go to the king, you will be with me. I will present you to him and tell the assembled warriors your name. They will acknowledge you as numbered among the Suevi."

The whistling stopped. Otto hurled himself past the shirt and embraced his father. He was speechless with joy. He would no longer be a boy. He would be a warrior. He had no words with which to thank Badurad.

The night before he left on his mission, Odila took out the braid in her husband's hair and went through it with a fine comb dipped in water in which wild violets and chestnuts had been boiled. They sat leaning over the hearth. Some of the lice she found she cracked between her finger and thumb nails, others fell onto the hot ash and exploded with a faint popping sound. When she had done, she plaited his hair and looked at him admiringly. She saw the desire mount in his eyes and shook her head.

"What you are going to do is a sacred mystery," she told him. "Stay purified but keep yourself in readiness for me when you come back."

Her lips were very soft and gentle as she kissed him.

In the morning, Badurad leaped onto his immaculately groomed horse with the light splintering off his armour as he moved. He rode slowly between the ranks of his clansmen gathered to wish him well and into the forest where he faded from their sight among the dark pines.

He knew where the sacred site was located. They all did, so that they could avoid it. But this time he headed straight for the valley where scores of rounded boulders many paces across thrust up through the ground. Some said they were the skulls of giants buried upright in the earth, others that they were the stones they had flung at each other when they had fought. However they came to be there, they lent a brooding sense of menace to the valley which rose to a narrow pass between two low cliffs. It looked like a hill that had been cleaved with a mighty axe, exposing its bones. A foaming torrent ran out of the ominous gap.

Badurad stopped his horse and looked into the dark maw through which he must go. His heart beat faster in his chest and his mouth became suddenly dry as a sense of superstitious awe grew within him. In the battle line facing a yelling enemy, in the hunt approaching a cornered boar, he did not know fear. But he was about to arrive at a place where gods and shades and men came together. Forces beyond his understanding and control would be at play. He waited a long while considering whether he could live with himself if he turned back, so great was his terror. But with a sigh of resignation, he touched his heels to his mount's flanks and urged it into the stream. He had not mastered his fear; he had accepted it. Going on was better than losing his reputation, without which his life would be unliveable.

He rode upstream into the deathly chill of the cleft in the rock that the sun never reached. The rough walls either side of him were green with dripping cushions of moss that dulled all echoes. The silence was thick around him other than for the gurgling and splashing water. It sounded to Badurad as if someone or something was whispering and laughing beneath the surface. He clenched his teeth and began to shiver. He was relieved to feel the temperature rise several degrees as he passed through and was in the open once more.

He found himself in a wide, level meadow bounded by rocky escarpments in all directions. Ahead of him was a holly hedge. It was so closely planted that it would be impossible for a man to force his way through it unharmed. He rode closer and saw hawthorn and brambles twined between the tree trunks to make it even more formidable. The dense mass of glossy holly-leaves edged with spines was clearly intended as much as a screen to keep the secret of what lay within as a physical barrier. He turned his horse to the right and began to ride slowly along looking for an entrance. He soon realised the barrier was circular and after half a mile, he saw three tethered horses ahead. He eased his sword in its scabbard and approached them.

A group of men were sitting on benches near the grazing animals. A steaming cauldron was suspended over a fire from which a thin spiral of fragrant smoke arose. One of the men stood up and opened his arms wide in greeting. He was dressed in a long, grey tunic. He threw back the hood as he rose. His head and face were completely hairless, even to the absence of eyebrows. He was so thin that the outline of his skull and facial bones could be seen beneath his skin. The tendons of his neck tightened and released like bowstrings as he spoke. At first glance Badurad had thought he was an old man but it was not so. He held himself very straight, his shoulders squared, his keen eyes were bright; he could not have been much above forty. Badurad began to give his name and rank but before he could utter more than a word, he was stopped.

"You have nothing to tell us; no lineage and no battle-fame. Neither do these men from elsewhere…" he gestured to the others looking curiously at the newcomer with the fine sword. "Here you are nameless under the gaze of the gods." He indicated two robed men tending the cauldron over the fire. "We are servants of the servant of the gods. Vow in your heart to say not one word unless invited and to obey without question the instructions you are given and thus be welcome. Vow in your heart that you will speak not one word of what you see or hear in this place and thus be received with joy. If you cannot give your oath, go now and never come near again as you value your life in this world and your place in the world to come. Man, will you stay under these conditions? You may answer."

"I will," Badurad replied.

The priest smiled and nodded.

"Then dismount. We shall see to your horse. Come; sit with us now we are all gathered together."

Badurad nodded a greeting and took his place on a bench. He looked around. Three of the company were dressed and equipped similarly to himself. He did not know any of them. He rightly guessed that they were warriors sent by their kings as he had been. He noticed a brook flowing out from behind the hedge a few yards away. Part of the banks on either side had been cut back to form a pool. He glimpsed what seemed to be a sort of gate concealed among the holly branches.

Still standing, the priest looked down on them, nodded his approval and began to speak. "All know of the grove of the white horses and that it is a place where gods reveal their will to men. Tomorrow each of you will harness one horse to the sacred chariot. The high priest shall mount it and let the holy steeds go where they will within the grove. The direction they take and how they behave will make clear the intentions of the gods. What they say, if indeed, they speak at all, is not of your concern. Once you have completed your task, you will leave the grove and not look back. Your mounts and weapons must stay here; they will be looked after. Now sit," he ordered. "You must be hungry. We have food for you."

One of the other robed men lifted the lid off the cauldron and spooned thick gruel into four wooden bowls. He handed them out.

"Eat," he grunted.

Badurad tipped the bowl to his lips and began to suck up the vegetable stew it contained. It tasted bitter but he persisted until it was almost gone and then....

A hand on his shoulder was shaking him awake. He tried to sit up but his arms and legs seemed incapable of obeying his will. He was dragged into an upright position. A drinking horn was pressed to his lips.

"Here," a voice said. "Empty it, take it all down."

Badurad tasted fresh milk; he swallowed it in hurried gulps. The mist in his head tore into shreds and drifted away and he became aware of his surroundings. It was dawn. He stood up, staggered a little and shook his head. One of the priests stood in front of him. He pointed to an indeterminate spot a few yards away.

"Go over there and piss," he commanded. "When you're finished, come back here." Badurad did as he was told. "Now strip and immerse yourself in the purifying waters; right in, head under."

He stepped off the bank into the pool. The water was deeper than it had looked and came up to his chest, the cold driving the breath from his lungs. He leaned forward and ducked his head under, held himself there for a few seconds and climbed out gasping. He went to pick up his clothes but a length of coarse cloth was thrown to him before he could reach them.

"Dry yourself," came the order.

The sun was up but there was no warmth in it. Badurad stood with his three naked companions. He made an effort to relax and stop shivering. The hairless priest stood in front of them unsmiling. He held a broad axe in his hands.

"You have eaten the magic potage which makes men sleep soundlessly and deeply. In that sleep, no-one mumbles or cries out things close to his heart others may overhear. Noble chieftains, fierce warriors you may be but to the gods you are as new-born infants. That is why you will go naked into the grove. There you will see the sacred chariot under its canopy and four white horses. Each horse wears a head stall with two silver rings. You will approach one of them and lead it to the chariot. You will thread a pair of traces through the rings and secure them. Once this is done, depart the way you came. Do not look back."

Unseen hands on the inside swung the gates open and they stepped through. Badurad took a deep breath and tried to convince himself that the tingling in his arms and the weakness he felt in his knees was not fear but as the result of the plunge into deep, cold waters when he had been barely awake.

Within the ring of holly was another of oaks. Some were huge trees in the prime of their lives, festooned with mistletoe, still covered in green and yellow leaves, in spite of the season. Others were ancient beyond counting, barely alive, gnarled and twisted into fantastic shapes. A spring of clear water emerged from a jagged boulder in the centre of the inner circle and ran across the open expanse and out into the streambed in which they had bathed.

Near it stood an arch of green boughs housing a brightly painted two wheeled chariot. The chief priest stood close by it. He was a tall man robed in white matching his head of long, snowy hair crowned in a wreath of greenery. His beard fell to the silver rope around his waist. He lifted his arms in blessing and they bowed. The guardians fell back and closed the gate, standing reverently either side of it.

Now that Badurad had entered the inner sanctum and had neither been struck down by lightning nor the hand of a god, he relaxed and began to look about him. Far off to his left he saw a fine white horse, its hide unblemished with any spot of a darker colour. The hair of its mane had been dressed to fall in plaits across its neck and its well-combed tail flowed almost to the grass beneath its hooves. Badurad walked calmly towards it, admiring the animal's flawless lines as he came nearer. It stood watching him with dark, intelligent eyes. The horse raised its head and snuffed the air through dilated nostrils. Badurad lifted an unhurried hand to grasp the head collar. Without warning the horse stretched out its neck and snapped at him, only his battle-trained reactions made Badurad whip his fingers out of the way of those clashing teeth. It reared and pawed the air above his head before swivelling on its back legs, dropping down and dancing a few paces away, arching its back, snorting and kicking out.

He heard the high priest call from a distance.

"Remove that man. He has no place here."

Hands grasped him by both arms as the two guardians ran him out, slamming the gates behind him. And there he stood, proud Badurad; naked and breathless, confused and ashamed.

The priest with the axe indicated his clothes and horse.

"Dress now, mount up and go."

Badurad obeyed but as he was about to move off, the man took hold of his horse's bridle.

"This has happened before. It is not unknown nor does it tarnish your honour. The gods speak through the horses in many ways all of which must remain unsaid outside the grove. Return to your people and think no more of it."

The reunion between Odila and Badurad had not been the happy celebration for which she had hoped. There was a shadow on her husband but Odila was wise enough neither to comment nor to ask what was wrong.

In spite of the assistant priest's advice, Badurad could think of nothing other than what he saw as his humiliation in the sacred grove. Had the gods singled him out as uniquely unworthy? Or had it been as the priest had said, not without precedent? He was still inwardly consumed by his struggle to understand as he rode at the head of his people into their winter camp.

Chapter 3

The legionary on watch over the Principalis Dextra gate of The Second Lucan Legion's permanent camp stamped his cold, damp boots in a vain attempt to shake some of the dewdrops off his helmet and the shoulders of his sodden, red military cloak. He had been walking the seven paces across the raised walkway behind the double leafed gate since midnight. Every five minutes he met his fellow sentry coming the other way in the middle but they did not speak. His arms ached from the weight of the shield and two javelins he carried but he was not unhappy. The legion's marching season was over for this year. He could look forward to spending the cold months sleeping in a warm wooden hut and not in a draughty, leather tent in some forest miles from the gods knew where. Yes, there would be daily training, fatigues and route marches but there would also be ample food and wine and some leisure in which to enjoy them.

Dawn was not far away. Soon he would be stood down and eating his breakfast of freshly baked bread and bacon, then excused duties until the afternoon, once he had cleaned and dried his kit. All in all, things could be a lot worse as he knew from ten years of army experience. He looked over to the eastern horizon willing the sun to appear.

The ground had been cleared of trees for at least a mile from the camp on all sides. To the east, where the sentry stared into the darkness, the land rose gradually to the tree line of that endless German forest. To the north, the silver snake of the Rhine slithered, a little under two miles away. To the south a small, nameless stream looped around two sides of the camp and ran into the great river. Beyond the stream, a collection of tents and huts housing wine shops, brothels and the dubious commercial enterprises of the camp-followers had mushroomed almost as soon as the legion had marched in ten days ago. To the west, the ground was ploughed and dotted with modest farmhouses. Some of the legionaries had taken their end of service bonuses, married local women and now farmed practically in the shadow of the walls. They felt protected so close to the legion, had a ready market for their produce and could keep in touch with friends still serving.

Behind its ditch, rampart and log palisade with artillery towers at each corner, it was home to nine cohorts made up of centuries of eighty heavy infantrymen and their officers, four thousand eight-hundred men in all. The foot-soldiers were supported by three hundred and sixty auxiliary cavalrymen with four hundred horses and one hundred artillerymen with their scorpions and ballistas. Some of the men were immunes; soldiers permanently relieved of manual labour and fatigues in view of their special skills. There were engineers, farriers, clerks, medical orderlies, butchers and cooks. There were mules and oxen, carts and heavy wagons. All the necessary parts of the Roman military machine.

The area of deforested ground the camp dominated was just above the spring flood plain of the Rhine. It boasted four wells, two granaries, other storehouses, stables, workshops, quarters for the men and officers, bathhouses, latrines and the Praetorium; the commanding officer's quarters. It shouted out a message to the native population; here was Rome's power, permanent and irresistible.

It was located at one end of a bridge over the Rhine. It was not a particularly large or important bridge and it often needed to be rebuilt after the recurrent floods subsided but it could accommodate eight men or four horses crossing abreast. A small log-walled outpost had been built at the near end of the bridge. It held quarters for twenty men and had a low, central tower bearing an iron brazier in which to light a signal fire in an emergency. It had never been intended as a strongly defensible position, only to give a warning to the legion in the event of hostile activity on the far bank. The nearest thirty yards of the bridge planks could be lifted off and thrown into the water, the oil-soaked timber in the brazier lit and the legionaries back in the main camp within half an hour if they marched in double time.

The tops of the far pines grew visible in black silhouette against a thin grey band of light that crawled across the sky. It grew paler and higher until a yellow glow announced that full sunrise was imminent. Long shadows spread inky fingers out from the base of the forest and then shrunk back as the orange ball of the sun finally showed itself. With the new day, the camp stirred to life. The smell of wood smoke wafted up to the gate as cooking fires were lit. The daily sounds of the garrison could be heard; the clop of hooves as horses were led out of stables, the clanking of metal and the usual shouting of centurions and their seconds in command, the optios. The sentry was impatient now. His empty stomach was rumbling and the weariness of the long hours on duty suddenly weighed heavy on him. But very soon the guard would be changed. An officer would lead six soldiers up the ladder to relieve the night-watch but only after the replacements had breakfasted, kitted up and then been inspected.

Just as he heard the rhythmic thud of approaching boots on the ground below, he caught a flicker of movement at the edge of the forest. He looked harder and leaned out over the parapet, propping his javelins on the timberwork and shading his eyes with his free hand. There was definitely a small group of men and vehicles emerging from between the trees. They were too far away to be much more than shapes but that did not really matter. What mattered was that nothing friendly had ever come from that direction. The main routes were to the south and west or followed the course of the Rhine. To the east was mile upon mile of hostile wilderness and mountains as far as the Danube, where things were much worse.

"Alarm!" he shouted and picked up his weapons. The ladder creaked behind him and an optio commanding the changeover guard was leaning over his shoulder peering out into the distance.

"What do you see?" he demanded.

"There, some men have come out of the forest."

The optio turned on his heel and shouted at one of his men still at the base of the ladder.

"Put down your shield and run for the centurion, now."

The man sped away.

"Faster you idle sod," the optio bellowed after him and had the satisfaction of seeing the legionary try to increase his speed.

The centurion arrived at a rapid rate just short of an undignified run.

The legionary of the night-watch was now sandwiched between his optio and his centurion. He stiffened to quivering attention.

"What is it, optio?" the centurion asked.

"This man has seen something odd coming out of the forest, centurion."

Only when this explanation had been given did the centurion speak directly to the sentry.

"Well lad, tell me all about it."

"Saw movement, shouted for the optio. He looked with me and called for you, centurion."

"And what have you seen worth dragging me away from my breakfast?"

"Sir, you can see them clearer now; looks like some carts with men around them. But why are they coming from over there, sir? I mean, there's nowhere for them to be coming from, so to speak."

The centurion stared at the distant figures now definitely moving towards the camp.

"Are you one of the men who have just come on duty?"

"No sir, been on stag all night."

The centurion turned to his junior officer.

"Optio, take this man's name..."

"Gods, what am I supposed to have done wrong now?" the sentry thought glumly.

"...after being on watch overnight, he was still alert enough at dawn to notice something out of the ordinary and draw an officer's attention to it," the centurion went on. "Commendable behaviour in any soldier; remind me make sure his action is noted in my written report to the senior centurion. Well done lad."

A heavy hand slapped the doubly relieved legionary on the back and he was dismissed

Justus Cordius and his men were as surprised as the look-out had been to see them when they came out of the skirts of the forest with the camp only a mile away. They had intended to reach the river and then follow it downstream until they found it but they had strayed a little to the east. The previous night they had halted only a few hundred yards inside the forest's edge without realising it, hence their emergence at first light.

"That's it boys, The Second Lucan's waiting for us to knock on the door," Justus said.

"What's their proper legion number?" one of his men asked.

Justus shrugged. "No idea, they're just The Second Lucan."

"Where's the First Lucan then?" another voice enquired.

"All gone getting on for twenty years ago, apart from three-quarters of a century of poor bastards who crawled back from Parthia with their eagle; they went east under Marcus Antonius."

The men became sombre as they remembered the often-repeated stories of how the best part of an army had died of cold, starvation or under the arrows that enemy horse-archers had hailed down on them in that disastrous campaign.

"The legion was taken off the list then reformed by Emperor Augustus. They recruited around Luca near the Tyrrhenian coast. So there they are, The Second Lucan. Let's go and say hello."

By the time the three wagons had threaded around the tree stumps deliberately left by the Romans to hinder an enemy charge down the slope from the forest, there were legionaries, one optio, a centurion and a military tribune on the walkway over the eastern gate.

To found a political career in Rome, it was desirable that young men of good families spent some time in the military. Favours were promised or called-in, patronage and votes offered, all to obtain a posting as a tribune in one of the legions. Some studied the trade of war, found the army to their liking and went on to high rank. However, the majority of them were impatient to return to Rome, learned nothing and left as soon as possible. But even the most uninterested of them had their precious few months of service to add to their curriculum vitae. Technically, a tribune outranked a senior centurion, though he may have no knowledge of strategy, tactics, or how to use his sword.

Justus climbed down from the driving seat of the first wagon and came to a sort of relaxed attention in front of the gate.

"Greetings to The Second Lucan; I am Justus Cordius and I have information which may be of value to your commanding officer."

The tribune stepped forward and looked down.

"Do you operate some sort of trading outfit, Cordius?"

"Indeed, sir, I do."

"Then I suggest you take your wares to the southern gate, the Porta Principa Sinistra. That's where camp-followers and traders assemble."

Justus and those of his men who had been in hearing began to laugh. Up on the gate, the optio glared at the legionaries daring them to join in. The centurion fought to keep his face straight. The tribune grew red with annoyance.

"What's so funny eh? What's so damn funny? I'll have you whipped!"

Justus calmed down and took a deep breath.

"The Porta Principa Sinistra is the western gate of a legion camp, sir. I believe you meant to say the Porta Decumana, that's the southern one; an easy mistake to make, sir."

"Are you trying to make a fool out of me?" the tribune demanded.

"No sir, you don't need me for that, sir," Justus replied.

A legionary spluttered the beginning of a suppressed guffaw but stopped abruptly when his centurion's vine-staff of office clanged into the side of his helmet.

"Carry on centurion," the tribune ordered. "I've no more time to waste on that clown."

He stalked down the ladder and across the parade ground with as much dignity as he could scrape together.

The centurion stepped forward and leaned his elbows on the top of the defensive timberwork. He had already noticed how Justus held himself and the well cared-for short sword at his side.

"What legion, citizen?" he asked.

"Led the fifth century of the Sixteenth," Justus replied.

"Oh, the Gallica eh?"

"The very same, all the men here with me served out their time, one way or the other."

"Well Former Centurion Justus Cordius, you should know better than to mock a tribune in front of the men," the centurion said with a wry grin.

"Apologies," Justus replied. "No disrespect meant to the finest tribune of The Second Lucan."

"Accepted; we'd better get you in front of the commanding officer as soon as possible. Open the gate for these sad old relics that had the misfortune to serve in a legion inferior to ours," he shouted down.

It was a long walk up the centre of the camp to the Praetorium for Justus and Calvus, one of his oldest comrades, who carried a heavy sack he held well away from his body and a smaller one that clinked and jingled. They were escorted by the centurion they had spoken with at the gate. Two guards in full armour with shields and javelins stopped them at the headquarters door.

"Centurion Lentus with former centurion Justus Cordius of the Sixteenth, and one of his men seeking an interview with Legate Publius Quadratus," Lentus told them.

"Wait here please, sir," one of the sentries replied and went inside.

"Stay outside for now," Justus told Calvus who put down his sacks.

They heard the muffled sounds of the message being repeated, boots on wooden floorboards and a door opening and closing. The guard came back and ushered them through a room in which four scribbling clerks barely looked up from their desks as they passed and stopped at an inner door. He knocked and waited. A voice called out for them to enter and they marched into the office of the legate, his commander with the power of life and death over every man in his legion.

The office was large enough for twenty men to sit down if a meeting of senior officers was called. Folding stools leaned against the walls, a central desk and chairs and a large charcoal brazier on a tripod against the winter chill filled the centre of the room. Behind it was an altar dedicated to Jupiter father of the gods and Mars his warlike son. A further door led into the legate's private quarters.

Legate Publius Quadratus looked up from his scroll littered desk at the visitors. He wore a deep blue tunic with Greek key embroidery in silver on the cuffs of the short sleeves. His neck was strong but slender and his head almost delicate, covered with a mass of dark curls. His brown eyes were lustrous and intelligent. At first impression, he had more the look of a scholar or philosopher than a professional soldier. The man sitting opposite him who gave them a peremptory glance over his shoulder was heavily built; shaven headed and wore the armour and decorations of a first spear centurion, the highest rank in the centurionate.

They stood to attention in front of the desk. It was Publius Quadratus who spoke first. His voice was deep and sonorous, demonstrating his early training in elocution and public speaking for which his father had paid private tutors a small fortune.

"Greetings Centurion Lentus, who do you bring with you?"

Cordius stood forward.

"I am Justus Cordius, sir. I have information which may be of interest to you."

"Go on."

"Two days ago, my trading convoy was attacked on the road to Augusta Treverorum. They made off with a wagonload of goods. We are a strong party; fifteen men, before we lost one in the fighting, and me, all former soldiers. We have travelled that route several times each year for four years. Once we had made our presence known, so to speak, the bandits avoided us. There are plenty of easier targets.

The first spear centurion spoke for the first time. His voice was harsh, raucous after years of shouting orders loud enough to be heard over the din of battle.

"Greetings Justus Cordius; I am Titus Attius. I regret your troubles and grieve with you for the loss of your man but why d'you think this is anything to do with my legate?"

"We were ambushed by a party of at least twenty. There may have been more concealed in the trees. Neither I nor my men recognised them as belonging to any tribe we had come across in that area. It occurred to me that they may be part of a larger raiding force or a reconnaissance in strength for an invasion.

"Late in the year for that," Titus Attius remarked.

"Yes, sir, but maybe they know that many of your officers and men with passes will soon be going home on leave until the next marching season begins. What better time to mount a quick incursion across the river?"

"He has a point, Titus," the legate said.

"We brought some artefacts with us and one of their heads. I thought you might be able to identify who they were…"

"With your permission, sir?" Titus asked Publius Quadratus who nodded his assent.

"Clerk!" the first spear centurion shouted in a voice which made the wooden walls of the Praetorium vibrate. The outer door opened and a head appeared around it. "Fetch Prefect Aldermar," Titus growled.

The door closed in an instant and the head was gone. Titus did not tell the man to hurry. He knew his reputation and authority made that unnecessary; the clerk would run full tilt.

"Where are these objects you wish us to see?" the legate asked.

"Outside with my man Calvus. In view of…"

"In view of one of 'em's a smelly head cut off three days ago now and you didn't want to stink up my commander's office; Calvus you say?" Titus broke in.

Justus nodded. The big centurion lumbered over to the office door and opened it.

"Sentry! Send in the man Calvus," he roared.

Then he turned to Lentus who had been standing silently at attention all this time.

"Be about your duties Centurion Lentus. You have done well in drawing this matter to the legate's attention.

Lentus saluted both officers, performed a smart about turn and left as Calvus arrived.

"Put those sacks on the floor and take a stool for you and Justus Cordius," the legate said with a reassuring smile.

Calvus looked apprehensively at Titus Attius. He knew a tartar when he saw one.

"You heard the commanding officer," Titus told him.

Calvus fetched a seat for Justus only and moved to stand against the wall.

"Never sat in the presence of a legate and a first spear; don't seem right," he explained.

Aldermar burst into the office. He was a tall German wearing the armour of a senior cavalry officer. His broad shoulders almost filled the doorway and his helmeted head brushed the lintel. He swept off his headgear freeing two thick braids of golden-red hair. He bowed to his commanding officer and acknowledged Titus Attius.

"You sent for me, gentlemen?" he enquired in almost accentless Latin.

"Take a gander into those sacks there and tell us if you know who the bits and pieces belonged to."

Aldermar tipped the bronze helmet and arms rings onto the floor and stirred them with one booted foot. He bent down and picked up one ring to examine more closely before letting it fall. He opened the other sack and lifted the severed head by its hair. He looked hard at the face for a few moments then gave a moan and covered his eyes with his free hand as if to hide his tears.

"It is…" he paused for effect, "…It is the head of my uncle," he croaked as if overcome by emotion.

Calvus and Cordius stared at him in horror. Publius Quadratus looked amused but Titus Attius sighed wearily.

"How many times do you have to be told you aren't funny?"

Aldermar grinned and shrugged. "The helmet, the arm rings, Suevi work, all of it. The tattoos tell me the dead man was from a good way north and east of the river."

"The Suevi tribe…" Attius began but the big German interrupted him.

"How many times do you have to be told that the Suevi are not one tribe but a confederation?"

Publius Quadratus spoke and demonstrated in a few words why he held command.

"Aldermar, what would your people do with this dead man's head?"

"A thief's head? We would stick it up on a pole to rot."

"We have none around here and if we bury it, some superstitious idiot is going to convince half the legion there is a curse on it. Select four reliable scouts and send them out to reconnoitre the area where

Justus Cordius and his men were attacked. They should have no trouble working back along the wagon tracks. I want their report in six days unless they come across a substantial party of raiders say, over two hundred, in which case they must be standing in front of me sooner, much sooner. Would any of them have a religious objection to taking this villain's head and throwing it away in the forest?"

"None at all, sir," Aldermar grinned.

"Good, then organize it" the legate went on. "Put everything back in the sacks, Calvus, and follow Prefect of Auxiliary Cavalry Aldermar. He will take the offending burden from you and give it to one of his men.

The German saluted and left with Calvus in his wake.

"Now Cordius, I believe you said one of your men was killed?"

"He was, sir; at the outset."

"Often that way," Titus Attius remarked.

They were silent for a few seconds remembering sudden deaths they had witnessed.

"He was a former legionary?" Titus asked.

"He was; a good solid infantry man, honourably discharged."

"You brought his body along with you?"

"What else? He was a comrade," Justus said sharply, offended that anyone should think he and his men would leave one of their own to rot on the forest floor.

Titus held up a hand in a sign of peace. "No offence was intended. All of us have had to leave good friends behind when we had to get out quick."

"Let him have his funeral honours under the eagle. Get the priests to organise it, Titus," the legate ordered

"Thank you, sir," Cordius said. "It will mean a lot to me and the others."

"And what will you do now?"

"I shall talk it over with the lads but it's pretty sure we'll cut our losses and head for home."

The legate nodded his approval and hunted around on his desk for a smooth wax tablet and a stylus. He scratched a few words on it and held it out to Cordius who stood up and took it from him.

"This orders the quartermaster to look over your stock and buy in anything he thinks we might need at a fair price. If you have any wine that is even half-decent he is sure to want it. After that, you may offer your goods to any off-duty legionary; they were paid the day before yesterday and some of them might even have a few coins left. Stay within the walls for the rest of today and tonight. The legion will feed your men and animals and then I suggest you head for home in the morning. "

"Sir, this is unexpectedly generous of you…"

"Not at all, Justus Cordius; the information you have given us might yet be of great value and in any case, you took the path of duty to go out of your way to report. You have my thanks."

Titus Attius stood up and led Cordius out. As they reached the door, Publius Quadratus called after them.

"Oh, and Cordius, you will leave by the southern gate which, as we all know is the Porta Decumana, referring to it as anything else will not be appreciated by my men."

Chapter 4

Justus Cordius and his companions sold practically their entire remaining stock to the quartermaster and the legionaries. He was pleased that all their amphorae of wine were taken into the legion stores. The heavy terracotta jars were difficult to transport and their absence would lighten the mules' loads on their way home. They even managed to sell the old bronze helmet and the thin, silver arms rings they had taken after the raid. The soldiers wanted them as souvenirs to impress their stay-at-home relatives and neighbours with lying tales of winning them in single combat against huge German warriors. Curly's remains were cremated during the evening and a priest handed Justus a glazed pot holding his still-warm ashes the next morning as they set off. They headed south towards Gallia Lugdunensis relieved that they had made a small profit, even taking into account the loss of one wagon. They passed through the Porta Decumana without ribald comment and drove off in the fine cold rain that had come on overnight.

Aldermar's scouts did not throw the severed head into the undergrowth. They came across a well-used path and rode along it until they came to a sharp bend over which hung an oak branch. They tied the head to it by the hair so that it dangled and spun, about the height of a mounted man. For the rest of the afternoon they grinned and laughed at the thought of the next traveller suddenly coming upon a disembodied grinning face dangling in front of them.

They were skilled trackers. Following the signs left by three mule drawn wagons was like riding up a sign-posted highway to them and they made good time to the ambush spot. They dismounted, scattering the feeding crows into the trees where they roosted and complained loudly. Three corpses lay at the side of the road. The fourth, headless, had been dragged into the edge of the undergrowth where it had been dismembered, probably by wolves they decided. The scouting party split and two horsemen took each side of the track heading north and east with an eye on the hoof-prints and footmarks which told a clear story. The mules had been galloping and then slowed to a trot. The men had been running at first then fell into a jog before they all stopped and milled about, probably examining the contents of the wagon. They broke off the track and headed in a more westerly direction. By late afternoon they had met up with others, lit fires and settled for the night. The scouts made camp in the same place.

At dawn they moved off following the raiding party which had made no attempt to conceal its tracks. Yet another group joined them, herding cattle and horses. Then they all changed direction and made haste towards the river. Aldermar's men kept on the trail to be sure that their quarry had not turned off and then debated what to do. They had found no evidence of a major force operating in the area and it seemed clear that this had been an incursion for whatever plunder the tribesman could grab before running for the Rhine. It was time to return to the legion camp.

On the evening of the fourth day since Aldermar had been given his orders to send out his scouting party, he sat in the Praetorium sipping wine diluted with hot water and honey. Publius Quadratus and Titus Attius sat with him around the legate's desk on which were placed the wine and water jugs and a plate of cold meat patties. The office was dimly lit by three oil lamps and pleasantly warmed by the glowing charcoal in the brazier. The two officers listened carefully as Aldermar gave them the gist of the verbal report he had received from his men on their return that afternoon.

"A straightforward raid with no aim other than taking plunder, according to my scouts," he explained. "Between sixty and eighty men in all who got away with one of Cordius' wagons and around fifty cattle and twenty horses…"

"And slaughtered a Roman citizen," Titus reminded him.

"That too," Aldermar acknowledged, "but all appearances say that there's no more to the incident than that. We have no reason to suspect any general unrest or hostile activity, no more than usual anyway."

Publius felt the side of the water jug. It was barely tepid. He shouted for his slave to fetch them more wine and another jug of the hot, sweetened water. When he had been served, he dismissed the man with a wave of his hand without thanks. He poured himself half a cup of wine and added an equal amount of the water.

"Help yourselves," he said and took a patty from the plate. He slowly chewed the spiced pork and pastry, eventually washing it down a gulp of wine before speaking.

"The marching season is over and I want to start out for Rome in ten days. However, I am not prepared to let this go. Roman citizens have been robbed and one of them killed, as you so rightly point out, Titus. I am sending a force across the Rhine to take appropriate action. Is there any chance of finding the guilty parties, Aldermar?"

"I could send some men over the river and look into it. It might take weeks to get any information but those responsible could be a group of thieves and outcasts who have already shared out the loot and gone their separate ways," the prefect told him.

"Right then," Titus said. "We go over, find some poor sods and let them have it. We can put the word about that this is what happens when arseholes decide to bugger about in our neighbourhood; might put the next lot off."

"It won't though, will it?" the German officer demanded.

"No, it will not," Publius told them both. "However, Roman citizens must be able to go about their business unhindered within the boundaries of the empire. When they are not, someone has to pay the price and Rome does not care who it is. That is the lesson we shall keep teaching them so long as they remain our enemies. What position does Lentus hold in the legion at present?"

"He leads the second cohort; next in line to me," Titus answered.

"Very well, he brought this matter in front of me in the first place so he will be the senior centurion for this expedition. Let him take his own men with another century to back his men up; suggestions Titus?"

"Send the twelfth; they could do with the experience and perhaps we should add a party of volunteer archers and slingers."

"Two things, firstly, no-one in the ranks will cross the river voluntarily and secondly, we have neither archer nor slinger units attached to this legion," the legate said.

No legionary would ever willingly go over into German territory. The dark, dripping forests with their ravines and bogs oppressed the Roman soldiers. They had a superstitious dread of the spirits that inhabited the wilderness beyond the Rhine and a healthy respect for the warriors who would oppose them. Above all, there was no profit in it. There were no cities to storm and loot. There was no gold to plunder. The women would not submit to being raped after a few slaps but fought like demons. Even after they had been forced, they would rise up from the ground and attack their abusers with anything that came to hand; they were big, powerful women and often their resistance resulted in the death of a legionary. There was little chance of bringing back any slaves to sell. The men battled to the death. The women cut their children's throats and joined their men in the shield wall or ran clutching their babies to them into the dark recesses of the forest where it would be madness to follow. No, from the common soldier's viewpoint, there was nothing for them in Germany.

"By volunteers, I mean men who are known to be good with bows or slings and who will not want to disappoint their First Spear Centurion when he asks them nicely to help out," Attius explained.

"I leave it to you, Titus but when they get back, give them two weeks excused fatigues by the order of the legate and of which order, you will no doubt express your disapproval. I want them ready by midday tomorrow. Light order, mules but no carts, supplies for six days maximum, the missile troops to carry no infantry weapons or shields. You will provide four reliable scouts, Aldermar. We shall be marching seven days after the attack on Justus Cordius; we must be seen to act swiftly as well as with sufficient force," said Quadratus decisively.

"And Lentus will command?" Titus asked

"No," the legate told him. "Overall command will rest with Tribune Longius."

Titus Attius sighed and shook his head. Quadratus spoke again but this time with an edge to his voice which emphasized there was no room for dissent or debate.

"Lucius Taurius Longius is coming up twenty years old. This is the end of his second season with the legion and he has told me he is happy to remain in camp over the winter. He is conscientious and has enough common-sense to know when to consult the greater experience of Lentus. If he is to progress, he must be given responsibility. I trust you will agree, First Spear Centurion Titus Attius."

"I apologize if I have offended you Legate Publius Quadratus. You command The Second Lucan, not me. After the shameful spectacle that tribune I shall not name made of himself at the Porta Decumana, I am pissed off with the whole tribe of tribunes."

"No offense has been taken, my dear Titus. I know you have the good name of the legion always at the front of your mind. Under Tribune Longius and Centurion Lentus, I anticipate a successful outcome. I believe it is time to wish you both goodnight; no doubt there are certain arrangements that can be made even this late in the evening. Titus, send the tribune to me, if you will."

Tribune Longius stood to attention in front of his legate trying to keep his face expressionless but failing to hide his excitement. Aldermar had told him that Quadratus wanted him for an important job and he should get over to the Praetorium as soon as possible. Longius did not have the appearance of a Roman aristocrat but he was of patrician blood on both sides of his family as far back as could be discovered. Young as he was, he had a deep chest and wide shoulders with the potential to be stocky and heavily muscled by the time he reached his late twenties. His cropped hair was chestnut, his skin fair and his eyes hazel. His nose had been broken and badly set as a boy when he was thrown off his horse. The bridge had been flattened and it was bent a little to the left. He looked as if he would be more at home in the ranks. However, he was an officer and keen to let everyone know he wanted to make his career in the army. Quadratus liked his energy and commitment.

"Tribune Longius, in view of the attack on a Roman trading convoy and the murder of a citizen and legion veteran, you are given command of a punitive expedition. You will leave camp at midday tomorrow with two centuries of infantry and as many missile troops as First Spear Centurion Attius can find for you. Four mounted scouts will be provided. Once you have crossed the river, you will march north for one full day and only after that reduce any settlement you come across. At the end of the third day, you will turn back making your way to the bridgehead. When you are again within one day's march of the river you will cease all aggressive action but may use what force you deem necessary to defend your troops. My clerk has a written order that you can collect when you are dismissed. Have you any questions?"

"What supplies will we be carrying sir?"

"Basic rations for six days on mules; no tents, you will all have to sleep wrapped in your cloaks and hope the weather is kind. The watchwords are fast and hard, tribune; fast and hard. Understand that by "reduce any settlements" I mean obliterate them and all their inhabitants. This is not a glorious and heroic mission but it is necessary to affirm Rome's dominion, understood?"

"Yes sir, I shall march with the men…"

"No, you will not," the legate cut him off in midsentence. "You will be on horseback wearing your best armour and cloak. There will be some prying eyes among the trees and they will see a Roman officer and his men. I want there to be no possibility of doubt that The Second Lucan mounted this expedition. On your return, Prefect of Auxiliary Horse Aldermar's men will pass the news along the river that this is what will happen when Roman interests are attacked. The gossip will soon spread and who knows? Someone might even pay attention. Is that all?"

"Yes, sir and thank you for giving me this commission."

"Not all, Lucius. Take a seat and have a cup of wine with me before you go."

He shouted and clapped his hands and the same slave scurried in to refresh the drinks. The legate mixed only the smallest amount of wine with the hot water and approved the way the tribune was not over-generous with his own proportion of alcohol. -

"So, staying in camp over winter, Lucius; Rome has no attraction for you?"

"I have never been to Rome, sir; my people are all from Luca."

"Indeed they are, how rude of me to have forgotten. That was what swung me in your favour when I had an unexpected vacancy in my tribunate; an officer from Luca for The Second Lucan largely manned by recruits from your area. It seemed an excellent idea."

They smiled at the thought and Quadratus rose to walk to the door with Lucius.

"A first independent command is never easy," the legate said as they crossed the room. "You have a good second in Lentus and three other experienced officers with you. You would do well to consult them but you are not obliged to follow their advice. It is you who makes the decisions for good or ill, not a committee. Remember that and Mars and Fortuna be with you."

Tribune Longius rode at the head of his two centuries resplendent in a mirror-polished breastplate and a nearly new cloak which fell from his broad shoulders to spread over his horse's rump. Thirty resentful or glum looking men with bows or slings and a train of twenty mules took up the rear. Once free of the camp, the scouts rode forward into wide positions, hardly necessary in the open ground leading down to the bridge. Titus Attius and Aldermar watched the column from the walkway over the Porta Praetoria, the northern gate of the camp. The scouts crossed first, the column followed and were soon lost to sight.

"Must be hard for you sometimes," Titus remarked.

"What is?" Aldermar asked.

"Well, seeing the lads going off to kill Germans, you being a German and all."

"I sometimes wonder about you Titus, I really do. You have been stationed here for years and it never sinks in does it? There aren't any "Germans"; it's just a handy label Rome uses. Over the Rhine there are Chatti and Bructeri, Quadii and Cherusci; they all have their own lands and they chop their neighbours into little pieces any time they can. Caesar's general Labienus invited my people to settle in Belgic territory. My grandfather led his horse in support of Caesar at Alesia where Vercingetorix was finished off. As a reward my family were made citizens. Those people over there have nothing to do with me and never did. Anyway, you aren't a real Roman."

"Of course I'm a proper Roman," Titus replied.

"No, you aren't. You told me you were born in Tarraco which, correct me if I'm wrong, is in Spain."

"Well, yes but I'm a Roman citizen."

"It's going to be hard for you when the legion gets transferred over there to kill Spaniards."

"Fuck off," said Titus.

"Right, I will but shall we have a flask of wine first?"

They walked across the parade ground together towards Aldermar's quarters.

Chapter 5

Badurad's people had been busy since their arrival in their winter quarters. They had unloaded their grain from the wagons and distributed it between three concealed storage pits. Rough fencing had been built to keep the cattle and horses from straying. They collected round stones from the riverbed and arranged them in circles for hearths and threw up their rudimentary wooden huts roofed with pine branches and bracken. The women collected moss and dried it around the fires to pad the sleeping skins they laid on the earth floors. Autumn ale was fermenting in the chestnut wood tubs. Gutted and split fish were drying on racks over smouldering oak bark fires. It was no part of Badurad's function as their chieftain to give detailed orders but the people came to him for advice and to settle disputes. If two families wanted the same spot on which to build their hut, they could either accept Badurad's judgement or fight. Provided Badurad phrased his decision carefully so that there was no loss of face involved, violence could be avoided. But if neither of the heads of families would give way, blood was shed and sometimes deaths resulted. So far, there had been none this year. Women worked. Warriors visited with their friends. Children and dogs ran about and got in the way. Within four days the community had put down its shallow roots and looked as if it had always lived there.

Odila was teaching Saxa how to make a needle from a sliver of deer bone. Mother and daughter's heads were almost touching as they squatted over the delicate work, using a precious steel auger to bore into the bone. From time to time Odila cast a concerned glance through the pale sunlight streaming in at the open entrance of their hut. Badurad was sitting outside on a log stool deep in thought as he sharpened one of his spears. For the first few days after their arrival he had been busy but now that the people were settled, he was once again silent and preoccupied.

The auger point passed through the bone without splitting the end. Saxa was delighted. She had made her first needle. She held it up and admired with a broad smile.

"Show your father," Odila told her.

Saxa jumped up and ducked through the entrance to stand beside him. She proudly held it out.

"Look father. I made a needle."

He lifted his head and looked at it, half smiled and said, "Very good," before returning to his spear blade and whetstone. Saxa was deflated. She had expected more from the father she loved. She turned back inside and sat by Odila who put an arm around her daughter but made no comment.

That night when they lay in their bed, Odila stared up at the roof supports almost obscured as the fire burned down to a few glowing embers. The children were asleep in the darkness on the other side of the hearth. Badurad had his back to her. He had not taken her in his arms since his return from the grove of the white horses. She reached out and laid a hand on his naked shoulder. A tremor ran through him at her touch but he neither turned to her nor spoke.

"Badurad, you are gone from me in spirit. Something weighs so heavily on your mind that you are being crushed by it. Or perhaps a spell has been cast on you. You must seek the help of the wise one."

He half-turned and smiled sadly. "I hear you, Odila. I shall think about what you have said."

The next morning, the sun was obscured by a thick blanket of grey cloud. The wind was settling in the northeast and the air smelled of winter. But Badurad woke in a more cheerful mood than he had for a long time. He rose early and jumped naked into the chilly river to wash. He splashed water over his body and head before ducking down below the surface to leap up spluttering in a glittering spray, his skin glowing pink from the cold. No-one passing by took any notice. Both men and women bathed naked in the running water most days unless it was iced over. Even in the depth of winter, some of the hardiest souls smashed the ice to lower themselves into the frigid water below. Badurad waded out and into his hut to dry and warm himself by the fire. Over breakfast, he teased Saxa and spoke warmly to Odila.

"Otto," he said to their son, "Fetch me four smoked fish and enough grain for four loaves. We are going to visit the seer today and we must not arrive empty handed. Oh, and bring both our axes."

He smiled at Odila who nodded her approval.

Father and son went on foot, Otto with their simple offerings and each with an axe on their shoulders. The axe heads were small but razor sharp and they used the long handles like walking staffs. They followed the river upstream through the series of valleys and climbed the northern escarpment of the last one. The going was steep. They were forced to bend double, use their axe handles and grasp at saplings to keep their balance but came at last to a gentler slope and then a plateau densely wooded with ancient, tall pines. It was gloomy and cold as they threaded their way between the closely crowded tree trunks. There was no sound; not a bird sang, not an animal stirred. After an hour's travel through the dim silence, they left the forest.

It gave way to a soaring, splintered rock face. At its base was a rough pathway of fallen rocks and gravel which they followed, glad of their rawhide shoes on the sharp stones beneath their feet. They reached a wide cleft cut by time and nature into the rock where a cascade of white water fell from high into a dark pool. The lichen-covered wall behind it was emerald green. No stream flowed out of the pool; the water plunged down into blackness and depths unseen. Wherever there was a ledge or a wide enough crack in the rock, heathers, larch and silver birch found a precarious foothold and somehow clung on and grew. Further into the fault in the low cliff face they could see a canopy of heavy logs had been built at its base, almost concealing the entrance to a cave. To one side lay a woodpile.

"Come on son, let's split some kindling for the wise woman," Badurad said.

"Is she in there?" Otto asked.

"Oh yes, look." Badurad pointed to where a thin wisp of wood smoke drifted from a crack in the rock and vanished into the air. "She'll hear our axes and when she thinks we've cut enough wood for her fire she might invite us in or she might chase us away."

Otto looked at his father to see if he was joking but Badurad had already selected a thick branch and was bringing his axe down on it. They shortened the long pieces, working together with alternative strokes until they had bitten through and then split the timber lengthwise into usable logs. They worked economically, expertly judging the best point to strike and prise open the grain. The length of the handles compensated for the lightness of the axe-heads. This work was second nature to them and neither of them was short of breath or sweating after an hour's labour. They stopped when a mellow voice called them from the cave mouth.

"So, you have listened to Odila, Badurad. I heard her advising you and was waiting. Enter."

Otto turned sharply but saw no-one.

"You also, boy," the voice added.

Father and son picked up their gifts and walked into the cave, ducking their heads. The fine gravel floor crunched under their feet. Ahead of them in the gloom, the flame of an oil lamp cast a faint yellow glow revealing the entrance to a second chamber. It was so low they were forced to crawl along a narrow corridor in the living rock, reaching their free hands out in front of them to feel the way. Just when his fear of the oppressive stony darkness was about to overwhelm Otto, the corridor turned sharply to the right and opened into a wide vault where he and his father could stand upright. It smelled sweetly of herbs and pine resin. It was lit by three oil lamps and a fire in a natural basin on the floor which was otherwise covered in deep sand.

The wise woman stood behind the fire. She was naked other than for a skirt made of wildcat skin. Her high-breasted body was painted in whorls and sigils. Bones, teeth and seashells were plaited into her long, pale-gold hair. The flickering light seemed to make the patterns on her skin move. She could not have been more than thirty-five. Otto was surprised; he had been sure that she would be very old. She gestured for them to sit and gracefully sank down, cross-legged. Her short kirtle rose up over her thighs and she was totally exposed. Otto stared. He was enthralled by her but his heart was still beating fast from the dread of that crawl through the dark into the unknown. She laughed and spoke directly to him.

"My body fascinates you, boy but you are afraid; of what, you do not know."

Otto looked away and his eyes widened as he saw what was displayed around the chamber. Costly skins and fine weapons, wine-jars and wooden casks, silver ornaments and strange flasks of some material he had never seen before gleaming green and red and blue. There was another person present. An adolescent girl dressed in a long white shift stood forward out of a dim recess and came to him holding out her hands. He was confused for a moment then passed her the fish and grain he and his father had brought. He glanced again at the treasures on view and was ashamed at how commonplace and paltry their offering seemed in comparison. Again, she spoke to him.

"You are mistaken if you believe what you bring is inferior. Your father understands what is truly valuable. I cannot eat wealth; now thanks to you, I shall have bread and fish for a few days." She made a gesture with her arms to include Badurad in the conversation. "I am grateful. I also thank you for cutting wood for my fire. How can I return your kindness?"

"I have come to you because I am troubled in my mind," Badurad said.

She drew some crystals out of a stone bowl beside her and threw them into the fire. They crackled and sparked and then the air was full of the scent of Frankincense.

"When did this come upon you?"

"After I assisted the priests in the grove of the white horses," he confessed.

"Then you can tell me nothing. The curse would fall on me as well as you if you did."

"I know and I will not break my oath but there is something I cannot understand that makes me wonder if the gods have turned away from me."

She stared at him in silence for a while. Just when it became unbearable, she spoke once more.

"You believe the gods no longer favour you?"

Badurad let his head fall.

"I do," he confessed.

"And yet here you sit," she replied. "Healthy, a fighter of renown, battle counsel to a king and respected chieftain of your clan; how can you be abandoned by the gods?"

"I know what you say is the truth but my uneasiness gnaws at me." He fell silent in turn and then blurted out, "How will I die?"

"What are you, what makes you Badurad?" she asked.

"I am a warrior," he answered without hesitation.

"Then expect to die like a warrior."

"But when, what time do I have left?"

The expression on her face changed to one of infinite sadness.

"You have asked me so you shall have your answer."

She pointed to a wooden trencher full of hazelnuts. The girl fetched them over and put them down beside Badurad. She handed him a large pebble.

"Take one and crack it open on the hearthstones," she ordered.

He broke open the shell. There was no kernel inside it.

"Take another."

He did and amongst the sharp brown fragments he found no nut, nothing to eat.

"The earth mother stores no food for you in her autumn bounty, man! She does not need to feed you through the coming winter days."

Badurad heaved a deep sigh and looked into her sorrowful eyes.

"I bless you for the truth you have told me but what of my son?"

The wise woman turned her attention to Otto. She indicted a stone near the centre of the fire.

"Spit on it," she told him.

He leaned forward, supporting his weight on his arms, feeling the heat of the fire on his face and dribbled a little spittle on the stone.

She clucked her tongue impatiently.

"No, sniff, hawk give me a big gobbet of your essence."

Otto did as he was told. She stared down at the lump of phlegm that steamed and bubbled until it dried up with a final hissing pop and all that remained was a silver skein.

"Your son will never carry his shield and spear in the ranks of the Suevi," she told Badurad with absolute certainty.

"He will not be a warrior?"

"I did not say that."

 "What is your name, boy?" she asked.

"Otto," he managed mumble from his suddenly dry mouth.

The wise woman began to shake and sway from side to side. Her body patterns writhed in the flickering lamplight as the shadows came and went as she shuddered. Her eyes rolled up in her head and two white orbs like pigeon's eggs glowed from her face framed by the snaking plaits of her hair. She croaked and growled as if from a place far away.

"Otto, killer of kings, the unchangeable fate of all men is already written and your destiny is borne by someone as yet unknown to you. A man is entering your life. He wears black plumes; black as the deepest night; black as death within the grave. Your spirit already knows him. Wherever he finds you, whenever he finds you, whatever you must sacrifice, go with him and he will set you on the path of your life's journey. This is the way the gods have chosen for you. Refuse to follow it and die, unremembered and unsung."

She slumped backwards. The girl caught her before her head cracked into the wall and lowered her mistress gently to the ground.

"Go," she told them calmly. "I have seen this before. The gods have spoken through her and she must have peace to restore her strength and for her own spirit to return to her body."

Badurad and Otto crawled out into the daylight and fresh air. They sat on the log pile, unspeaking. Otto was badly shaken by all that he had heard. He wanted to re-interpret what the wise woman had told his father but there could be no other meaning than the obvious one. Badurad's days on this earth were coming to their end. He looked at his father and felt his heart clench and grow heavy in his chest. He could not imagine what his life would be without his father in it and wanted to say so but could not find the words. Badurad stood up and smiled at his son.

"Let's go back," he said.

He strode ahead with a lithe, springing step as if a heavy burden had been lifted off him. Occasionally he would slash at a weed or dead branch with his axe and even sang snatches of well-remembered songs. Otto could not understand. His father had been warned of his imminent death and yet went happily through the forest as if he had no cares. Otto lagged behind desperate to ask what was going on in Badurad's mind but frightened to speak. They left the dim light that fell between the pine trees and came to the edge of the steep slope that led down to the most northerly of their winter home valleys. Badurad sat on a fallen tree trunk and let Otto catch up with him while he contentedly surveyed the small river flowing below. He lifted one finger.

"Listen," he said.

And sure enough, Otto caught the faintest sound of a human voice at the very edge of his hearing. It sounded like a mother calling a child. As they sat still and concentrating, the scent of wood smoke came to them. Badurad sighed with simple contentment, closed his eyes and lifted his face to the sky where the noon sun was trying to break through the clouds.

"Now you can ask me the questions that have been boiling up in you as we walked," he said.

"The wise woman told you that you are going to die and yet you seem happier than I have seen you for days, weeks even," Otto burst out in a rush of tumbled words, close to shameful tears.

"Dying in itself is of no consequence. A warrior knows death; it walks beside him everyday not as a friend or an enemy but like a man's shadow. It is simply there and nothing can be done about it. In any case, it is better to die in battle or the hunt while you are still proud and strong than to cough the rags of your life away in an old man's piss-soaked bed. But you're right; I am more cheerful because now I understand. Something happened to me in the grove of the white horses which made me fear that the gods had turned their faces away from me. It gnawed at my mind like a fox chewing away at its leg to try to escape a snare. But I was mistaken. The wise woman made it all clear. It was nothing to do with the gods but simply this world bidding me farewell. She has led me to know that what happened to me in that sacred place was the first sign. So, my son, my mind is clear and unclouded."

He smiled and patted Otto companionably on his shoulder but the boy would not be as easily reconciled as his father.

"How will I go on without you?"

A stern expression came over Badurad's face.

"You have been told. You have a destiny locked to a black plumed stranger. Look to his coming and follow your fate." He stared hard into Otto's eyes until his son nodded acceptance. They both knew this had the force of a blood-oath between them. Badurad softened and looked lovingly at Otto. "As for you and me, well, we have had many good days together. Appreciate them for what they were and store them in your memory."

He stood up.

"Time to go home and show a cheerful face to your mother and sister because doing otherwise will change nothing."

Chapter 6

Tribune Lucius Taurius Longius walked his horse across the bridge at the head of his column of men, his chest swollen with pride. This was it. This was what he had been born to do. He was leading soldiers into hostile territory in the name of Rome and the Emperor. His horse's hooves ceased clattering on the planks as he reached the far side and rode down onto the riverbank where he brought his mount to a halt and reviewed his men as they passed in front of him. A passable track had been worn by the desultory commerce that crossed between Greater Germany and the Empire at this point and led off northwards into the all-encompassing forest.

He was doing his best to look like a dignified and impassive officer representing Roman Gravitas, but a smile kept breaking out. The thump, thump of the legionaries' boots on the timber bridge made a pleasing martial rhythm; it wasn't a legion, not even a cohort but he was their commander and how fine they looked to him. The centurions brought them to a halt and doubled back to where the tribune waited at the bridgehead. They slammed to rigid attention.

"Your orders, sir," Lentus barked.

Lucius felt a moment of panic. Up to now it had been a sort of parade, not real, but these men were looking to him to lead them. His mind went blank. The missile troops were not at attention in dressed ranks. They were not the elite Cretan archers and Balearic slingers the army favoured. They were ordinary soldiers who had gained a reputation for being useful with a bow or a sling, largely as a result of their skill in hunting for the pot to supplement standard rations. Titus Attius had pulled them out of different centuries for this operation. They had lost their accustomed chain of command; their centurions and optios were back in camp. Longius made his first command decision. He looked at the uneasy mob carrying bows and slings and called out.

"Who amongst you is the best archer?"

They looked at each other and shuffled before one man was pushed forward. He was in his late twenties, a hardened professional; tall, gaunt and weather-beaten. He looked up at Longius and saluted.

"Your name?"

"Marcus Corvo, tribune."

"Very well Marcus Corvo, you now lead the archers and slingers. Keep alert to receive and carry out the orders that I or the other officers will give you. Choose the best of the slingers for your second and give his name to the centurions. My first order is that you get your men into proper ranks and straighten up."

Corvo saluted, performed a smart about turn and began to shout at his troops.

"You heard the officer. Pick your arses off the floor and try pretending you're soldiers."

Lucius relaxed. The men were going to do what he told them to; something he had not quite believed until Corvo gave him the proof. He looked down at Centurion Lentus.

"The track leads more or less north and that is our line of march. We shall stay on it and make the best time until an hour before sundown when we shall veer off to the east to make camp. Send the scouts ahead and tell them to keep a good look out. Even this close to the river there might be trouble. Let the column advance, centurion."

Lentus saluted and jogged back to his position, stopping for a brief word of explanation to the other officers. Lucius heard shouted orders and then the men hefted their shields and javelins and began to move off. The going underfoot was comfortable at first. The earth track had grassed over during the summer and a carpet of fallen pine needles and the first autumn leaves on top made it springy under the men's boots. At the end of the first hour, it came on to rain. Fat, cold drops plunged down from the dirty yellow clouds glimpsed now and then through the tree canopy. The archers immediately unstrung their bows and coiled the strings. Wet, they would stretch when the bow was drawn and it would be impossible to shoot with any force. To keep the coils dry, they shoved them inside their subarmalis, the padded shirt they wore under their chain mail armour. Lucius had been moving up and down the column and saw what they were doing. Although he mentally commended their foresight, the fact that over twenty of his force were no longer combat effective gave him food for thought.

After a further half an hour, the ground began to soak up the rainwater and soften. It was not so bad for the men at the front of the column, their boots barely broke the surface but the men who came after churned it even more as they passed until the mules and missile troop bringing up the rear were struggling in ankle deep mud. It was an object lesson in why the marching season ended when it did. Two hundred odd men and a few animals had cut the path into oozing furrows. If a legion had passed that way, the last men would be in it to the knees. Still, they kept up a good pace and were well clear of the river when the scouts judged sunset was approaching and led them off to the east looking for a place to bivouac.

They found a clearing made by two massive oaks that had crashed down in the same storm during the previous winter. Lucius ordered one third of the infantry to form a picket line and two of the scouts to ride around its perimeter. "Fast and hard" the legate had said so the men had not carried their entrenching tools to make a fortified temporary camp. Instead they would rely on sentries to give them warning of any attack and sleep in full armour with their weapons within reach. In spite of the rain they soon had small fires lit.. Although rotten with fungus underneath, many of the branches of the fallen oaks had stayed clear of the ground and had dried out so that they could be snapped off. These fed the fires and burned well once the surface moisture the rain had left on them boiled off.

Most of the legionaries were old hands and soon made lean-to shelters of pine branches with enough greenery on them to keep off the worst of the rain. Breeches, socks and the scarves they wore to stop their armour chafing at the neck were propped up on sticks steaming dry in front of the fires. Rations were served out from the mules' packsaddles. Under leaking canopies, the men chewed on cold bacon and stale bread washed down with watered, vinegary wine. They laughed or grumbled according to their individual natures but overall, they were not unhappy. They expected no better and had endured much worse.

The guard was changed after the first two hours and then every four hours. In the middle of the night, the rain ceased. At dawn, the last of the watches was replaced long enough for them to eat and warm up before they moved off, wending their way ever northward through the monotony of the dank, tree-filled landscape. They rested at noon. Lucius called in his centurions, their optios and Corvo.

"My orders are to march north from the river for a full day, which we have now accomplished, noon to noon. From now on our mission is aggressive. We are to destroy any German settlement we come across. There will be no prisoners taken and no loot. At the end of the third day, we are to return to base but there will be no violence shown to anyone when we are once more within a day's march of home. Is that understood?

He looked around, and everyone nodded.

"Very good; now, we cannot keep on in this stretched formation but neither will I split our forces. We will proceed on a broad front in three groups, each within hailing distance of the other. It is essential that no group moves too far ahead or lags behind. Unless attacked, no-one engages without informing me first. A scout will be assigned to the head of each group ready to act as a runner. The mules and such food and equipment as we have will be protected by your men, Corvo. I march with you and one scout assigned to me. Centurion Lentus, I suggest you decide on how to organise the men along the lines I have indicated, any questions?"

"Not a question as such, sir but I'd like to point something out."

"Go ahead," Lucius said.

"Going to be a lot slower, covering the ground this way, sir."

"You're right of course but we will be advancing on a broader front which will make up for it to some extent. Is that all? Well, get on with it then."

Lentus and the other officers spent the next quarter of an hour shouting and pulling men into line. Each group was made up of fifty infantrymen marching ten abreast, in a file five men deep and fifty yards distant from the next formation. Eight spare soldiers had been sent back to the tribune to act as close support for the archers and slingers in case of a direct attack on them. Bows were now restrung and at the ready, the slingers had unwrapped their leather slings from around their waists and held them at the ready. Each of them carried a pouch of army-issue lead bullets which could kill a man a hundred feet away with a strike to the head, even if he was wearing a metal helmet. The centurions' whistles shrieked and the new formation moved off.

Lentus had been correct; it was slower but there was little undergrowth between the trees to impede them. It was hardest for the men in the front who had to negotiate around fallen trees and such brambles and bracken as managed to find enough light to grow under the dense branches, so they were rotated in the usual Roman way. The second rank took the place of the first, then after a while the third replaced the second until each man had taken his turn in sharing the lead of his formation. The scouts ranged in front, constantly returning to report to the centurions and optios. They helped them to keep their relative distances and a reasonable straight line. They spoke almost no Latin but knew the key words necessary to advise the officers, even if they could not put them into a complete sentence.

After two hours during which five miles had been covered, a runner dashed back from the head of the formation and stopped to pant out a message. Lentus had ordered a general halt and requested that the tribune joined him to give his assessment of the situation. Lucius ordered the soldier to catch his breath and then follow on. He cantered his horse the two hundred yards to where Lentus stood waiting with a dismounted scout beside him. The centurion saluted then indicated the scout with a jerk of his thumb.

"This one reckons there's a farmstead or small settlement about half a mile out to the west of our present position, sir."

Lucius unhooked his legs from the saddle horns and jumped down. He looked at the scout and then at Lentus.

"Can you trust him?"

Lentus shrugged.

"Wouldn't be the first of 'em to change sides once he was over the river; but Prefect Aldermar would have given us his most reliable."

"Even so, best have a look ourselves, eh?"

Lentus frowned.

"No need for you to go along, sir."

"I'm not committing my men unless I know what they're getting into, centurion."

"With all due respect, Tribune Longius, it is not usual for a commanding officer to go on a hazardous reconnaissance mission."

"Your recommendation is noted. Send your optio along the line and have all the men rally to this point and stand-to. Someone fetch me Corvo, he might be useful. And get one of the lads to help me out of this," Lucius said, tapping his cuirass.

He was greatly relieved to have an excuse to take off his ornate breastplate and the steel back plate he had worn since they had left on the mission. His subarmalis was covered in oiled brown leather to help it stay waterproof. It was ideal as an outer garment for slipping through the forest. Corvo arrived and was told to leave his bow. On foot, Lucius, Corvo and Lentus, who had removed his distinctive centurion's helmet, followed the scout off to their left. He urged them to silence with a finger to his lips. They walked in single file for twenty minutes and then the German dropped into a crouch, moving cautiously. Finally, he indicated they should all get down and they crawled for a few yards. He gently separated a tuft of yellowed grass, peered through it and grinned wolfishly. He motioned for the others to move up beside him and look for themselves.

They were at the edge of a roughly circular clearing perhaps one hundred yards across. Near the centre was a low, thatched house made of pine logs and behind it stood a barn. The barn was also thatched and had no doors, just a simple gate across the only visible entrance. Crude fences had been erected close to the buildings to pen half a dozen cattle and two horses and keep them from straying. A faint haze of greyish wood smoke filtered through the thatch of the house roof and drifted away on the cold breeze. As they watched, a red-headed man with a wooden pitchfork over one shoulder walked from behind the barn towards the house. He propped up the fork beside the door and went in with a glance over his shoulder in their direction. They all shrank further down into their cover but did not look again. He had seen nothing.

"Let's get back a few paces," Lucius whispered and then felt stupid; he could not possibly have been overheard unless he had shouted at the top of his voice.

Ten yards from the edge of the clearing under the trees, they squatted behind the broad trunk of an oak.

"This is it then," Lucius said, trying to sound calm and sure the others could hear the hammering of his heart. "Lentus, what do you think?"

"We've only seen one man but there could be more inside and that log house will take some storming, particularly if there's only one way in and out. We'd better set fire to the thatch and finish them when they run out."

Lucius shook his head.

"No fire; the smoke will warn the whole district. The others will either vanish into the forest or assemble a force against us."

"Then we have to surround the clearing and send a few of the lads through that door."

"And that is risky?" Lucius asked.

"Always risky to be the first men in, sir," Lentus told him.

Lucius did not answer but stared at the leaf mould beneath his boots for a while. The others did not interrupt his silence.

"Corvo, could you hit one of those cows with an arrow from where we first saw them.

Corvo looked at the young tribune to see if he was joking.

"Sir, it's less than fifty paces; an easy shot," the archer replied.

"Could you deliberately wound it from that range rather than killing it?"

"I could sir."

"Good man, then here's what we are going to do. The entire column is to assemble at a convenient point two hundred paces from where we are. Ten slingers and archers supported by twenty legionaries are to make their way through the forest and take up a position behind the barn and the house. A further squad of the same number will come up to our observation point. Corvo will stand in the open and shoot one of the cows. Someone from the house will hear and come out to see what is wrong. I believe that he will run at you, Corvo but you must stand your ground. When he is close enough, one of your men will help you bring him down. Then we shall advance shouting, blowing whistles and thumping swords against shields. Anyone else in the house will take fright and run away from us right into the second group who will deal with them. Do you have anything to add, centurion?"

"With your permission, I will lead the group with Corvo and his men. The second group will be under the orders of the other century's optio. You, sir, should remain with the main force." Lucius frowned but before he could object, Lentus continued. "This seems easy enough but things can always go wrong. If this does, the lads will still have you, my optio and the other centurion to lead them."

Lucius puffed his cheeks out and sighed deeply.

"Very well, Lentus, I concede."

Three-quarters of an hour later, the dispositions had been made. The main body were still gathering but the assault units had separated and doubled up to their agreed positions. Lentus left plenty of time for the second party which had been out of his sight from the outset to make their way around behind the house and barn.

Apart from Lentus and Corvo, standing behind a convenient tree, the other men lay on the ground as near to the forest edge as possible.

"Off you go then, soldier," Lentus told Corvo who took two paces forward and stood in plain view at the edge of the clearing.

He drew his bow back until it creaked, took careful aim and released an arrow. It arced upwards then dipped to strike on of the cows through her udder. The poor beast bellowed in shock and pain, and half fell into a fencepost, snapping the arrow shaft. Another wave of pain went through her and she bellowed again, kicking up her back kegs and clumsily rushing around the enclosure in a futile attempt to escape her agony. The other animals felt her distress and panic ran through them. Within four seconds, what had been a peaceful scene of grazing cattle and horses had become a frantic, milling stampede, likely to burst through the fence rails at any moment.

Lentus was watching from cover. Corvo stood firm as the red-haired man appeared at the house door, saw him and ducked back inside. He came back out almost immediately armed with a spear and shield, whistling shrilly as he ran towards Corvo as predicted by Lucius. What none of them had foreseen were the two huge dogs that had responded to his whistle and now streaked across the open ground towards the archer. It was one thing to put an arrow into a standing cow, quite another to hit one of the dark blurs with lolling tongues and snarling jaws that raced towards him. Lentus stood forward and shouted.

"Fall back Corvo! On your feet men, shields up, on your fucking feet!"

The legionaries were up in an instant; short swords drawn and shields almost touching. The first dog leapt straight onto a sword point that sunk to the hilt into its chest. The second gripped the bottom of a shield and worried it until a downward thrust passed through its spine. It whimpered and lay still. The spearman had seen the Romans and tried to slow his onward charge. A second man, older and holding an axe, had joined him and was twenty paces behind. He managed to stop dead in time for a slingshot bullet to shatter his right knee. He fell sideways, screaming. The leading man was taken in the chest by two arrows and killed instantly.

"Forward march," Lentus yelled and repeatedly blew his whistle. The soldiers drummed the flat of their swords against their shields and advanced. As the line passed over the man with the destroyed knee, one of them leaned over without breaking step and casually killed him with a stab to the base of his throat.

A group of six people fled the house and ran towards the back of the barn.

"Silence!" yelled Lentus.

A few seconds later, the sound of some faint cries came to him. They continued their unhurried, relentless march around the barn and met the other party of soldiers, standing among the bodies of an old man, two women and three children, all killed by missile fire. The optio stepped forward, came to attention and saluted.

"That all of 'em?" Lentus asked

"Yes, centurion, no-one escaped."

"Well done, send a couple of lads to have a gander inside the house and barn."

Two soldiers were told to double up. As they trotted away, Lentus shouted after them.

"Oi, take care before you stick your heads in there, still might be some monster inside itching to have your guts out. The rest of you, start collecting up the bodies. And Corvo, will you please put that poor cow out of its misery, don't you have any heart, man?"

Since he had rejoined his troops, Lucius had spent his time marching up and down in a frenzy of suspense. It took all his disciplined resolve to stop running up to Lentus when he saw him approaching at the head of his men.

"Centurion Lentus reporting, Tribune Longius," he said with a flourished salute, copied by Corvo who stood slightly behind him.

"Make your report, centurion," Lucius replied.

"Objective achieved without any casualties. We have accounted for eight Germans and their livestock sir. In accordance with your orders, we did not fire their dwellings."

"All went according to plan, then?" Lucius inquired.

"Nearly, sir; they set two big hounds on us. They nearly got poor Corvo but the lads dealt with them."

"A narrow escape then, Corvo," the tribune remarked.

"Funny how fast you can move with a couple of damn big dogs snapping at you, sir.

"I hope I don't have to find out," Lucius replied and turned to Lentus again, "And the bodies?"

"Put 'em all in the house along with the livestock after we'd cut their throats, left 'em all in one big heap. Then we just shut the place up. Oh, and the optio wrote "Second Lucan" on the door with charcoal and drew an eagle on it; very good at drawing that optio is. There will be no doubt that it was us, sir."

"Thanks to you both; pass on my congratulations to the men on a job well done."

They marched out until the scouts reported a good place for an overnight camp. It was beside a small lake with a narrow river running into it. Beside a sandy beach, a rickety jetty like an old man's skinny, bent finger ran a few yards out into the lake There were two tumbledown wooden buildings beside it. Smoke curled out of a hole in the roof of one but there was no sign of any inhabitants. They were all gone along with their boats if they had any, their nets, traps and fish-spears.

"Must have seen or heard us coming," remarked the optio who drew so well.

No-one bothered to answer him; it was so obvious it had not needed saying,

The second hut was full of racks of smoked fish. They pulled it down to use for firewood and cooked up a fish stew for all. There was a mild holiday mood among the men. With the lake at their back, they needed to post less sentries overnight and the fish had been a welcome change of diet. Lucius commandeered the remaining hut for his quarters. A soldier was detailed to help him off with his armour, which he would sleep without since they were reasonably secure. The temporary orderly looked disapprovingly at the weather- tarnished metal helmet, cuirass and back plate.

"Looking a bit grubby, sir," he said. "I could polish it up if you like; have it ready for you first thing."

Lentus passed him as he squatted under his rudimentary shelter using a mixture of spit and olive oil on a piece of doeskin to brighten up the armour.

"Got a new job, brown-nosing the tribune, have you?" one of his comrades said.

"Bugger off; he's not a bad lad for an officer is Boxer," he replied, turning the helmet in the firelight to admire the shine.

"Thought he was called Tribune Longius," another soldier remarked.

"He is," the first one said, "but a lot of the lads call him boxer. Seen that nose of his? All over his face, poor sod."

They all laughed.

"Here, give us a go," a newcomer said, picking up the back plate.

Lentus smiled and went on his way without comment.

In the morning, Lucius mounted his horse wearing newly gleaming armour. The legionaries had even untangled and combed through the crest on his helmet. They surreptitiously admired their handiwork.

The lake and the river feeding it ran roughly north. The trees were more widely spaced near the riverbank, so the column could march six abreast as one combined unit. Orders were shouted and the lines shuffled off, swinging into a steady rhythm once the leading men had got up to speed. They marched cheerfully deeper into Upper Germany, knowing that tomorrow they would turn for home.

Chapter 7

Odila was no happier in her household than before Badurad and Otto had gone to visit the wise woman. Yes, Badurad was restored to his former self; the gloom was cleared away. He smiled, he talked, teased Saxa and walked around the camp greeting his friends. But Otto was withdrawn and self-absorbed as if the cloud from his father's mind had blown over his. And worse, her son and his father seldom spoke to each other. But sometimes Odila thought she saw a conspiratorial look pass between them as if they shared a secret. She said nothing. Her love for her family was deep and genuine but she was the daughter, partner and mother of warriors. The traditions of her people dictated how she lived her life. If Otto had a problem, he must solve it or go to his father for advice. That was how it was. Her son was nearly a man and had already freed himself from her influence. The only woman who could ever discuss private matters with him would be his future wife.

She sighed and shook her head. It was time to forget her troubles and get to work. Today, she and many of the other women were going to gather chestnuts. There was a grove high on the western slopes of the next valley upstream and the husks containing the shining reddish nuts inside them were beginning to fall. They would have to be brought in as soon as possible before the wild animals took them. There were twenty-seven wives and mothers in all in the party, half of them carrying babies in slings on one hip. Sixteen girls of various ages came with them along with a dozen boys under ten, and a one-armed man with his hound in case wild boar were about. They had woven baskets in wooden frames with straps on their backs. By the end of the day, they hoped they would be heavy with the bounty they were going out to forage. The cheerful body set off; the inevitable late comer rushing breathless to catch up, dragging a reluctant child by the hand. They moved upstream along the riverbank and through the neck of the escarpments on either side into the next valley past some cattle grazing on the sparse late pasture. They climbed steadily for nearly an hour, stopping to rest on the ridge before moving on through the inevitable pines. No-one knew if the chestnut grove had been planted deliberately but there were over forty well-grown trees with a carpet of bright green spiky globes spread over the ground between them. They represented a rich harvest but everything comes at a price; the needle-sharp spines would make fingers bleed before they were all gathered in.

Odila looked back. From her elevated position, she could see the farthest half of the village over the intervening high ground. The roofs of the huts steamed in the growing warmth of a cloudless morning. The river seemed very blue from up here. A few tiny figures moved about, too far away to be recognisable. Someone tossed hay over the stock pen fence. Odila took the basket off her shoulders and bent to the day's work.

The scouts galloped back to the Roman column and flung themselves off their horses, gabbling in their excitement. They kept pointing upstream and shaking their lances. Lucius and the other officers gathered and tried to make sense of what they were being told. "Castra, Castra!" one of them kept shouting, using the Latin word for "camp".

"I think they are trying to tell us there is some sort of native settlement up ahead," Lucius suggested.

The scout understood something of what Lucius had said and began to nod his head in assent. He smoothed over some of the sandy earth underfoot with his boot and began to scratch in it with his lance butt. They bent over to study what was being outlined in the dirt. A wriggling line was clearly the river; beside it were some circles and stickmen with shields and spears. Lucius squatted and pointed at the crude drawing of the warriors. He held up his other hand with the fingers and thumb splayed and looked inquiringly at the scout. The German shook his head and clenched and unclenched his right hand three times.

Lucius stood up. "I believe he is trying to tell us that there is a sizable village nearby with at least fifteen warriors, possibly more."

"If they have fifteen armed or half armed men, you can double that number with all the great hairy bastards that will come at us with an axe or a hoe," Lentus added.

"Halt the men where they are and get them in close order, Lentus," the tribune told him and leapt into the saddle. He indicated that the scouts should lead him to where they had seen the German village.

"Tribune, I must protest," Lentus said.

"Centurion Lentus, do you have a horse?"

"No sir…."

"But I do. I shall be back as soon as I can. Keep a good look out in my absence."

Lucius made his horse rear on its hind legs then spin before cantering off upstream, the scouts on either side of him. The horsemen soon passed out of sight. Lentus vented his irritation on his optio who accepted the dressing down philosophically then turned on the nearest legionary and shouted at him. The legionary remained silently at attention; he had no-one to take it out on.

The group of three horsemen was back in little over half an hour. The tribune's expression was serious; a deep vertical line creased his forehead. He dismounted and the officers ran to him. The legionaries edged as close as they dared to try to overhear.

"What we have here," Lucius explained, "is a half-moon shaped valley around two hundred paces long. It follows the river on one side and rises steeply on the other. At the head of the valley there is a break where the water flows through. I counted twenty huts but I could not see them all from my vantage point. The entrance nearest to us is half a mile away. What further information would be helpful?"

"Are the huts arranged in any sort of pattern?" Lentus asked.

"No, not so far as I could see."

"The wind is blowing in our faces, centurion," Corvo added.

Lentus acknowledged his comment with an appreciative nod.

"My turn to ask a question," said Lucius. "Is the force we will be facing strong enough to do us any real damage?"

"They shouldn't be too troublesome if we can hold formation. The problem is, we shall have to break ranks in order to pass around their huts and, as you've said, tribune, there's no order to them."

Lucius turned to Corvo. "Why is the wind direction worth noting?"

Corvo looked a little nervously at the centurions and optios before replying. He was unsure whether he was part of this council of war or not. He cleared his throat and spoke up.

"I've done this a couple of times before, Tribune Longius. As Centurion Lentus says, the problem is there are no proper lanes between their dwellings and that hinders us in keeping formation. What we usually do is we set them alight as we advance. This drives the enemy out in front of us and makes sure there is no one hiding to attack us in the rear. But we can't do that today because as soon as we fire the first few huts, the smoke and heat will blow back in our faces and we'll be blind, sir, so to speak."

"Corvo has got it dead to rights sir, couldn't have explained it better myself," Lentus confirmed.

Marcus Corvo blushed for the first time in many years.

"Could we get around them through the forest?" Lucius asked.

"Not unseen sir; a settlement this size is bound to have hunters or woodcutters out," Lentus answered.

Lucius put his hands behind his back and wandered over to the river. He stood staring across to the far bank for several minutes. When he returned, he had a stick in his hand. As the scout had done previously, he began to scratch on the ground with it. His map was more detailed than the first one. Lucius looked around at the faces staring down and used the stick as a pointer while he spoke.

"Right, gentlemen, this is what we do. We advance to within fifty paces of the valley mouth. There is a steep ridge butting right up to the path at that point. We deploy eighteen infantry and six missile troops there to prevent a breakout. That will allow a triple defensive line the width of the path with the slingers and archers up on the ridge. The rest of us double time right through the village to the far end keeping close to the river. There we leave the same number of men to protect us from any stray hostiles in the upper valley. The main force now turns through ninety degrees and attacks on a broad front back the way we came; infantry in front, archers and slingers behind them using every vantage point they can to lay down fire on the opposition. We use the river to protect our flank. We can burn the huts as we go because the wind will be behind us. Fast and hard, as the legate ordered and charge right over anyone who gets in our way

There was a muted cheer from the legionaries close enough to have overheard. Lentus spun round.

"Shut up you lot. What do you think this is; the fucking pantomime? Optio, take the name of the next man who says a word…or grins in an insubordinate manner. Corvo, get your men to tie some bundles of dry twigs together into faggots for kindling and detail off your rear and advance men. Optios, centurion, form the men up, sort out the guard parties and let's get going. Oh, and the lads can stroll till we're up close. No marching in step and banging around with shields; gently does it."

Badurad and two friends lounged on the riverbank near the centre of the village enjoying one of the rare warm days for the time of year. They were watching one of their companions who stood naked and waist deep in the middle of the stream fishing with a spear. Each time he plunged it below the surface and brought it back with no fish flopping on the barbs, they laughed and shouted ribald comments. The fisherman's jaws were clamped tight to stop his teeth from chattering. He had been in too long and was chilled to the bone but his pride would not let him give up.

Otto was on the opposite side of the settlement. The cattle had been dispersed into the upper valleys until the ice and snow arrived when they would be brought closer in but the horses and four oxen were penned behind a wooden fence near the huts. Otto had been given a colt last year. It was now coming up two years old and he was beginning to school it. He held it on a long line attached to its halter and clucked and whistled between his teeth to get it to circle him at differing paces; now a canter, now a walk. After he had finished, he was going up into the forest to bring back yet more of the seemingly endless supply of firewood everyone would need over the fast-approaching winter. His axe, little more than a hatchet on a long handle, was propped against the rudimentary gate of the enclosure.

Over one hundred souls were going about their business around him. Women ground grain or scooped the excess foam off the yeasty liquid in the ale vats. Some men were skinning a buck hanging from a frame by its back legs; or rather, one was working at it while the others gave him helpful advice. A few boys ambushed each other with toy spears. Some girls had their heads together in a giggling group, falling silent if an adult walked within hearing of them. Old folk sat outside their huts stretching arthritic limbs to the healing warmth of the sun.

Soon it would be time for the midday meal.

The Romans halted two hundred paces from the settlement, hidden from it by the curve of the path and the ridge of higher ground. No orders were shouted and no whistles blown. Instructions were passed in quiet voices repeated down the lines of men. Calloused hands eased swords in their scabbards and took a firmer grip on javelins and shields. They were waved on with hand gestures and moved as silently as they could until the fifty-pace mark Lucius had talked about was reached. The rear-guard halted and took up its position. The main force went forward, missile troops nearest the river since they carried no shields, all now marching in step and accelerating into first, double time and then a fast jog as they burst into the winter camp of Badurad's clan. They were forty paces in before they were noticed and another ten until the first shouts and screams rose up from the few shocked people who had seen them and begun to scatter, some for shelter, others to find a weapon.

The level of noise grew as the Romans ran onwards. Badurad knew that sound and what it meant. He and his two friends sprinted for their huts and armed themselves as quickly as possible. The fisherman was too slow. He was within three floundering paces of the bank when a well-aimed javelin struck him in the chest and knocked him back into the water to float gently downstream. The men absorbed in dressing the deer carcase looked up to see a wall of Romans rushing towards them. They were overwhelmed, killed with javelin thrusts and trampled by the thudding boots before they had properly risen to their feet.

The head of the valley was reached, to the great relief of Lucius. He had been cantering his horse in the middle of his running troops, desperate to avoid barging any of them to the ground and slowing the momentum of this mad dash. The centurions and remaining optio yelled out orders and the troops deployed. The second guard took up their position and the bulk of the legionaries formed two ranks with the archers and slingers behind them, now on the side farthest from the river. Sparks were struck, the faggots lit and lobbed into the air to land on the nearest roofs. Yellowish smoke rose and thickened into rolling, choking clouds. Orange flames burst from the sun-dried bracken thatch. The screaming and shouting intensified as the first Germans ran out to die in a hail of javelins, arrows and slingshot.

"Let the men advance Centurion Lentus!" Lucius shouted. "Keep your dressing."

The centurions' whistles shrilled and the steely line of armed men began to cut through the village and its inhabitants like a band saw. They were halfway through when they met their first organised resistance.

Badurad had assembled the surviving twelve of his warriors in a line between two of the largest huts. He was bare-headed but wore his fish-scale armour and carried his sword. Ranged alongside him were men with shields and spears; a few were partially armoured. He stared into the billowing smoke through stinging eyes and caught the first glimpse of the soldiers grinding inexorably towards him like some nightmare dragon of impenetrable scales and fiery breath.

The Romans saw him and his men, shrugged their chainmail into a more comfortable position on their shoulders, crouched and drew swords ready to engage. A mounted officer appeared behind them.

"Halt," he bellowed. The legionaries held their positions. "Centurion," he yelled, "Get Corvo to clear this rabble out of the way."

Badurad heard a Roman carrying no shield but with a crest like a fan on his helmet shout something.

A gaunt soldier holding a bow walked around the end of the shield wall; a dozen slingers and archers following him. The slings whipped round at arm's length just once and released their bullets as the first arrows flew. Half of Badurad's men fell. He looked at the dead and wounded one either side of him and made his decision. These enemies had come to destroy him and his people for no reason. There was no blood feud between them. He had killed no Roman nor had he raided their territory but what did not matter to them? They were inexplicable; like a storm or a plague they came and wreaked havoc then they were gone. If Rome was a force of nature and could not be defeated, it could be defied. He held his sword high, screamed his war cry and ran at them, his warriors closely following. At the instant of impact, a whistle blew and the legionaries leaned forward pushing out with their shields. The weight of the charging Germans shoved them back into the legionaries' bodies but did not break their line. The short swords flickered out through the gaps like vipers' tongues. Badurad and his forlorn hope fell, bleeding their lives out into the earth. Roman boots marched over the bodies. A stamp to the throat or a downward thrust in passing finished off the wounded and the line of death rolled on, seeking further prey.

Badurad lay on his back. Blood pumped out of wounds in his chest and the side of his neck was ripped open. He used his sword to heave himself onto his knees and then to his feet, swaying, head hanging, struggling for every ragged breath. His immense will was focussed on one thing only; his enemies should have neither his body nor his honourable sword to gloat over and despoil. He managed three staggering steps, dragging it behind him and let himself fall headlong through the side of a burning hut. The roof poles crashed down on him, throwing up a wave of flame and completing his warrior's pyre.

Otto's first reaction to the onslaught had been to run and find his father but he quickly realized that was useless; he would never find him in the smoke and confusion. He pulled the halter off his colt's head and smacked it hard on the rump. The screaming and the reek of blazing thatch terrified the animal. It bolted towards the higher ground. He opened the gate of the pen and stood aside as the half dozen horses inside barged each other to get out in a frantic stampede. The oxen lumbered around in a bellowing circle.

Faint screams and rising smoke made the foragers rush to the edge of the chestnut grove and looked down towards their homes. They could see fire moving in a line of yellow flames and behind, the gleam of armoured men chopping and thrusting at any figure who stood in their way. The women screamed and wept; some fell to their knees but Odila watched impassively. She understood what was happening and knew that there was nothing to be done; nothing down in the village could be saved.

"Come on," she shouted harshly. "Get up and run. Stop that stupid noise or we'll be dead as well. Come on!"

She cajoled and bullied them deeper into the grove and out the far side, climbing higher up until a ridge hid them from view of the village. Breathless they collapsed in a hollow, clinging to each other and sobbing.

"Odila, I must go down," the only man with them said.

"To die?" she asked.

He nodded. "Yes, with my brothers; can you imagine the shame of being the only man who did not oppose them?"

"Go then," she said, "but leave me your knife and don't lead them to us."

"What do you reckon's going on here then?" a legionary of the upper valley guard asked the man on his left.

A lone warrior was loping steadily along the river path towards them with an immense black hound keeping pace with him. He carried a shield and two spears. As he came closer, they could see he was going to run straight at them.

"He's only attacking us!" another one said.

They began to laugh until their optio ordered silence and they all stared at the solitary figure growing larger by the second as he approached.

"Archers," the optio shouted, "knock 'im down.

Two stood forward and fired their arrows. As soon as they were airborne, the warrior swerved in mid-stride and raised his shield. Both shafts missed him and plunged quivering into the turf. A slinger fired. His bullet went right through the shield, rocking it back with the impact but failing to hit the man behind it. When he was ten paces away from the Roman triple line the warrior hopped sideways and flung a spear. It arched over the first rank and stuck in the shield of a second rank legionary. But that was all he achieved. Two lead bullets and an arrow at almost point-bank range took him down. His hound ran back to its fallen master, whimpered and licked his dead face. They shot the dog as well.

"Bloody idiot," a legionary said and spat at the ground beneath his feet.

The optio hit him so hard on the head that his helmet rang like a bell and he staggered.

"Would you do what he did?" the officer asked. "No, you fucking wouldn't. That was a brave man; show him some respect."

Lucius had kept immediately behind the centre of the constantly breaking and reforming infantry line as they advanced. From his vantage point high on his horse's back, he saw an old, bent man with scrawny arms and legs standing in front of an old woman defending her with a kitchen knife. He watched them fall to two of his men who casually thrust them into a burning hut with their javelins. He saw a legionary strike down a young woman and catch the baby she held in her arms before it hit the ground then cut its throat and toss it, pinwheeling through a blazing roof. He could feel the blood draining from his face and suddenly his mouth was full of vomit. He swallowed it back, burning his throat and fought the faintness that made him rock in his saddle.

"Mars, is this your true face?" he thought, appalled.

He looked around and saw his men going about this butchery as if it was all in a day's work. Then he understood that it was, exactly that; a day's work and if he wanted to serve as an officer of Rome, it must be his work too.

"We give you this blood in sacrifice great Mars," Lucius muttered under his breath, hoping to appease the god of war for the weakness he had momentarily shown.

The action was nearly over. The initial fires were burning low and there were no roofs left to fire. The legionaries were ordered to break ranks, form small groups and hunt down survivors. One such knot of three men found Otto.

He still stood with the gatepost at his back holding his axe across his body in both hands. He watched them impassively as they came nearer and spread out in front of him. He had never seen Romans before. They were smaller than he had expected after all the stories he had heard about their victories under their great general, Julius Caesar. But people now said that Caesar was a god which explained why his armies swept the lands clear of all who opposed him. Otto was not impressed by what he saw. He accepted that they would shortly kill him but he wished his enemies were heroic in stature and bearing. They were not. Their boots were black with ash, their faces smeared and filthy and their swords fouled with brown stains. They gave off an odour of smoke, sweat and the metallic scent of blood.

They saw a German like all the others; tall, blond and with those horrible blue eyes like chips of ice.

"He's a big 'un," one of them said.

His companion looked more closely.

"Bit of a boy, that's all; look, he hasn't even got any peach fuzz on his face."

"Bloody big boy, that's all I say," added the first speaker. "Come on, Tubby, sort him out."

They both turned to the middle soldier in the group. He was short, barrel-chested and had only the vestige of a squat neck.

"Why me?" he complained.

"Oh go on, it'll be a laugh. Chop 'im down at the knees, they're about level with your shoulders."

"Bastards," Tubby muttered and stepped cautiously forward.

Otto did not stir as the Roman closed in. He could see only his eyes above the top of his shield and his sword held out at the side, level and ready to thrust. More legionaries emerged from the thinning smoke and stood back to watch the fun. Tubby was in sword strike distance of Otto. His eyes narrowed slightly at the moment he made his move. It was enough for Otto who had been trained by his father to look out for such signals on an enemy's face. He half turned to avoid the blade and stepped to the Roman's left. Tubby had leaned forward and advanced his right foot to get all his weight behind the blow, but since he had missed, he was off-balance. Otto banged the end of his axe handle down on the toe of Tubby's boot. The legionary yelped and fell sideways through the fence. A huge roar of laughter burst out of the watching soldiers. Otto did not strike at his fallen opponent but took his place with the post at his back again; calmly waiting for whoever would come next.

A horse's head and neck appeared through the murk. It came forward revealing the rider. He jumped nimbly down from his saddle, looked around and walked towards them. At that moment, a gust of wind blew the air clear and the sunlight struck down on him.

"What's so funny?" he asked the soldiers who immediately clammed up and came to attention.

Otto took in his fine armour but most of all, the helmet he wore; silver and gold with an ornate crest of black plumes that had been plucked from the tails of several roosters. They nodded and shook as he moved. Blades of sunlight splintered from their glossy surfaces which made them even blacker; black as the deepest night; black as death within the grave. Otto dropped his axe, stepped across the three paces that separated them and knelt. He lifted up his hands held together as if in prayer and looked inquiringly into the face of the man who held his destiny. Lucius did not know what was happening but without thinking about it, he clasped the boy's hands in his own. Otto stood up, smiled broadly, nodded and took hold of the tribune's bridle, holding his horse for him.

Lucius was as amazed as the legionaries. They all stood in silence staring at this German oddity. Lentus bustled up and took everything in.

"Alright, alright, what's all this?" Tubby what the bloody hell are you doing, mending the fucking fence? Get on with it the lot of you; no-one's sounded the recall have they?"

The soldiers melted away, cheerfully grinning, to get back to the sports of prodding in woodpiles and haystacks for any hidden survivors to kill.

Lentus looked at Lucius and then at Otto who was calmly holding the tribune's horse. He drew his sword which had remained in its scabbard throughout the operation.

"Want me to finish him, sir?" he asked in the tone of someone offering to do a favour.

"I think not," he replied.

"Oh, going to do 'im yourself are you sir?"

"He gave himself up to me," Lucius told him, as if that would explain why the boy was not to die.

"Gave himself up?" Lentus snorted. "These Germans don't do that, never. Kill him now or he'll cut your throat as soon as we're back in camp, if not tonight. They make shit slaves, Germans."

But Lentus had gone a little too far. It sounded to Lucius that the centurion was issuing an order. He fixed the man with his best superior stare.

"Thank you for giving me your opinion Centurion Lentus. I do not believe I asked for it. Recall the men and have them assemble here where there is room for them all. Oh, and I noticed some horses galloping about in the confusion. Let them be captured and brought along."

Lentus tried to keep his face impassive but his pinched lips turned down at the corners. He was angry at being put in his place by this youngster who obviously thought he was Alexander the Great because he had seen his first action. He saluted stiffly and turned smartly on his heel before striding rapidly away and issuing a stream of orders. The men drifted up out of the smoke which was now little more than occasional thin wisps like rags shaken out on a gust of wind. They had brought three horses with them which they led into the pen. Although the scouts had received no orders to engage, they had done so gleefully, cutting down anyone they could. They now had trophies tied to their saddles; scalps of bloody hair, right hands. The soldiers fell in and the roll call was taken. They were all accounted for; none missing, none injured. Lucius turned to mount his horse. Otto passed him the reins and cupped his hands to help the tribune into the saddle.

"Well done men," he called in a voice loud enough to be heard by all. "You will be pleased to know we are now proceeding back to camp but before we do, there is one more task we need to accomplish; Centurion Lentus!" Lentus stepped forward and saluted. "Detail some men to slaughter those oxen and butcher a couple of them. Load the hind quarters up on the horses. Tonight, we feast, lads."

He was rewarded by a cheer but the sour look did not leave the centurion's face. They marched out of the valley and picked up the guard they had left fifty paces down the river path.

"Any problems optio; anyone tried to get past you running away or surrendering?" Lentus asked pointedly.

The optio looked puzzled. "They're Germans, centurion, they don't never give in…."

"Very good, optio, well done you and your men; Centurion Lentus, get them to fall in at the rear of the column," Lucius intervened, barely able to contain his annoyance.

The day after the soldiers left, Odila and the others came home. Their huts were circles of ash and half burned timber. There were few recognisable bodies left but they knew Badurad by the sword still clutched in his charred right hand. They hunted out anything that might be useful and made a pitifully small heap of axe heads, knives and tools. They found half a dozen skillets and cooking pots that had not been destroyed. They had no shelter, no warriors to defend them and hardly any property left. They might have despaired but they did not. There were a few cattle in the upper valley, their grain stores were left untouched and Otto's colt together with two other horses were found grazing on the lower slopes.

They had enough to come through the winter. In spring they would find their kin and their lives would go on, never knowing why the disaster called Rome had fallen upon them. They carried out the funeral rights for their dead and moved out of the ill-omened valley.

Chapter 8

The column marched back the way they had come along the river path until they reached the fishing place where they had bivouacked the previous night. The original inhabitants had not returned. The legionaries and their officers did not relax either on the march or in making sure they set out enough sentries overnight. They were all very aware that they were still days away from the legion camp and in hostile territory. They lit fires in shallow trenches and fed them with wood until the embers were white hot before roasting the ox haunches over them on improvised spits. The fat dripped down and flared, sending a rich odour of cooking beef through to cold air. The legionaries' mouths filled with saliva and their bellies rumbled until the cooks decided they were done. Gangs of men lifted the sizzling meat clear of the fire and they began to hack it up and gorge. No-one offered Otto any food but neither did they prevent him from taking his share. When he picked up the butcher knife to slice himself a steak, the nearest men to him recoiled and put their greasy hands on the hilts of their swords, then looked sheepish when the German boy dropped the knife and walked away with a bloody, steaming lump of meat to eat in seclusion.

Otto was ravenous and tired from keeping up with Lucius' horse all day. Once he had eaten his fill, he washed his face and hands in the river and lay down to sleep in front of the door of the hut the tribune was using. He was anxious. He did not understand these men; their speech or the relationships between them. The legionaries had armour and swords which made them rich noblemen in his eyes. But there were other Romans who carried no shields but had thick sticks with which they struck at them. Since the legionaries did not draw their swords and kill the men who hit them, they could not be noble. Only one of them rode a horse and had a breastplate and feathered helmet so he must be the leader.

He was glad that his mother and Saxa had been away when the raid took place. They would survive and their lives would continue. His mother's family was numerous and powerful and they would find room for her and his sister. Badurad's end had been fated so there was no point in mourning what had been decreed for his father. As for himself, he had found the man with the black plumes as had been foreseen. Whatever happened next would be his destiny. Since it could not be changed, he must accept it as something to be endured or enjoyed like a warrior and the son of Badurad. He slept dreamlessly and awoke refreshed.

They marched on a slightly different route from their outgoing journey, partially for security but mostly because the scouts had found a short-cut that saved them several hours. Otto ran beside Lucius again and either held his horse or stood beside his when he was dismounted. Although the men were happy to be going back to base, there were some grumbles.

"No loot we were told but Boxer's got himself some nice horses." a soldier said quietly to his mate but unfortunately for him, not quietly enough. Lentus overheard.

"Were you expressing disapproval of Tribune Lucius Longius?" he asked.

"No, centurion; wouldn't dream of it."

"Glad to hear it because if you did, I would have to hit you like this…" Lentus told him and lashed him across the back of the thighs with his vine-staff. The legionary hissed with pain and bit his lip but did not break step.

They reached the bridgehead without incident. Before crossing the men were told to fall out and smarten themselves up as best they could.

"First Spear Centurion Attius is not going to chew my balls off because you lot look scruffy," Lentus told them.

While they were gathered in an informal group doing their best to clean up their kit, Lucius walked his horse into the middle of the busy men.

"Centurion Lentus," he called, "when we get back to camp ask Prefect Aldermar if he wants to buy those three horses we brought back. If he doesn't; have them sold to one of the traders. The price you are paid for them is to go into the legion funeral fund."

"Understood, Tribune Longius," Lentus replied, smiling, "and thank you on behalf of the men."

They did not make too bad a show as they entered through the Porta Praetoria before being dismissed. Lucius sent a legionary to the Praetorium to inform the legate of his return and that he would report as soon as he had cleaned up. Otto walked beside the tribune's horse looking around him in amazement. He had never attended a gathering of more than three hundred human beings in his life; and that had been in a forest glade. There were close to five thousand in the legion camp. Everywhere he looked soldiers were marching or walking in off-duty groups. He passed armouries where sweating men hammered glowing metal over their anvils in showers of sparks, barrack huts; laid out in precise lines with lounging soldiers at their thresholds. He saw so much he could not register it all. To him, the camp was a vast city thrumming with confusing activity. They arrived at the stables where a groom took Lucius' horse. There were hundreds of other mounts inside or in the nearby pen. It seemed to Otto as if every horse in the world was in sight or hearing. And then there was the negligent display of what was to him, immense wealth. Steel weapons and iron tools everywhere, casually carried or stacked, harness and saddles, mail shirts and helmets wherever he looked; it was impossible to take in. He wondered if this was Rome, so much power and riches were gathered in this place.

Lucius saw Otto staring wide-eyed and open-mouthed. It amused him. He tapped the boy on the shoulder and gestured for him to follow. They made their way to a group of four single storey wooden buildings. They were built of pine planks and roofed with locally made clay pantiles. The roofs swept down at the front and verandas had been constructed underneath the overhang. Lucius strode briskly up the two steps of one and flung open the door of his quarters. There was one large room where the tribune ate and slept, behind it, a kitchen and servant's cubby hole. The room held a bed, a table, two chairs and a desk. An altar in one corner bore an image of Mars and a shrine to the ancestors of the Longius family. A military chest and a tripod for heating charcoal completed the furnishings. Otto was still studying them as Lucius took off his cloak and threw it on the bed.

"Atrexes!" he shouted for his body slave,

A tall man with tightly curled black hair bustled in from the back room. He smiled broadly but not with his eyes; they were furtive, darting constantly around, they lighted upon Otto standing just within the door and lingered on him a moment. Lucius held his arms out at his sides and without being ordered, Atrexes began to remove his master's armour. Once his cuirass and back plate had been unbuckled, Lucius bent forward with his arms in front of him and Atrexes pulled his subarmalis over his head. A pungent waft of stale sweat filled the room. Lucius sighed with relief and moved his shoulders to relax them.

"Bath I think, Atrexes. Fetch my blue tunic, a fresh loin cloth, clean boots and my best cloak. I shall report to the legate as soon as I am fit to be seen…and smelled."

Atrexes brought the required clean clothing and linen then pointed at Otto.

"And what of …" he let the rest of the sentence hang in the air but his distaste was obvious.

Lucius looked at Otto who was trying to make sense of all the unfamiliar items in the room. He was covered in the dirt and dust of the road. His simple leather tunic covering him from one shoulder and down to the knees was shiny in places and well-worn. His shoes looked passable; his mother had sewn them only a few weeks ago.

"Well, he won't do dressed like that will he?" Lucius mused aloud. "Find him an old tunic of mine and take him to the soldiers' bathhouse when we are finished."

"And what is he supposed to be doing here?" the slave asked spitefully.

"Whatever I require, Atrexes." Lucius snapped.

The bathhouses were primitive when compared with the marble edifices of Roman cities but the legion was proud of what they had been able to do with wood, stone from the riverbed and local tiles. In the essentials, they matched anything in the empire; plentiful fuel for the furnace and a constant supply of clean, fresh water. The officers' bath slaves soaped and rinsed his body and Lucius went into the hot room where water was poured over an open trough of hot stones to supply the steam. Finally, he moved to the cold plunge from which he emerged gasping to stand while his naked body was towelled. Fragrant oil was poured on him and then he was scraped clean with an ivory tool designed for the purpose. Atrexes and Otto had been standing by all the while and now Lucius called his personal slave forward to dress him.

The tribune ran the palm of his hand over his chin and decided he would be shaved tomorrow. The legate would not mind; after all, Lucius had only just returned from a mission. He repeated it in his head, "returned from a mission". He liked the sound of it.

The soldiers' bathhouse was similar to the officers' but had more wood and fewer tiles. The single slave attendant offered basic services; handing out towels, replacing the hot stones in the steam room and making sure the furnace slaves kept busy. Legionaries usually bathed with their best friends to oil and scrape each other's backs in the absence of anyone else to help. A pair of them were just finishing when Atrexes and Otto walked in.

"Here, what's this then?" one of them shouted. "This bathhouse is for soldiers, not slaves and bloody Germans!"

"If you don't like it, complain to Tribune Lucius Taurius Longius, not me," Atrexes retorted.

"Talk to me like that and I'll kick your arse," the legionary threatened.

Atrexes fawned, what else could he do? He had no rights, no status; he was property and that was all he was. If one of them decided to kick him he could do nothing. If he dared to fight back, they would say he had attacked them and then he would be crucified.

"Apologies masters but what can I do? I have my orders," he whined.

"Alright then," the other soldier said. "But watch your lip."

"Yes, I will; thank you, thank you…"

He had not wanted to take Otto to the bathhouse, he had no wish to help him and now yet another of the countless humiliations of his life had been heaped on him. Atrexes was in a foul mood. He gestured for Otto to strip and shoved him into the cleaning room where he tossed a bar of coarse and gritty soap at him and pointed at the hot water ewers on a shelf. Otto had watched Lucius and knew what to do. But he had never used soap before and did not keep his eyes firmly closed. His discomfort made Atrexes laugh as he led him into the steam room, half blinded after rinsing. There he sat, not knowing why at first but then beginning to appreciate the heat slackening the taut muscles of his neck and shoulders. The cold plunge was something familiar to him. He submerged for a long while, bubbles surfacing from his nostrils, before he burst upwards and climbed out of the bath. Atrexes flung him a towel.

Atrexes watched Otto drying himself and sighed appreciatively. Naked, the youth was magnificent. The proportions of his body were almost perfect. Smooth, adolescent muscles rippled under his flawless white skin as he worked with the towel. The greatest of Greek sculptors, Praxiletes himself, could not have wished for a better model. Atrexes took down a flagon of oil and a scraper. He had intended to ignore that part of the bathing process or watch the boy struggle alone. He smiled at Otto and began to stroke oil onto his body and legs and demonstrate how to use the tool to remove it with the dead skin.

"It's called a strigil," he said, holding up the scraper. "Can you say that? Can you say strigil? It's what we always use, gently but firmly like this. Can you do it? No, I don't believe you can, you need my help, don't you?" he crooned as he worked on Otto's back and thighs. When he had finished, he patted Otto's shoulder and offered him the tunic Lucius had told him to bring. It was green with some embroidery at the neck and sleeves. It was faded but clean and serviceable and by far the most luxurious garment Otto had put on. It was a winter tunic. Mid-calf length on Lucius, it came to just below Otto's knees. It was tight across his shoulders but altogether, not a bad fit. Otto beamed with delight and nodded at Atrexes in the absence of being able to thank him in words.

"Not at all, my boy; you like it don't you? Haven't I been kind to you?" he said and led Otto out of the bathhouse once he had laced up his shoes. "Here," he told the attendant slave, "throw these into the furnace," indicating Otto's old clothes with the toe of his boot. They walked through the lines to the tribune's quarters, Atrexes still holding the strigil and flagon of oil.

Lucius had gone straight back to his hut after the bathhouse and written some notes on a wax tablet. He would refer to them when making his verbal report to Quadratus. He was going to have to tell him about the horses which had been taken in contravention of his orders… and the German boy. He did not quite know what to say about him so decided to leave that until last. He stood up and buckled on his best parade sword in its ornate scabbard and marched up the Via Praetoria.

Centurion Lentus had seen his men to quarters, stood by while the mules he had requisitioned were handed over after a meticulous examination by one of the transport-section who then went on to check their pack saddles and harness before giving him a receipt. He found his optio and gave him his orders for the rest of the day and then went to find First Spear Centurion Attius who was in his office going over supply and medical reports. He was pleased to see Lentus as his arrival meant the paperwork could be ignored for a while. They saluted each other and Attius told Lentus to sit, pulled his own chair around from behind his desk and poured them both a cup of wine.

"First things first, are all the lads back in one piece?" Attius asked.

"Yes, all accounted for without a scratch."

"And how did Tribune Longius do?"

Lentus was suddenly standing on quicksand and he knew it. If he said the wrong thing in the next few moments, his career could well be over.

"First Spear Centurion Attius, it is not for me to comment on the performance of a senior officer in the field."

Attius threw back his head and laughed.

"That's an old soldier's answer Centurion Lentus but look, here we are sitting sharing a jug of piss pretending to be wine in my private office. Now, between you and me, how did he do?"

Lentus shrugged; he was not in a position to avoid his superior officer's question.

"He did well, very well. He took charge when he had to and he listened when he had to. We were in the middle of sorting out this German village, blood and skin all over the place, and I thought he was going to puke but he swallowed it back…."

"He actually swallowed it?"

"Yes, I saw his throat moving. Anyway, he got on with it. The lads call him Boxer."

"Boxer?" Attius asked with a puzzled look on his face.

Lentus pushed his own nose sideways with his index finger. Attius grinned.

"Oh, I get it. Always a good sign if the lads give an officer a repeatable nickname."

Legate Quadratus was patiently listening to his tribune's account of the expedition. Lucius was going into infinite detail as if he was recounting a great battle to an historian. The legate understood how important it was to the young man that he missed nothing in the retelling. After all, it had been the tribune's first independent command. As he half listened, keeping a rapt expression on his face, his mind drifted across the years to when he had been so very youthful and so intensely earnest.

Back in the tribune's quarters, Atrexes motioned Otto to place his hands flat on the desk and lean forward, waving the oil flagon at him. Otto thought that this was something to do with Roman bathing and complied. Behind him, Atrexes lifted up the front of his own tunic and bunched it into his belt. He let his loin cloth drop to the floor at his feet. He anointed the tip of his erect penis with some of the oil, put down the flagon and lifted Otto's tunic up to his waist. Clasping the boy by the hips he stroked his penis up and down in the cleft of Otto's buttocks. After a shocked moment of disbelief, Otto clenched tightly. Atrexes put one hand on the nape of his neck and pushed him further forward, bent over the desk.

"Come on now, be nice. I was nice to you."

He grasped the shaft of his penis with his free hand to help guide it in.

Otto trembled, astonished and horrified. His scrabbling fingers came into contact with the brass and ivory stylus Lucius had left on the desk and seized it. Half turning, he lashed out behind him. The improvised weapon struck Atrexes in the right cheek, went through, scored his tongue and knocked out a tooth on the left side of his jaw. The point jammed in the new gap.

They stared at each other for a moment in appalled mutual non-comprehension.

Atrexes tried to protest but his mouth was flooded with salty blood. In his agony he could not speak or cry out, only burble and moan. He did not understand what had he done to deserve this. He had been gentle with the boy and helped him. Why had this young savage turned on him?

Otto's eyes were flashing blue fire and his lips were curled in a wolf's snarl. He saw Lucius' service sword in its scabbard on the bed and lunged for it. As the steel blade came free with a hissing sound, Atrexes guessed what was going to happen next and ran for it. He fled out of the door, down the veranda in one jump and hurtled towards the Praetorium where his master was, hoping for sanctuary before this German madman cut him down.

Chapter 9

Attius and Lentus lifted their heads at the explosion of voices outside; men were hooting, cheering and catcalling. Attius rose to his feet, frowning. There was clearly some serious breach of discipline going on. He would stamp on it, instantly. He flung open his door, Lentus at his shoulder. The sight he saw outraged his sense of what was proper in a well-run legion camp. A man he recognised as Tribune Longius' body slave was sprinting up the middle of the street. His arms and legs were pumping. Spatters of blood flew back from his open mouth and ran down one cheek onto his sodden tunic. Behind him, and gaining fast, a German with a naked sword was in pursuit. The centurions looked at each other in bewilderment then stepped outside. As Otto flew past, Lentus kicked the legs from under him. Attius stretched out his hand and grabbed his wrist, wrenching the sword from his grasp. Otto smashed into the packed earth and the breath went out of him. They dragged him to his feet. As each of them pinned one arm, there was a burst of renewed cheering from the off-duty legionaries who had been making all the racket.

"How did he get into the camp?" Attius asked, shaking Otto.

"He's the tribune's boy. He brought him back from the raid," Lentus told him. "I knew he'd be trouble."

Quadratus and Lucius had heard vague sounds penetrating from outside but ignored them until the general cheer when Attius and

Lentus had dropped Otto and disarmed him. Irritated, Quadratus shouted to his clerks to ask what was going on but received no answer. He opened the inner door to see them crowded in the main entrance staring out into the street. They scattered back to their desks like a flock of startled birds when they heard their grim-faced legate approaching.

Atrexes had reached the steps of the Praetorium. The guards had seen him coming, pursued by an armed German and had dropped into defensive position, shields up and javelins levelled. Atrexes stumbled to a halt, pointing at his ruined face and making incomprehensible sounds as he tried to explain and to beg for his master.

Quadratus looked out at his camp and almost let his jaw drop at the sight in front of him. Over the heads of his guards, he saw a panting, bleeding civilian kneeling on the ground and lifting imploring hands. To add to the bizarre sight, there was something sticking out of his face. Behind him, Attius and Lentus were marching towards him restraining a German youth he had never seen before. His first thought was that the prisoner in the grip of his centurions must be a fanatic who had somehow broken into the camp to assassinate whoever he could. To cap it all, both sides of the Via Praetoria were lined with grinning soldiers

"Restore order, First Spear Centurion Attius," he called.

Attius nodded at Lentus who tightened his grip on Otto. Attius released his, saluted the legate, turned on his heel and faced back down the street.

"You will stop this shameful conduct right now. Report yourselves to your centurions or optios to beg pardon for your disgraceful behaviour, all of you. Get going," he bellowed in a voice loud enough to be heard up on the southern gate. The soldiers shoved each other out of the way in their haste to be out of the basilisk gaze. They were going to have a hard few days until their first spear centurion was satisfied that they understood how angry they had made him.

"Has anyone the slightest idea of what is going on here?" Quadratus asked, icily.

"The bloke what was running away is Tribune Longius' personal slave, sir, and the one who was after him with a sword is the tribune's German boy he captured," Lentus replied with a certain self-righteous air. Had he not said all along that Otto's throat should be slit?

"Is this true?" the legate demanded.

"Well... yes... sort of... sir," Lucius said, stumbling over his words."

Quadratus glared at him.

"We shall discuss this disgrace inside but not in my quarters," he pointed at Atrexes who was now pale and nearly fainting from his pain and loss of blood. "I don't want him dripping all over my floor. We'll use the outer office."

They trooped in after him.

"Wait outside all of you," he ordered the clerks.

Quadratus folded his arms and looked at each member of the assembled group in turn. Lucius was clearly anxious. Atrexes' head was beginning to droop. Attius was a mass of seething outrage. Lentus seemed to be almost smiling. The German looked outside of himself with fury.

"Can we try to make some sense of what has been a public entertainment up to now?" Quadratus asked and looked first to Atrexes. "What do you have to say for yourself?"

Atrexes pointed at his wounded face and tried to speak but he could not articulate properly; gouts of blood fell from him mouth.

"It's probably because he's got that thing stuck in his face, sir," said Lentus and stepped over to the injured man. When he tried to pull the end of the stylus out of his cheek, Atrexes screamed and fainted, bouncing his head off the floor with a dull thud.

"Thank you so much, Centurion Lentus, very helpful," Quadratus told him sarcastically and looked at Otto. "Is it remotely possible that you speak Latin?"

Otto snarled and began to curse Atrexes in German.

"I thought not," the legate continued. "To summarize, we have an incomprehensible slave who is now lying unconscious and a

German who does not speak our language. I do not call that progress, gentlemen."

He shouted for one of the clerks to fetch Prefect Aldermar and folded his arms, before glaring at Lucius.

"So, you brought this German into the camp, did you Tribune Longius? If you wanted a boy to keep you warm on the long winter nights you could have brought another slave from one of the brothels outside out stockade".

. "No sir, it's not like that sir…"

"What is it like then?"

"He surrendered to me at the village sir…."

"Germans don't surrender," Attius stated with absolute certainty. "I'm afraid you've got the wrong end of the stick this time, Tribune Longius."

Lucius felt cornered between his legate's disapproval and the centurion's disbelief so he went on the attack.

"Well this one did, First Spear Centurion Attius," he snapped.

"I see," Attius said. "In my twenty years of service on the Rhine not one single, solitary German has ever surrendered to me but they drop their axes and put up their hands to you. What's your secret?"

Lucius grew red in the face but before he could say something that everyone would regret, Aldermar strode in, saluted the legate and took in the scene. He nodded to Otto, looked at him appraisingly, greeted him in his own language and asked his name. They conversed for a minute or more.

"If you are ready prefect, yet again I must rely on you to act as translator and enlighten me, if you will," Quadratus requested.

"Certainly sir, I already know some of it…"

"How?" asked the legate

"Amongst other things, because of what this young man," Aldermar indicated Otto, "was roaring as he chased the slave up the Via Praetoria with every intention of removing his head. That is still his intention, by the way. A couple of my scouts heard and told me. You might like to know that all of my men want to cut this slave's throat the first chance they get."

"What crime did he commit to merit death in the eyes of our entire cavalry?" Quadratus asked.

"He tried to have sexual relations with the boy," Aldermar replied.

"What just for trying to bugger him?" Attius demanded with a snort of laughter.

Aldermar looked uncomfortable and the colour rose in his face.

"Gods, he's blushing!" Quadratus thought.

"You must understand, gentlemen, that Germans are an extremely moral people in such matters. No young man approaches a woman until he is over twenty years of age and the young women are equally chaste. As for practices such as Attius mentioned, any man found guilty of attempting to act in such a way would be bound hand and foot and his body flung into a bog to sink into ignominy."

"Well, you learn something every day," Attius said. "Good job they don't apply that rule in Rome. It would be half-empty."

"If this German lad is such a proud warrior, then why did he surrender to the tribune?" Lentus asked.

Aldermar lifted one eyebrow and briefly laughed.

"Ah yes, another misunderstanding," Aldermar said and turned to Lucius. "Tribune Longius, did Otto… that's his name by the way; it means "Prosperous" … did he lift his hands up to you, both palms pressed together?"

"Yes, he did."

"And did you clasp them in your own?"

"Well, yes, he was surrendering you see…"

Aldermar shook his head.

"No, he was not…"

"Told you," Attius interrupted; glad to have been proved right.

"…He was not surrendering," Aldermar went on. "He was offering himself to you as your sworn companion. When you took his hands, you accepted him. Otto is now your liege man until death. He will defend you with his life; if you fall in battle, he will not leave the field alive. In return you must feed, shelter and arm him. He is of a noble line among his own people so you may not treat him like a servant although he will perform tasks he does not regard as demeaning. Congratulations, Tribune Longius, Otto has honoured you for as long as you both live. What I do not know, is why."

"Well, Lucius, you really have given yourself a problem, haven't you?" Quadratus chuckled. "Perhaps next time your legate says no loot and no captives you will hear and obey."

"It is not entirely a bad thing, sir," Aldermar told him. "My cavalrymen take the tribune's actions in accepting Otto as an enormous compliment. He has gone up highly in their estimation and that reflects on every Roman officer in The Second Lucan,"

Quadratus instantly caught the implication of what he was being told. They all relied on the loyalty of the German auxiliary cavalry and especially the scouts. Anything which could reinforce that loyalty was to be gratefully accepted.

"You said you did not know what moved this…Otto, is it?" the legate enquired, noting Aldermar's nod of agreement before continuing. "…to perform such an action. What can have decided him to commit himself to Tribune Longius in so formal a manner?"

Aldermar interrogated Otto who recounted the story of the wise woman and her prophecy. The Romans did not understand anything that was being said but they saw the prefect's expression change and that he took an amulet he wore around his neck from under his tunic and kissed it. They began to be apprehensive.

Aldermar repeated the story. How a witch had looked into Otto's future and seen that a man wearing black plumes would lead him to his destiny. Almost immediately afterwards, Lucius came to Otto's village with black rooster tails on his helmet crest. It was beyond doubt that he was the man that the Fates had chosen to guide Otto on his life's journey.

No-one dismissed the omen, no-one scoffed, and certainly, no-one laughed. Augurs and priests of Rome read the future in the livers of ritually slaughtered animals and in the flights of birds. An acceptable blood sacrifice could influence a man's future for the better or could be forever ruined by a curse inscribed on a lead sheet, dipped in blood and then hidden where the victim would pass by it every day. They all knew with absolute conviction that what was said by those who had the second sight must be respected.

In living memory great Caesar himself had scorned a prophecy. Told not to leave his home on the day of the Ides of March, he had walked out into the street and seen the man who had warned him.

"The Ides of March are here, my friend," he called, "and so am I!"

"Yes, Caesar, the day has come but it is not yet gone," the seer replied.

Within half an hour, Rome's greatest general lay bleeding to death at the foot of the statue of Pompeius Magnus, his former rival.

Aldermar's words brought the dread of the supernatural upon on them to varying degrees. They made the sign to avoid evil and looked silently at Otto to see if there was some clue in his face to tell them why he had been singled out by whatever gods he worshipped.

Quadratus broke the mood. "Well, it seems, Tribune Longius that I cannot admonish you for bringing young Otto into my camp since you were acting in accordance with the will of some local god. We would not be wise to offend this unknown deity. However, your domestic affairs need to be put into good order and under the circumstances, I hesitate to intervene."

Lucius looked down at Atrexes for a moment and prodded him with his toe. The unconscious man moaned and began to stir.

"The continued presence of this man in the camp will be prejudicial to discipline. Centurion Lentus, I need the services of two legionaries," Lucius said firmly.

Lentus shouted out the door and a pair of men trooped in. They had the old soldier's shifty, "who, sir; me, sir?" look about them as they came to attention smartly and stared into the distance over the top of the centurion's head.

"Tribune Longius has a job for you," Lentus told them.

"Take this man," Lucius said, indicating Atrexes, "and put him outside the gate. He is not to re-enter."

They saluted and dragged him to his feet.

"Here, there's something sticking in him, sir," one of them said, gripped the protruding end of the stylus in his fist and yanking it as hard as he could. It came out with an audible crunch breaking one of the teeth that had been jamming it in on the way. Atrexes screamed and passed out again.

"What shall I do with it, sir?" the soldier asked holding out the bloody object.

Otto stepped forward and took it. He lifted the wounded man's head and wiped the stylus clean on Atrexes' hair before spitting in his face.

"He really bears a grudge, doesn't he?" Attius remarked.

The fainting slave was hauled away to popular derision and thrown through the Porta Decumana. He crawled to the riverbank near the camp followers' shantytown and tried to bathe his punctured cheek before passing out once more.

"I applaud your decision, Tribune Longius. Clerks! Get back to work and find an orderly to scrub this office. No stain will be left, understand?" said the legate and turned to the assembled officers. "That was all very diverting in a repulsive sort of way. We shall adjourn to my quarters and take a restorative cup of wine."

"What about the German?" Lentus demanded.

"Aldermar, please tell him to go back to the tribune's quarters and wait for him there." Quadratus requested then turned to Lucius. "Either you must learn German or he must learn Latin, your choice."

"One of the Roman farriers has been dealing with my men for so long he can get by in most German dialects. The tribune can borrow him as a part-time tutor." Aldermar suggested.

"Excellent," the legate agreed, "please see to it, and now our wine awaits us."

And the wine flowed. Quadratus was a few days away from starting his long journey to Rome where he would spend the winter months with his family and friends and was in an expansive mood. His personal servants, guards and a cavalry unit would travel with him along with the legionaries and other officers granted leave. Once they reached the settled areas of southern Gaul, most of them would go their separate ways until recall the following March. Therefore, there was no point in hoarding his wine stores. Not that he drank too much, never forgetting the dignity of his rank.

Lucius was far from being a hardened drinker and two cups of wine were enough to overcome his normal reserve in front of his commanding officer and the centurions who were vastly more experienced than he was. He mentioned the oxen they had slaughtered for barbecuing and the horses they had used to carry the meat.

"Always a sound idea to supplement the men's rations in the field, Lucius; what became of the horses?" Quadratus asked.

"I bought them in for remounts, sir." Aldermar told him.

"So, you made a profit on the transaction, tribune," the legate said with an edge to his voice.

"No sir," Lentus replied. "Tribune Longius instructed me to add the money to the legion funeral club funds."

Quadratus nodded.

"All in all, you seem to have done well, Tribune Lucius Taurius Longius but be careful of courting popularity among the legionaries. They may begin by liking you but in the end they will hold you in contempt. Not that I am criticizing the decisions you made, you understand. It is a general observation. Centurion Lentus, is there anything arising from the expedition to which you wish to draw my attention?"

"Well, sir, I was discussing things with First Spear Centurion Attius when all the nonsense broke out so we were interrupted. I think having our own missile troop turned out to be very useful. One of the legionaries stood out as a leader sir, Marcus Corvo. In the absence of us getting some proper archers and slingers, auxiliaries like, I was going to ask if we could do something to make it a bit more permanent," said Lentus.

"What do you think?" the legate asked Attius.

"I've long had the idea that we need something along the lines Centurion Lentus suggests but it's how to organize it….

"What about we form an additional century of skilled missile troops? They would act as normal infantry but have extra training so they could be deployed in their special role if necessary," Lucius said.

"Think about it, Titus and take a look at this man Lentus recommends. If he has the qualities and he can read and write, appoint him to the centurionate to lead the unit. Let me know what you think by letter while I'm on leave. I was going to bring a few hundred or so recruits with me when I come back in the spring. If having our own archers and slingers is a viable, step, I can take that into account in selecting them. If we go ahead, I will want Tribune Longius to take oversight of the new unit and report directly to you in my absence." Quadratus instructed.

"They'll still have to be trained in all the basics," Attius observed.

"Agreed. Well, young Lucius, what will you do over the winter without a personal attendant who can understand you?" said the legate, changing the subject.

The tribune looked moodily down into his half-empty wine cup.

"Fuck knows," he replied, half to himself.

The others burst into laughter. Lucius looked around at them blankly, not understanding what was so funny.

Quadratus wiped the corner of one eye and looked at the embarrassed youngster.

"Oh Lucius; one mission over the Rhine and you've come back a foul-mouthed old sweat!"

While the officers were holding their informal conference, two German cavalrymen passed out of the camp on foot. They were looking for Atrexes and they found him easily enough, sitting on the riverbank. The bleeding had stopped and his pain had subsided to a fierce throbbing in his cheek and jaw but he was in despair. How had this come about? If the boy had not wanted his attentions, he only had to say so. Why all the violence over something so commonplace? He doubted whether he could survive in this alien place. He had been born a slave in the household of the tribune's father and had known no other way of living. Perhaps there would be some business owner among the camp-followers who needed an educated servant. A tiny glimmer of hope flickered in his mind. His face would heal, although it would be scarred but how many around here had his skills? He could cook, act as a valet; he could read and write. Perhaps all would yet be well.

Then he saw the pair of big men with yellow beards and long plaits coming towards him along the riverbank, grinning and purposeful.

"Oh no, please no more!" he thought to himself.

They laughed as they cut off his penis and stuffed it in his mouth before dragging him into the river and drowning him; they would not honour him by giving him his death by a warrior's blade. Once his struggles had ceased and they were sure he was not breathing, they let him go. The body of Atrexes floated gently downstream into the Rhine, his name and thirty years of service to the Longius family almost immediately forgotten.

A knot of bored legionary sentries had gathered on the walkway. They had watched, intrigued.

"Wonder why they did that to him?" one of them asked.

"Don't know; he must really have pissed them off," his mate said.

Chapter 10

With the agreement of the legate, Attius called a general parade of the entire legion the next morning. Quadratus spoke first.

"Come to the front Legionary Marcus Corvo," he called.

Corvo fell out from his rank and doubled up to the foot of the rostrum where the legate stood, Attius beside him.

"Legionary Corvo, your leadership, coolness and good soldierly conduct during the recent expedition across the Rhine has been drawn to my attention. I commend you and you will receive double pay this month."

"Thank you, sir," Corvo replied and saluted.

He was about to return to his position among the massed troops when Quadratus stopped him.

"Remain where you are Corvo," the legate commanded and then addressed his entire command. "I shall be returning to Rome in a few days. On my departure, First Spear Centurion Titus Attius is appointed Camp Prefect and your commanding officer. All military authority rests in him. You will obey his orders without question. Yesterday's display somewhat shook my confidence in the professionalism of The Second Lucan. I trust that it will be restored… very shortly. To that end, I am now handing the parade over to First Spear Centurion Attius."

Attius saluted him; Quadratus returned the salute and marched away without looking back, his red cloak billowing out behind him. Attius glared at the men then shouted in a voice that echoed off the far walls.

"You have heard your legate. He is not happy with some of you. That means that among you are some poor excuses for soldiers who have made me look bad in front of my superior officer. I do not like that. I do not like those men who have made the legate question your professionalism because that means he's questioning mine. Now, I can search through the off-duty rosters until I find out who was laughing and jeering and disturbing the peace or those responsible can admit their guilt. I am now dismissing this parade but those soldiers with bad consciences, stay where you are. Parade, dismiss!"

The legionaries clattered off, shields banging against javelins; leaving a forlorn group, dotted here and there and looking very small in the rapidly emptying parade ground. There were one hundred and forty men left where over four thousand had been assembled just moments before.

"Get yourselves up close and in some sort of order; like soldiers do, if any of you know what I mean. Where are the carpenters?" he yelled.

Two men scurried up carrying an open wooden chest between them. It was two feet wide, four feet long and three feet high. They dropped it at the foot of the rostrum and left as quickly as they had arrived. Attius came down and walked around it examining it closely. He gave it a kick.

"Well made that; Legionary Corvo, I have one of these, how many will I need to have twenty in all?"

"You will need nineteen more, sir," Corvo shouted in reply.

"And if I want twenty-five altogether?"

"That would take an extra twenty-four, sir"

"Very good Corvo; you can count. Can you also read and write?"

"Yes, sir, I can."

"Even better," Attius told him then turned to the men ranked in front of him.

"I am having twenty-five of these chests made. They are to be placed strategically on the parapets of the stockade. You are going to fill them with stones from the river. I want round stones as big as you can comfortably hold in one fist. Now, you are saying to yourselves, that isn't so bad, we can get them out of the pissy little stream just outside the gate. Well you can't. You bastards can march down to the Rhine and fill up your baskets with as many as you can carry. When my twenty-five boxes are filled level, the job is done. Oh, no wine and barley-bread only until you're finished. Legionary Corvo is promoted temporary acting optio reporting to me and me only with immediate effect. Temporary Acting Optio Corvo, get your men busy, they've stood about in idleness all morning."

The tutor Aldermar had recommended for Otto was Martellus Flaccus. He was a decanus, a corporal, with fifteen years of army experience. He had been a farrier in civilian life and after his basic training was declared immunes and practised his craft in the legion's cavalry. He was deep-chested with sloping shoulders and massively developed forearms. Martellus loved horses and he loved the army. He woke in a good mood each morning and never let a day go by without thanking the gods for the life they had given him. He had only one fault. Every few months he would drink impossible amounts of wine, or local beer if no wine was to be had, until he collapsed and had to be carried back to his billet to sleep it off. Since sleeping it off generally took more than a full day, he had been granted an unofficial medical status which meant that on the two or three days each year when he was too sick and hung-over to stand, he was classified as being on the sick list. This suited everyone. His masterly skills compensated for his occasional weakness. He had his head shaved of its dark hair once a week, was missing his bottom front teeth and liked to sing filthy songs in a low voice while he worked. He was a generally affable man who seemed older than his thirty-eight years. The troops called him "Uncle" behind his back. He knew and he did not mind,

He became a different man entirely when faced with a horse which had been misused. Any rider who brought a wounded or bleeding animal to "Uncle Martellus" was well advised to have a good explanation. He had once broken a cavalryman's foot with a hammer for jagging at his mount's bit so fiercely that the corners of its lips were split.

When he was called to Lucius' quarters, he stood at relaxed attention on the veranda. He wore a leather apron over his uniform and exuded a strong smell of horse. Martellus listened politely to Lucius' suggestion that he spent an hour or so a day with Otto then shook his head with a rueful grin.

"That won't do at all, sir, begging your pardon. I'm not a schoolteacher. I can't sit in a room with the lad and learn him anything."

"I am disappointed that you feel unable to assist me, Decanus Flaccus," Lucius replied stiffly.

"I didn't say that, sir, not at all. Why doesn't he come over to me at the stables everyday? He can learn a bit of the trade and he'll pick up our lingo in no time if I'm asking him to pass this or hold that, you see if he don't."

"That seems a much better idea, Flaccus. Would you please explain it to him?"

Lucius listened to the interchange between Flaccus and Otto in German without understanding a word but judging by the worried expression on Otto's face and the way he kept pointing at him that the suggestion was not well received. Martellus scratched his head.

"There's no such thing as German like there is Latin sir. It's different languages sharing lots of the same words but not all of 'em, so to speak. His talk is a bit unusual to me but as far as I can understand, he don't want to leave you unprotected all day long. Says that would not be honourable sir, very big on honour these Germans in their own odd way."

"Gods above and below; I'm in the middle of a legion camp with thousands of comrades around. What does he think is going to happen to me?"

"I'll repeat that to him as best I can, sir."

After what seemed to Lucius an interminable discussion in which even he could make out that words and phrases were being repeated as they tried to make themselves understood to each other, Martellus smiled and nodded at Otto then spoke to Lucius again.

"He says in that case it will be fine as long as you promise not to leave the camp without him."

Lucius rolled his eyes and sighed.

"Tell him I agree."

At the end of the further interpretation, Martellus turned to Lucius for the last time.

"All sorted, Tribune Longius; he's going to come over first thing tomorrow morning to make a start. Two things though, if I'm any judge he isn't wearing anything under that tunic so better get him a loincloth, in view of all the scandal. Oh, and those soft shoes he wears might be grand for running about in the forest but he's going to need a pair of regulation boots.

Tribune Lucius Taurius Longius thought everything was now settled. He was wrong. The quartermaster's clerk refused to hand over the boots.

"He isn't on the strength, tribune. My stores are for legionaries and cavalrymen. He ain't neither of those now, is he?"

"He is attached to my staff," Lucius told him.

"And that would be as what sir, infantry or cavalry?"

"You are being insolent."

"No, sir, I am not. I am simply stating the regulations. I can't hand out kit to anyone who just comes along and asks for it. Not unless they have a chit, sir and are on the strength."

"Very well, soldier; since I do not have all day to argue with you, I shall buy a pair of boots. How much are they?"

The clerk sucked his teeth and shook his head.

"I can't sell off legion stores just like that, sir; bribery and corruption that is, very serious offence."

"What is the answer then? Decanus Martellus Flaccus says that Otto has to have them."

"Why didn't you tell me that right away, sir? Give me a chit and I can issue a pair to a farrier's assistant. Doesn't have to be a sworn-in soldier you see; an assistant could be a civilian auxiliary."

Otto had never worn anything on his feet as heavy as army issue hobnailed boots. He had trouble walking in them but at the same time, he was grinning widely and seemed to be proud of his new footwear.

Lentus and Attius watched Temporary Acting Optio Corvo lead his punishment detail down to the Rhine. The men were in full armour, helmeted and carried wicker baskets on their backs.

"Did you order him to make 'em wear full marching order sir?" Lentus asked.

"No, I didn't tell him anything; just what I wanted done and that he was in charge. Let's see if he makes a pig's ear of it," Attius replied with a chuckle.

An hour and a half later, Corvo arrived back at the gate with a group of twenty men. Half of them formed a cordon with shields and javelins at the ready, the other ten struggled with the first load of stones as well as their heavy kit. Attius had been waiting for them. He kicked the side of the chest.

"Get this up in the middle of the walkway over the Porta Praetoria and fill it up," he commanded.

While the soldiers were busy, he drew Corvo aside.

"You've only got half of 'em working Temporary Acting Optio Corvo, what's the idea?"

"If the German's are watching from across the river, sir, they'll see that sixty men are on watch at all times. That'll put them off the idea of a hit and run attack, sir."

"How would they manage that, it's all open ground?"

"They could come across upstream, mass in the forest and make a rush to cut us off from the camp, sir."

"And what would you do if they did?"

"With a hundred and forty men we could fall back in good order to our bridgehead fortress and send a signal."

"So why did you march back with the first load, Corvo?"

"Because now I know how long it takes. The next lot I send up won't be able dawdle and pull the wool over my eyes."

"Impressive, Temporary Acting Optio Corvo; carry on," Attius told him.

Throughout the rest of the day, the carpenters produced more containers and the legionaries more stones until the light began to dim as evening approached.

"You do understand that with only half the men working at any one time it's going to take twice as long?" Attius asked Corvo.

"I consider it worth it to keep my unit secure, sir" he replied.

"But they'll be on barley-bread and water for twice the time as well."

"That's their fault for behaving like arseholes in the first place, sir," Corvo told him.

Attius noted that Corvo had said "my unit". He went to see Legate Quadratus.

"Marcus Corvo, sir, shaping up very well in the first task I've given him. With your permission, I'd like to confirm his promotion to optio but not assign him to a century. He can be directly under my command for the moment so I can see exactly what he's made of."

"Very well, Titus, I leave it to your judgement." He handed Attius a sealed scroll. "This is a commission appointing Lucius Taurius Longius to the command of missile troops. If in your judgement Corvo is the man we need, set it all in motion before my return. If not, well, that is the tribune's misfortune because an unassigned tribune he will remain. I shall be gone the day after tomorrow so it's all up to you until the end of March anyway.

The next day Corvo paraded his men in the cold early morning drizzle. Before they could march off, Attius loomed out of the softly falling skeins of rain with his hands behind his back under his cloak.

"Marcus Corvo," he boomed, "You are no longer a temporary acting optio." He paused long enough to take in Corvo's attempt to hide his disappointment before continuing. "Legate Publius Quadratus has made your promotion permanent."

Corvo stood taller and saluted his first spear centurion. But Attius had not finished.

"Optio Corvo, you are improperly dressed where is your officer's helmet crest?"

Before Corvo could reply Attius stepped forward and handed the transversely worn horsehair crest denoting the rank of a centurion or optio.

"Here you are, Corvo," he said quietly. "Wear it with pride."

Otto stamped over to the stables early on the morning of his first day with Martellus Flaccus. The new boots seemed to crash into the ground of their own will and he felt he had to lift them very high to compensate for their weight when he took the next step. He entered the open-fronted forge soon after the charcoal fire had been blown back to life with the mighty leather bellows slung over it. He walked into a wave of heat which was pleasant after the damp, chilly air outside. He looked around but could see no-one. There was a horse tethered to a ring set into a pillar. It was a huge, bay stallion. All the horses the German cavalry rode were massive. They had to be to carry their heavy, armoured riders.

The horse turned its head and rolled back one eye to catch a glimpse of Otto. It stamped the ground with its two front hooves, each bigger than a dinner plate, shaking the long hair on its fetlocks. Otto went forward slowly, letting one hand slide along the horse's flank and over its shoulders and neck until he reached its head. He slowly stroked the broad forehead while he spoke to the stallion telling him how powerful, how handsome he was. The great animal calmed and nodded its head in time to the caressing words.

Martellus had arrived but stood back and said nothing, watching the German boy and the stallion. His long experience had made him a good judge and he could tell that he was looking at a born horseman. The farrier was pleased; he warmed to Otto from that moment.

"Ave Iuvenis," he called and repeated in German that he had just said, "Hail, young man."

Otto's education had begun. That night he returned to Lucius' quarters, stood in the centre of the main room and, frowning in concentration, said his first words in Latin; "Hail Tribune Longius."

Lucius smiled, "Hail Otto," he replied, watching the broad grin of achievement breaking out on the boy's face.

To the salutes and fanfares of those of The Second Lucan remaining in camp over the winter, the legate, his officers and legionaries marched out of the Porta Decumana; not to return until spring. When the gate had shut behind them, the men on parade expected to be stood down. They were disappointed. Attius looked around slowly with what he thought was a benign smile on his face. The spirits of the soldiers sank. This could not possibly be good.

"Well, boys," he began, "here we are comfortably housed for the winter. Good, tight roofs overhead and plenty of supplies, charcoal and firewood to cook with and keep us warm. Sounds perfect doesn't it? Perfect for soft civilians maybe, but not for the hard men of The Second Lucan. I know in my heart you do not want to laze about for months on end and lose your fitness for combat and your fighting edge. Optio Corvo tells me that the stone-gathering fatigue will be finished today. Therefore, the second and third cohorts will assemble at sun-up tomorrow ready to undertake a twenty-mile route march. That is, ten miles out and ten miles back. Optio Corvo will march alongside the head of the first century of the second cohort as I have another task for Centurion Lentus. The day after tomorrow, the fourth and fifth will have their turn followed by the rest of you. I do not like to disappoint any of my boys. That is all, dismissed."

A short while later Lentus came into Attius' office.

"A word, sir?" he asked.

"What is it?" Attius replied.

"I think that the centurions will be unhappy about the presence of Optio Corvo taking a lead on the march tomorrow… if I may say so…sir."

"Why is that?"

"In case he's reporting back to you on them; it's like you have no confidence in your officers...or so it seems…to some…sir."

Attius shook his head and laughed.

"Can you tell me, Lentus," he said, "how it is that men who've fought their way up through the ranks to the centurionate can behave like a mob of temperamental Greek actors at times? I didn't know you were all so bloody sensitive. You don't like Corvo being there either, do you?"

Lentus stiffened to attention.

"Truth to tell, First Spear Centurion Attius, I do not."

Attius laughed again.

"I'm not going to tell you or anybody else what I've got in mind. Have faith in your First Spear Centurion. Is that all?"

The next morning was bright and cold under faded blue skies without a cloud in sight. The four centuries marched out under the gaze of Attius. Corvo stood on the left of the optio leading the second century in place of Lentus. Six hours later they were back, chilled to the bone, splashed with mud, hungry and weary. Whatever task Attius had wanted Lentus to do must have been forgotten because he had received no orders all day.

The following day, the designated cohorts stood at attention awaiting the command to set off when Attius called out to Corvo.

"Optio Corvo, you will march at the left of the leading centurion: carry on."

Lentus visited Attius again that evening but this time smiling broadly and cradling a flask of the best wine he could find in the camp followers' taverns.

"Would you drink with me, sir?"

"Of course; you look like a man who has something to celebrate."

"Well I think I understand. This is all about Optio Corvo; you're testing him."

Attius held out a wine cup.

"Fill it up, Lentus and let's drink to plans and plots."

Every day, Optio Corvo left camp out with the route-marchers and every day he made it back. On the very last day, when the tired, wet and hungry men stood to attention waiting for Attius to dismiss them, he walked over to Corvo and looked him up and down. Marcus Corvo had been a spare, sinewy man before the gruelling marches day after day, had begun. Now he looked almost skeletal. The bones of his face were prominent under his stretched skin and dark half-moons under his sunken eyes demonstrated his fatigue. He was managing to hold himself to attention but only just. Attius noticed one of his kneecaps trembling because his racked thigh muscles were strained to their limits. But he had endured and accomplished what had been required of him.

Attius leaned in close and spoke directly to the exhausted man.

"You've marched one hundred miles in the German winter without a rest day, Optio Corvo. That takes some doing. Spend tomorrow in your bunk or in the officer's bathhouse; report to me the day after."

He stepped back and gave the order to dismiss all troops.

Chapter 11

Otto was a changed youth by the time December came. He no longer walked in his boots as if an inexpert puppeteer was pulling his strings. He had advanced in his informal Latin studies to the point where he could manage a simple conversation and he had learned much more than just the language from Marcellus Flaccus. First of all, he now knew that the camp of The Second Lucan was not Rome but only one of scores of military bases spread across the empire, although he had no conception of the distance between Gaul and Egypt. Initially, he had talked with Marcellus solely in German but they spoke more and more in Latin as time went by.

Marcellus had explained that sex acts between men and men or women and women were tolerated as long as there was willingness on both sides. When a slave was involved, a master could do as he pleased.

Otto was horrified. How could this possibly be accepted by honourable men? "I think that is disgusting," Otto responded.

Marcellus grinned and commented, "The whole legion knows that, young man. But listen to me, change your way of thinking. If you don't like the way we Romans go about something, keep your mouth shut."

Otto learned that Romans allowed the worship of foreign gods provided there was no disrespect to the Gods of Rome. He learned that

Emperor Augustus ruled and that all soldiers swore an oath of allegiance to him.

"Then he is the king," Otto said.

"No, no, no," Marcellus shouted. "He's not the king. Romans have no king. Romans will never let any man be a king over them. You mustn't say that, ever."

Otto thought that since there was no-one above Augustus and he held the oath of every soldier, denying he was the King of Rome was stupid. But then, much of what he was learning about Rome and its ways was so strange he sometimes wondered if it were all true.

As his confidence increased, he felt free to wander about the camp watching all the different activities when his allotted time with Marcellus was over. He observed the cooks preparing more food than he had ever seen in one place before and doing it day after day. He liked to spend time with the scouts and cavalry who had made something of a mascot of him but most of all he haunted the area where arms drill was held. Sturdy posts were set into the ground for the legionaries to attack with wooden swords and shields under the critical eye of the training officer. The first time he watched, Otto had stood quietly to one side. The next day, after hesitating for half an hour, he lifted a spare practice sword from the bin. He was surprised at how heavy it was. He took a firm grip and set about slamming it into one of the posts. The training officer saw him out of the corner of his eye but neither approached him nor said anything. When the session was over, he went straight across to the Praetorium and spoke to Attius who was with Corvo and Lentus going over requisition lists, a never-ending task.

"The thing is, sir, I need a ruling. That Otto attended training today. He's not on the strength but he is sort of attached. So, do I chase him away and have a word with Boxer… I mean Tribune Longius, sir?"

"He's a German when all's said and done," Lentus growled. "The last thing we need is any of them learning Roman army skills."

Attius looked at him with one eyebrow raised. "And what good would knowing what we know do 'em anyway? They're big and brave but they're still a hopeless rabble."

"Supposing they learned discipline and organization…." Lentus began to say but Corvo could not resist interrupting.

"With all due respect, disciplined and organized Germans? That's never going to happen…"

"…And even if that miracle occurred, where would they get their arms?" Attius continued, with a shake of his head. "They would need three legions' worth of kit minimum and where would that come from, eh? They're so poor they haven't got a pot to piss in so they couldn't buy 'em." He turned to the training officer. "As I understand it, that young man's supposed to be some sort of sworn bodyguard to the tribune so he'd better be able to handle himself for Boxer's sake. Give him the basics in sword, shield and javelin and leave it at that."

So Otto was allowed to join in weapons drill with the legionaries. He learned to grip the practice sword properly and hold it level as he struck. No easy task since it was double the weight of a standard issue blade. He learned to thrust and never to slash, to use his feet to add to the force of the sword and the shield he carried. The training officer had to admit that in a few weeks, Otto was more than adequate but it was with the javelin he excelled.

His first toy had been a wooden spear. He had grown up with spears always within arm's reach and they were almost an extension of his own body. The heavy Roman javelin was different to those he had used before. It had a thick wooden shaft into which was pegged a length of soft iron ending in a small blade. When the blade hit the target the peg snapped, dropping the shaft. If it struck flesh, it caused severe injury. If it went into a shield, it stuck leaving an unwieldy length of iron impossible to remove. Otto examined the javelin he was given and hefted it, trying to establish the point of balance. The target was a straw-filled sacking dummy suspended with ropes to a frame twenty paces away in front of the palisade wall. Some humourist had added a pair of straw plaits and a grinning, painted face.

Otto stepped up to the mark, drew the javelin back and squinted along the iron rod to the tip of the blade, lining it up with the target. Although he had not arrived at the peak of his physical strength and still had a lot of growing to do, the weeks of training had hardened his muscles. The breadth of his shoulders and the length of his arms gave him extra leverage over the older and more compactly built legionaries. He took a deep breath, steadied himself and waited.

"Release!" the training officer shouted in his ear.

In one instinctive motion, Otto brought his throwing arm up and around, shifting his weight from his back to his front foot and let the javelin fly. It hummed through the air. The heavy blade struck the dummy dead centre. The impact was so powerful that the straw man was lifted up, still with the javelin attached, and flipped completely over the horizontal pole to which it was tied. The rest of the legionaries cheered. The training officer cut the javelin out of the tattered dummy and discarded it. They were one-use weapons but could be recycled after the armourer had straightened the iron rod and fitted a new peg. He marched ten paces back and gave Otto a fresh javelin. Again, the dummy flew up and jerked on its ropes, scattering straw. The cheering had brought a crowd of spectators, amongst them Lentus and Corvo. Another ten paces back, another powerful strike but at fifty paces, the crowd fell silent. Otto was now throwing from well beyond the accepted effective range of the weapon.

"Release!" the order rang in his ear.

The javelin flew from his hand but not too fast for the eye to follow like the first throw. This time it soared upwards and seemed almost to hover at the highest point of its flight before it plunged with ever increasing speed and force and tore the ragged target from its ropes. It fell in a fluttering heap, pinned to the ground. A long moment's silence was broken by a roar of cheering.

Lentus turned to Corvo with a sour look on his face.

"And that's why you don't teach Germans how to use our kit," he said.

Marcus Corvo had worked long days for Attius. He had drilled men on the parade ground. He had inspected used equipment deciding what was reusable and what should be scrapped. He had reconciled column after column of figures in the legion's accounts. He had supervised maintenance repairs of the camp fortifications. He had written reports on every aspect of the legion's activities. He had learned a lot and grown in confidence. Perhaps most importantly, he had earned the respect of the rest of the officers and men after his epic series of route marches.

Attius was running out of testing assignments for Corvo so it was a relief to him when a messenger carrying a reply to his letter to Legate Quadratus arrived. Attius had written that Corvo was performing well and there was no doubt that he was fitted to the rank of centurion. He had asked the legate to confirm the promotion and to ensure that on his return in the spring with the new recruits, he also brought sufficient specialized equipment for a dedicated missile unit. He took the parchment scroll out of its leather carrying case and began to read it while the messenger stood at attention in front of him. Attius was occupying the Praetorium in the absence of the legate. The charcoal braziers gave off a pleasant warmth which made the messenger's sodden cloak begin to steam, filling the room with the smell of wet wool. Attius sniffed and looked up at the man. A dew drop hung off the end of his nose and his cheeks were red, almost raw after days of hard riding in the bitter wind.

"You look knackered, soldier. Take your horse over to the stables and tell them to attend to it. Then go over to the cavalry barracks and get them to feed you and give you as much hot spiced wine as you want. You sleep here tonight. Any nonsense, just say it is by order of Camp Prefect Titus Attius."

"Yes sir, thank you sir," the weary man replied and hurried away.

Attius finished reading. After the usual greetings, the legate hoped that Titus enjoyed good health and all was well with The Second Lucan. He confirmed Corvo's promotion and that he would consult on what equipment would be required to arm a unit composed of both archers and slingers and ensure it was brought with him in the baggage wagons. He looked forward to being back with his legion around the middle of March and offered his good wishes.

Titus shouted for a clerk to docket and pigeonhole the message then send for Optio Corvo and Tribune Boxer. The nickname Lucius had acquired had stuck. It was how everyone referred to him other than in official meetings and documents. He liked it. He had spent his early youth being self-conscious about his lop-sided nose but now he regarded it as a sort of mark of distinctiveness and pride.

When he and Corvo walked in, Otto was behind them.

"What are you doing here?" Attius barked at him.

"I'm with 'im ain't I?" Otto replied, pointing at Lucius who had not noticed he had been followed into the office.

"Sir," Attius shouted, "You must say "Sir"."

Otto looked at him unperturbed.

"I'm with 'im sir, alright?" he enquired in a friendly tone.

"Gods above and below, Boxer, I thought he was learning our language. He speaks it rough as rats."

"He's mostly learning off the men sir. They're not big on grammar and also, they think it's funny to teach him every foul word and expression they can. It isn't easy, sir but he is getting better by the day," said Lucius in defence of his youthful companion.

"And while I'm on the subject, why is he sleeping out on your porch? Give the lad a room, man. He'll freeze."

Lucius shrugged.

"He prefers it sir. Says it's too warm inside. I had to fight to get him to take an extra blanket."

Attius grunted, scribbled something on a wax tablet and shouted for a clerk, "Here, he said handing it over. "Read it and get on with it." Then he turned back to Otto. "You, go and stand by the door." The youth smiled and obeyed, even coming to attention.

"Right, take a seat, Optio Corvo and you, Tribune Longius; the meeting can now begin, at last. Well Corvo, I've got some good news for you. Legate Publius Quadratus has authorized your promotion to centurion. You will take charge of a mixed century of archers and slingers. What do you say?"

Corvo drew a deep breath. "May I ask two questions, sir?"

"Of course," the First Spear Centurion said, a little deflated. He had expected an enthusiastic acceptance but on reflection, it was more like the thoughtful Corvo he had come to know to make sure of his ground before committing to anything,

"Will this be a regular or an auxiliary century?"

"Regular, optio; I thought that would be understood."

Corvo beamed and nodded.

"And it will be full-time and full strength?"

"Yes, the men serving under you will be permanent transfers from other units plus new recruits coming in the spring. It may end up slightly bigger than normal though not above one hundred men in all."

Corvo rose to his feet, eyes bright with joy. He saluted and held out his right hand. Attius took it and they shook.

"My grateful thanks to Legate Quadratus and to you sir; especially to you for all the time you have spent over the last few months preparing me for this promotion," Corvo said with feeling.

"What, even the route marches? Let's drink to your future success Centurion Marcus Corvo."

The cups came out and were filled with spiced wine and hot water. They were rapidly emptied to be filled once more. The officers leaned back enjoying the moment. Then Attius reached on to his desk, picked up a scroll and tossed it to Lucius.

"Here is your commission Tribune Lucius Taurius Longius. The legate has designated you to have special responsibility for the missile unit under Centurion Corvo and also to act as second to the Artillery Commander so you had better report to him and begin to learn the ropes."

It was the turn of Lucius to flush with pleasure and grin.

"Thank you, sir."

Attius waved the gratitude away.

"It's one of the greatest pleasures of an officer's military life to witness the promotion of worthy young men…" he held up one finger in emphasis. "…worthy young men, let's drink to 'em!"

The clerk came back carrying a sacking bundle he had fetched as ordered on the wax tablet he had been given. He handed it to Attius, saluted and went out.

Attius unwrapped the coarse cloth revealing a red leather belt with a silver buckle and a matching scabbard holding a wide-bladed dagger. The weapon had begun its life as regulation issue but the handle had been cross-lapped with red leather strips and the pommel covered in embossed silver. He withdrew it from the scabbard. The blade shone in the lamplight and the razor-sharp edges and point were flawless; not a knick or a dent. Satisfied, he pushed it back and beckoned to Otto who came over to where the three officers sat. He held out the belt with the scabbard and knife to the youth.

"Here," he said speaking very slowly and clearly, "Take this to defend your master. It is a prize for your javelin skill."

Otto understood and reached out but then withdrew his hand. He looked at Lucius who nodded his approval. Only then did he take the gift, clutch it to his chest in both hands, smiling widely with pleasure and bow to Attius.

"What did he stop for?" Attius asked.

"He can only accept a gift of arms with my permission," Lucius explained.

The senior officer sighed and shook his head.

"Rather you than me, Boxer," he said. "Why don't you all piss off now and get drunk?"

The next morning, Lucius woke late with a burning throat and a demon hammering the inside of his head with a sledgehammer. He sat up and felt his stomach heave. When he had at last finished vomiting sour wine and bile, he washed his face, dressed and contemplated his breakfast of bread, cheese and water. He pushed the plate to one side and forced himself to his feet. The cold air outside rocked him back on his heels but after a few deep breaths he began to feel a little better. He made his slow and careful way over to the artillery lines and introduced himself to the commander.

Cestus Valens, Commander of Artillery Second Lucan Legion, was a sturdy man in his early forties with a round, jolly face under a few strands of white hair. He looked like a benevolent doctor or teacher. His manner was in tune with his appearance. He was always cheerful and friendly, even in the most extreme circumstances. He was also a talented and efficient killer, and proud of his profession. He smiled at Lucius and returned his salute.

"And what can we do for you today, young Boxer?"

Lucius showed him his new commission.

"As you see, sir, I am to second you."

"First of all, forget the sir; Cestus will be fine. Now, what do you want to do; learn the trade of destroying enemy strongholds and killing men at long range or fanny about?"

"I want to learn."

"Right ho, that's the ticket. Are you any use at mathematics?"

"Not bad."

"Get better. The effective use of artillery is theoretically based on mathematical principles. In practice, the theory falls to the ground when it's too cold or too wet or the wind veers. Only experience can teach you how to allow for the conditions you face. I'll lend you some geometry texts to get your head around. Now for smashing things up, we have the Onager and Ballista both of which hurl rocks. For knocking over people we don't like, we have the Scorpion which is basically a dirty-great crossbow. We can also fire pointed bolts with the ballista at longer range than the scorpion; not so accurate but when they hit someone, everybody knows about it. Where would you like to start?" Cestus took Lucius by the arm and led him over to a large wooden machine under a lean-to roof. "We'll take a look at this onager shall we? By the way, we tend to turn in on ourselves in the artillery. The men are slow to take to newcomers but once they understand you're serious, they'll open up to you and then you'll really begin to master the business."

Centurion Marcus Corvo walked at a stately pace as befitted the dignity of his rank with his vine-staff under one arm, in conversation with First Spear Centurion Titus Attius. They were making an informal inspection of the camp, keeping to the log pathways which had been laid down against the mud. From time to time Attius would spot something of which he disapproved and would roar out a command that had legionaries suddenly scurrying to obey. The rest of the time, he was listening carefully to Corvo. He had asked the newly promoted officer what ideas he had in respect of his new command and was pleased at the detailed thought Corvo had already given the matter.

"My century must be fully trained as infantrymen and be able to stand in the line of battle with javelin, sword and shield."

"Agreed," said Attius. "That is essential."

"But when we are on manoeuvres, the men should be excused all fatigues."

"Why?

"Suppose, sir, the legion is engaged on building a marching camp, the best use for my men will be to act as armed look-outs. In the event of any incursion, they can deploy their slings and bows to slow up any hostile activity before the enemy get too close. They need to be used in threes and fours for this to be effective. If they are excused the labour of building the marching camp, they do not need to carry entrenching tools, which means they can have their bows, slings and ammunition with them ready for use.

"And where would you post them in the line of march?" Attius asked.

"Depends on the terrain; in open country they should be out wide semi-scouting but if we're in thick forest, wherever you think best to put them, sir. Missiles aren't a lot of use if you can only see for a few yards between the trees, sir."

"That's true…"

"Then we will need leather bow cases and beeswax; as much beeswax as we can lay our hands on…."

The senior officer's mind began to drift. It was December and he had a lot on his mind.

Chapter 12

Like any other legion, when The Second Lucan was in the field the course of the legionaries' days was prescribed by military necessity. At the sound of reveille, every man and every officer had his duty. The marching camp in which they had slept overnight was dismantled. The palisade was taken down and the individual sharpened stakes loaded onto backs, mules or wagons. The earth they had dug out to build a ditch and rampart was shovelled back where it had come from. The ground was levelled and tents folded for transportation. The solders armed themselves and were fed. The horns blasted out the calls, the column formed and marched. They never failed to build a temporary fortified camp each night and it was always obliterated the following morning so it could not be used as a stronghold against them.

Even their battles followed a pattern, although their opponents did their best to disrupt it. The legion formed up on a broad front three to five men deep with reserve units immediately behind in the centre. Additional troops were posted to strengthen each flank with the cavalry lurking behind them waiting the order to burst out. Each legionary in the front rank was so close to his comrades that the edges of their shields touched. Centurions carried no shields, only their swords and vine-staffs. They stood out in front of their men to give them confidence until the general engagement. They slipped back into their centuries when the enemy closed.

When the roaring mass of barbarians was thirty paces away, the order to release javelins was given. The front rank hurled their spears into the packed mass of their foes. If enough fell dead or wounded to make them hesitate, a second volley followed. Finally, the two forces engaged man to man. The Roman short swords stabbed out over or between their massed shields. If a legionary was downed, a second rank man jumped up into the gap to take his place. Every ten minutes or so the centurion blew his whistle and the front-rank men pushed forward then stepped back to be replaced by fresh soldiers in a slick, well-practised movement.

The savage tribesmen were faced with a shield wall several men deep and never had an exhausted legionary fighting in front of them. If they looked up, they could see the golden eagles held aloft in the centre of the Roman formation and their officers in their glittering armour mounted on fine horses. As well as the whistles, horns blew calls to which the ranks of their implacable enemies manoeuvred.

The bravest and biggest of the enemy were first in the charge and the first to fall. As the battle progressed, the quality of the Romans' opponents deteriorated. Eventually, the stragglers' courage failed and they turned their backs to quit the field. Then a cry of "Pursuit and melee" rose up from the centurions. It was a death sentence for the fleeing remnants who died of a sword thrust in the back or were quickly overwhelmed by small groups of legionaries if they tried to stand and fight. The cavalry was released to cut them down with their lances and long swords, mercilessly following them for miles. The recall was sounded only when the legate decided he had seen enough blood for one day.

It did not always turn out perfectly for the Romans. Sometimes they were forced to fight on the retreat until they reached more favourable ground. Sometimes they were quickly surrounded and had to fight in a square formation. But overall, the final result was rarely in doubt. If they were attacking a fortified position, they used their engineers and artillery or stormed it. If they were advancing across a river, they built a bridge or found a ford.

The Romans had the equipment, tactics and organization to take on their enemies in the field and triumph. Courageous warriors fought as individuals, running forward to achieve immortal glory. Legionaries were dispassionate; simply efficient workmen plying their trade.

Who were these legionaries; these routinely brutal rapists, looters and killers of the very old, the very young and anyone in their way? Most of them enlisted in their late teens. Strict rules of eligibility applied but if Rome was threatened, these were relaxed with the exception of two. No runaway slave could serve in a legion on pain of crucifixion if found out. No non-citizen could be a legionary but in time of dire need, legal fictions could be created to get around this restriction, as Caesar showed when he was desperate to reinforce his armies in the Gallic War.

They were lads with a sense of adventure. They were second sons who would not inherit the farm. They were slum boys who had never eaten every day or had a decent set of clothes until they joined up. In amongst them were older men with a useful trade they could no longer exercise at home for some reason. Although they might be above the age limit, recruiting officers would turn a blind eye to have a skilled metal or leather worker on the muster rolls. Harsh physical training and brutal punishments soon forged them all into the military force Rome needed.

Titus Attius had over three and a half thousand such men in camp. For the first few weeks, the luxury of sleeping under a roof and not having to march for five hours a day was enough to keep them happy but they soon became bored. The officers arranged training exercises and competitions to keep them occupied but the weather was against them; impossible to hold games in mud covered with a layer of frost or iron-hard earth beneath a foot of snow. Under these conditions, the men had nothing to do with their time and as a result discipline weakened day by day. Some lost all their accumulated pay illegally gambling. Accusations of cheating and knife fights followed. Good comrades quarrelled over next to nothing and the fists flew. Every morning the number of men with split lips and black eyes on parade increased. They had all "slipped on the ice".

A punishment frame was set up near the Praetorium and every other day a defaulter was led out to be tied to it and receive his allotted number of strokes. Whipped but not scourged; scourging was almost always a death sentence. The instrument used was a long lash with sharp pieces of bone and metal, nails, glass and even teeth woven into it. Each stroke lacerated the flesh and it took very few to expose the spine and ribs. Few recovered, and of them most were permanently crippled.

One man was condemned to execution. In a drunken fury he had snatched a centurion's vine-staff from under his arm, flung it down in the mud and stamped on it. The centurion had kicked him half the length of the Via Praetoria before Attius had stopped him. The sentence was carried out by the corporal and men who shared a tent with him on campaign. The legion formed a hollow square and the punishment party lined up in two rows in the middle. Each of them was armed with a pick-axe handle. The guilty man was brought out, his crime read aloud and then he was shoved between the lines of his old comrades. They beat him to death. None stood back or failed to strike hard. If they had, they would have shared his fate. It was over noisily but quickly. When the screaming, grunting and thud of wood on flesh faded into silence, they stood around, spattered with blood, panting clouds of steam and looking down at the wreck they had made of the companion with whom they had soldiered in good times and bad. Titus Attius stepped forward.

"This man not only defied his centurion but wrenched the symbol of his office from him and despoiled it. His was a crime against all the legion stands for. It was sacrilegious as well as contrary to military discipline. Let his remains be flung on a dung-heap and his name erased from the muster rolls."

That had concentrated the men's minds for a few days but they soon broke out again. On top of the daily problems, the seventeenth of December was approaching and with it the festival of Saturnalia.

During Saturnalia, the world was turned upside down. In Rome, slaves sat in their master's chairs and demanded to be served. People put on ridiculous clothes and wore them in the streets. Dignified leaders of society played pranks and gave silly gifts. Most people drank too much and went to too many parties. On the twenty-fourth when the fun officially ended, they bitterly regretted their behaviour, promising never to be so stupid again – until next year. If Attius was troubled, in the camp followers' shantytown they were rubbing their hands together in anticipation of the money they would strip from drunken legionaries who would remember nothing the next morning; not even that they had been robbed and cheated.

When the civilians of a Roman city cavorted around the streets, drunk, hilarious or both, there was little lasting harm done. But the result of a legion on the border of hostile territory giving itself over to a week's revelry could be catastrophic. If the tribes across the river got wind of it, even allowing for the atrocious weather, they might mass and attack. It would be a massacre. The obvious thing to do was to ban the legionaries from celebrating Saturnalia but this was impossible.

Practically, they would not stand for it and would probably mutiny and there was another reason. All Roman festivals were religious in origin, even the chaotic, orgiastic Saturnalia. To ban it would be an impious action which might well offend the gods; no-one was prepared to risk that. The officers made what preparations they could. A stockade roofed over with planks was constructed inside the camp. This was the temporary drunk tank. Fire pits were dug and oxen purchased to roast. The wine stores were checked. Fortunately, there was enough for a double ration to be issued for the week of the festival. Prefect Aldermar agreed that his men would take no part in the celebrations in return for the legion funds paying for their own winter solstice party, to be held a few days later outside the walls. Instead, they would patrol the forest edges and the banks of the Rhine ready to report any signs of incursion.

The day of the seventeenth dawned cold and bright with a keen east wind, ice on the horse troughs and stream but no sign of snow. Attius stood in front of his expectant men. He looked around with a stern expression on his face then grinned, flung his head back and roared, "Io Saturnalia!" The legionaries shouted the traditional greeting in response, "Io Saturnalia!" They drew their swords, beating them against their shields. Attius let the thunder roll over him for a few minutes then lifted his hands for silence which eventually fell.

"Well boys, we're a long way from home but we can still have some fun. Those contraband dice boxes half of you have hidden in your kit can come out for Saturnalia. Anyone who loses all his money will not do without. We'll be roasting two oxen every day and the wine ration is doubled..." He had to fall silent as a second roar of cheering and shouting broke over him. When it had subsided sufficiently, he continued. "...The Porta Decumana will be open from the beginning of the third watch of the day to the end of the second night watch. One cohort at a time, you may leave the camp and booze or shag yourselves silly as I'm sure most of you will. No blades of any kind are to be carried by off-duty men, not even a fruit knife. Any soldier found in possession of one will be severely punished. Armed patrols will circulate the shantytown for your protection. And lads, if one of your mates is too drunk to stagger back to his billet, do the decent thing and carry him home. At the beginning of the third night watch the gates will be closed and the patrols withdrawn. If you are still out then you're on your own. That's it. The senior centurion of each cohort will now come forward and draw lots to decide who goes first. Dismiss!"

The priests were guardians of the water clock and sundial and timekeepers for the legion. Each twenty-four-hour day was divided into three-hour watches, summer or winter. A clerk in the Praetorium had the duty of turning over the hourglass so it was precisely on time that the gate was opened for the third cohort, who had drawn first position, to enjoy their debauch. The stood more or less in formation wearing tunics, cloaks and boots eager to go. They catcalled the guards and told them to hurry but they stood firm until the signal was given.

The heavy wooden gate was dragged back and the crowd surged over the bridge to be lost in the alleyways between brothels and wine shops. As the light began to fade, torches on poles blazed, raucous singing and music drifted back to camp. Pimps and barmen stood outside their establishments shouting their wares; the most accomplished near-virgins, the best almost-Falernian wine were definitely on offer. Some half-dressed women stood in the entrances, trying to smile and beckon as they shivered in the cold. The soldiers circulated and their money flowed in a steady stream into the pockets of the proprietors of these places of dubious entertainment. The patrol on provost duty had a quiet time, overall. There were a few fights and they were forced to execute a bouncer on the spot; he had been too rough throwing a soldier out of his master's bar. They were glad enough to form up to return to camp when the horn sounded recall. There are few things worse than being sober and on duty when everyone else is having the best of times.

The crowd wove and staggered its way back to barracks in reasonable order. The gate was closed and there was no-one drunkenly beating on it for entry in the middle of the night, this time. In the morning a soldier was found lying behind a wine shop in a pool of frozen vomit. He had taken on too much sour wine and gone outside to relieve his stomach of it, passed out and died of the cold. Two deaths on the first day of Saturnalia, the civilian barely counted, and the gate guards engaged in only one scuffle, it had been better than expected. Attius was pleased. The third cohort men were pale and hung over the next morning. The soldiers who had not yet had their turn mocked them. They couldn't take their drink like real men. Some of them were offered lumps of bloody, fatty beef for breakfast and the rest laughed at their nausea. The second day watch came to an end and the next crowd of eager revellers moved through the open gate. This was repeated over the next few days. The bathhouses operated night and day offering some relief for the symptoms of over-indulgence. By the time each party had recovered, the more sedate offering of roasted oxen and a generous wine ration in camp was almost a relief.

On the fourth evening of the festival Otto was using one of the camp latrines. Each of them was a narrow hut in which half the floor space was taken up by a rectangular pit. Over it was fixed a full-length bar to support the back of the thighs while the men squatted. The pit was nearly over-flowing and stank, even in the draughty cold of the winter. At least it was not buzzing with blowflies crawling over buttocks and into eyes and mouths like in summertime. It was closed from the outside air with an old leather tent flap and lit with one smoky oil lamp casting a guttering light on the half dozen pots filled with supposedly clean water that held sponges on sticks for wiping everyone's backsides. Otto was alone, staring down at his booted feet and just finishing his bowel movement when he felt a blast of cold air as someone came in. He did not look up. Three legionaries were at the entrance. Two were in the mellow stage of drunkenness but the third was a flask of wine ahead of them and was looking for a fight. He was short and barrel-chested with a thick neck. His blood-shot eyes rested on Otto and he grinned evilly.

"That's that German bastard who whacked me on the foot and made me look a right twat in that shite-hole of a village," he said.

"Oh, come on, Tubby, don't make trouble…" one of his companions began but he was too late.

Tubby took three strides across the latrine, grabbed Otto by the ankles and hurled him backwards over the bar on which he had been sitting. His shoulders and the back of his head hit the surface of the semi-liquid ordure with a slapping sound. For a moment he was held, staring up in astonishment, but then he slipped underneath. He thrashed and floundered until his legs came free and he managed to get his feet under him. A great bubble of stench filled the latrine as Otto grabbed the bar and hauled himself free. He was plastered from head to foot in shit, his ears, mouth and nostrils full. Tubby lifted a boot to kick him back under but his mates pulled him away.

"That's enough!" one of them shouted.

"Come on; it's a joke. Io Saturnalia!" he yelled as they dragged him outside.

Otto stood in the middle of the floor dripping, stinking, humiliated and enraged. He poked his head through the door-flap to make sure no-one was about then slunk out. Keeping to the shadows, he made his way towards the open gate. The guards were all at one side, pushing and shoving a group of drunks who thought it would be funny to climb up onto the rampart from the outside. Otto darted past them, down the slope of the rampart and under the bridge. In the frigid darkness, he could make out the faint glow from the frozen river. He walked in a crouch to the centre and stamped hard. A splintering fissure opened up and he fell forward, thigh deep in the invisible water beneath. He let himself fall full length and as the ice cracked around him, he forced his body into the current, letting its burning chill wash the filth away from his body. He turned and twisted, trying to get as clean as possible in spite of the agonizing cold. He took in gulps and forced them back out through his mouth and nostrils, until at last he could bear the pain of the icy water no more. He crawled to the bank and pulled himself to his full height at the side of the bridge. He climbed up to the gate and forced himself to stroll as nonchalantly as he could past the guards who were now back at their posts.

"What's up Otto, fallen in?" one of them called but as he went by, the sentry wrinkled his nose. "Shit yourself first and then fallen in maybe?" But by the time he made his remark, Otto was already gone.

He made his way home and went in through the back of Lucius' quarters. He took a bucket, filled it with well-water and flung in his boots and a block of soap. Then he took a clean tunic and loincloth from the small supply of clothes he had been given and walked over to the bathhouse. Passing a fire pit, he stripped, balled up his wet clothes and threw them into the blaze.

A bare-foot, naked man carrying a change of clothes was not the strangest sight the attendant had seen in the past few days and, in any case, he was a slave and could not risk making any comment. Otto poured hot water over his head and body, soaped himself, rinsed the scummy lather away and went straight into the hot room. Five times he repeated this until he felt as clean as he was going to for a long while, then he plunged into the cold pool. When he emerged, he called the slave.

"Cut off my hair and shave my body." he ordered.

"I'm not the barber, master. He will be here in the morning…."

"Cut off my hair and shave my body."

There was not much body hair to remove and the attendant did as he was asked, very nervously; terrified that he would nick the very white skin of this young giant. Who knew how he would react if he was cut?

Otto looked down at the coil of his Suevian Knot lying at his feet.

"Burn it," he said.

Otto had no money to pay the man for his service so next morning he cut a thick slice of beef from the hindquarters of a roasting ox and took a loaf of fresh bread. He gave them both to the bathhouse attendant who was ecstatic; never in his life had he held so much food in his hands.

He had not burned the long plait he had cut from the German's head; he had sneaked out and sold it to a trader for a few coppers. Eventually it would make its way to Rome and be sold to a wigmaker who paid a premium for blond hair.

Chapter 13

Lucius looked at his shaven-headed and sullen companion the next morning and decided it was better not to ask. Martellus said he liked the new look.

"Much more Roman, Otto my lad; you look almost like one of us now."

Otto tried to smile but it was more like an enraged beast raising its hackles. As Lucius before him, Martellus thought it better not to press the issue.

Aldermar came to visit Lucius.

"Tonight, my men are going outside the camp to feast the re-growth of the sun. Beer, roast pork and riotous behaviour; you're invited, tribune ..." He held up one hand before Lucius could reply. "...Don't think of saying no. You are honoured with this invitation because you have chosen a German as your war-companion. A refusal would be an insult only to be wiped with bloodshed. Otto would be forced to defend you; he would probably be killed as well and then I would be forced to hunt down and behead half a dozen of my men."

"You are joking?"

"I may be but then again, perhaps not; you know how unpredictable and ferocious we Germans are ..."

"I should be delighted to attend and my thanks to the auxiliary cavalry for their generous invitation."

At midnight, Lucius sat on one of the log benches arranged in a circle, sweating in the light of an immense bonfire contemplating the huge hunk of roast pork in one hand and the horn of ale in the other. Aldermar sat on one side of him and a cavalryman on the other. A hand slapped him in the back, almost knocking him off his seat and a voice yelled in his ear, "Drink Roman, eat, be at home among us." He smiled and waved his ale horn in acknowledgement. The beer seemed to fill his stomach and lie there, heavily. He belched loudly to relieve the tightness in his belly to the approval of the unknown man sitting beside him who gave him another slap on the back.

Once they had eaten their fill, drunk and drunk again, the Germans began to enjoy themselves in their own ways. Some used their long cavalry spears to pole-vault the bonfire with mixed success. Those who cleared it were cheered, those who fell in were dragged out to general laughter. One massive warrior swore he could lift a horse. He peered drunkenly around for a horse to prove it but there was none. He stripped to the waist flexing his muscles so his tattoos writhed in the dancing light then invited as many men as could to hang on to his back and he would march around the circle of the seated spectators. He staggered around as he had boasted he could with three men clinging to his neck and shoulders. There were wrestling matches, feats of strength and agility; high jumping and long jumping from a standing start. One man had been wiping the pork fat of his hands onto his plaits all night and when he leapt through the fire, they burst into flame. His friends dowsed them with ale before he was too badly burned. This was generally reckoned to be the highlight of the entertainment.

As the hours passed, the fire burned lower. The men sat in their rows drinking steadily as the old tales of gods and heroes were told. The mood, if not sober, became more reflective. Suddenly a man stood up and called out to Otto. There was a moment's silence then nearly all of them shouted, as if demanding an answer.

"What's he say?" Lucius asked Aldermar who was looking serious.

"He wants to know if Otto is ashamed of being a Suevian since he cut off his hair."

Otto stood up and walked forward so that everyone could see him. He gave a short speech and sat down again as a roar of approval washed over him. Lucius looked enquiringly at Aldermar.

"I'll give it to you as close to word for word as I can. He says he did not cut off his Suevian Knot willingly; this was forced on him and he feels the dishonour keenly. When he has avenged himself, everyone will know and he will not be ashamed to sit among such mighty warriors as the German cavalry."

"I don't like the sound of that," Lucius said.

"There will be blood, without doubt," Aldermar replied, cheerfully. "Let's drink to it."

December made way for January in bitter winds and falls of deep snow. There was little Titus Attius could do to keep the men active in such conditions. But their mood had changed. They were no longer bored and aggressive like they had been in November; they tended now to a morose state akin to depression. Orders were obeyed, kit kept in good order, fatigue parties accomplished their tasks but it was all done with no lightness of spirit. They were going through the motions with an unexpressed longing for spring.

Before he had arrived in the camp, Otto had never come across writing. Priests used runes for religious purposes but there was no place in his people's world for the everyday skills of reading and writing. It intrigued him. He asked Martellus who said it was beyond his skill to teach him. However, once an idea entered his head, Otto would not let it go. He wandered the camp badgering whoever he could for help and he did pick up a certain amount. He could scratch his name and a few words on a wax tablet within weeks.

Lucius was pleased at his young companion's new obsession. So far, Aldermar's prediction of trouble had not come to pass and as time went by it faded from his mind. It had faded from Tubby's as well. For days and weeks after he had attacked Otto, he was tense; expecting a move against him at any time but nothing came. When their paths crossed, Otto neither avoided his gaze nor showed any sign that there was anything lying between them. Tubby's nervousness subsided and was replaced by contempt. For all the big talk about these Germans being so tough, when it came to it, they knew who was boss.

February's weather was even worse than January's. The snow fell thicker but soft and clinging. The prevalent wind had shifted to North-west so the temperature rose slightly and wet air blew in off the North Sea. The days seemed even shorter, although they were not, and it was very dark under the lowering skies as soon as the hidden sun sank in the afternoon.

Otto had been brought up to believe that there was no nobler way to fight an enemy than face to face in a clash of shield walls where strength, courage and skill combined to give victory. But his father had also taught him the value of ruse and subterfuge; the art of the ambush where a warrior became a ghost, laid his foe low unseen and was gone, leaving pain and terror behind him. He watched Tubby, learning his routines and searching out the weak point that would inevitably be revealed. His patience was rewarded. Tubby liked to go to the bathhouse as late as possible in the evening so he could scuttle across the camp swathed in two cloaks, carrying as much of the glow of the hot room as he could into the hut where he slept with thirty others. One night of swirling snow he trotted towards his billet and reached out a hand to the door latch when he felt a white-hot strike of pain lance down the right side of his head. Before he could instinctively clutch at it, a punch to the back of his neck drove him headfirst into the doorpost and he fell, stunned. He thought he heard the creak of boots in snow behind him but by the time he got to his knees and looked back, there was nothing to be seen in the blinding white flakes, falling and falling as if winter would never end.

At first light, an ear could be seen displayed on the lintel of one of the latrines. It was fixed with a horseshoe nail. Beside it, "Io Saturnalia" was deeply scored into the wood in crude lettering. When Otto went over to Martellus' workshop later the same morning, the auxiliary cavalrymen gathered and when they were all there, they shouted "Hail Otto!" three times then dispersed, joking and laughing.

Tubby was outraged and complained to his centurion.

"If you want to make a serious charge against anyone, you'll have to see Camp Prefect Attius. Better get your story straight for your sake."

It was a formal affair. Titus Attius sat behind his desk flanked on one side by Lucius and on the other by Aldermar who was there to translate if necessary. Otto stood to attention in front of the desk to the left and Centurion Lentus marched in Tubby, his head heavily bandaged. Lentus did a lot of stamping and saluting before leaving the wounded and aggrieved legionary at the right side of the desk.

"What is the nature of your complaint, soldier?" Attius asked.

"Sir, this German bastard..." Tubby pointed at Otto,"....came up behind me in a snowstorm and cut off my ear. He nailed it up on the door of the jakes, sir; the door of the jakes!"

"I hear you," Attius told him. "You say he came up behind you, did you see him?"

For a moment Tubby hesitated. His eyes flickered along the line of officers. He licked his lips and sighed. It would have to be the truth.

"No, sir, but it was him."

Attius nodded.

"Do you have any witnesses?"

"Well, no sir, it was late on and like I said it was snowing really heavy and …no sir, no witnesses but after all, sir, I'm a serving Roman legionary. Who the fuck is he? Begging your pardon, sir," said Tubby in a desperate attempt to be believed; all the more so since he was speaking the truth.

Attius ignored the outburst

"Were there any tracks or other evidence to point to this young man as your attacker?

"No sir, like I said…the snow…And…" Tubby's voice trailed into nothing and he stood staring straight in front of him.

"To sum up, you say it was the German known as Otto but you did not see him, you have no witnesses and no evidence to support your claim, have I got it right?"

"I would like to speak if I may, Camp Prefect Attius," Lucius intervened.

"Go ahead, Tribune Longius."

Lucius turned to Lentus.

"Centurion Lentus, when we attacked that German village last year, a legionary engaged Otto as we now know him in combat. Is that correct?"

"Yes sir, it is."

"Who was the legionary?"

"It was this man, sir," Lentus confirmed gesturing to Tubby.

"What was the result of the duel between them?"

"The German lad whacked the man on the foot sir and he fell over a fence rail, as I recall. The other lads laughed sir; very funny it was."

"Thank you Centurion Lentus," Lucius said and turned to Attius. "That's all I wanted to say, sir. I think it speaks for itself."

"Speaks volumes, tribune, speaks volumes," Attius replied and looked hard at Tubby. "This lad made you look a pillock and so when someone had a go at you, you blamed him. Case dismissed; now piss off out of my sight." As Tubby marched to the door, he called after him "You'd better pray Otto doesn't have an accident any time soon because if he does, you cop for it."

He turned his glare on Otto.

"If Tubby had been invalided out after what you did to him, I'd have had you crucified. You can fuck off out of my sight and all."

When the officers were alone and the wine cups had come out, Lucius mused aloud.

"I wonder what really happened."

Aldermar, Lentus and Attius looked at each other and began to laugh.

"How do you all know and I don't?" Lucius asked. "Why is it I never find out until it's all over?"

"Youth and innocence," Aldermar said. "Shall we tell him the story together or shall I do the honours?" he asked the others.

"Go ahead, Aldermar, light his lamp for him," Attius replied.

"Very well, one of the latrines is found in a disgusting state with shitty footprints crossing the floor. The same night Otto is seen coming back in through the gate from the river soaking wet and smelling like a ripe turd. The next morning, Otto has no hair and is in a foul mood. Tubby is known to be a mean drunk and he had a skin-full that night. Otto tells the cavalrymen he did not cut off his Suevian Knot voluntarily. Tubby gets his ear sliced. It is nailed to the door of the same latrine which was found in a filthy condition. All the Germans hail Otto. Conclusion; Tubby shoved Otto into the latrine pit so Otto cut his ear off; probably using the dagger with which you presented him, sir," Aldermar finished, smiling at Attius.

Attius grinned. "Tubby got what he deserved in my opinion which you never heard me say. Make sure Otto knows he won't get away with it twice, Tribune Longius; for everyone's sake," he advised Lucius.

Tubby was passed fit for service as soon his wound had healed but had to wear a padded skull cap to stop his helmet wobbling due to the lack of his right ear.

At the beginning of the last week in February, as if a switch had been thrown, the snow turned to rain overnight. The gravel-filled drainage trenches the engineers had constructed when the camp was built carried the excess water away from inside the palisade and for the first time in months the parade ground looked evenly brown, not dirty white. The Rhine swelled and roared, bursting its backs at points and carrying whole trees and swollen-bellied dead animals spinning down to the sea at its mouth. The bridge vanished under the floodwaters. Everyone hoped it would survive the battering it was getting but it was obvious that large scale repairs would be required, at the least. The fort at the bridgehead had to be evacuated because water was coming in under the gates. After three weeks, the rains abated and the river level fell but it still flowed at the furious rate of a galloping horse.

By mid-March what was left of the bridge was clearly visible. Whole lengths were untouched but there were substantial gaps between them. The chief engineer went out in a boat with a long pole and sounded the bottom. He came back to report to the camp prefect.

"Not too bad; we need to sink forty new piles into the riverbed. Once that's done, it's just a matter of constructing the cross braces and covering them with planks. You'll have to give me a wood-cutting party and enough oxen or mules to haul the timber."

"How many men will it take?"

"Two centuries worth plus as many extra as necessary to protect them in case of trouble, I should say."

"Seems a lot for a few bridge piles…."

The engineer took out a wax tablet and scribbled some calculations on it.

"Twelve hundred feet of trimmed heavy timber for the piles themselves, twice the length of lighter wood for bracing plus planks to lay across plus enough to build a couple of piling barges and drop-hammers; it's a fair old amount when everything is taken into account…. better have the carpenters along as well…"

"You can have all the men you want as long as our bridge is back in commission before the legate returns," Attius told him.

The works began. They identified one hundred suitable trees in the nearby forest; oaks for piling, pines for the rest. But it was not simply a case of the legion's experts walking into the skirts of the forest and marking the timber they wanted to cut. Danger lurked out of sight of the camp. Twenty specialists in four parties made the selection but each of them was accompanied by a full century of infantry and ten missile troops. No group strayed beyond horn call of the others so they could quickly assemble in numbers to defend against any attack. Within six days, men with adzes, saws and axes swarmed over a pile of tree-trunks at the riverside trimming and shaping them. Two square rafts were moored out on the water. Each of them held a gantry from which a heavy, stone-ballasted log fell, end-on, to hammer the thirty-foot piles into the riverbed. After each blow, punctuated by a reverberating thud, straining legionaries winched it up and let it fall again. Inch by inch the piles were pounded into the silt, mud and shingle to form the firm supports on which all depended. It rained, a watery sun shone, it rained again but the construction teams laboured unceasingly. The bank was trampled into ankle deep mud which made the work heavier and more dangerous. At least getting the timbers into the river where they were needed was easy enough; they were simply floated out attached to a series of ropes.

Two rowing boats were anchored, one upstream and the other downstream of the bridge where the works were underway. They carried archers and slingers to protect the toiling legionaries. Onshore, two scorpions and two ballistae covered the far bank. Lucius shared the command of the battery with Cestus Valens. He was praying for some movement across the river during his spells of duty so that he could give the order to fire but none came.

The morose lethargy that had overtaken the legion after Saturnalia was gone. There was a sense of busy purpose about the camp. It was as if the bridge repairs had shaken everyone out of a walking sleep and they were now hurrying to catch up in all sorts of ways. Attius ran the quartermasters and clerks ragged counting and recording stores and drawing up accounts of what had been used and what remained. Equipment was checked and repaired or replaced as necessary. Weapons were polished and sharpened or new ones forged. During this period Otto had gone into the forest and returned with two long, straight branches cut from a fallen ash tree. He peeled away the loose, dried bark and spent several days smoothing and shaping them. When he was satisfied, he heated them in a fire and slathered them with beeswax he had begged off Centurion Corvo. He ended up with two perfectly balanced and straight six-foot poles which he took to Martellus.

"These are my spear shafts; I made them," he said.

"And I can see what a good job you've done," the farrier replied.

"But they don't have blades…."

"I can see that an' all…"

Martellus made a pair of socketed blades to Otto's specification, each four inches long and two broad at their widest point. Otto tapered the ends of his spear shafts and fitted them himself. Martellus was doubtful.

"Don't you think they are a bit on the small side?" he asked but Otto shook his head.

"No, big enough to kill. Light to carry all day; thank you."

Titus Attius walked the length of the newly repaired bridge which smelled strongly of pine resin. He jumped up and down in the middle and expressed himself satisfied when it did not collapse under his substantial weight.

Aldermar visited Lucius down by the riverbank.

"It's about Otto…."

"Oh no; what's he done now?" Lucius asked anxiously.

"Nothing, he hasn't impaled the faces of any slaves or cut appendages off legionaries for weeks…"

"That isn't funny you know."

"Well Tribune Longius, as it so happens, it is… to everybody except you. But the reason I want to talk to you is to ask what are you going to do with him when the marching season starts? He'll want to go with you but you can't let him take the field in just a tunic and boots; he's going to need some decent protection.

"You see, this is where it gets difficult, Aldermar. He can't wear standard issue kit; he isn't a legionary nor is he one of your cavalrymen. I don't quite know what to do."

"Can I make a suggestion?

"Please do."

"First of all, it's your duty to arm your companion. He's made his own spears and some of my boys think that you are being a bit mean with him because of it. Pay for one of the saddlers to measure him up and make him a decent subarmalis and then give the cavalry a gift, a good size pig will do, and they will sort him out a mail shirt. By the way, did you notice he's letting his hair grow again? When the light's right, it almost looks like some sort of fuzzy beard's breaking out on his face as well."

Lucius tipped the saddler enough to keep him drunk for a week and was outraged at the cost of the pig but gritted his teeth and paid up. It was worth it to see Otto, bright-eyed with excitement wearing his mail shirt, cinched in at the waist by the belt Titus Attius had given him, holding his two new spears and trying to look like a dignified warrior, in spite of his beaming face. When Lucius gave him a dark blue scarf to wrap around his neck to stop the mail links chafing, his joy was boundless. Otto felt that he had served an apprenticeship over the winter. He had learned the language of the legion, trained with and been accepted by the men. Now his lord was rewarding him with a man's possessions; armour and the right to bear arms in his service. The wise woman had said he would never carry a shield in the ranks of the Suevi but Otto would like her to see him now, dressed as a warrior of the highest rank.

Attius had sent scouts out to look for the approach of the legate's column shortly due to return with fresh men, equipment and supplies for the coming season. He was not going to be found with the camp and the men left in his charge in less than excellent condition. A lathered horse galloped up to the Porta Principalis Dextra to report that Legate Quadratus was one day's hard ride away. That meant three days march for a body of men encumbered with heavy supply wagons.

The news caused an orgy of cleaning and inspecting. Centurions shouted at optios, corporals and legionaries that they weren't going to be the one caught on the hop when the legate arrived. The men became infected with a sort of frenzied fever to polish everything in sight, to arrange things in straight lines and square corners and have the barber shave them until their faces were raw.

The hour finally arrived when they assembled in gleaming ranks under the eagles as the gate was opened and their legate entered the camp to a flourish of horn calls.

Chapter 14

It took two full days for the end of the legate's column to come into sight He had brought fifteen hundred men with him, some returning from leave but over six hundred recruits. They had marched either from Rome or Luca and felt like veterans by the time they reached the Rhine. Not all of them were raw youngsters. Some had served their term and received their honourable discharge but found nothing for them in civilian life so they had re-enlisted. These men were not a problem provided they were fit enough. But the length of engagement had been ten years until very recently so most of them were "ten-year" soldiers and still relatively young. Amongst them was a small number of evocati. These were former officers or legionaries of exceptional merit who had been invited to remain with the legion after their time was up. Their position in the structure was not closely defined but they were always available to support the officer corps and steady the troops in times of extreme emergency. There were two new tribunes. One was keen but knew nothing and soon got in everyone's way. The other had three personal servants and a wagon loaded with furniture, carpets, silver dishes, glassware and wine. He would be a very popular young man as long as that fine wine kept flowing.

As well as personnel, there were wagons loaded with grain for the coming campaigning season, metal ingots, weapons and an innovation. The standard mail shirt with double thickness shoulders was being replaced throughout the Roman armies by the new lorica segmentata. This body armour was made up of horizontal metal plates that slid over each other, looking like barrel hoops with a separate piece covering the upper chest, back, and shoulders. The individual iron and mild steel strips were held together with brass buckled clips and straps. One hundred sets were available, initially reserved for centurions and optios. They were of a standard size so the armourers had a busy week making alterations but there was only so much they could do; no amount of letting out and lengthening straps was going to make an average size fit around the deep chest and massive shoulders of Titus Attius. His was made up for him from scratch with his bronze and silver medals welded to it. Centurion Lentus grumbled. The new armour was difficult to put on and who knew if it would protect him as well as his familiar chainmail? Still orders were orders and within ten days, the centurions and optios on parade wore their lorica segmentata, if not with pride, then with sceptical acceptance.

Corvo ended up with one hundred and five men under his command but four of them were specialist arrow and bow makers. Among the supplies were two barrels of bow staves and one of arrow heads. There was also a cartload of lead pigs and twenty bullet moulds for the slingers. His optio was an expert with the sling so Corvo could put one hundred men into the field led by two specialist officers and their technical support. He was more than satisfied. His only complaint was the scarcity of beeswax. The quartermaster had a permanent indent for it.

"You lot bloody eating it or what?" he would complain when yet another of Corvo's legionaries put in a request.

This was the time of year when good artillery officers took every machine to pieces and rebuilt it; Cestus Valens was one of the best. Human hair torsion ropes were rewound and replaced if showing signs of over-stretching. Wooden slides were smoothed down and greased. Metal fittings were examined and new ones forged if necessary. Lucius had arrived at the depot dressed as a smart Roman officer with Otto one pace behind him as usual and stopped in his tracks in surprise. Cestus was wearing a leather apron over a worn tunic and boots spotted with grease. He was helping five other straining men to lift a ballista off its chassis. Lucius said nothing but went back to his quarters and changed into his oldest tunic. Otto followed suit. The pair of them spent the next six hours in hard physical labour. Lucius learned more about the mechanics of artillery in that one day than he had taken-in by observation and reading over the entire winter. The men changed their attitude towards him after he had spent a fortnight working alongside them. Previously if he had wanted to know something he had been forced to ask. Sometimes the answers had been vague or grudging. But now they began to volunteer information they thought might be useful to him. He was becoming one of them; an artilleryman.

Over a flask of wine Cestus offered more wisdom.

"Every artillery piece is made to a standard specification but they're all different. It's almost like each one has its own character. See that scorpion?" he asked, pointing at one exactly like all the rest. "He's the most accurate. No matter which crew mans him, that scorpion fires truer than any of them. Why is that?" he shrugged. "No-one can tell but by putting aside the dignity of your rank and working on them with your own hands you get some understanding of each one. That could be the difference between victory and defeat."

By the beginning of the first week in April, the last of the civilian haulage contractors had left along with the men who had come to the end of their service and were returning to their homes with a cash gratuity or a smaller amount of money if they had elected to take up land grants in Gaul. Publius Quadratus now commanded a fully manned and equipped legion together with its cavalry and missile troop support able to undertake all required military activities on a two-hundred-mile front along the Rhine. His legion was divided into nine cohorts. The first cohort had centuries of one hundred and sixty men in them, not the usual eighty. It also contained most of the immunes specialists; blacksmiths and the like. The first expedition of the year was always undertaken to show the flag. Two cohorts were sent out. One to patrol a hundred miles upstream, the other the same distance downstream for no other reason than to let the natives know that Rome was not only still there but there in force.

The pattern for the season was set. Forces marched out in the spring rain and the summer heat. They criss-crossed the whole area within the legion's nominal control. Sometimes they were called on to support friendly local tribes against incursions, sometimes they were ambushed but never seriously opposed. The sudden attacks coming from a steep defile or the gloomy forest edge of a clearing were mounted by warriors wanting to make a name for themselves. Even though the Romans were never at risk of defeat, the tribesmen could return to their villages boasting that they had defied Rome. There were losses, gnat bites compared with the strength and manpower of the legion but even so, comrades and friends pointlessly lost from the Roman point of view. But as far as the raiders were concerned, any legionary cut down was one less to have to deal with in the future. They directed their main effort against officers. Lentus came in with a fearful slash through his left eyebrow. An axe blow had slid off the rim of his helmet, cut his face and dented his shoulder armour. The doctor stitched his wound and pointed out that if he had been wearing mail and not his lorica segmentata, his collar bone would have been broken. Lentus said that if he had been wearing his mail shirt, he would probably have been able to get out of the way. Centurions and optios were easily identified by the transverse crests on their helmets. They carried no shields and looked like easy pickings. Their losses were disproportionately high as compared with the rank and file. By the end of the month of Sextilis, seventy-five men had been killed or so badly wounded that they received a medical discharge once their wounds healed but nineteen centurions and optios had been killed or disabled.

Attius and Quadratus kept a running casualty total and, although the death of any man was regretful, their casualties were negligible in strict military terms. The sorrow felt when a jar of incinerated ashes, the remains of a brother, or a son was delivered to relatives hundreds of miles away never crossed their minds. The legate was able to report his sector "at peace"; as far as the German border could ever be truly pacified. It appeared as if The Second Lucan was totally isolated in the vastness of the territory but a regular trickle of dispatches passed between the legion and army administrative headquarters at Augusta Treverorum. Sometimes the riders brought letters from home. Although these were welcome, they seemed irrelevant; talking of events and people who would not seem real until the recipient stood in the open door of his home and saw his family and old friends face to face. All the information coming out of headquarters supported Attius and Quadratus' opinion that things were as quiet as could be hoped for, although neither of them believed that this relative calm would last.

Lucius undertook his share of field duty. Now that he had been given specific responsibilities, his command was firmer than it had been. However, he listened carefully to the advice of his experienced officers. If they were patrolling in relatively open territory, he rode his horse. Otto acted as his groom in the field, marching or loping tirelessly beside him all day long. He had decided that the nickname

"Boxer" had been bestowed on Lucius as a mark of honour and used it every time he spoke to him, to the amusement of anyone in hearing. If they were operating in forested areas, Lucius marched with the men; an officer on horseback would be a ready target for a solitary arrow or spear from a dense thicket. In either case, Otto had a further use. His rudimentary Latin was far in advance of any of the German scouts so he acted as translator. Unfortunately, his vocabulary was straight out of the barracks. On one occasion, a group of possibly hostile warriors had been sighted in the next valley. The scout reported to Otto. He called Lucius who gestured for the nearby senior centurions to join him.

"Boxer, sir, there's about twenty dodgy looking fuckers in the next valley over," he told him.

The other officers grinned widely. Lucius was embarrassed and for once showed his annoyance at his constant shadow.

"That is no way to make a military report," he snapped.

Otto looked hurt.

"But I called you "sir", Boxer and they're there alright, so what's your problem?"

"Just shut up," Lucius shouted and walked away.

One of the centurions slapped Otto on the shoulder.

"Don't worry son, you're doing a grand job."

Lucius grew closer to Otto over the summer. They were constantly together and the more they spoke, the greater the understanding between them. However, Lucius was an upper-class

Roman trained practically from birth to reserve his friendship for, as his mother would have said, "people like us." It did no good to become too close to the lower orders; plebeians, freemen, let alone slaves. So where did Otto belong in this rigid order? The concept of a warrior-companion was alien to Lucius but the relationship was an honoured tradition among the northern tribes. Otto had belonged to a family of minor nobility; that was obvious by the way the German cavalry treated him. It could be said that he and Lucius were of equal standing in their own societies. Army life had softened Lucius' prejudices; he had seen dangerously useless young men of his own class fail and displays of intelligence and expertise from his social inferiors. But Otto…he was not a slave, not a servant but could he truly be a friend? Lucius thought long and hard about it without coming to a decision.

The legion veteran farmers working land near the camp brought in their hay and watched the sky anxiously, hoping the weather would hold up until the wheat could be harvested. On clear days, wavering lines of storks could be seen flying down to the salt marshes of southern Gaul for the winter. Flocks of other birds passed over, high up among the clouds, making longer journeys. Some crossed over the Alps to spend the cold months down in Africa. The air began to smell fresher and the days shortened, almost imperceptibly at first. The quartermasters hurried to replenish their stores before the snow and ice returned. Wagonloads of grain, of hay, of firewood trundled in through the gates. Yet more audits, accounts and indents were made up;

checked, countersigned and filed. Men reported that their old mothers were dying and it would be the decent thing to do to give them leave. Earnest looking legionaries stood to attention shamelessly lying to their officers who had heard it all before and regarded them with cynical eyes. Unscrupulous officers based their decisions on whether to accept a leave request on the size of the bribe they were offered. Centurions passed the provisional lists up to Titus Attius who referred to Legate Quadratus for the final say.

Lucius was listed for home leave and although he was pleased, he foresaw a problem and went to talk it over with Aldermar. They sat with a flask of wine Lucius had brought with him in Aldermar's office in the cavalry lines; a cubicle with basic furniture, smelling of horses and leather and with wisps of hay on the floor.

"I need your advice," Lucius began.

"Of course you do else you wouldn't be sitting here sharing your not too dreadful wine with me. Come on then, young Boxer; what's troubling you? Is it a woman? 'Course not. Have you gambled all next year's pay away? Did you…."

"It's about my going home over this winter and Otto…"

"You don't intend to leave him here over the winter?" Aldermar quickly interrupted.

"I don't know what's best; that's what I want to speak to you about. Let's face it; he's bound to cause me some problems back in Luca," Lucius said.

Aldermar took a deep breath and a deeper draught of his wine before responding. "So, let me understand you; he's good enough to accompany you on every mission you've undertaken. To run beside your horse, to march with you, to carry messages up and down the line, to work with the scouts and always, always, have your back but he won't fit in at home in Luca."

"That's putting it a little harshly," Lucius replied.

"Oh, is it Boxer? If you don't take him with you when you go on leave, in his eyes and the eyes of my men you have as good as said that he is unworthy to be your companion. He will be shamed. The only decent way to break your bonds is for you to offer him a princely gift and formally bid him farewell as if you were never going to see each other again. I don't believe you want to do that."

"Why is it always so serious and complicated?" Lucius complained. "But you're only telling me what I know; I have a duty to him in return for his loyalty. And what's he had out of it so far but food and shelter, a few clothes, a pair of boots and mail shirt? The only mark of recognition he has is the dagger Titus gave when he showed himself to be better with a javelin than any man in the legion. You and my conscience are both telling me it's time I did the right thing by him." Lucius rose to his feet and sighed. "But I dread what he's going to say when I introduce him to my family…"

Aldermar laughed.

"He'll probably ignore them and piss in your fishpond. Thanks for leaving the wine," Aldermar shouted cheerily to the retreating back.

Two days later he was called out of the stables by one of his men.

"Look at that," he said.

Otto was riding a tall grey gelding, deep-chested with a flowing white mane. He made the horse turn in a figure of eight to show off its paces and then leaped out of the saddle at Aldermar's feet. He held the reins and patted its neck while the horse tossed its head and snorted puffs of steam into the crisp morning air.

"Boxer gave it to me. We go to feast with his people until spring," Otto told him, beaming with pride.

Lucius stood to attention in front of Legate Quadratus' desk. Otto, also at attention, was a respectful distance away by the door.

"You will begin your journey to Luca at first light tomorrow. A column of men recruited out of your own district will be following. When they arrive, they will be in holiday mood but they are still soldiers and subject to military discipline." He handed Lucius a scroll in a leather tube. "This letter is to the city magistrate. It informs him that should any matters arise involving men of The Second Lucan, Tribune Lucius Taurius Longius is to be consulted. Use your judgement. Don't put the civilians' backs up but don't let them cheat and swindle our lads. Is Otto to go with you?"

"He is, sir," Lucius replied, taking the scroll and pushing it under his belt.

"I am glad. You are a professional soldier now, Lucius. Comradeships on which you can rely should be valued above everything... and everyone." He gave the tribune a piercing glance. "Our truest friends in the legion would not always be acceptable outside of the military but you must make your family appreciate how priceless they are within it. Do you understand me?"

"I think I do, sir," Lucius replied.

"Very good," the legate told him then commanded Otto to stand forward. He looked the young German up and down and nodded his approval.

"You are very different from that wild boy who chased the slave to my Praetorium steps last year. You have grown and filled out. How well can you speak our language?"

"More better than before, sir," Otto said in his thick accent.

"I hear the improvement but you must continue with your studies. Learn from Tribune Longius, or Tribune Boxer, as everyone seems to prefer. Over this summer you have marched with my soldiers and been of service to them in the field. You are not of the legion yet you have cheerfully shared the fatigues and dangers it faced. However, legionaries are paid for their efforts and you have not been rewarded, as yet. So here is a gratuity in recognition of all you have done." Quadratus handed over a soft leather purse. "It contains one hundred and fifty silver denarii. That is about half a year's pay. You are not entitled to the full amount since you cannot give your oath under the eagle."

Otto's mouth dropped open. He had some idea of the value of money after his time in the camp but had never dreamed of owning such a fortune.

"Thank you, sir, thanks to you," he said, his words coming out in a rush.

"On what will you spend it?" Quadratus asked.

Otto had no hesitation in replying. "A helmet and a long sword; I have horse."

"Oh no, that will not do," the legate said and shouted for a clerk who stuck his head around the office door. "Write me out an indent for a cavalry helmet and sword for this young man," he ordered then turned again to Otto. "You must take another name, you know. We Romans have two or three and it's awkward you having just one…"

"I believe it may be right for him to take my family name, sir. As if he were a freedman acknowledging his patron…" Lucius suggested.

"Exactly so, Otto Longius it shall be."

They left at dawn; their horses fresh and newly shod and leading two pack mules. It would take them a month to ride to Luca if all went well. They would stay in the established military roadhouses where they and their mounts could expect good food and care and, above all, security overnight. The roads could be lonely, particularly at this time of year, and even two well-armed men would be in danger from robbers when darkness fell. The infantry column encumbered with wagons would travel at a slower rate and could be expected to arrive after fifty days on the march.

Lucius and Otto rode south-east, the low sun in their eyes, both of them excited in their own ways to be free for a while, on the road and answerable to no-one.

Chapter 15

Although they had spent a year in each other's daily company, Lucius and Otto had not spoken much because they had no common language. Later, Lucius was occupied with his duties, Otto was busy learning and training and when they were in the field there was no time. Now they had thirty days or more of being together with no-one to distract them. Otto was happy to ride on in silence, frequently drawing his long cavalry sword and swishing it through the air to practise different cuts and slashes.

"It's called a spatha, that type of sword," Lucius remarked as one whistling downward slice came too close to his leg for his liking.

Otto held the weapon upright and examined the blade as if knowing its name called for a closer examination. He sighed and sheathed it, to the relief of Lucius.

"It is a blade only for king or high warrior. Legionaries are better armed and armoured than the highest born of us," Otto said wistfully in response.

"Do you miss them, your people?"

Otto thought for a while then shook his head.

"It would be good to know my mother and sister still live. They were not in village when you fell on us."

This was a subject that they had never mentioned. Lucius was uneasy about speaking of the day they had first met. It was like a boil he did not want lanced; better to let it fester than to be told a truth he did not want to hear. He still could not completely understand why Otto had offered his loyalty in the middle of all that smoke and blood and anguish. Surely he must harbour some resentment, some desire for revenge. He looked back over his shoulder and then ahead. The track they were on was empty in both directions. If Otto had vengeance in mind, this would be his ideal place and time.

The roadhouse they reached that evening was nearly empty apart from half a dozen soldiers scattered around the dining room where a fire blazed in the great stone hearth. After a hot meal and two cups of spiced wine with very little water, Lucius felt relaxed and expansive. He broached the nagging question.

"Do you hate us for what we did to your village?"

Otto looked at him with his pale, cold eyes a puzzled expression on his face.

"It was will of the gods; soldiers were their instruments. If I hate you, I hate the gods who sent you. That is great sin. In any case, you know I am fated to follow this path…."

"But your father…?"

"…Was mighty warrior. He died sword in hand; that I know. You are soldier of Rome. If you are killed in battle, your family will not hate enemy who brought you low. They understand that it is end of road you set your feet on when you joined the legion."

Lucius laughed. "I'm sure my mother would be annoyed."

Otto looked scandalized. "Boxer, do not say things disrespectful to mother!"

They travelled at a steady thirty miles a day resting on every sixth day to give their horses and their own backsides time to recuperate. Well south and east of their starting point, Otto saw his first building constructed entirely of masonry. It was a u-shaped three storey roadhouse with a screen wall enclosing a stable yard. The walls were built of dressed stone blocks in-filled with brick around the windows and door frames. The roof was covered with red pantiles.

Lucius rode straight into the yard but Otto turned his horse to the right and slowly circled the perimeter, gazing up at the walls. When he finally came into the stables, Lucius was already unsaddling his horse. Otto looked apprehensively at the underside of the roof above his head but was reassured by the sight of the rafters holding it up. They were made of wood; a material he knew and understood. Before they went inside, he pushed a corner stone. It did not budge.

"Why it isn't it falling over?" he asked.

Lucius pointed at the thin line of mortar visible in the joints of the stonework.

"The builders make a paste of sand, lime and water and rest the blocks on it. When it dries, it grips them together."

Otto looked at him sceptically then scratched at the mortar with a fingernail. None came away; he grunted, satisfied but only for the moment. Lucius spent the rest of the evening explaining what he knew of building techniques. Every answer seemed to bring a fresh query out of Otto and he had exhausted his sketchy knowledge by the time they went to their beds.

They travelled through Germany, the Belgic lands and deep into Gaul with the mountain ranges well to the east of them. Each stage displayed new and unheard-of wonders to Otto and generated an endless flow of questions. Lucius answered them as best he could. He soon grew bored with dredging up scraps of information to feed into his companion's hungry mind. Then it occurred to him to use Otto's curiosity to improve his Latin. If he did not frame a query with correct grammar, Lucius refused to answer until he did. Lucius had to supply vocabulary as well; Otto had never seen an aqueduct, did not know its function and could not fairly be expected to know what one was called. The improvement was startling. But nothing they had seen so far had prepared Otto for his first sight of a Roman city.

They were now travelling on new, well-paved roads which were easier on the horses but did mean that their shoes wore out faster. They smelled Lugdunum, the Roman trade and military hub, long before it came into view. A faint scent of smoke, of animals, of metal and of humanity drifted on the easterly breeze. It intensified as they walked beside their horses up a long incline, reached the top and saw the city for the first time. Otto was astounded. From their vantage point they could see the defensive walls with gate and corner towers surrounding the innumerable roofs of houses, factories, barracks and warehouses.

The facades of temples rose up in stone dominating the other buildings. It was home to thousands of permanent residents, swelled by itinerant traders in every type of goods imaginable and legion after legion marching through from north or south. Otto was frightened as they rode through the heaving streets looking for an inn, although he would never admit it. His heart was hammering and his breath came short. Such noise, such stink, so many people; the sensations bearing down from all sides panicked him. But he could see that Lucius was taking it all in his stride and forced himself to go on as if unconcerned.

At dinner, Otto asked if Luca was as crowded and reeked as badly.

"No," Lucius laughed, "it is a quieter place and the sea breezes keep the air sweet, most of the time." Otto did not completely understand what he had been told but decided to ask no more, for once. He remained subdued until they left after two days, to his great relief.

They were now riding down the Via Agrippa; part of the network of military roads connecting Lugdunum with the Atlantic, the Mediterranean and strategic strongholds in the recently conquered territories. There was more traffic in these parts. They gave way to imperial couriers galloping between relay stations where they could change horses, they moved off the carriageway to let columns of soldiers pass by without hindrance but disdainfully forced civilians aside. Eventually they turned east onto the Via Antonia on the final few stages heading towards Italy and home.

They had the mountains to their left and the sea to their right as they made their way to the port of Forum Julii. Otto spent one entire day riding with his head twisted to one side marvelling at the troubled sea, rolling and heaving as far as the horizon. He woke the next morning with a stiff neck. But if he had been impressed with his first sight of the Tyrrhenian Sea, it was as nothing to his delight at the sight of the harbour of Forum Julii. Roman warships, huge triremes and sleek, fast liburnians, bobbed in the choppy swell and fretted at their mooring ropes, huddled behind the shelter of the stone breakwater. Fishing craft moved among them, dwarfed in comparison. One three-decker was hauled up onto a slipway with its enormous hull exposed while the barnacles and weed were being scraped off it. Otto saw squid and octopus for sale on the dockside for the first time. He was repulsed and thought Lucius was joking when he said they were good to eat. He also learned that the sea was salty after trying to drink from it using his cupped hands. Lucius had sat back to watch his companion's experiment without warning him, looking forward to the inevitable result. Otto choked and spat and without thinking, tried to wash his mouth out with even more seawater. The disgusted look on his face made Lucius laugh out loud, which earned him a reproachful stare.

Their coastal path led them north and east now, around the head of the Tyrrhenian, always with towering cliffs and defiles inland, until they turned south again and through the Apuan Alps. On the fourth day out of Forum Julii, Lucius reined in his horse at the crest of a pass and pointed to the funnel shaped valley below. Two rivers split around a compact city surrounded by farmlands and protected from the north and east by the forested foothills of the mountains they had just traversed. The sun shone, making the roofs and temples glow in the golden light and the indigo sea sparkled away to the far horizon where it merged with the paler blue sky.

"Home," said Lucius. "This is Luca; we have arrived."

Otto stared down for a while then turned to his companion with a concerned look on his face.

"I have seen many new sights and I now understand how ignorant I am. Nor do I speak good. I hope I will not shame you in front of your family, Boxer."

Lucius remembered his legate's words on the value of comradeship.

"You won't, Otto you won't. Remember you have been honoured by First Spear Centurion Attius and by Legate Publius Quadratus. You've stood by me on the march and in the field. I will not forget that as soon as I walk in my father's house," he said and saw the young German break out in a faint smile but he still seemed nervous.

Mid-afternoon, they entered the city by one of the landward gates and rode through the forum with its temples and magistrate's court before turning right and moving up a steady incline. The shops and commercial premises grew fewer as they climbed; the houses farther apart. They came to a suburb where nothing could be seen except high blank walls pierced by stout, solid gates. There were no pedestrians on the streets, no pedlars or street-vendors calling their wares. Lucius had taken the lead and turned up a side street until he reached a black gate reinforced with iron and indistinguishable from any other. He stopped his horse and kicked out with his boot instead of dismounting and knocking. A panel opened and a face peered up at him.

"Greetings Janus," he said to the porter. "Open the back gate and tell the stable boy I'm home."

He moved off without waiting for a reply. They turned again down a narrow alley and stopped at a pair of wider gates which were hauled open by unseen hands. Lucius, followed by Otto holding their mules' lead ropes, walked their horses into a paved yard where a boy was busy unlatching the double doors of a stable large enough for half a dozen animals. They dismounted and stretched; their journey was over.

Otto looked around. A grid of crushed seashell paths ran across a large garden divided into flower and herb beds. Fruit trees were planted in what seemed a random display but had been carefully placed to give the effect of a natural grove. Shrubs growing in carved marble urns were dotted about and a stone fish spouted water up through its mouth to fall back into a pool in which carp glided. A small building stood under the shade of a trimmed cypress and beyond it the main house. It was a single storey structure. The external walls were rendered with mortar and painted a warm buff colour. Vines were trained up the sunniest aspect on a trellis. They were far south of the Rhine but it was still early November and winter, although not a winter such as Otto had ever experienced. To him, it seemed as if they had travelled back through the seasons to summer. They walked around the side of the house to the main entrance. Two steps led to a terrace under a portico and the front door. It stood open revealing a long rectangular hall painted with scenes of forests and huntsmen. The death masks of Lucius' ancestors stared out of niches in the walls. The central floor area was taken up with a shallow pool lined with a mosaic of sea creatures. They stepped inside.

The family stood in a formal group, smiling and waiting to greet the son and heir. The smiles slid off their faces as they saw the bulk of an enormous blond stranger looming over their Lucius who stepped forward and shook hands with his father, Vitius.

"It is very good to have you home safe and well, my son," he said. "I did not know we were expecting you to be accompanied by a guest..." he added in an enquiring voice looking directly at the tall German blocking the light in the doorway.

"Oh, this is Otto, father," Lucius replied and waved him forward.

"Greetings noble father of the Tribune Lucius Taurius Longius," he said and held out his right hand.

Vitius looked at it, glanced quickly at his son who was smiling and took the proffered hand. Otto shook it warmly, causing the older man to gasp at the pressure.

A very young woman in the family group giggled until she was nudged into silence with a reproving glare from what was clearly her mother. The last of the party was an older lady who shared a strong facial resemblance with Vitius. Otto was introduced to all three in order.

"This is my sister Poppaea," Lucius said, "and my mother Sabina Pulchra…" Sabina looked at Otto like the doe cornered by the hounds painted on the wall behind her, "and finally but not least in importance my grandmother Aelia Clodia…"

Otto had towered over Poppaea and Sabina when he greeted them but he knelt to Aelia and gently took her hand.

"Greetings lady, I am Otto, the sworn companion of your grandson, Tribune Lucius Taurius Longius called Boxer."

Aelia smiled and raised him to his feet. She craned her neck to look up at him.

"I am well aware of my grandson's name and rank, Otto but I have never heard him called "Boxer" before…."

"That is the name given him as a mark of honour in the legion, lady," Otto explained.

She raised one eyebrow.

"Is it indeed? Well, we shall get used to it no doubt." She placed one hand on Sabina's shoulder. "My daughter-in-law thinks you are going to murder us all. Are you going to murder us?"

"No lady; why would I do that?" said Otto, looking puzzled.

"Because, unless I am very much mistaken, you are German and everyone knows Germans kill and destroy for the pleasure of it."

Otto looked into her unafraid, smiling face and burst into laughter.

"Oh lady, I did not know you were joking at first."

Sabina did not appear to be much reassured and glared at her mother who ignored her.

"In any case," the old lady said, "both of you smell of horses and sweaty bodies so go bathe and be sure to put on clean clothes before we eat.

Chapter 16

Janus the porter was also the family bathhouse attendant and had lit the fire to heat water as soon as he could after the young master and his friend had arrived. Now Otto and Lucius sprawled on the stone benches in the small steam room letting the heat melt the aches and strains out of their muscles. They both sighed with pleasure as they relaxed.

In the main house, the atmosphere was tense.

"I will not have that savage in my home, Vitius. Do something." Sabina demanded of her husband.

"What do you suggest?" he asked.

"Throw him out, or have the slaves throw him out. I don't care as long as he goes from under my roof before he cuts our throats."

Vitius held up one hand for calm.

"I'm sure Lucius would not…."

"Lucius? Lucius?" Sabina spat. "What does he know?"

Vitius raised his voice.

"He is a grown man and a soldier. Publius Quadratus would not have given him his own military responsibilities if he did not respect his judgement…"

"Well then that German animal can go and stay with Quadratus but I refuse to let him spend one night under my roof."

Vitius frowned but said no more. He turned on his heel and left the room.

Fresh out of their baths and wearing clean tunics, Lucius and Otto were ushered into the dining room by Pinerus, the family major domo, who also acted as secretary to Aelia and Vitius. He had been with them all his life and although now freed, did not choose to leave "his family". The room was decorated with views of a garden full of flowers and birds shown through false window frames painted onto the walls to deceive the eye. Otto ran his fingers over one of the scenes and smiled. Three couches and two low chairs were laid out around the table. They took their places with Otto on a chair next to the couch on which Lucius lay back and directly opposite Sabina and Poppaea who shared their couch. Sabina reclined with Poppaea sitting upright at the foot. Vitius had the last couch and Aelia took an ornate chair of her own. Pinerus poured the wine, clapped his hands and dinner was brought in. There were sliced loaves of bread, a baked mullet, roasted fowls, a platter of spiced sausages and dishes of olives, pine nuts and vegetables. There were several smaller bowls of fermented anchovy sauce.

Pinerus supervised the two slave women serving the food, poured the wine, bowed and left. Everyone except Otto took some bread dipped in the fish sauce. Following the others, he tried it, pulled a face and gagged. Vitius and Lucius laughed a little.

"It is what we call garum; an acquired taste," Vitius told him.

The family began to talk across the table. Most of it was too quick for Otto to catch. He could manage quite well one-to-one, but the crossflow of several people speaking at once still confused him.

It was unfortunate that the sausages had been placed in front of Otto. He took one and bit into it. He licked his lips and took another, then another and kept eating until they were all gone. Poppaea watched, smirking but fascinated. Sabina's fear had turned to resentment and she glowered across the table at him but Otto was too busy putting away sausage and bread between gulps of wine to notice. Vitius rang a small bell by his hand. Pinerus came in.

"Yes master?" he intoned in his mellow voice.

"Ask the cook if there is any more sausage," Vitius asked.

"Yes," Sabina spat. "It appears that our so-called guest has eaten the whole plateful. If there are none left in the kitchen, perhaps you might bring in a bullock for him or a couple of whole pigs."

"Please," Vitius began, "he was not to know that the dishes are shared…."

"Naturally he wasn't," his wife broke in. "How could he know how civilised people behave at table? He is a low barbarian and I am surprised at you, Lucius, for showing your lack of respect for me and your family by bringing something like him under our roof. There, I've said it," she finished and glared around the room defying anyone to contradict her.

In the shocked silence following her words, comprehension broke in on Otto; all the sausages had not been meant for him. He blushed deeply.

"I am sorry. The plate was put in front of me…." he began but Sabina cut in once more.

"Oh, don't apologize, next time we'll have a trough filled up and put outside on the step for you."

Otto flushed even deeper red. Lucius put one hand on his shoulder to reassure him.

"Pinerus, please have two mattresses and some blankets placed in the summerhouse," he said and rose to his feet. "Otto, take some bread and those roast fowls." Lucius picked up the wine jug and two cups. He looked directly at his mother. "You have insulted my sworn companion and you cannot do that without equally insulting me. I shall not sleep under this roof and the protection of our household gods until you invite both of us back," he said and walked out with an unhappy Otto following.

"Oh, don't be so melodramatic," she called after him. "There's no heating in the summerhouse, you'll freeze."

"I doubt it will be as cold as on the German border, dear," Aelia told her daughter-in-law in a quiet voice.

Vitius glared at Sabina, his face white with anger but he mastered himself and said nothing in front of the rest of the family and servants. They would speak later, in private.

Some wooden garden benches had been brought into the summer house for storage. By the time they were dragged into position, Pinerus arrived with a slave carrying their mattresses and blankets. Two beds were made up. The benches were too short for Otto whose feet would dangle over the end of his but both he and Lucius had slept under far worse conditions. There was still some light in the sky and it was too early for sleep so they sat companionably eating and drinking.

"I am sorry to have eaten all the sausage," Otto said and looked at Lucius with such a sad expression on his face that Lucius burst into laughter. After a moment's pause Otto joined him.

When Vitius opened the door and stepped in he saw the two of them wiping their streaming eyes between guffaws.

"You did get through a hell of a lot of sausages," Lucius managed to gasp out.

"But they were so good," Otto responded after two attempts.

Vitius sat down beside his son who filled his wine cup and handed it to him.

"Sorry, father, you'll have to share with me."

Vitius drank a little then looked over at Otto.

"I apologise. I am humiliated that a guest has been made unwelcome in my home," he said.

Otto waved the chicken wing he held in his right hand magnanimously.

"The lady is right. I do not have good Roman manners. And she thinks I will do harm to all of you, the grandmother warned me."

"I must say you are taking it very well…"

"It is not of great importance, sir. Boxer and I are comfortable here and I must not take offence at the words of his mother."

"You all have to understand that Otto is sworn to me for life, father. He will fight alongside me to the end if necessary, neither would he ever do anything to wound me or my family. That is why he let mother's harsh words wash over him; for my sake. If any man had spoken to him the way she did, he would be dead by now. If Otto did not kill him, I would," Lucius said in a matter of fact manner.

Vitius looked at the muscular, hard-faced young man beside him striving and failing to recognise in him the cheerful boy his son had been not so long ago. Otto noticed the strong facial resemblance between them, except for their noses. He thought of his own father who he would never see again in this world. A pang of sorrow went through him but he shook it off, wondering why the will of the gods was so cruel at times.

"Lucius, neither I nor the rest of us have seen you for nearly two years. You've changed but I suppose we still think of you as the boy who left us. Please make peace with your mother."

"Not unless she accepts she has wronged Otto."

Vitius sighed. "Well you can't stay in the summerhouse for your entire leave…"

"I shall go over to the city garrison barracks in the morning and arrange billets for us there."

"I don't think you can just do that…"

"But I can, father. I am a tribune of The Second Lucan; the most senior serving military officer in the city."

Vitius sighed as that truth sunk in. He rose to his feet.

"Very well; but take breakfast with us before you go…both of you, sleep well."

In the night, Otto heard a shutter rattle and snuffling at the door.

"What's that, Boxer?"

"Nothing; it's Ursus the guard dog. Janus sets him loose overnight, get your head down… early start."

They prodded the stable boy awake at cockcrow and sent him to fetch two buckets of water from the well. They washed, spluttering at the sharp cold of the water in the chill dawn and unpacked their armour and weapons from the pack saddles which had been left in the stable overnight. The boy watched entranced as they transformed themselves into glittering warriors while he polished their hob-nailed soldier's boots.

"Saddle our horses for after breakfast," Lucius ordered and they strode together around the side of the house.

They clattered into the dining room carrying their helmets under their left arms. The family was once more assembled. Otto seemed even huger in his mail shirt and Lucius looked older and more authoritative in his cuirass. They put their helmets on the floor beside them, shifted their scabbarded swords out of the way and sat.

"Why the display of military pomp?" Aelia asked.

"I have to introduce myself to the magistrate and hand him a letter from Legate Publius Quadratus," Lucius told her.

"Whatever for?"

"Some legionaries are due to arrive on leave. He will have to consult me before sentencing any of them that get into trouble with the law."

"The magistrate has to consult you, brother?" asked the incredulous Poppaea.

"Our Lucius is the highest-ranking army officer in Luca," her father told her.

She giggled.

Sabina stood up and walked around the table to Otto. Her face was strained and her lips pursed into a thin line.

"My husband and my mother in law have pointed out to me that I have broken the sacred rules of hospitality towards you and I...."

Before she could say any more, Otto came to his feet and took her hands in his own. Her eyes widened in momentary panic. He was so tall that her head did not come up to his shoulder and her hands had vanished completely in his broad fists, although he grasped them gently.

"Lady, you are right to say I know nothing of your ways. But as many times as I tell you I will do your family no harm you will always fear me. If you and Boxer will agree, I will sleep in the little house. Then I shall be nearby in case of danger but make no problems, yes?"

He released her hands. She flushed and went back to her seat without replying.

"Well said, indeed, Otto," Aelia told him and all the family smiled with relief.

The table was set with jugs of milk, fruit juice and water, bread, butter, cheese, olives and cold meats. Otto winked at Poppaea and passed a platter of bread across the table to her mother.

The stable boy trotted beside them as they rode down into the city. He would hold their mounts while they were with the magistrate. The clerk sitting at his desk in the waiting room smiled politely at them as they marched in.

"If you would take a seat, gentlemen, his honour will see you in your turn"

Lucius looked around the spacious high-roofed hall. A dozen or more people were arrayed around the walls on marble benches, some clutching papers which they hoped would prove their case, some staring morosely at the floor, others twitching with impatience. An ornate door at the far end of the room opened. Everyone sat up watching an elderly man bowing himself out. He closed the door behind him, turned, and walked out into the square with a satisfied expression on his face.

Lucius nodded to Otto who marched over to the door, banged on it three times with his fist, flung it open and stepped into the office. Lucius followed to a muted chorus of disapproval from those who had been waiting for much longer than they had, just to be pushed aside. Soldiers were always so arrogant; it was a disgrace!

The portly occupant of the inner office sat open-mouthed at the abrupt entry of the blond giant. He winced as hob-nailed boots crashed down on his ornamental floor. Otto closed the door behind Lucius and stood rigidly to one side. Lucius marched up to the magistrate's desk, came to attention, saluted and handed over the scroll he had been charged to deliver.

"A letter from the noble Legate Publius Quadratus to the Chief Magistrate of Luca, sir," he barked.

His honour opened the leather scroll case with hands that shook a little, read quickly then looked up.

"Says here you're Tribune Longius; are you the son of Vitius?"

"I am, sir."

"Also says I have to liaise…"

"Not "have to", but that you are requested to consult me if any of my soldiers misbehave while on leave in the city."

"Well, there we are then. I shall, of course comply. Are you staying at your family home?"

"I am; you can contact me there. I thank you on behalf of my legate for your cooperation, sir."

Lucius threw another salute, crashed his boots down on the mosaic head of a nymph, turned and marched out followed by Otto who closed the doors behind them with an echoing bang. Everyone glowered at the two of them but felt it wiser to say nothing.

"Goodbye, and thank you citizen," Lucius told the clerk politely as they walked out into the pale sunshine.

The stable boy led their horses behind them as they strolled over to the main gate and the military guard quarters. The centurion in command lacked one eye, which explained his posting to a garrison command.

"A courtesy visit, I am Tribune Lucius Longius." Lucius told him. "I simply wanted to let you know that I am here and that a number of men on leave from the Second will be arriving shortly. You will be given the list by the transport officer in charge of the party."

"Centurion Decimus Massus. Understood, sir and thank you; another few weeks of wrestling drunken legionaries into the cells," he replied half rueful, half smiling.

"Surely the city-watch is responsible for policing?" Lucius enquired.

"Technically yes, but in practice one of your lads can sort out half a dozen watchmen so we get roped in to assist. Might I ask how things are going on the Rhine, sir?"

"Difficult as ever, Centurion Massus; did you serve there?"

He put one hand up to his empty eye-socket barely covered with a black patch.

"No, I never did; got this in Africa. Your bodyguard, he would be a German then?"

"He is; one of the Suevi people."

"Gods above and below but he's bloody big. Are they all that size?"

"Tell the centurion how old you are Otto," Lucius said with a laugh.

"I am now seventeen," he replied with a salute to the one-eyed officer.

The centurion made the sign to deflect bad luck.

"Let's hope you reach eighteen safely but what size will you be if you reach twenty-five?" he asked.

The interview finished on that note. Otto and Lucius walked across to where their horses were being held.

"Why did the officer make that sign with his fingers?" Otto asked.

"To keep bad spirits away; a lot of people believe seventeen is an ill-omened number. You can rearrange it to read "VIXI" which means "I lived". If you have lived, you must be dead; bit stupid really,"

Otto raised his eyebrows and shook his head. Was there no end to the complications these people made of daily life?

"Boxer, I want to buy something before we go back."

"Well, you aren't short of money. What do you want?"

"I want boots with no nails so they will not break your mother's floor pictures," he said, pointing at his feet.

"Now that is a good idea," Lucius replied.

The ill-tempered cobbler told them he had nothing remotely big enough to go around Otto's feet and in any case why did they want new boots? The ones they were wearing were perfectly good. When it became obvious there were not going to leave empty-handed, he reluctantly got up from his bench and rummaged around in the back of his shop.

"Try these," he said when he came back throwing a pair of red, soft leather boots to Otto.

They were his exact size.

"Made them last year for another freak of nature but he never collected them. Now you, soldier, let's look at your feet," he told Lucius.

Once fitted, they discussed how much; the cobbler named his price. Lucius laughed and made a counterproposal. The tradesman walked to his open door and spat into the street.

"That's what I think of your offer," he said.

Lucius pointed out that by his own admission, Otto's boots were technically second hand and, in any case, when would the next giant come in wanting footwear?

They finally agreed, shook on it and paid. Otto looked doubtfully at the small pile of change that had been poured into his palm. Once out of the shop, he showed it to Lucius.

"Look, I gave the man coins for his boots but he has given me many more coins," he told him.

All the way back home, Lucius tried to make Otto understand that coins had differing values and the concept of "change". In the end Otto shrugged and gave them to the delighted stable boy.

"That's quite a lot of money to give him," Lucius told him.

"You just told me they were small coins that cannot buy many things," he said, bored with the whole idea of money which he thought too complicated for a man to waste his time on.

When they returned some changes had been made. There was now only one bed in the summer house but a charcoal brazier and an oil lamp had been added to the furnishings. A rudimentary rack had been constructed in the stables for their weapons and armour. They changed and went into the house. Lucius chatted with his family while Otto sat feeling out of place and staring down at his new boots. Eventually he stood up and wandered out into the garden. Around the back of the house he found storerooms and slave-quarters. Some women were washing clothes but they looked away and said nothing when he greeted them. He poked his head through an open door and saw the cook sitting at a table with Pinerus. They did return his salute but it was clear that his presence was unwanted. He strolled around by the porter's lodge where Janus was sitting on a stool dozing in the pale sunshine but it was what he saw next that really aroused Otto's interest.

Behind a low hedge at the side of the porter's quarters was a high-fenced pen in which lay the biggest dog Otto had ever seen. It was a Molossian Mastiff; slate grey with a heavy head on a thick neck that sloped into a deep chest. Otto peered over the fence.

"You must be Ursus," he said.

The dog opened one red-rimmed eye and licked his pendant jowls. He slowly got to his feet and stared up at Otto. He sniffed the air and raised his fringed lips on one side to show his fangs. A low rumble emerged from that massive body. He weighed one hundred and sixty-five pounds, his shoulders stood three feet above the ground when he was on all fours and his front legs were almost as thick as Otto's wrists. The German looked at him with open admiration.

"What a dog you are," he told the beast, reverting to his native tongue. "A dog like you should be running down a wild boar in the forest, not shut up like this. But are you brave? Maybe you are just big like an ox but with no fire in you, let's see."

He reached down and slid back the bolt locking the inward opening door to the pen. He moved away half a dozen paces and waited. He heard shuffling and snorting then one black clawed paw hooked back the door and Ursus stood there, free. Otto laughed aloud and shouted.

"Come on then, here I am."

The dog put his head down, lifted it and bayed. The sound shook Janus awake and he nearly fell off his seat at the sight of Ursus hurtling towards the young master's guest. He watched frozen with shock as Ursus flung himself at Otto. They collided, going down together in a snarling, laughing heap. Janus scurried for the front door shouting for help at the top of his voice. Everyone ran out and the slaves followed by Pinerus appeared round the side of the house.

Otto had bent his knees and braced to receive the dog's first leap. He had gripped the loose skin on either side of its neck to keep its teeth from tearing out his throat but he had been deceived at the bulk and power of his adversary. Ursus knocked him off his feet. He fell backwards desperately hanging onto his grip. The household watched in horror or excitement, according to their tastes, as the two figures locked in combat rolled over and struggling for a purchase, gravel flying up from scrabbling boots or paws. Ursus kept up a continuous growl interspersed with frantic barks. Otto was shouting in German when not laughing. Both showed open jaws full of strong, white teeth. The dog managed to get on top and advance its foam slathered fangs within an inch of the strange man's face but Otto got a forearm in between them, blocking the final, thrust from that mighty neck which could have been fatal to him. With a quick movement of his knees, he knocked the animal's back legs aside and twisted so that he was now above it, still with his forearm across the dog's gullet. He let his weight bear down and cut off its breathing. Ursus' legs scrabbled frantically in the air but grew slower and fell still as he used up the oxygen in his lungs. With a grin of triumph, Otto slid off and lay on his back with his arms stretched out either side of him. Ursus lurched to his feet and took Otto's throat in his jaws but he did not bite down. He felt the man's hand come up and massage the root of one of his ears. He released his grip and wagged his tail. Otto stood up, panting and grinning.

"Good dog," he said. "Good dog, let's have a drink."

They walked companionably back to the pen where Otto refreshed the water in Ursus' bowl.

Sabina turned to her husband.

"If anyone ever wanted proof that Otto is a monster we all had it today; two beasts fighting in our garden."

When Janus let him out at nightfall, the dog ran straight to the summer house where he whined until Otto opened the door for him. After licking his new friend's face, he laid on the floor peacefully beside him all night long apart from his forays around the garden when he thought he heard or smelled something that needed investigation.

Chapter 17

The next morning, when everyone had calmed down, Lucius and Vitius sat facing Otto who did not understand their concerns about his wrestling match with the mastiff.

"What I want to know," Vitius asked, "is what did you think you were doing?"

"For the sport, to test myself against him …." Otto replied with a shrug.

"You do know Ursus could have killed you?" Lucius put in.

"Have you watched wolves fighting?" Otto asked, answering the question with one of his own. Lucius shook his head. "When wolves try each other's strength, the loser goes still and shows his throat. The winner grips the offered throat and then releases it; as with wolves, so with dogs. Ursus and I now respect each other." Otto went on.

"It seems to me that your companion has more experience of such things than we do, my son" Vitius said.

That was the end of the discussion. However, the slaves smiled and nodded at Otto as he went about the house and garden. For them, the fight between man and dog was the sort of spectacle they had heard was displayed in the arena but never hoped to see themselves.

Otto sat alone on a stool in the atrium under the projecting roof. A soft rain was falling. He rested his elbows on his knees and looked down at the mosaics, thinking. These Romans were so different. He understood that challenging Ursus had been something none of them would ever do but why was that? They were the best of soldiers but where was their warrior pride? He could make no sense of them. On the edge of his vision he saw Janus open the gate to admit a figure hooded against the rain in a blue cloak. The owner of the cloak came up the steps into the atrium and unclasped the ornate brooch holding it in place at his neck. He pushed the hood back. Otto saw that he was a young man with thickly curled hair wearing a blue tunic edged in gold fringes and a matching leather belt and boots. He held out his cloak to Otto at arm's length.

"Here, take it," he said in an abrupt tone.

Otto looked directly at him. He did not like the newcomer's manner or his appearance. He had rings on the fingers of both plump hands and a petulant mouth. Otto decided he was not worth troubling over and returned to his examination of a fish depicted in minute tiles on the floor. Each small tile was nothing in itself but when a number of them were cleverly placed next to each other, the difference in their colours transformed them into an image. Otto admired the skill of the artists who could make fish and men and horses and gods on a floor, of all places.

"I told you to take my wet cloak," the man shouted and threw it down beside Otto. "Now pick it up and have it dried out."

Otto looked up, shook his head and pushed it aside with the toe of one boot. The newcomer grew red in the face and so enraged that he shook and danced from one foot to the other.

"I'll have you whipped," he shouted, "I'll have you whipped until your bones are bare…."

Lucius hurried out to see what the commotion was all about.

"Greetings Servius," he called out. "Whatever is wrong?

Servius pointed at Otto.

"This slave," he snarled, "has shown me the most damnable insolence. I want him flogged…"

"He isn't a slave," Lucius interrupted.

"Well, one of your soldiers then… whatever he is, he can't behave to me like that."

Otto laughed. "I am Otto, war-companion to the Tribune Lucius Taurius Longius, called Boxer. Who are you?" he asked with amused contempt. He felt he had the measure of this young man who could not control himself and was so soft his flesh shook when he stamped his feet.

"He is my oldest friend, Otto and should be treated with respect," Lucius told him.

"Then let him earn some, Boxer," Otto replied.

The visitor looked as if he might either burst or break into tears. With a hard glare at Otto, Lucius picked up the cloak and led Servius into the house with one arm over his shoulder. Otto heard Sabina's voice wearily saying, "What has he done now?" and then all was silence once more. He went into the summer house feeling sorry for himself and lay on his bed, one arm flung over his face. After several minutes, he heard the door open and looking up, saw a slave carrying a high-backed stool and cushion followed by Aelia. Her servant placed the seat for her. She sat and he lit the charcoal brazier, even though the afternoon was not cold. Aelia smiled at Otto as her attendant departed.

"Oh dear," she said kindly, "how hard it must all be for you. What on earth happened with Servius?"

Otto told her and she laughed aloud.

"He is a pompous ass, always has been. The problem with Servius is that he is the only child of a rich father who was in turn the sole heir of a rich man. His is the third generation of privilege and he believes in his own importance above everything else…."

"What does he do?"

"Nothing; he has money and property so he has no need to do anything. Even if he wanted to, I doubt that he would have the will and intelligence to achieve much."

"But Boxer is the only son of a rich man and he is a soldier; an honoured officer…"

Aelia laughed again, gently.

"We are not rich," she said.

She saw the expression of disbelief pass across Otto's face. He looked into her eyes with his own, so pale that the blue of them seemed almost colourless in bright sunshine.

"My father was Badurad, a war counsellor to a king. He was accounted wealthy among our people because he had a sword, a mail shirt and a horse. Lady, you are rich."

Aelia sighed. "We have status Otto and land but not as much money as you might think. We have to keep up our position in society and that costs a lot. Lucius contributes from his pay so we are comfortable but far from rich, as you believe. Two bad harvests means we have to borrow and it takes three good ones to repay the loan. Now, tell me how you came to be my grandson's companion and I will tell you all about my family."

He recounted everything; the wise woman, her prophecy and his father's demand that whatever happened he must follow his fated path.

"Very well, I shall think about what I have just heard. Do you know that some years ago there was a civil war in Rome and the empire?"

"Yes," replied Otto. "People said that the Romans' bloodlust was so great that they turned on each other because there was no-one left to slaughter in the whole of the Gallic and Belgic lands."

Aelia pursed her lips and tilted her face for a moment before continuing.

"That is, of course, a view. However, there were great men in Rome at that time whose power was equally balanced. The richest of them was Crassus who was killed in far eastern lands. Pompeius Magnus fought Caesar and lost his life. Then the Divine Julius was murdered and his heir, the present Emperor we call Augustus, fought with the Antonian family for control of the empire. Everyone in Rome was forced to take a side, whether they wanted to or not. My late husband, Vitius' father, chose the Antonians. They lost and so did he. His villa in Rome, his estates and his gold were confiscated by the victors. We barely escaped with our lives. My parents owned this house and our farms outside the city so here we came to seek refuge. When they died, we inherited and here we live now. You see, Otto, there are degrees of wealth as there are of poverty. By the standards of my youth, I and my family are poor." She rose to her feet. "Tomorrow, I shall visit you and tell you a great story you will understand and enjoy."

She was as good as her word. The next day, she began to recount the fall of Troy.

"Achilles' mother told her son that if he sailed away to fight in this war, he would fall but his fame would last forever. If he stayed home, he would have a long and happy life but his name would die with him. He chose glory…"

"Of course, what warrior would not?" Otto enthused.

Aelia laughed gently. "I knew this would be a story close to your heart."

They spent many afternoons together while Otto was in Luca. Listening to the old lady's tales and conversing with her improved Otto's Latin to the point where only his persistent accent showed he had not been brought up speaking that language. Sometimes their cultures clashed.

"Why do you Germans hate us Romans?" she asked.

"We do not," he replied.

"Why then do you cross the Rhine to kill and plunder in Roman lands?"

Otto snorted in derision.

"Roman lands? We have raided and fought wars across the river since the beginning of time. The Belgic people are our cousins who decided to stay in territory they had conquered in the south. Then you Romans come and when we do what we have always done you say we are your enemies. No-one invited Rome into our world…."

Four days after his first visit, Servius called again in the early evening. He pointedly ignored Otto.

"I have arranged a little celebration, madam, to welcome home our Lucius," he told Sabina.

"Spending the evening with a group of young men with nothing better to do than to drink too much wine and misbehave, you mean," Sabina laughed.

"Perhaps a little wine will be drunk but in a good cause," replied.

"And that cause would be what?"

"Enjoyment, lady, recreation, relaxation after the harsh military discipline poor Lucius has endured…."

"Go on then; as if anything I could say would stop you."

While Lucius dressed to go out, Otto went over to the summer house, changed into his soldier's boots and buckled his pugio dagger around his waist under his cloak. He caught up with the other two just as Janus was letting them through the gate.

"I don't remember inviting you, whatever your name is," Servius snapped looking at Otto for the first time.

"I go where Boxer goes," Otto replied.

"And who told you that you may call the noble Tribune Lucius Taurius Longius by that name? You really take a lot on yourself for a barbarian, don't you?"

"Come on, Servius, Otto is my sworn companion of course he must come with us."

"Even when he is unwanted? My, what a faithful dog you are; heel boy, heel," Servius said spitefully.

Half a dozen urchins were waiting in the street. They held pitch-soaked torches, as yet unlit, to guide the gentlemen through the dark streets. They would be paid a few coppers to accompany them to the place of their night's entertainment and would then wait outside as long as it took to see them home again. Only then would they be paid; unless their "gentlemen" had lost all their money at dice or simply chased them off.

The moved off downhill, crossed the square and turned left past the garrison barracks and into a narrow street that followed the curve of the city wall. The torches were lit with flint and steel. They gave off a yellow guttering light and the air was full of the pungent odour of burning pine resin. Wavering shadows danced before them off the walls until they stopped at a door identical to all the others but heavily reinforced with iron straps. Servius knocked and a hatch opened. A pair of hard eyes reflecting the torchlight examined the party.

"Welcome Master Servius," a harsh voice said as the door was thrown back.

They found themselves in a room about ten feet square. It was empty other than for a pair of stools, an oil lamp on a bracket and lines of hooks on the walls from which cloaks hung. There was a second door, equally massive, opposite the street door. Two heavily set men with an air of suppressed violence about them took the newcomers' cloaks. One of them stopped in front of Otto.

"No slaves admitted, sirs, sorry but house rules," he said.

"He's not a slave," Lucius told him. "He is the son of a German noble visiting my home while I'm on leave."

"You don't say?" the doorman responded. "Well, if you vouch for him fair enough." Then he noticed the dagger on Otto's belt and pointed at it. "Visitor or not, no weapons on the premises; we look after it, you not worry, savvy?" he said very slowly and loudly in case Otto spoke no Latin.

Otto looked over at Lucius who nodded so he reluctantly handed over his prized knife. The second man opened the inner door and a blaze of light fell into the cubicle with a sound of music and a sweet perfume.

"Welcome to Calypso's Island," he said as they stepped through into an enclosed garden. The space was bounded by high walls on three sides and a low house with a red glow passing through closed shutters at the windows.

In the middle, under a canopy warmed by charcoal braziers, a dozen men of around Lucius' age reclined on couches or lay on mounds of pillows on a rich carpet. Torches flamed in wall brackets to illuminate the scene. The other guests wore garlands of artificial flowers on their heads and held goblets. Girls passed among them pouring wine and offering snacks and sweets from trays. Two female flautists accompanied by a man with a lyre sat on stools to one side making music for their indifferent audience.

"Noble youth of Luca," Servius called out as he stepped forward, "friends, brothers of the wine-cup, greet our Lucius, returned from the ice, snow and sudden death of the German border."

They greeted him with a cheer and cleared a space for him in the centre of the party. No-one made room for Otto who found himself a seat on an unoccupied bench at the edge of the canopy. The girls passed with their wine jugs, laughing as they pushed away the interfering hands of the partygoers sliding up their thighs or squeezing their breasts. Sometimes one would throw some crystals on one of the braziers and a perfumed smoke arose from it with a hiss and crackle. The hours passed. The drinkers became more raucous. Some vomited in dark corners, wiped their mouths, staggered back into the light and shouted for more wine. Otto noticed that one after another of the young men would disappear into the house for several minutes then return looking sheepish or proudly muttering comments to their friends.

Servius was drunk but that had not blunted his malicious streak. He had been throwing surreptitious glances at Otto sitting sober and aloof for some while. He called a serving girl over to him.

"Fetch your mistress," he demanded.

She went into the house and came back with an older woman, dark, slight and richly dressed, with eyes like two jet beads. He spoke to her, she nodded and disappeared. Servius wandered over to Lucius, sat beside him and put one arm around his shoulders.

"Lucius, my oldest friend, I apologise."

"For what?" Lucius asked blearily in his half drunken state.

"For getting off on the wrong foot with Otto, that tame German of yours. In fact, if you don't mind, I'd like to make it up to him."

"Decent of you… take it kindly," Lucius slurred.

Servius smirked and rose to his feet, walking over to Otto.

"For the sake of Lucius…Boxer… we must be friends so I've arranged a pleasant surprise for you. Come with me."

Otto looked suspiciously over at Lucius who noticed, smiled and raised his wine cup. Otto took that as assent, not realizing that Lucius was so far gone in drink he was doing the same to anyone who caught his eye. He followed Servius into the house.

"This beauty is Calypso" he said, introducing Otto to the mistress of the garden.

"Hello, my handsome hero," she purred at him taking one of his hands and leading him to a small door. "There's a special treat waiting for you inside."

With that, she opened the door and pushed him in the small of his back. He took an involuntary step forward. The door closed behind him. The room in which he found himself was small but well-lit, the walls painted with scenes of half-men, half-goats pursuing naked women through a forest. There was a bed and a padded chair. There was a girl; a girl with her hair parted in the middle and falling in two thick blond braids to her waist. She too was naked apart from a belt of some sort of animal skin around her waist. Her breasts were high and small, immature, and if she had yet grown any pubic hair it had been completely removed. Her long, slender legs made her tall, above Otto's shoulder. She looked at him with blue eyes almost as pale as his own.

Otto was appalled.

"Maiden, what are you doing here?" he asked in his native language.

"Maiden?" I was taken by the Romans when I was ten and put to work here at the age of twelve. What sort of "maiden" has been used by men who prefer children to women? You are of the Suevi?"

"I am."

"Then shame on you for coming to a place like this. At least I was forced…"

The door burst open and Servius fell into the room two others half drunken youths. He took in the scene and was suddenly angry. In revenge for the incident with the wet cloak he had planned to stripe Otto's naked backside as he lay on top of the girl. He dropped the garden-cane he had been holding behind his back to the floor.

"What are you talking about in that jabber of yours? You're supposed to be warming her up for me. Thought I'd show what Romans do to Germans. We fuck 'em, fuck 'em all because that's all you're good for," Servius told him.

He slid around Otto and shoved the girl down onto the bed. She bent her knees and opened her legs as he fumbled at his loin cloth.

"Go on, Servius, give her a right seeing to," one of his friends sneered.

As Otto turned away, he looked right into her eyes and saw there was nothing there; no pain, no hope, no spark of life. Her soul had been slowly and agonizingly destroyed.

Calypso was waiting for him in the corridor.

"Looking on not to your taste then?" She said, "Still Master Servius is getting his money's worth."

"Men pay you to lie with these girls?" he asked in disbelief.

Calypso threw her head back and laughed stridently. He caught a waft of foul breath and saw the blackened, rotten teeth at the back of her mouth. He shuddered.

"Of course, they do. This is a brothel, that's what it's for."

"Then I will buy her."

Calypso laughed again, briefly.

"She's already paid for."

"No, I mean I will buy her from you."

"Oh, fallen in love, have we?" her eyes glittered at the possibility of making big money. "So, what's your offer?"

"I have two hundred Denarii…."

She put a hand on his arm and shook her head. "Stop there. She earns me more than three times that in a year. She's fourteen now and she's got at least another two years in her, maybe more, her being a big strong one, before she's too used up and I have to sell her down the market." She fell back a little at the baleful glare on his face but recovered her bravado. "No, sonny, it seems to me that none of this is for you. My advice is; go home and don't think of coming back 'cos you won't be let in. I can see trouble coming a mile off and you're it."

Otto knocked on the inner door and was admitted to the entrance cubicle. He picked up his cloak and his dagger was returned.

"Nice knife that, where'd you get it?"

"It was a gift from my First Spear Centurion."

"I thought the other bloke said you was a German noble," he said suspiciously.

"Auxiliary I expect, mate," his colleague explained. "They have a lot of them in the cavalry."

Otto squatted beside the wall with the group of boys waiting to light their torches and see their employers back home through the dark streets. Eventually Servius and Lucius came out into the cold night air. Otto was pleased to see that Servius had vomited stale wine down the front of his tunic and would be forced to walk all the way, wet and stinking.

Lucius did not appear until noon the next day. He was pale and red-eyed. He refused food but drank jug after jug of water before vanishing into the hot room of the bathhouse for two hours to sweat the alcohol out of his system. Later, sitting with Otto and his father in his study, he still looked a little fragile but his eyes were no longer blood-shot and his headache had mercifully subsided.

"By the way," Vitius asked, "whatever happened to that slave I gave you? Atrexes wasn't that his name?"

Lucius looked uncomfortable and avoided his father's eye.

"He didn't work out. I had to let him go," he mumbled after a pause.

"Let him go in far Germany? I wonder what happened to him…"

"I don't exactly know," Lucius said truthfully but not wanting to pursue the topic.

"I do," Otto intervened. "He tried to dishonour me, to use me as a wife. His manhood was cut off, stuffed in his mouth and then he was drowned."

There was a long moment of shocked silence. Lucius had never heard these details before. Vitius was horrified at Otto's casual tone of voice.

"You did that to him?" he gasped.

"No, not me; I just stabbed him through the face with a stylus. It was the cavalrymen who finished him. They took it as an insult to all Germans because Boxer had accepted me as his companion." He looked very hard at Lucius. "Any disrespect shown to me should be a matter for Lucius to deal with but they took it out of his hands. Any disrespect from anyone," he repeated for emphasis. "Like last night…."

Lucius groaned.

"Oh please, Otto, no: I don't remember much about it after the first hour. If I did or said anything to upset you, I'm sorry. Don't blame me, blame the wine."

Otto smiled and nodded his head. He was now sure that Servius' crude and cruel mockery had not been done with the knowledge or connivance of Lucius, which greatly relieved his mind. But he did not forget the cane. He had guessed how Servius had planned to use it on him.

Chapter 18

Otto accompanied Lucius on several more social outings but he made sure he was always cautious, always sober. He never could never work out exactly why Servius had been so determined to humiliate him on that first night so if Servius was present, Otto stayed outside with the boys who carried the torches, no matter how long he had to wait. Lucius took less and less pleasure in nights spent drinking with his old friends as time went by. After the initial excitement of seeing them all again, he quickly realized they had nothing but school days in common. He thought they had never quite grown up. They thought he was too rigid and reserved. He had become a soldier; hardened by exposure to strict discipline and frequent scenes of violence. They were the sons of prosperous provincial officials as they had always been. Nothing had changed for them. It sometimes made Lucius feel a little lonely and when he did, he turned to Otto for comradeship.

When Lucius was called on to appear in front of the magistrate because some soldier on leave had broken the law, it was always done with full military ceremony. Lucius and Otto rode into the square in their best uniforms attended by the delighted stable boy who always received a tip from Otto for holding the horses.

"You give him too much," Lucius complained.

"It is the duty of a warrior to be generous to those who serve him," Otto told him with a shrug.

They went into the magistrate's office and court with much saluting, thumping of boots on his prized floor (which made him shudder) and clashing of armour and weapons. The cases were petty for the most part. Drunken fights or property damages which were settled by monetary compensation if the soldier had provoked the incident, if not, they were dismissed out of hand. One crime was serious. A soldier had attempted to rape a woman in the backyard of a bakery. Her husband, the baker, had heard her screams and ran through the shop in time to save her but took a fair bit of punishment in the ensuing fight.

The accused legionary stood with a smug look on his face while he listened to the evidence being given against him. He looked sideways at the tribune standing to attention beside him and was sure the officer would tell these civilians where to get off. He was wrong. In the iron grip of Otto, he was frogmarched to the garrison headquarters with the baker, his wife and the magistrate following on. The magistrate's clerk carrying a wax tablet and stylus to take notes for the official record completed the small procession. Lucius explained the matter to Centurion Massus who led them into the guardroom. The prisoner's tunic was ripped away and he was made to kneel, arms outstretched, with a burly soldier hanging on to each of his wrists. Lucius and the optio acting as guard commander consulted.

"How many, sir?" asked Massus.

Lucius was not entirely sure. "Enough to give out a strong message that honest women are to be left alone, but not enough to make him unfit for service."

"Fair enough," he said and took an expert look at the man's back and shoulders. "Twenty it is then. I'll keep the count."

He nodded at the soldiers who took a firmer grip. "One!" he bellowed and his vine-staff swished down and scored a diagonal red line across the prisoner's white skin. He worked methodically, alternating his blows to right and left so that they left a neat herring bone pattern from shoulders to hips. The guilty man remained silent as the first few blows thudded into his flesh but he began to groan aloud as more and more rained down. Once the count had reached ten the centurion began at the top again but reversing the angles of his strokes. Blood began to well up at the intersection of the welts. The clatter as the clerk fainted and dropped his writing materials did not distract him from his precise work.

"Twenty and all done, sir," he said at last. "Leave him to me, we'll get the medical orderly to have a look at him and send him home tomorrow, if that's agreeable."

Lucius turned to the baker's wife and pointed at the battered soldier slumped on the floor.

"Madam, he has been punished, are you satisfied with the penalty he has suffered?"

She said that she was and so was her husband in answer to the same question. A large lump was coming up on the back of the unconscious clerk's head where it had bounced off the tiles. So, as a matter of courtesy, Otto carried him back to his master's office where he was laid on a couch in a side room to recover.

"Thank you, Tribune Longius. Justice has been quickly and fairly done, I do believe. This sort of distasteful crime can lead to rioting if it is not handled properly," the magistrate said, shaking Lucius' hand

"Only doing my duty, sir," Lucius replied.

"You may be surprised to know the number of officers who would have turned a blind-eye. The military have difficulty in telling the difference between civilians and the enemy at times, my compliments to your noble family."

A tremor went through him as he heard hobnailed boots stamping down on his polished floor as Otto and Lucius threw their farewell salutes and performed a smart about-turn.

Even in what was to Otto the balmiest winter he had ever known the days shortened and grew colder with more frequent and prolonged rain until late December arrived. One morning he got up and threw his tunic on to go over to the bathhouse when he saw Janus wearing his clothes back to front.

"Io Saturnalia" the porter shouted across the garden.

Otto felt his spirits sink. "Io Saturnalia!" they all called out as he came into breakfast. He grunted something in reply. Pinerus sat in his master's place while Sabina and Vitius served him. Poppaea came to the table with her brother's helmet on her head. It kept falling forward over her eyes and the whole family laughed each time. Otto excused himself and left the room as soon as possible. This was only the beginning.

Visits were exchanged with all the neighbours every afternoon. Torches on poles were thrust into the ground and illuminated the garden for the incessant flow of noisy guests until late into the night. They were often bizarrely dressed and behaved absurdly. Normally dignified fathers of families appeared wearing necklaces of old shoes, prim wives and mothers sported hats from which strings of vegetables dangled. They gave each other useless gifts; a brush with no bristles, a spoon with holes drilled through the bowl. The offerings were received with elaborate courtesy, as if they had been things of beauty or value. Strolling entertainers; jugglers and acrobats were invited in to perform and then went around demanding money from the spectators. Servius arrived with half a dozen musicians in tow. A pantomime was performed in the square. A woman wearing only a string between her legs cavorted lewdly with a man who had a huge stage penis tied to his hips. From time to time he walked to the front of the stage and waggled it at the audience who went into shrieks of laughter and catcalls. There was some sort of plot to the play but no-one paid much attention to it.

Otto kept out of the way as much as he could but it was impossible to avoid everyone. The festival seemed interminable but at last it wound down and he was left with a small clay pig and a pair of women's shoes with no heels he had been given as mementos.

He had now lived in the Roman world for eighteen months. At first, he had not been able to see past the invincible legions that had swept away the tribes of Gaul and converted everything to the Roman view of how the world should be ordered. Now, he thought he knew them well. They were not the supermen he had believed them to be. Individually, they were no better than anyone else. He was no longer overawed. He was growing in experience as well as age and gaining the confidence of early maturity. He was beginning to feel that his opinions mattered and the urge to speak out.

At dinner on the last night of Saturnalia, the family ate together served by Pinerus and the maids in the usual way. The days of frolic and misrule had exhausted everyone and all seemed happy to return to their normal routine. The food was leftovers; half an ox tongue pickled in brine, sliced, cold black pudding, smoked fish and the inevitable garum for which Otto never developed a taste. Poppaea kept hiding yawns behind her hand, Sabina was wearing more make-up than usual to hide the puffiness around her eyes but both Lucius and Vitius had dark half-circles below theirs. Too many late nights, too much rich food and far too much wine had taken their toll. Only Aelia was serenely untouched.

"Well, Otto what did you think of your first Saturnalia?" she asked.

"It isn't my first; that was last year in the legion camp."

"And did you enjoy it?"

"No," he said and added no more.

The family were surprised into silence by his abrupt tone to Aelia. He had always shown her courtesy and obviously had a lot of respect for her.

"Oh, I don't believe you," Poppaea chimed in naively. "Everyone loves Saturnalia."

"I don't," Otto replied. It would have been better if he had let her remark pass.

"Why is that?" Vitius demanded.

"I don't want to say."

Perhaps it was because he was tired or a little liverish that Vitius became irritated and pressed the point.

"Since you are under my roof as a guest of my son, I feel that I am entitled to an answer."

"Sir," Otto replied, "I am grateful for your hospitality and out of consideration for the ladies, I have told you I do not want to say more."

"Father..." Lucius tried to intervene but Vitius brushed him aside with a wave of his hand.

"That's as maybe but I demand the courtesy of a reply to a reasonable question," he persisted.

Otto looked him straight in the face and for the first time Vitius received the full glare of those pale eyes with sparks of fury dancing behind them. He forced himself not look away.

"Last year I was caught unaware by a legionary who tipped me upside down into a full latrine pit. I sneaked out of camp, broke the ice on the river and sank myself under the water to wash away the worst of the filth. I was forced to burn my clothes and have all my hair shaved off; Io Saturnalia, noble Vitius, Io Saturnalia!"

Sabina's mouth fell open. Poppaea's head dropped and a bright red flush mounted from her bosom up her neck.

"That is atrocious!" Aelia exclaimed.

Vitius turned to his son.

"I hope you had the man who did this punished to the fullest extent."

Lucius looked around the table and thought he would have to say something so why not the truth?

"Let me describe a chain of events to you. Otto appeared one morning with his Suevian Knot cut off and his head shaved. Shortly after, he asked if his mentor could teach him some writing skills. He made very good progress in a short time. On a dark night of swirling snow, an unknown hand sliced the right ear off the head of a legionary returning from the soldiers' bathhouse. He couldn't identify his attacker. In the morning the ear was found nailed to the lintel of the latrine door with a crudely lettered sign over it saying, "Io Saturnalia".

Now family, never ask Otto if he carried out this act of revenge. He would not answer with a lie but if I hear out of his own mouth that it was indeed him, I am bound to report it to the legate and he will be condemned to suffer execution."

"Surely under the circumstances…" Vitius began.

"If anyone maims a soldier of the empire off duty, he must die. There are no exceptions, especially for non-citizens."

The dinner party broke up quickly and sombrely but Aelia registered the information that Otto had begun to learn to read and write. It gave her an idea.

Two days later she appeared for her afternoon with Otto carrying a scroll.

"The tales of Aesop are written in this book. He was a very wise slave who wrote stories about animals that tell us something of men and women and the mistakes they often make. Would you like to read them with me?"

She did not tell him it was a children's book. He read them aloud, painfully and haltingly. Aelia corrected him with gentle patience. In the course of a few days, she barely had to guide him at all.

"That young man has become a project for you, mother," Vitius remarked.

"If he is fated to share my grandson's life, I want to equip him as best I can. In any case, he is quick and has a retentive memory. Who knows what he may yet make of himself?"

The first day of February was miserable; dark skies overhead, a cold wind and waves of drizzle passing. Near midday, Janus was startled by the tramping of boots in the street and was at the point of opening the door to see what was going on when he heard a shouted order and the boots stopped with a crash. Three heavy thuds made the door shake and he opened it to see a centurion glaring at him out of his single eye.

"City Garrison Centurion Decimus Massus requesting an interview with the noble Tribune Lucius Taurius Longius," he said then turned to the four legionaries with him. "Stand at ease!" he bellowed.

Janus stood staring at him open-mouthed.

"Jump to it sunshine; the army hasn't got all day to wait for you," Massus demanded.

Janus scuttled into the house and gave his message. Lucius hurried over and asked the centurion and his escort to come inside.

"In we go lads," he told his escort. "Don't knock anything over with them javelins."

Lucius walked into the house, the centurion took off his helmet and followed him into the dining room. The four soldiers took up a position guarding the entrance. Janus stared at them for a while and then ostentatiously examined the front of his door. He was sure that one-eyed soldier must have made dents banging on it with that stick he carried.

"Pinerus," Lucius called. The major-domo appeared almost instantly. "A flask of wine and some snacks for this officer and me, please." Lucius requested. While they waited, he turned to his visitor. "Your men could go around to the kitchen and get a bite themselves, if you don't object."

He did not, went out again and addressed them

"Right you lot, it's your lucky day. The tribune says you can go round to the kitchen where you will be served with some grub; mind your manners. Stack your shields and javelins here under the shelter of the roof. Off you go."

Pinerus had arrived with a tray which he placed on the table.

"Is that all, sir?"

"Just tell cook four hungry soldiers will invade the kitchen any moment. She is to feed them well"

At which point Vitius came in and was introduced.

"I'll leave you to your military matters," he said, shooing away Poppaea who had been lurking in the open doorway trying to see what was going on. She still did not quite believe that her brother was an officer to whom other ranks had to defer. She found it absurd; he was just Lucius!

"A courier came in this morning with army mail for you, sir. I took the liberty of receiving it on your behalf," Massus said handing over two leather scroll cases. "You will see the seals are unbroken."

Lucius pushed the tray bearing sliced, spiced sausage, cheese, bread and dates across the table. He poured two cups of wine. Massus drank and started on the bread and cheese. Lucius read the first letter.

"To the Noble Tribune Lucius Taurus Longius, Greetings. You are hereby ordered to assemble all troops of The Second Lucan Legion currently on leave in the magistracy of Luca on the last day of February and proceed on the first day of March to Lugdunum where you will join my column prior to proceeding to legion headquarters. In the event you arrive in Lugdunum before me, you will report to the senior officer there and arrange to await me. I also send warrants for you to hire four mule wagons and buy sufficient supplies for one hundred and thirty men for twenty-five days to the account of the legion, payable in Lugdunum. You will keep all receipts for inspection. Trusting that your relations with the City Magistrate are cordial, you will liaise with him and take his advice in respect of the civilian haulage contractors and commissaries to be employed.

I look forward to our rendezvous in Lugdunum and hope that you have profited from this period of leave with your family.

Signed; Publius Quadratus Legate Second Lucan.

P. S. On my supposition that Otto is returning, I propose to make him an "attached civilian support" assigned to you, then we can at least pay him something for his efforts in the field. See you soon, my Boxer."

Lucius passed the letter to Massus who read it

"I have the muster-rolls in safe-keeping, sir and the equipment they brought with them is in storage. I'll start getting hold of your lads. I'll use my men to get an acknowledgement from all of them that they know the date they must assemble with their kit. I suggest we tell them to come in three days early then we'll have time to round up the column-dodgers and the poor saps who have fallen in love and think they want to spend the rest of their lives in the arms of some farmer's daughter."

Lucius showed the letter to the family.

"So soon?" Sabina complained. "Surely they can't mean the end of February; the weather will be awful..."

"Your legate seems to have a good opinion of you, Lucius," his father said. "But I wonder how you'll rise to be a broad-stripe tribune and maybe command your own legion one day if you remain an artillery specialist."

"I'll never command a legion; grandfather saw to that when he chose to support the Antonians, but there are other ways of advancement. An army needs a master of artillery as much as a master of horse. War brings unexpected opportunities."

Aelia said nothing but next day she sent for a scribe who was ushered into her room for a private conference. He left after half an hour with money chinking in his belt purse. He returned several times over the next two weeks and conferred with her. She refused to tell anyone what was going on.

Lucius started to earn his army pay again. Everyday he strode or rode into the city and consulted the magistrate or Decimus Massus. Frantic chaos began to give way to order. After prolonged negotiations, corn, bacon, oil and wine were bought in sufficient amounts. Two four mule wagons and two six mule wagons were provisionally hired. It was only at the very last minute that the owners suddenly demanded additional money for their animal's fodder. But although Lucius was young, he was not green. He stood up and turned to the magistrate who was there to record and attest to the legality of the proceedings.

"Is there a skilled tradesman in the city who could build me half a dozen handcarts?

"Well, yes tribune, but I…"

Lucius interrupted him, turning to the hauliers.

"Thank you for your time, gentlemen but your services will not be required. With two-man handcarts and what they can carry on their backs, my men will manage without you."

"All the way to Lugdunum dragging their own supplies? Please, young sir; we all know that you're bluffing," said one portly carrier with a complicit smirk.

"You are talking about experienced soldiers. Do you think that it is any real hardship for men of the legions like them?" Lucius told him sharply and with that he left the meeting.

Two hours later, contracts were signed on the original terms.

The days of February rushed past, seeming to accelerate as the deadline for departure approached. On the fifteenth, Servius demanded that Lucius spent an evening with him for a farewell drinking session.

"I'm too busy," Lucius replied.

"No you're not; that's just an excuse. You can't do anything at night when the magistrate's office is shut and all the business types are lying in bed snoring on top of their fat wives. Come on Lucius, you're my oldest and dearest friend…."

"Oh, alright but I'm not making session of it. I need to keep a clear head."

"That's the way," Servius said and named the wineshop where they would meet at eight.

The tavern was in a side street leading off the square. Lucius went in at the appointed time but Otto would not go in with him. Otto kept his distance if Servius was involved.

"I'll wait for you," he told Lucius who no longer tried to persuade him that his friend was not so bad.

The full moon rose at nine. High in the heavens, an immense silver ring surrounded it. Otto knew this for a sign of great cold. One side of the street was so brilliantly lit it could be noon but the shadows on the other side seemed thicker, stygian by contrast. He stood in the shelter of a deep doorway further down the street to avoid the frost he was sure would soon fall and was lost to sight in the gloom. After a further hour had passed, three men walked up to the shivering boys waiting beside the wineshop door ready with their torches to light the gentlemen's way home.

"Wasting your time, lads, on a bright moonlight night like this," one of them said in a friendly voice. He thrust his hand into his tunic and brought out a few copper coins. "Here take these and get yourselves off before you freeze to death."

The grateful boys vanished into the maze of streets behind the square, happy to be heading home early with something to show for their evening spent hopping from one foot to the other against the numbing chill. The men drifted across street and found concealment. Time passed. The night grew colder. Glittering powder like shaken salt covered the flagstones in frost. Suddenly the door opened and a shaft of yellow light accompanied by a burst of warm air flooded out to be instantly cut off as the door was quickly slammed shut to keep the heat in. Servius and Lucius stood on the pavement in the moonlight. The three men surged towards them out of the shadows. Servius saw them first. He flung his purse down. The string at its neck snapped and a few silver and gold coins fell out, reflecting splinters of light off the ground.

"Here, take it; take it all," he yelled and sprinted off down the street without looking back.

The men hesitated at the sight of the money, giving Lucius just enough time to wind his cloak around his left arm to give himself some rudimentary protection. They fanned out. One drew a knife and grinned as he closed in.

Otto was on the move now, drawing his pugio as he sprinted towards Lucius. The thief struck his first blow but Lucius took it on his padded arm and lashed out with his right fist catching his attacker on the cheek bone. He reeled backwards but that allowed one of his partners the space to slash with his own blade. Before he could defend himself, it sliced across Lucius' chest from left to right on a downward arc. Then the full power of Otto at a run hit the knifeman in the back and drove him into the wall. He heard his ribs splinter as massive shoulder hammered him against the stonework and he fell. Otto wheeled in time to see the third member of the gang step towards him with a cudgel raised in both hands. He stepped close in under the blow and thrust his dagger into the man's upper belly. He ripped sideways to free the blade. His victim howled and clutched at his gaping wound trying to push his intestines back in. The first man who had struck at Lucius saw that this night's work had gone badly wrong and decided to make a run for it. As he spun on his heel, he noticed Servius' purse. He reached down to grab it up but that move was fatal. Otto stamped on his clutching hand, pinned it to the ground and stuck him in the angle of his jaw with his wide-bladed knife. A jet of blood shot high into the air. He was dead before it hit the wall.

Otto picked up the purse put it into his tunic. He saw that Lucius was deathly pale and that blood, black as ink in the moonlight, was sheeting down from his gashed chest He dragged the cloak off Lucius' arm and bound it as tightly as he could round his wounded body. Then, half dragging him, Otto ran for the guard barracks. As he drew closer, he saw the pair of sentries on duty standing by a glowing brazier.

"On me, on me!" he yelled repeating what he had heard shouted out by the legionaries when they were hard-pressed. "On me, rally on me!"

Three minutes later, Lucius lay on the guardroom mess table. The knife wound had divided his chest in two by a furrow from which a thick flap of flesh fell open. The medical orderly poured wine vinegar over it and Lucius fainted, which saved him a great deal of pain while he was being tightly bandaged.

"Need a surgeon, sir," the orderly told Centurion Massus.

Half an hour later, groggy from the poppy juice he had been given, Lucius looked down at the line of black horsehair stitches holding the pursed edges of his wound together.

"Looks much worse than it is," the surgeon said cheerfully. "Right across the front of his ribs but it didn't pierce his innards, thankfully." He produced a clay pot with a close-fitting lid. "Garlic oil in honey; rub this on and bandage him with clean linen every day and he'll be up and about in a fortnight and fully fit in a month. In the meanwhile, he should take it easy; mustn't open his wound. I'll give you some more poppy juice for him but go easy, only four drops a day in watered wine. That's it boys, now, whose paying?"

Otto fished a gold coin out from Servius' purse.

"Is this enough?"

"Oh yes, I have no problem in accepting that handsome emolument for services rendered."

A squad of legionaries was sent round to collect the bodies.

"All dead?" Massus asked.

"The one with the smashed-in chest said he wasn't so I gave him a kick in the head for telling lies. And what do you know? He was lying 'cos he turned out to be dead as well."

"You're a bit of a handful lad, aren't you? Did for all three of them on your own and them armed as well." Massus said to Otto who shrugged.

"They had fallen upon Tribune Boxer. He has my oath."

The centurion patted him on the shoulder.

"Then he is a very fortunate man. You'll have to stay here tonight. In the morning we'll go and square all this with the magistrate and organize a litter and an escort for the tribune."

The magistrate was shocked.

"In Luca? In the centre of the city?" he exclaimed. "Such things never happen here. Where was the night-watch? In any case, I am relieved to learn that the tribune's injuries are not life-threatening. You're sure they're not?"

"Who can say sir?" the centurion answered in a gloomy voice. "I've seen many a fine lad on the road to recovery suddenly take a turn for the worse and then…" he snapped his fingers.

His honour went pale and missed Massus' grin and wink at Otto.

"I shall have to take formal statements for my court records. I presume there were no witnesses?"

"No, sir," Otto told him. "Do you know a young man called Servius who calls himself a close friend of the noble tribune?" The magistrate nodded. "He was there but when those men closed in, he flung down his money and ran off into the night wailing." Otto pulled Servius' purse out of his tunic. It was black with dried blood. The magistrate looked at it with distaste as Otto placed on the corner of his desk. "Would you please give this to him and tell him that Otto returns what he left behind when he ran away and left his friend to die. Use those words, sir."

"Of course," he agreed, with no intention of doing so.

Chapter 19

No-one was particularly worried when Lucius had not returned home by morning. It would not be the first time a night's carousing had gone on too long and he had slept it off at a friend's house. Janus grinned as he heard a knock at the garden door. No doubt his young master would be outside, red-eyed, hung-over and wanting a bath. He opened up with a greeting on his lips, was grabbed by the tunic and hauled sideways into the street, out of view of anyone in the house. He looked up reproachfully at Otto and then saw the centurion and a file of legionaries, four of them holding a litter. The officer stepped forward.

"Now listen; you will walk quietly into the house and tell your master that someone is at the gate demanding to see him. You will do this with no show of fear or panic. Go!"

Vitius stamped down the gravel path behind Janus, irritated that he had been dragged out of the comfort of his study into the cold air. Stepping into the street he instantly took-in the soldiers, Otto, the litter but no Lucius. His heart turned over but he reacted as a Roman should. He pulled himself up to his full height, squared his shoulders and tried to make his face expressionless.

"Greetings Centurion Decimus Massus," he said without a tremor in his voice although every instinct wanted to make him rush over to the litter he was sure held his only son.

"Greetings Vitius Longius," Massus replied. "Tribune Lucius Taurius Longius was badly injured last night in an attempted robbery. He has been treated by my medical orderly and a civilian surgeon. They confirm that his wound is not likely to be fatal. I ask if you wish to inform the ladies of your household before my men carry your son inside."

"What happened…" Vitius began but Massus cut him off.

"Perhaps explanations can wait until he's out of the cold air, sir?"

"Of, course, of course; Janus, run for Pinerus and tell him to get a brazier into Master Lucius' room. If your men will follow me, centurion, we'll get him comfortable."

The women assumed their masks of Roman fortitude as well as Vitius had, although Sabina's eyes were bright with tears. Poppaea was pale and trembling but she held her chin high. Lucius was lifted into his own bed with surprising gentleness by the tough legionaries. The soldiers left and Pinerus was summoned to arrange for the household slaves to give Lucius a bed bath and clean linen. His slashed and bloody tunic had been burned on the sentries' brazier.

The family gathered in the dining room. Massus had ordered his men to return to barracks and tell the optio he would be back shortly. He removed his helmet and held it on one knee. Wine and bread were served by a shaken Pinerus who was allowed to stand by the door and hear the story. Otto sat by Aelia.

"It appears," Massus began, "that as Tribune Longius left a tavern in the centre of the city, he was set upon by three armed robbers. He was badly cut across the chest but according to the surgeon, no internal organs were touched. Otto got him to the sentry post and he was taken into the guardroom where his wound was cleaned and stitched up. That is it, ladies, sir, in brief." He sat back and waited for the inevitable questions.

"Have these felons been caught?" Sabina asked anger now surmounting her fears for her son.

"In a manner of speaking, my lady," Massus told her with a chuckle. "Otto Longius, your son's oath man as he calls himself, killed them. My lads collected up the bodies."

"Otto killed three robbers, all on his own?" Poppaea squeaked.

"He did, with brute force and his army issue dagger," the centurion confirmed.

All eyes turned on Otto who looked uneasy at the attention.

"And Servius?" Aelia asked.

"He flung his money down at their feet and ran away," Otto growled.

There was a long pause. Massus and Vitius looked at each other appraisingly.

"So being unarmed, and therefore unable to assist, the noble Servius sacrificed his purse to distract the thieves and ran for assistance. Is that what you are telling me centurion?" Vitius asked.

"The magistrate's formal report has not yet been written. It will undoubtedly read along the lines you have stated," Massus replied.

"This is not right! This is not the truth…!" Otto exploded.

Aelia gripped his forearm, feeling the muscles bunch as he clenched his fist.

"Be silent, Otto, there are things here you do not understand. I shall explain later."

He turned a baleful glare on her but softened when he saw the earnest entreaty in her expression. He asked to be excused as he needed to bathe. They all saw his slumped shoulders as he left the room.

"Has the surgeon who attended my son received his fee?" Vitius enquired.

Again, Massus chuckled, a brief throaty sound.

"Yes, indeed he has; in gold! Otto paid him from what I suspect is the purse of Servius. He picked it up off the street and handed it over to the magistrate this morning."

"Please excuse me," Vitius said and left the room.

"So, centurion, we are to thank Otto for saving my grandson's life?" Aelia asked.

"Without doubt, lady; if he had not been there and willing to face death or injury himself, the tribune would have been slaughtered and his body searched for whatever coins he had on him."

Sabina shuddered. A tear ran down Poppaea's cheek. She brushed it aside, annoyed at showing her weakness. Vitius returned from his study and placed five gold coins down on the table in front of Massus.

"I will not insult you, Centurion Decimus Massus, by offering you anything other than my sincere thanks and a promise of continuing friendship for what you have done to assist my son. Would you please accept this donative on behalf of the litter carriers and others of your legionaries who were involved?"

"My thanks to you, sir; your generosity will be greatly appreciated by the men but not as gratefully as I accept your offer of friendship. It honours me."

Once the centurion had left, the family doctor was summoned. He examined Lucius who was now fully conscious and in no pain unless he tried to move.

"A neat and clean job," the doctor said. He sniffed the ointment jar and closed the lid. "Call me if he becomes fevered, otherwise, let nature do her work. Bathing is strictly forbidden until those stitches are removed."

"When will I be able to take up my duties?" Lucius asked.

"A month, six weeks; who knows?" was the unwelcome answer.

Lucius demanded to see Otto, alone. He took his right hand in both of his and looked up unblinking into those pale, impassive eyes.

"When the fates sent you to me, my friend, it was for my sake not yours. I owe you my life."

Otto smiled and shrugged.

"The future will tell us if you are right, Boxer."

Later, Aelia came into the summerhouse and sat next to Otto who was brooding about the injustice of Servius not being made to answer for his cowardice.

"Achilles sulking in his tent," she began with a smile. "Now listen carefully to me young man, because what I have to say is important. Luca is a small city. Only around twenty noble families live here. The father of Servius is the head of an important house, he is wealthy and influential. If his son is publicly shamed, he will be resentful. He will cast doubt on your account of the event. Some will take his side; others will oppose him. The city will be split into factions and all civic harmony will be lost. That is why my son and Centurion Massus have agreed to a version which saves the face of the unworthy Servius. You heard Vitius offer friendship to Decimus Massus who accepted it; a new social link has been established. This is how things are accomplished; by people forming webs of mutual support. You put great store by honour and I admire you for it but Otto it is a sad truth that we all, and I mean all, have to compromise. Do you understand that word?"

Otto shook his head.

"It means that we have to let things go or leave things unsaid for the common well-being. It is part of being "civilized"; by which I mean fit to live in a city alongside many other people. Learn this lesson and take it to heart. Now if you believe that Servius will not have to account for what he did, think again. He knows," she paused to let her words sink in "and so will everyone else, even though it is never said aloud. Consider his daily shame. Is that not a punishment?"

Otto smiled at last. "You are very wise, lady."

Aelia laughed briefly.

"Thank you Otto but I am not. I am, however, well-educated for a Roman woman. I was my father's only child and so he had me tutored as if I had been a son, unusually for a girl of my class. But why would parents go to the trouble and expense with daughters? Roman women of even the highest rank take no part in public life. It is not our way. Poor Sabina and my granddaughter have never read a serious book, think of that! They can write a brief letter or read an invitation but that is their limit, as it is with nearly all the ladies of this city and no doubt of Rome as well. I am determined you shall do better, but enough of that for now. Consider this, you are a warrior as is my grandson but Servius is not. Also, he had no weapon. What practical use could he have been? It is probably for the good that he ran away; one man injured is better than two, don't you think? I must go now as there are preparations to be made for later. This evening, you are invited to feast with us. Pinerus will escort you when it is time."

The major-domo came to the summerhouse door carrying a garland of dried flowers.

"Put this on your head, Master Otto, it is the custom," he said handing it over. Otto placed it awkwardly and Pinerus adjusted it so it sat squarely and walked beside him to the house. "This is a formal occasion to thank you for what you did. If I may, I advise you to enjoy it and speak from your heart," he said quietly.

Vitius was waiting at the door. He embraced Otto and kissed him on both cheeks.

"Welcome Otto Longius," he said, using that adopted full name for the first time and led him to the head of the table where he was duly seated in the master's place.

Sabina kissed his hand and poured his wine. Poppaea kissed his hand and put down a brimming bowl of hot sausages in front of him.

"All for you," she told him with a giggle.

Aelia beamed at him and bowed her head in greeting.

"Thank you all," Otto said. "Would anyone like to share these sausages?"

He was rewarded by a burst of happy laughter. When dinner was over, some hours later, it was Sabina's turn to take his hand and lead him through the house to a guest room. His clothes were hung in a closet and his few belongings arranged on a nightstand.

"Sleep well, defender of my son," she said.

"My lady…" the startled Otto began but she silenced him by putting her index finger on his lips.

"Sleep well," she repeated.

Ursus the mastiff sniffed at the door of the summerhouse and whined for the loss of his night-time friend.

After three days, Lucius was bored and his wound itched. He became fretful.

"I need to know what's going on," he kept repeating. "There's so much to do before the end of the month."

He sent Otto down to the barracks with a message for Massus. This was the first of innumerable trips to and from the city which were annoying for Massus who had better things to do than read a wax tablet handed to him by the big German and then send him back with another written message in reply. By the twentieth of February, Lucius was on his feet.

"I'd better go down to the barracks today and see what's going on." he said at breakfast.

"Don't be foolish," his mother told him.

"Foolish, mother?" he said in a loud voice. "You do know that I have to lead my troops to Lugdunum on the first of March?"

"Out of the question," she responded with the maddening calm of a mother who knows best.

"I have my orders and I shall obey them. I will take my men out of Luca on that day whatever you say or try to do to prevent me."

The family doctor was called in to persuade Lucius that what he wanted was impossible.

"You could not wear your cuirass," he said.

"What about my subarmalis? Lucius countered.

"Is it made of leather?"

"Yes, of course it is."

The doctor shook his head. "Ill-advised; it could hold your sweat against your wound so the humours of your body would be unable to dissipate and turn inwards causing putrefaction."

"Very well then, a tunic and leggings under my cloak will have to do. As long as I can put my helmet on so the soldiers can see me; you will allow that?"

The doctor threw his hands up in dismay.

"But how will you get into the saddle?"

"Otto can boost me up."

"If you are determined no-one can stop you but I tell you now, you are not fit to ride to Lugdunum for five hours a day. The prolonged motion of the horse will tear your stitches open."

"I appreciate your advice doctor but I have my orders."

"I know you do, Lucius," Sabina said. "But the legate can't possibly order you to do something which could lead to your death."

"I rather think he can, my dear," Aelia told her, dryly.

"What about a cart...?" Otto put in. Sabina saw her son's eyes light up at the idea. She gave Otto a look which would have instantly withered a full-grown oak. "...There are mules in the stables. If you had a cart, you could rest in it when riding was giving you too much pain. That way you wouldn't be holding up the column. We can only travel as fast as the slowest wagon in any case."

"And how are you going to manage two horses as well as driving a cart? It's impractical," Sabina told him going back on the attack but the surety had gone out of her voice.

"We'll take Passer with us."

"And who is this Passer?"

"Passer is the stable boy, mother," Poppaea advised.

"Oh, is that his name? Well, it doesn't matter since he's a mere child."

"He is nearly thirteen and a well-grown, handy lad," Lucius told her, beginning to warm to the idea.

Sabina played her ace of trumps. "Your father will never allow it."

At first it appeared that she was correct. When Vitius was consulted, he was not happy.

"I gave you Atrexes, Lucius and look what happened to him. I do not want to send another of my household slaves to die in Germany."

"Ask Passer," Otto suggested.

"Ask a slave!" Sabina was outraged at the thought. It was practically admitting that their property had the right to make independent decisions.

"Free him and then ask him," Otto suggested.

Sabina turned to her husband with a mute appeal to end this nonsense now but Vitius was thinking about it. Passer was the son of the cook. She had been pregnant when he had bought her, with a few other items, at the auction of an insolvent estate. She had been a bargain and Passer had cost him nothing. If he freed the boy and gave him the choice, then his conscience would be clear. Either he stayed on as a servant costing next to nothing in wages, or he went off with Lucius. If he ended up cut to pieces somewhere hundreds of miles away, it would be as a result of a decision he took as a free person.

"Fetch cook and Passer," he ordered Pinerus.

They stood trembling in the porch. If the master called for a pair of slaves to be brought in front of him, it was not likely to end well for them.

"This concerns Passer, you are here solely as a witness," he told the cook with a reassuring half-smile.

"What has he done master?" she pleaded

"Be silent, woman. Now Passer I intend to give you your freedom today. Once this interview is over, you will walk to the court with me where I will formally record your manumission. Do you understand?"

"Yes, master, thank you master," the stunned boy finally managed to say.

"Good, now, I am asking you as a free man to decide what you want to do. You may stay in my house as my groom. You will live and work as you do now but at the end of every month you will be given a small amount of money to pay for your labour in addition to bed and board. Or you can go to the army in Germany with Master Lucius and Otto Longius as their servant. You will no longer be under my charge. I warn you that their lives are hard and dangerous. What do you choose?"

"The army, Master Lucius and Otto," he said in a rush, the words tumbling over each other.

"Very well, from this moment I have no more responsibility in the matter. You must look to my son for all your needs, serve him well."

Sabina silently went to her own room and did not come out for the rest of the day. Vitius walked into the court and within a few minutes Passer had a stamped certificate of manumission. That afternoon he went with Otto to search out a suitable cart. They turned heads as they made their way through the town. The tall, broad German dressed as a Roman with a slim boy, his head a mass of dark curls, who barely reached his companion's shoulder.

They found what they wanted; a two-wheeled cart with an oiled canvas cover supported on iron hoops. It would make a relatively comfortable and dry vehicle in which Lucius could rest if necessary and sleep overnight. It was high enough above the ground to allow enough space for Otto and Passer put their bedrolls underneath. The cartwright guaranteed to overhaul it and grease the axles. He fitted a new trail so that a pair of mules could be harnessed to it. All the work was done by the next day as promised. The purchase of transport and the certainty that he would be able to take his men out of the city on the appointed day revitalized Lucius. Each of the following days, he dressed in his warmest tunic and marched around the garden for an hour and then up and down the street.

On the twenty-sixth of February, a day of fine rain, he felt strong enough to go down to the barracks. Massus and his optio sat in the guardroom behind a folding table. The optio had the rosters stretched out flat and weighted down. A single file of soldiers was moving up to him. When a man reached the front of the queue, he fished his identity disc out of the leather pouch around his neck and handed it to Massus. The centurion read the name aloud, and the optio pricked it on his list. The disc was returned and the next man shuffled up.

"Good to see you up and about, sir," Massus said, standing up and saluting.

Lucius waved him back to his seat.

"How is it going?"

"Very well; we've accounted for nearly all of 'em. One confirmed dead; trampled by an ox. Not much of a loss in my opinion. A soldier who isn't quick enough to dodge a big cow is next to useless. On the other hand, four volunteers. They look likely enough lads."

"Good, provide them with basic equipment and the legion training officer can decide if he wants them when we get to Lugdunum."

"I'll need you to sign for their kit, sir."

Lucius sighed, remembering the saga of Otto's boots but scratched his name on the docket before making his way home.

There were five optios and seven corporals among the returning troops. Massus gathered them out of the hearing of the men.

"This tribune is a decent bloke, not one of your posh timewasters. A fortnight ago he got himself split open in a fight outside a city tavern. It's only his stitches holding him together so, what I'm saying to you is don't make his life harder than it is. You all know what I mean. And if you piss him about he'll set Otto on you."

"Who's this Otto, centurion?" a corporal asked.

"He's the German lad who stuck a stylus in that slave's face and chased him through the camp with Boxer's sword," one of the group replied on Massus' behalf.

"And he cut off Tubby's ear for pushing him into the shithouse pit," another said.

"They never proved that," one of the optios added.

"Well," said Massus, "you learn something new every day, lads. Doesn't surprise me, though; he's bloody huge and a real hard case. He only killed two of the scum who went for the tribune with his pugio and the other one by smashing him into a wall."

On their last night at home everyone's mood was sombre with the exception of Passer who was bursting with excitement. He had packed and repacked the mule cart a dozen times. The mules themselves were resplendent; teeth and hooves polished and their coats gleaming. He had displayed his new clothes and boots to the slaves and his mother. She was torn between dread that she would never see her son again and ecstatic dreams of what his future might be now he was free.

As Otto was sorting out his few possessions in his room after dinner, Aelia came in. She was carrying a scroll case which she handed over. The case was copper, covered in leather and designed to protect the contents against the worst of weather.

"Inside this case is a distillation of wisdom," she said. "On the scroll it contains are written fifty quotations from the works of great thinkers; Zeno, Diogenes, Lucretius, Cicero and many more. They spent their lives trying to understand what it means to be a human being and live wisely in this world. I selected them and a scribe has written them out on best Egyptian paper for you. Do not read the whole thing at once. Select just one, study it with care and then think about it before going on to the next. And while you are turning it over in your mind, look at the people around you and how they behave, consider your own actions with honesty. Only then will you be able to judge the value of what you have read. I hope that some of these words will strike a chord in your soul and bring you enlightenment."

"I will treasure it, thank you," Otto told her, holding the gift reverently on both hands. "But why have you taken such pains to be my friend and teacher, lady?"

"The Fates sent you. I wish to be their servant in helping you on your way...and I like you."

As daylight broke, they rose from the breakfast table. The mule cart was already hitched up in the street. Otto said his farewells and stood by the horses. Lucius saluted the death masks of each of his illustrious ancestors, received his parents' blessings and strode out. Otto cupped his hands for his foot and eased him into the saddle. The incense burned low in front of the altar of the household gods as the family prayed together for the safety of Lucius to which they added the names of Otto and Passer.

At the city gate, the legionaries were waiting in a column four abreast bent around the square with the wagons taking up the rear. Passer pulled up behind the last of them. Massus handed up a satchel of receipts dockets and muster rolls. He saluted.

"All in order sir and I wish you a safe journey. Remember me to Titus Attius if you will with my good wishes."

"I shall, Centurion Decimus Massus. Please accept my grateful thanks for your unwavering support."

The hinges of the gates squealed as they were opened and the troops marched off in the growing light.

"I told those lazy bastards to oil those gates," Massus thought to himself. "I'll have their guts for embarrassing me like that."

Chapter 20

For the first hour, the column trudged on the level past ploughed fields waiting for their spring planting. Lucius rode easily. He complacently congratulated himself. Doctors were always too pessimistic; it kept their patients calling them back and increased their fees. But the ground rose. Subtly at first, the road started to climb towards the low foothills and the farther Apuan Alps they must cross to come to the Via Antonia and Gaul.

Behind his mules, Passer was grinning from ear to ear. Otto dropped back to check on him.

"What are you so pleased about?" he asked.

"I've never been so far from home before, Master Otto. It's exciting isn't it?"

They had covered five miles.

Lucius' horse had to work harder uphill. His pace became less regular and sometimes a hoof slid on a wet stone and he had to adjust his balance. Lucius was forced to lean forward in the saddle. At first, he began to feel a series of pinpricks across his chest. Each one was the result of his stitches pulling under the play of the muscles moving under his skin. They merged together into a throbbing harmony and then a line of hot pain. Three hours out of Luca the column stopped on a plateau so that the men could rest and have something to eat.

"Otto," Lucius said quietly so no one else could hear, "I don't think I can get off."

Otto dismounted without replying, stood by Lucius' horse and held out his arms. Lucius slumped sideways lifting his thighs free of the saddle horns and letting himself fall. Otto took his weight effortlessly and gently deposited the wounded man on his feet.

"Well done Boxer; I didn't think you'd get that far."

Lucius took two faltering steps then pulled himself upright and made his slow way to Passer and the cart. A short ladder was hinged to the tailgate up which he climbed and gratefully stretched his length on the mattress inside. At the end of the break, Lucius called the senior optio to him.

"Get the men on their feet. We've got no palisade poles so we can't make a standard marching camp but even though we're close to home I want us secure overnight. We'll get another three hours in before we have to call it a day so liaise with Otto here later on and he'll go ahead and find us a good place to halt." He noticed the man's quick look of unease at Otto. "Don't worry, optio, he knows what he's doing."

Lucius spent the rest of the day in the cart. Even that was not without discomfort. If a wheel went into a rut, the shock sent a wave of pain across his chest. Some of the men had looked askance when he did not reappear, mounted at the head of the column.

"Great for officers; lolling about in that thing while we slog up these bastard hills," one muttered to his mate.

"Well, that's what they're like aren't they? Soft shits the lot of 'em when it comes to the hard graft; too tired to ride his bloody horse while we march," was the reply from the side of his comrade's mouth.

Otto found a flat area with a stream running icily through it and a solitary, enormous boulder in the centre. With the great rock at their backs and the wagons and cart in front of them, they were as safe as they could be. It was unlikely that such a strong force would be attacked but they needed to be on their guard. There was always the chance of a hit and run raid by a gang of robbers after weapons and equipment.

Lucius sat stripped to the waist on the steps of the cart. Passer had removed his bandage and was busy smearing the garlic and honey paste on a clean one before binding him up again. Several of the legionaries caught a glimpse of the jagged red lips of the slash held together by a wandering line of black stitches that crossed his chest. Word quickly got around, with the usual exaggerations; "Poor old Boxer's nearly chopped in half, saw it meself, 'orrible to look at".

Once it sunk in with all the men that this tribune was the celebrated "Boxer", of whom they had heard such entertaining gossip and that he was genuinely injured, their attitude changed. Next morning the senior optio and his second approached Lucius.

"With your permission, tribune, it might be a good idea to put your cart in the centre of the column. Then we can find you quicker if there's a problem…and you aren't on your horse… it might be easier for you, sir," he suggested nervously.

Passer duly moved up with legionaries marching in front and behind him. They climbed for another day, the road steeper at every turn. Again, Lucius endured another three hours in the saddle. Otto found them an overnight halting place once more and the pattern of their days was set.

On the fifth morning, it was discovered that one of the recruits had slipped away in the night. This led to a discussion among the officers; the case was not straightforward. Technically, he was not a legionary since he had not completed training and been assigned his number, so he was not a deserter in the usual meaning of the word. However, he was on the ration roll and had been given the basic kit that he had taken with him. He had definitely stolen legion stores. So, deserter or not, he was a condemned man. Lucius made a decision.

"Go and find him, Otto," he ordered.

He returned just before the midday break, slowly riding the length of the column with a legionary's equipment festooned around his horse and person. A pair of boots with the laces tied together was slung around his neck. He brought his mount up alongside Lucius and saluted. Lucius shouted for the senior optio to halt the men and come up to him, bringing the other officers.

"This will be instructive," he told them and turned to Otto. "Come on then, what's your story?"

"The runaway was quite a long way back. He must have heard my horse so he tried to hide behind some rocks but he left enough tracks for a child to follow. He cried and said he did not wish to be in the army and his feet hurt. So I left him there out of kindness. I did not want him to be executed, Boxer, sir."

"And what's all this kit dangling off you and your horse?" Lucius asked.

"Ah, as I explained to him, if he did not want to be a soldier, he had no right to any of it and must give it back. He refused at first but when I got off my horse he handed it all over."

"What did you leave him?"

Otto knitted his brows together in a frown as if he did not understand the question.

"Nothing…well his tunic for decency," he said, finally.

"So, to summarize, Otto, you left him wearing only a thin tunic, no cloak, barefoot, with no weapon and no food or means of making a fire, four days from home halfway up a mountain. And you did that out of kindness."

"Yes, I did."

"And you do not think that is a death sentence?"

Otto threw back his head and laughed.

"A Suevi boy Passer's age could handle that and he's a grown man."

"Thank you Otto, my friend. Take the kit over to one of the supply wagons," Lucius told him and waited until he was out of hearing before addressing the dumbstruck officers standing by. "The worse thing about that is he really believes he has done the poor sod a good turn, dismissed."

Eventually, the highest point of their route was reached and they began to descend. This was easier for the marching men and better for Lucius. Now he was using his back muscles to hold him upright in the saddle there was less stress and strain on his chest. Once they set out on the broad and well-paved Via Antonia, it was better again and by the time they branched onto the Via Agrippa, Lucius was riding all day. Although his health had visibly improved, he still exuded a miasma of faintly sweet, stale garlic. Passer re-bandaged him every evening. The inflamed edges of his wound looked less angry as they began to knit. The day arrived when he climbed into the saddle and dismounted completely unaided, to a cheer from the watching legionaries.

The smudge of brown smoke which lay over Lugdunum finally broke over the horizon. They arrived late in the afternoon and reported to the barracks where the usual, smooth Roman organisation swung into action. Lucius handed over his paperwork to the quartermaster who bustled away with the hauliers to pay them off. A centurion ordered the ranks of legionaries off to their billets at a quick march. Lucius sent Otto to the stables with the horses and was sitting on the tailgate of the cart wearing only his boots and a loin cloth, about to have his bandage renewed when two figures in dazzling breast plates and helmets came around the side and stopped in front of him. Legate Publius Quadratus looked at his tribune in frank amazement.

"What in the name of Dis have you been playing at, Tribune Longius?" he asked.

Lucius started to come to his feet but the legate told him to stay where he was.

"There was an attempted robbery, sir. I was cut about as you can see."

The legate stepped closer and examined the damage for himself.

"When did this happen?"

"It was on the evening of the fifteenth of February."

"Two days after the Ides of February, so what are you doing here?"

"Sir, your orders were perfectly clear. I was to leave Luca on the first day of March to make the rendezvous with you."

"That they were. And have you travelled all the way in this cart?"

"No sir, I rode my horse for as long as I could each day. I am pleased to report that for the past few days I have mounted and dismounted unassisted and ridden for six hours."

"What is that appalling stench?"

"Ah, that would be me. I have to smear garlic oil on my dressings and I cannot bathe until the stitches are removed."

"In which case, stay where you are and I'll send the garrison surgeon over; come to my quarters when he has examined you and you're sorted out."

He turned on his heel and strode off with the other officer who had not spoken.

"Boxer, was that the Emperor?" Passer asked.

"No, that's the legate, the most important officer in the legion. And do not call me "Boxer" all the time."

"But Otto does and so do all the soldiers. They all call you Tribune Boxer or just Boxer. Is it because of your nose, sir? You look like a boxer."

"Shut up!" Lucius snapped.

The surgeon was a middle-aged man with greying temples and big, red, hands that looked like they should belong to a ditch-digger. In his wake an orderly carried a wooden box of instruments and medicines.

"Been travelling with a dead goat have you?" he demanded then gently stretched the skin either side of the line of stitches between finger and thumb.

"When did you receive this injury?" he asked.

Lucius told him.

"When did you set out on your journey to Lugdunum?"

Lucius told him that.

The surgeon clucked his tongue and shook his head. "And I suppose everyone told you not to, but you just went ahead. In my opinion you are an idiot, sir. But a strong and very fortunate one: I see no reason to delay removing this first-rate stitching."

He clicked his fingers. His orderly produced a bottle of distilled wine vinegar and poured some out onto a piece of lint. The surgeon wiped the wound clean and then with a pair of scissors and forceps took every black, knotted horse-hair stitch out. A few small beads of blood welled up and were wiped away by the orderly.

"There we are, sir. My professional advice to you is to take a bath as soon as possible for the benefit of the rest of us as much as your own; otherwise carry on as normal."

"When can I wear my armour?" Lucius asked.

"Oh, right away I should have thought. Put a square of clean linen under your tunic every day for ten days and if you see the slightest sign of pus, leave off the subarmalis and breastplate and see a doctor who is as good as me as soon as possible."

Otto returned. "You are no longer sewn together; that's good. The horses are in the stables and the head groom says he will make room for our mules. We can park the cart outside. The optio in charge of officer accommodation has shown me our quarters. Do you want to go and look at them, Boxer?"

Passer smirked so Lucius clipped him around the ear, but not too hard.

Half an hour later, Otto and Lucius luxuriated in the baths. The attendant had baulked at admitting Otto but Lucius had a word in his ear.

"He is the only son of a powerful German warlord. We don't want to risk offending him, now do we?"

Passer was on the veranda of the rooms they had been assigned polishing boots and armour under the watchful eye of the optio. He was there to ensure the security of all the officers' property during their temporary stay but he decided to relieve his boredom by supervising Passer.

"Not like that lad; whoever taught you to polish boots? Put some effort into it, the best thing to make 'em shine is elbow grease..."

Lucius and Otto were unrecognisable when they stepped outside their quarters bathed, shaved, hair neat and, in Lucius' case, lightly perfumed. Shards of light sparkled off their mirror-bright kit. Lucius threw Passer a coin and told him to get himself something to eat and come straight back. The optio pointed out the legate's rooms. The guard announced them and they walked into a combination office and reception room. It was sparsely but comfortably furnished, warm and well lit. They saluted.

Publius Quadratus stood up with a wide smile on his face and ostentatiously sniffed the air.

"Is that you Boxer?"

Lucius laughed. "What a relief to feel clean and be able to wear my uniform again sir, thanks to the surgeon you sent me."

"And you are sure he has passed you fit for duty?"

"Yes, sir, there is one minor precaution I must take and I'll be sure to follow his advice."

"Good," the legate said and turned his attention to Otto. "I am pleased that you have rejoined us, Otto Longius."

"I am happy to see you again, sir. And where else would I be if not here by the side of Tribune Boxer?"

Quadratus eyes widened in surprise. "I can hear you have not been idle during your leave. I must congratulate you in the improvement in your Latin."

"Thank you; the noble lady Aelia, the tribune's grandmother, has spent a lot of her time helping me."

"Very good but gentlemen, I forget my manners," he indicated the other officer in the room, who they had seen previously just after their arrival.

"Please greet the noble Tertius Julius Fuscus. He has been given to us by the Emperor to act as my second in the legion with the rank of Senior Tribune. Tertius, I present Lucius Taurius Longius, tribune with special responsibilities in regard to artillery and missile troops and his companion Otto Longius."

Tertius stood up and stepped forward. He looked about thirty years old, slender, immaculately and expensively turned out and so tall that he could look Otto directly in the eyes. He saluted Lucius who returned the salute and then they shook hands. He followed this with a slight bow to Otto but also took his hand with a not unfriendly but penetrating look.

"Well, now that we all know each other, shall we sit and take wine?" the legate suggested.

"If you will not be offended, legate, I would prefer to return to our quarters now that we have greeted each other," Otto said.

"As you wish, Otto; no doubt we shall be seeing a lot more of each other in the coming months."

When they were alone with a cup of wine in front of each of them, Quadratus began to speak.

"I did not introduce you to Tertius by the mule cart, Lucius because you would have been at an embarrassing disadvantage considering your unsavoury state. I want the air clear and no ill feeling between the two of you, so I shall be frank. Boxer, there was never any possibility of you being promoted to Broad Stripe rank. You're too young and your family's political history is against you. Both of those problems will diminish over time. So, harbour no resentment towards Tertius; he has not usurped your place. Tertius has been on permanent garrison duty in Italy during his entire career, so far. He is an able administrator and an expert theoretical strategist. I know that he will prove to be of great support to me but he has never served in a legion on active, frontier duty. It is to his credit that he accepted this offer of promotion knowing that it would take him to the German border; somewhat less comfortable than home. Tertius, Boxer is the most able of my tribunes; I want you to assist him to develop his expertise in the organisation of a legion. Boxer, I want you to aid Tertius when it gets dirty and dangerous, but discretely. The men must see that he is your superior officer. Now gentlemen, can you willingly agree to proceed as I have outlined?"

They looked at each other for an appraising moment then Tertius held out a hand to Lucius who took it.

"Very well, now then Lucius, tell us how you come to return to me practically hacked to pieces," Quadratus said cheerfully.

Lucius began to recount the story. When he reached the point when Servius had run away and left him standing with his cloak wrapped around his left arm, Quadratus interrupted.

"Don't tell me, Otto stormed up like Mars himself…"

"Yes, sir, just as you say; he smashed one into a wall and broke in his ribs and killed the other two with his pugio."

"Excuse me," Tertius enquired, "but I don't quite understand where Otto Longius fits in…"

The legate laughed.

"Nobody does but we are very glad of him. Our auxiliary cavalrymen regard the relationship between him and Lucius as a compliment to them all, which helps cement their loyalty. Better tell him that story as well, Boxer."

Tertius listened fascinated.

"Oh, there's a lot more to say about these two, Tertius," Quadratus remarked.

"But, if I may, why do they refer to you as "Boxer", Lucius. It strikes me as disrespectful…" Tertius suggested

"The nicknames the men give officers are usually unrepeatable and never used to their faces. "Boxer" is the reverse of what you think, Tertius. It signifies that they have some regard for him. In any case, once we are in camp, if you ask for Tribune Longius, three-quarters of them will not know who you mean."

They stayed in Lugdunum for a further three days to let men and animals recuperate and then made their way out on the arduous road to their destination in the face of spitting rain. They were two hundred and ten experienced infantry with their officers, and fifty-three raw recruits all travelling with their lumbering wagons loaded with military supplies…and Passer's mule cart. Down on the coast by Forum Julii the first whispers of spring were on the air when Lucius had passed through. Now they seemed to travel back in time towards mid-winter as they crawled their way to the Rhine. The trees seemed even barer of leaves, the drizzle of the coast turned to sleet and hail. Ice formed on damp tents and water buckets overnight. The land around them grew less settled, bleaker and more forested. When not covered with treacherously thin ice, every stream they crossed was swelling with the arrival of the first snow melt waters tumbling off the slopes of the Alps.

It was particularly hard on Tertius. He had never been so cold and damp. He had never lived in the wilderness with a large body of other men. The crude realities of their everyday living disgusted him. There were insufficient men to construct a marching camp and rampart big enough to enclose their wagons so the wagons themselves became their rampart. They drew them into a rough rectangle pushed tightly together. They crammed the spaces between the wheels with thorny branches to prevent attackers crawling in underneath. All the men and animals crowded into this inadequate space: cooking, eating, washing and defecating cheek by jowl.

Over their evening meal, Quadratus, Tertius and Lucius were discussing their progress.

"We are covering a reasonable amount of ground under the conditions," the legate remarked. "Still, it cannot be easy for you, Tertius."

"How do you keep a disciplined distance between officers and men under these conditions?" he asked.

"You don't," Lucius replied with a shrug. "If you are squatting over a fallen tree having a shit and a centurion comes up asking for an order. You give it, salute and then finish your personal business as best you can after the interruption. The men are judging you at all times, particularly when you're new. You have to show them you can cheerfully take the hardships as well as they can."

"Arriving at the right balance takes time," Quadratus said. "Eventually, one simply acts and the men respond."

Lucius gave an example two days later. A wagon started to slip sideways over the edge of a frost covered, muddy slope leading down to a raging stream of brown water in the ravine below. Lucius had been riding knee to knee with Tertius when he saw the beginnings of the slow-motion disaster. He leapt out of the saddle and flung his reins to his superior officer.

"Take my horse, sir" he yelled and ran towards the wagon. "Drop your shields and on me!" He shouted to the nearest men. They gathered around him. "You, you and you, jam the shafts of your javelins under the wheels on the uphill side and hold it steady. The rest of you, get that cover off.!" They hauled the canvas aside. The wagon was loaded with barrels and kegs of sundry ironware; arrow and spear heads, tools, ratchets and gearwheels. He jumped up on it. "Right, get 'em over the side." The legionaries began to manhandle the cargo. "On the track!" he bellowed. "What's the point of chucking them down the fucking slope? That's the way boys," he laughed and helped heave at the heavy barrels. "That'll do; we've lightened it enough," he told them when a quarter of the load was off. He hopped down to the ground. "Right, let's give it a shove and get it straightened up. Carter, wake up those bastard mules!" They got their shoulders braced and dug their boots in "One, two, three, heave! One, two, three, heave!" he chanted to the crack of the driver's whip. The wheels slipped and skidded but found purchase and reluctantly turned. The wagon lurched forwards, a yard away from the edge and back onto the safety of the track. Slathered in mud to the knees, Lucius put his hands on his thighs, bent forwards and took several deep breaths to regain his wind. He noticed one of the men he had been yelling at was an optio. He straightened up and saluted him. The salute was returned.

"Well done optio, and your lads. If your centurion agrees, I suggest three days off fatigues for these men, you know who they are. Perhaps some of the interested spectators who have done nothing so far might care to reload the cargo and get us moving?"

"Yes, Box... sir," the optio shouted back.

Quadratus had joined Tertius and spoke to him quietly.

"Tribune Longius works alongside the men using appalling language and when the emergency is over, he reverts to the formality of his rank. And even though he is sweaty and mud-covered, the optio salutes him and calls him sir. This is what we were talking about the other night."

"I did not think to dismount and help," Tertius admitted.

"Nor should you; the men have known Lucius since he was eighteen and completely raw. You are a mature officer of higher rank; he has his manner with the men and you will develop yours."

As they marched north and west, the forest closed in around them. Dark pines, rank upon rank ran from the edges of the track into the dim recesses of the forest. The bases of their trunks were thick with ivy and brambles where the gales had brought some trees down to let a little sunshine enter. The spirits of the men dampened as the overwhelming dank solitude hemmed them in. Even at noon there was little light falling on them from the grey skies, it was claustrophobic.

It became more difficult to find a reasonably secure camping ground every afternoon. The experienced legionaries knew that the nearer they got to their destination, the more the danger grew. Close to their permanent camp they were always under the scrutiny of unfriendly eyes. The main routes in and out were equally watched and there was no doubt that their wagons laden with stores and equipment would be the prize of a lifetime for an enterprising warband. They were valuable enough to encourage several tribal groups to combine their strength in the attempt. Quadratus called a meeting of all officers. Tertius asked how far out they were and what was the average distance travelled each day. He then sat down with a wax tablet and stylus taking no further part in the discussion. Various proposals were put forward and all talked down. Finally, Tertius stood up and addressed the assembly.

"If I may, Legate Quadratus," he began, "we are seven days from the security of our permanent camp at our rate of progress of twelve miles per day; a total of eighty-four miles. This distance could be covered in two days by a man on horseback riding hard. In two days' time we shall be sixty miles from camp. A body of cavalry can cover that in a day and half and be with us when we are forty miles out. If we act now to put this plan into effect thus, we shall have the added support of mounted scouts and a screen of horsemen for our run in. Admittedly, this is not ideal cavalry country but no doubt our men are used to operating in such conditions. We also have the added benefit of being able to request infantry reinforcements if we run into serious trouble at the last minute."

There was a long silence during which appreciative glances and nods of approval passed between the other officers.

"This sounds the best solution we have for our potential difficulties, Tribune Tertius Fuscus. I shall adopt it. Who is to ride for the camp?" Quadratus said.

"I suggest Otto Longius. He is a native speaker of the local language, useful if he is intercepted and is well known to our troops."

"Ah, but he will not leave the side of Tribune Lucius Longius; his oath prevents him."

"I think he will, if I may speak with him?"

Otto was summoned. The plan was explained and he shook his head.

"How can I abandon Boxer, sir? Honour forbids me."

Tertius smiled. "Otto Longius, you are bound to do all you can to preserve the life of Tribune Longius, is that not correct?"

"Yes, sir, it is,"

"Then the best way you can support him is to bring us cavalry. Tribune Longius is in peril here, as are we all; he needs the protection they will bring. By undertaking this mission, you are fulfilling your promise. By refusing, you are leaving him in danger."

Otto looked over to Lucius who solemnly nodded his approval.

"I ride," Otto confirmed.

He left off his mail shirt and helmet to give his horse less weight to carry and armed only with his two spears, galloped away from the column. He had with him a rough map of their line of march and a written message for Titus Attius.

"Neatly done," the legate told Tertius. "I did not believe that you would be able to persuade him."

All worked exactly to plan. They entered the Porta Decumana without incident behind a screen of one hundred auxiliary cavalry. The myth of Tribune Fuscus' ability to come up with ideas to get the legion out of trouble was born.

Chapter 21

Entering the camp felt like a homecoming to Lucius but inevitably, things had changed. The "useless" young tribune who had arrived last year had over-wintered with the legion. His boyish face had thinned and hardened, he was taller and more confident.

"Greetings Lucius Taurius Longius," he said offering his right hand.

Lucius looked at him blankly for a moment without recognition. He held out his own hand and struggled to recall the name he had barely bothered to commit to memory.

"Tribune Soranus, isn't it?"

"Rufus Vulso Soranus; I'm not surprised you had difficulty in remembering me. We barely passed a dozen words last year."

"I'm sorry…"

"Oh, don't apologise. All I did was to get in everyone's way at first but five months under the command of the camp prefect have taught me a lot."

"Yes, exposure to Titus Attius tends to be educational…"

They laughed briefly.

After three days of settling back in, Quadratus invited all the senior officers to a formal dinner in his quarters. Otto was also summoned to attend.

"Otto, my friend," the legate said, "yet again your status causes me a problem. This is an evening for my staff, and yet here you are and rightly so I believe. I am never sure if you belong to this legion or not. You have taken no oath under the eagles nor are you a citizen and yet you willingly rode through miles of dangerous country to bring me support when I needed it. What am I to make of you?"

"Nothing sir, with respect; I remain what I always was, the oath companion of Tribune Longius."

But Otto was far from being the ignorant boy who had first loped into camp beside the tribune's horse. He now spoke fluent Latin, could read and write and he had seen something of the Roman world. He had lived in the home of an upper-class provincial family. His viewpoint had widened along with his understanding. Only his loyalty to Lucius remained unaltered.

Stories of what had happened in camp and to the men on leave were swapped. Titus Attius was delighted that the pugio he had given Otto had sent two villains to the underworld. Then Lucius remembered to pass along the regards of Centurion Massus. "Centurion Decimus Massus, with one eye? Where did you come across him?"

"He commands the Luca city garrison," Lucius replied.

"Does he now?" mused Titus and then paused before turning to Quadratus. "May I tell a tale, sir?"

"By all means, let us hope it is instructive," the legate answered.

"Very well then, Africa, gentlemen; heat, flies, sand and elephants as well as ferocious opposition from the native inhabitants are what we faced back then. Imagine two legions formed up side by side showing one continuous front to the enemy with rocky escarpments protecting both of our flanks. Their horse archers rode up, wheeled and discharged a volley before breaking away. They did this time after time. Our losses weren't serious because they stayed too far back, barely within effective range. But what they did do was kick up a bank of yellow dust that rolled over us obscuring our view. So, there we were, gritty throats burning with thirst, when a bloody huge grey shape loomed through the dust cloud in front of the legion to our left. It was a war elephant with a platform on its back full of bastards firing bows and chucking spears at us.

To be fair to the lads, they held their ground. The elephant was being peppered with javelins which slowed it down but it was still coming on. The poor beast was not happy. It curled its trunk up and lifted its head to trumpet and a lucky throw, which turned out to be damnably unlucky, got it up through the roof of its mouth. It took a few more steps forward and fell dead. Of course the line broke; no-one wants to be underneath a dead elephant when it hits the ground. Hordes of barbarians swarmed over and around it and flooded through the gap. They managed to drive such a wedge that half of the legion Massus was serving in was cut off from the rest of us. Barbarians they might have been but they were not stupid. They manoeuvred to contain the bulk of the legions and directed their main attack against the lads who had been cut off. This is where "Cyclops" Massus comes in.

A ricocheting arrow had hit him in the eye. He pulled it out but what he did not know was that his eye had come with it. The arrow fell free and Massus was left with his eyeball swinging from its cords on his cheek and blood everywhere. Well, he really lost it at this point. He called down the curses of the gods on them and went forward with his sword. Anyone in front of him must have thought he was a demon; covered in his own blood and with this horrible eye rolling around in the middle of his face. No-one would stand against him and the nearest ones tried to get out of his way. This made more and more of them turn back the way they had come until it became a panicked stampede. Well, that turned into a general rout. We regrouped and advanced. Then the order for melee was given and we chased them down and slaughtered them in their thousands. Decimus Massus was awarded a silver spear for saving the army. Here's to him." Attius finished, raising his wine in a toast.

"Somewhat of an obscure posting for such a man, the garrison of Luca," Tertius commented.

"You could say so, Tribune Fuscus, but it's a quiet life and perhaps he knows the Lady Fortuna will never again smile on him like she did that day."

Centurion Lentus approached Lucius one morning. He saluted briskly.

"I believe I have a man in the eighth century who can out-throw Otto with a javelin, sir."

"Do you now? I'll go and find him."

As he walked across the parade ground with Otto at his side, Tertius asked him what was going on.

"A javelin contest sir, you might like to watch."

Lentus stood at the end of the range with a knowing smile on his face. A brawny legionary with powerful sloping shoulders stood next to him. Lucius looked the legionary up and down; the man was composed, eager to show off his prowess.

"Centurion Lentus, this is hardly fair. I believe you have been training your man for months while Otto has not picked up a javelin since we left last autumn…."

Otto laughed, picked up the nearest weapon and hefted it in his right hand. He took half a step and launched it with a roar as it left his grasp. The javelin whistled through the air, arced high over the target and stuck quivering, six foot up the palisade wall fifteen paces beyond it.

The new contender Lentus had proposed looked disappointed; he was never going to best that throw.

Lentus saluted. "I believe we should call it a day, sir," he said, his face expressionless.

"Don't be downcast, soldier" Lucius told the legionary on whom Lentus had pinned his hopes. "Otto is a foot taller than you and he's still growing, as far as I can make out. The only thing that will beat him is an artillery bolt thrower."

They smiled at the quip and any ill-feeling was avoided.

Tertius noted another example of how easily Lucius related to the men. He would never have thought to address the legionary directly. He knew he was too stiff, too firmly upper-class to be able to do so freely. And he also had the intelligence to know that he should not try. He would content himself with being an active and thorough officer and hope the legion would come to appreciate him for those qualities.

The arrival of Tertius had changed the dynamic in the legion officer corps. Before his appointment, Lucius had direct access to the legate and took his orders from him. Now he fell under the command of Senior Tribune Tertius Julius Fuscus. Tertius was careful not to throw his weight about but he had to impose himself on the legion. It was not an easy path for him to tread, particularly since all the officers and men knew this was his first tour of border duty. Lucius was mindful of the legate's words when he and Tertius had been introduced and showed the newcomer unwavering support. This was noticed but did not alter the fact that some of the senior centurions were undecided about the new tribune. In their eyes, only battle showed a man for what he was.

Lucius spent more of his time than ever with Cestus Valens and the artillerymen. He had developed his mathematics and expertise to the extent that his comments were now taken seriously. He also kept close contact with Centurion Corvo and his mixed force of archers and slingers. He could not handle a sling, no matter how hard he tried but he became more than competent with a bow. If he should ever be demoted, he could take his place among the archers as the equal of most of them, though below the best. Tertius disapproved of an officer working alongside the men while dressed in an old tunic, dismantling and greasing a catapult. He had been trained to believe that such behaviour was prejudicial to discipline. With some vague idea of mentioning to Lucius that his appearance and actions were inappropriate, he went across to where he stood with Valens, head bent over a bench studying a wax tablet covered with triangles and scribbled figures. In spite of himself, Tertius was intrigued.

"It's always the same calculation, sir," Valens explained. "Weight of missile, tension on the rope sinews, maximum range possible."

"Can you not simply twist the ropes tighter?" he suggested.

"Ah, well, then we bring in the other consideration; the structural strength of the weapon, sir; too much tension and it will rip itself apart," Lucius informed him.

"But if we...." Tertius went on and was surprised to find that a full half hour had gone by while they discussed the intricacies of hurling death up into the air to rain down on an enemy.

"Do you think it is necessary to labour alongside the men and out of uniform, Tribune Longius?" he asked at last.

"But if I don't know how these machines should be assembled and maintained, sir, how will I know if the men are doing it properly?"

Tertius smiled. "Therefore, it is necessary, tribune and you are to be commended for your attention to detail, as are you Cestus Valens."

"Thank you, sir," Cestus replied. "We like to pretend that our knowledge of geometry excuses our sometimes less than officer-like appearance."

The Second Lucan trained its recruits, exercised its infantry, maintained its fortifications and showed the flag. Sorties in strength along the banks of the Rhine or into the forest were always dangerous but an essential activity. The sight of Roman power should kill any rebellion in the egg. Largely speaking, it did.

On the last day of May, the second cohort, supported by sixty of Corvo's mixed missile troops and commanded by Tribune Tertius Julius Fuscus left the Porta Principia Dextra to patrol the Roman bank of the Rhine for a distance of fifty miles upstream. Prefect Aldermar had seconded three scouts to the mission. Quadratus ordered Lucius to take part.

"You can have a look at Centurion Corvo's men in the field, Boxer, make sure they are in good form," the legate had said but they both knew that Lucius was also there to back up Tertius in case things went badly.

Since Lucius was marching, or rather riding, Otto was at his side; he would be of use in translating for the scouts. Lucius offered his two-mule cart to Tertius since it was small and light enough to go where the supply wagons could not. Passer demanded to drive it. When he was told he could not, he looked so despondent that Otto thought an explanation was necessary.

"You are not a warrior and the mules and drivers are the first targets that raiders aim for."

"What is the use of being free if I can never do anything of my own will?" he said.

So Tertius rode out at first light with five hundred and forty men, accompanied by twenty mules carrying entrenching tools, sharpened poles for the basic structure of a palisade and food supplies; and one cart loaded with extra food, arrows and slingers' bullets driven by a thirteen-year-old boy.

"Your slave does not lack courage," Tertius said to Lucius pointing at the grinning Passer, high up on the driver's seat.

"He's not a slave, sir. He demanded to come along because he's now a free man."

Tertius looked askance. "Your domestic arrangements are unique, Lucius," he remarked.

Five abreast with the transport mules dispersed along the length of the column, they passed out of the bright May sunshine into the gloom of the forest. They planned to follow a route they had used previously which took them forty miles as the crow flies from the camp and five miles inland of the river. The disadvantage was that it was ripe for ambush, since they were known to have made use of it. The scouts ranged ahead and, on either flank, constantly criss-crossed each other's paths on the hunt for any sign of danger. The legionaries were all on high alert, their tension almost palpable. But there was also an advantage in following this previous way through the endless monotony of trees. The track had been beaten down and was easy to follow. Overnight halting places were quickly cleared; in the two years since the legion had been this way, saplings had grown up in the clearings where they had spent the night but they were easily cut down and added to the palisade.

Tertius ordered fires to be lit. "Inevitably, we are being watched. They all know where we are, so there is no reason for the men not to have the comfort of some warmth and light."

The only incident that occurred was early one morning when a wild pig and half a dozen of her litter rushed across their path. Some of the soldiers asked permission to hunt them down. Tertius refused.

"For all we know, they have been chased in front of us by the Germans for that very reason. Fifty paces to the side of our column, you men would be out of sight and ready to have your throats cut."

Mid-morning on the third day, they turned to the east and broke out of the overhead canopy by early afternoon. They felt the sun on their faces and the sight of the blue dotted with white clouds above them as a blessing. There was something about being constantly surrounded by trees on all sides with the canopy of their tangled branches overhead which was profoundly depressing to the spirits of the legionaries. They angled towards the river and came in sight of it late in the afternoon. They made camp. There was the danger that they would relax now that the back of their march was broken but Tertius anticipated that. He trebled the sentries

"We can see little in the forest and are more vulnerable in the open. One is as bad as the other. We cannot drop our guard."

They now travelled with the Rhine on their right flank and the skirts of the forest on their left. The scouts surged in and out of the trees constantly on the move; if there were to be trouble, it would most likely come in a screaming rush from between the pines. Their track was wide and free of undergrowth. It was regularly used by civilian traffic going up and downstream. The day passed. They broke at midday to rest men and animals and then resumed with the sun at its zenith. In the late afternoon a treeless hill came into view ahead of them. It was about one hundred and fifty feet high, its steep sides yellow with flowering gorse bushes and a crown of bramble, furze and alder on its summit. The track bent around it so that the hill lay between the soldiers and the river. As they came nearer, Lentus made his way up to Tertius and Lucius at a brisk pace. He fell into step beside their horses and saluted.

"An optio reports one of his men thinks he saw movement near the top of that hill, sir."

Tertius began to turn his head to look at it but noticed Lucius was studiously avoiding looking in that direction and stopped.

"Nothing from the scouts?" he inquired.

"No sir, but they're all in the forest."

"I see. Centurion, how many men do you think could hide in that thicket up there?"

"Dunno, maybe a couple of hundred…" Lentus suggested.

"I think more. I think they could have a force up there that would equal our own, or no-one at all."

"We could cut inland, sir…."

"Rome does not move aside for a few barbarians, let alone the suspicion that some of them may be nearby…."

"Sir, if we...Boxer…" Lentus pleaded, suddenly afraid that this untried officer was going to lead them into a trap.

Lucius' voice rang out like a hammer striking an anvil.

"Centurion Lentus, you forget yourself. The noble Senior Tribune Tertius Fuscus commands here. Address yourself to him."

Lentus pulled himself to a taut attention then bowed his head briefly.

"My pardon sir, I intend no disrespect."

"I am glad to learn it. Now, centurion, if I may finish what I was saying. We do not move aside but we alter our dispositions according to the circumstances. Prepare to adopt a marching box formation eight men broad, two ranks deep. Put the transport animals in the centre. The rear ranks to face forward but to be ready to about turn if necessary. Get Corvo." He came running up. "String your bows and ensure you all have sufficient ammunition. Fall-in on either side of the transport to protect it. On your own initiative, deploy your men where they will be of most use if we come under attack. Lentus, halt the column and carry out the manoeuvre, quick as you like."

Orders were shouted, whistles blown and in a very short time with an immense clatter of shields and weapons the caterpillar of men and animals had turned itself into a mobile fortress. They reached the foot of the hill and heard a roar of frustrated rage and anguish from the top of it.

Four hundred warriors had lain concealed in the brambles and thorny scrub for two days. They had held their collective breath, as the Romans' scouts had ridden around them jabbing their lances into the tangle. But the cover was too thick for them to enter on horseback. The ambushers' reward for enduring the cold night and the days lying still, always with a thorn sticking into them somewhere, was to see their enemy come into view, wary and prepared to fend off an attack. If they had been able to hurtle down on the cohort while it was in line of march, they would have had a more than even chance of fragmenting it and cutting the scattered groups of legionaries to pieces. But with the formation Tertius had adopted, the odds of success were loaded heavily against them. Scores of men erupted out of the dense cover but they did not attack. Promising the Romans destruction on another day at the top of their voices, brandishing spears and axes, they drifted away down the far hillside and upstream to vanish into the forest. Thirty or so young warriors desperate to make a name for themselves and a few older fanatics who should have known better, made a ragged charge at the Roman flank. They were repulsed with heavy losses. Many more were brought down by lead bullets and arrows fired by Corvo's men as they tried to scramble back up to safety. It had been a disaster for the Germans.

A dozen legionaries had received minor cuts and grazes. Tertius pointed to the top of the hill.

"Good place to camp, I think."

In the morning they dragged the enemy corpses to the summit and flung them into the undergrowth before setting fire to anything which would burn. The wind was behind them and they marched for several hours with the smell of smoke in their nostrils.

In camp once more, Lucius was invited to drink some wine in Tertius' quarters. The Senior Tribune raised his cup.

"To you in thanks for backing me up when it mattered."

Lucius laughed politely. "It was nothing, chain of command and all that but you now have the undying loyalty of the second cohort forever."

"Why?" Tertius demanded.

"Because of taking that hill and turning it into a funeral pyre; that smoke will have been seen for thirty miles in every direction. The soldiers like the way you, "showed 'em what we're all about." They will follow you anywhere. But as far as the Germans are concerned, congratulations on becoming perhaps the most hated Roman officer on the Rhine."

They drank more of Tertius' best Falernian wine and began to talk more intimately.

"Why the fascination with artillery?" Tertius asked.

Lucius sighed. "My promotion prospects are not good. The artillery is far from glamorous, as you pointed out when we were dismantling that catapult, but if I master the skills, there is the vague possibility of an appointment to a general's staff as a master of artillery. You heard the legate when we first met. I shall never lead a legion; politics. Thank you grandfather," he said and raised his cup in mock salute.

Tertius pulled his stool closer and leaned forward, speaking intently in a low voice.

"You are not alone in having troublesome ancestors Lucius. My own grandfather was a rabid supporter of Pompeius Magnus against the divine Julius Caesar. He was on Pompey's staff in the Civil War and about to embark for Greece with his legions when he had the good sense to drop dead before his ship sailed. My father was a very young officer who took the chance to desert, word of it got out and hundreds joined him on a desperate march to Rome. He threw himself on Caesar's mercy and the fact that he had a cohort of experienced soldiers with him no doubt helped him get his pardon. So, I have a grandfather who was willing to take up arms against Caesar and a father who was a celebrated deserter. No-one really trusted him afterwards, no matter how much they praised him for joining the "right" side."

"But you have been able to rise to your present rank, in spite of all that," Lucius said.

"Yes, because my family remained in Rome and kept their money. Rome is where the decisions are made, not in some provincial city. And the money buys influence and pays for favours granted…"

"Grandfather lost all ours, or rather it was confiscated. He was a dedicated Antonian and when Marcus Antonius went to Egypt that was the end for us in Rome. Fortunately, my grandmother's people had property in Luca which has stayed in the family" Lucius told him.

"Your family owned a house in Rome?" Tertius enquired.

"Yes, on the Esquiline Hill, I believe."

"And what was your grandfather called?"

"Taurius Vitius Longius, my father is Vitius Lucius Longius and you know who I am."

"Would you mind if I make a note of these names?"

Lucius was doubtful but did not want to offend his senior officer and possible new friend by refusing. Tertius understood.

"Lucius, those were troubled times, to say the least. The stories that come down through families are often a false version of what actually happened. I have a younger brother who is beginning to make his way in the court system. He could make discreet enquiries on my behalf. Let me write to him, perhaps some good may come of it."

Lucius shrugged. "I don't want you to waste your time but thank you for the offer. Please let your brother loose on the records."

"Good, then here's to the rehabilitation of the noble Longius family!"

The clinked wine cups and drained them together.

Chapter 22

While Lucius and Tertius were laying the foundations of a future friendship, First Spear Centurion Titus Attius and Centurion Lentus, leader of the second cohort, stood side by side on the walkway gazing out over the silent landscape. The Rhine reflected a metallic glow by the light of the rising moon. As it climbed higher in the sky, the cleared area around the camp resolved into the long black shadows of tree stumps interspersed with brilliant patches flooded with such bright moonlight that all colour was bleached from the ground. The two men were cloaked against the damp chill of the night air. The sentries had moved away, leaving the officers room to talk in private.

"It's difficult to know what to do if a soldier questions an order or shows he's unhappy with it," Attius said.

Lentus looked at him with some surprise. "Not so, sir; if any of my men did such a thing, they would get a beating at the least," he responded.

There was a long pause.

"Ah, yes, you're quite right; a legionary would get a damn good hiding. Of course, centurions cannot be beaten by superior officers. That would destroy all respect their men might have for them," Attius continued.

"The legion would turn into a rabble," Lentus agreed.

"That's the way of it. Mind you, a centurion can be reduced to the ranks and then flogged. No-one would want to see that, of course. Apart from the shame to the man concerned, it would reflect badly on the reputation of the legion he's serving in. Me, I'd rather fall on my sword."

"Well yes," Lentus said, suddenly uneasy about the direction of this conversation. "But he would have had to do something bloody serious."

"Something like interrupting a senior officer giving an order in the field and then appealing to another officer?" Attius demanded. The blood drained from Lentus' face until it was as pale as the moon above him. The First Spear Centurion put one arm across Lentus' shoulder and went on. "Tricky things, tribunes; we both know that nine out of ten of them are playing around for a year to help their civilian careers in Rome but then there are the others; the ones who will go on to high command. It's hard to remember that even an experienced centurion just can't afford to put that sort right," he paused again to let his words sink in. "How long have you served, Lentus?"

"Twenty years," he croaked.

"Saved any money?"

"Yes, enough," he said.

"If I were you, I would think about turning it in. A centurion's honourable discharge bounty is worth having and if you've got money put by, you should be able to live well, probably get some public appointment outside of Rome; damn expensive place Rome. Goodnight Centurion Lentus."

Two days later, a courier going up to headquarters was accompanied by former Centurion Lentus with his paperwork signed and countersigned. Lentus was gone. Replacing a centurion did not impose any difficulty on Titus; so many men achieved the rank only to be killed in the following few weeks or months that finding someone to fill a gap was routine. Tertius and Lucius saw a connection between the brief spat on their last sortie and the sudden disappearance of Lentus who had seemed like a fixture in The Second Lucan. They asked Attius about the matter.

"An effective legion needs an effective centurionate, gentlemen and it is the duty of the first spear centurion, and no other, to make sure all the officers under him are fitted to their positions. Former Centurion Lentus was a good soldier and a brave man but he had his faults. He was increasingly inclined to think he knew best at all times." Attius grinned. "He was wrong of course; I'm the one who always knows best."

"But I made no complaint against him," Tertius said.

"No more you did sir, neither did Tribune Longius but anything soldiers overhear is repeated and all gossip comes to my ears sooner or later. Lentus should not have expressed doubt at your order not should he have turned to Tribune Longius. He is fortunate that matters have ended as they have. May I help you further, gentlemen?"

"I intended no disrespect to you…" Tertius began but Attius stopped him.

"I know that, sir. You did not want to let an injustice go unchallenged but in this case there has been none."

Passer's behaviour was another disciplinary matter that needed attention. When Lucius and Otto were on duty, he ran wild. His household tasks took up a fraction of his time and when they were done, he explored, interfered, asked questions at the wrong times and became a general nuisance. There were complaints. Lucius shrugged them off but they persisted. At last he and Otto sat Passer down for a serious talk. After the preliminary accusations on one side and blanket denials on the other, they reached an impasse. Then Lucius had an inspiration.

"Passer, what do you want to be when you are grown up?"

"I'm going to be a soldier," he replied firmly.

"That's not possible. You aren't a citizen; all legionaries must be citizens."

"Of course, I am. Your father freed me. I have the paper…."

"Passer, you are no longer a slave, that is true but that does not make you a citizen."

"Well, that can't be right."

"Boxer would not lie to you, don't be insolent," Otto told him.

That ended the argument but dashed Passer's spirits. Lucius looked at the unhappy boy and sighed. He could not leave things there.

"You could join the navy; you don't have to be a citizen to do that."

"Don't want to," Passer told him abruptly.

"Why not?

"Can't swim."

"You'd be on a ship."

"Might fall off."

Lucius was coming to the end of his patience and Passer was looking sulky. It might have ended with a slap "to wipe that look off your" face but Otto intervened.

"What part of your work do you like best?" he asked the boy.

"Looking after the horses... and the mules," Passer replied, visibly brightening.

"So, if you cannot be a soldier, would you like to work with horses?"

"Yes, I suppose so," Passer said reluctantly.

Otto turned to Lucius. "There is the answer, Boxer," he said.

"What exactly?" Lucius asked; he had now passed from annoyed to bored with the discussion.

"We take him to Martellus."

They exchanged salutes with the master farrier who glared at Passer.

"You again; I thought I told you to clear off – permanently?"

"Decanus Martellus Flaccus is an expert in shoeing horses...." Lucius began but Martellus snorted.

"I am a farrier. I do a lot more than that. I correct their gait. I tend them when they are sick and I keep them in the best condition they can be."

"Indeed, Martellus; I was just trying to explain to Passer here...."

"Would you like to explain why he's such a pain in the backside, sir?"

"I can do that," Otto interrupted. "He is young and runs around like an unbroken colt because he has no one to train him. He knows a little of horses and would like to learn more. Will you teach him?"

Martellus looked passer up and down as carefully as if examining a young horse being offered for sale.

"Do you want to be initiated into my craft?"

"Yes, please, sir," Passer said without hesitation.

Martellus smiled and then shook his head, looking at Lucius.

"I don't know if that would be fair to the lad. The trade's not what it was; too many slaves doing the work now. Who wants to pay a master craftsman his due when you can buy a cheap slave to do his job? Of course, the results will never be as good but most people either don't know enough about it or don't care."

"There must be some opportunities," Lucius suggested.

Martellus puffed the air out of his cheeks and scratched the bristles of his shaven head with one sooty finger.

"Well, I suppose slaves need expert supervisors and then there's racing stables and stud farms. Their stock's too valuable to leave in just anyone's hands…. "

"Will you train him?" Lucius asked trying to disguise the pleading tone in his voice.

"Alright, I'll do it. I'll take him on as my apprentice for five years. At the end of that time he will know enough to be able to earn some sort of living if he pays attention and works hard. What do you say boy?"

"Oh yes, sir, I will try my best, sir."

"Very well; we have all heard you give your word. As an apprentice he should live under my roof but that's not possible in an army camp. He'll have to sleep in the hayloft; I can arrange a cot for him. Now the premium, let's say, one hundred denarii per year, five years so five hundred denarii and we'll draw up a contract.

"Five hundred denarii?" asked the astonished Lucius.

The master farrier looked grave.

"Sir, Passer is not a member of my family by blood or marriage so he's not entitled to my special consideration. You expect me to open the secrets of my craft to him and teach him its practice. Surely you understand that education comes at a price and mine is not excessive."

"When you put it like that…"

"I do, and the five hundred up front please. Without being morbid, you could be knocked on the head next week; these are the Rhine Borderlands after all." Everyone made the sign against evil. "We will both have a copy of his contract and it will state my obligations to him in respect of the premium paid and his duties to me for the full period of five years."

Lucius looked at Passer. "Now, Passer, if you decide to do this, Decanus Martellus Flaccus becomes your master. You are not in bondage to him; you remain a free man but you agree to be under his tutelage and obey him for five years until you have mastered the farrier's craft. Let each of us hear you say that you accept these terms. If you do not want to, we shall have to think again."

"Master Lucius, I was a slave in your father's household until he made me a free man and now you pay a fortune so that I can earn my living in the world? I agree; my heart is so full of gratitude to your noble family. May I take the name of Passer Lucius Longius on my contract to honour you?"

The legate was consulted as a matter of courtesy. He had no objection.

"I hear that the boy was becoming a major irritation; at the least this will keep him occupied."

Otto had decided to sleep outside under the porch again fearing that the comforts of Luca had softened him. He had bought a folding bed to keep him off the floor and kept an oil lamp beside him. He opened his case and took out "The lady Aelia's scroll" as he thought of it. Passer had received his contract that day and Otto was in a thoughtful mood. He scanned the scroll and his eye caught one particular item.

"Those who claim to own their fellow men are looking down into a pit forgetting that justice should rule the world.

Zeno."

He put everything carefully away and extinguished his lamp. Before he slept, he considered what he had read. It was the stupidest idea he had ever come across. It was obvious that there must be slaves and if there were slaves, they had to have owners.

When he woke in the morning, Zeno's words had remained with him but his mind had worked on them during his sleep. Otto asked himself why it was "obvious" that some men were bound but others free. There was no answer other than that this was the way things were. He wrestled to find sense in the words that Aelia had thought so important for him to read. He remembered his family slaves. They were not ill-treated but he could not recall the name of a single one of them. He could picture them. Tall, blond or red-headed for the most part, speaking the same language as his family, dressed like them; in every way similar but they were not at liberty. They were lesser because they accepted their state, he decided. But supposing enduring their lowly status was an act of courage; holding on to life in the hope that one day they would again be free? In a perverse way, that was honourable. As for looking into a pit, how better to describe Servius, thrusting and grunting over the belly of the German girl in the brothel? He was so deep in his need for dominance that he could never climb out. He needed to prove his power over her and to show Otto that he too was less than Servius. Slaves were other, slaves were inferior. The girl was German, Otto was German therefore he, Otto, was other and of no more account than she was. The last thing that came to mind was Passer. Having been born a slave, then freed, he had been told that one of the few ways to earn a decent living once he had mastered the trade Martellus was teaching him was to become an overseer of slaves. It was absurd. Otto did not arrive at any conclusions but had a greater respect of Zeno.

By the end of the first week after Passer left them, the quarters Lucius and Otto shared were a mess. In spite of the boy's tendency to wander the camp getting into trouble when he wasn't occupied, he had done a lot of boot and belt polishing, armour and saddle cleaning, horse grooming and floor sweeping. Trying to do it all themselves as well as performing their military duties was too much. And it had to be said that Lucius was not a lot of use. He had never needed to do these mundane tasks himself and lacked both the skill and the patience.

"Come on," he said to Otto, "we'll have to go to the slave traders among the camp-followers and see if we can buy someone to help us out."

Otto thought of Zeno and hesitated but what alternative was there? He shrugged and followed Lucius out of the Porta Decumana.

A figure they had not seen before stood on the far end of the bridge opposite the camp gate. As they drew nearer, they saw that he was not of any great age but sadly worn down by life. His cloak and tunic were threadbare. He was very thin and his lips blue in the cold wind. He wore a soldier's belt but no weapons and had a scuffed satchel hanging by his side. As Lucius drew level he saluted and tried to come to attention but could not. His left leg bent outwards below the knee and was badly bowed.

"Good morning, sir," he said.

"And to you…. ex-legionary?" Lucius asked, stopping beside the stranger.

"Ex-decanus, sir, for all the difference it makes."

Lucius put his hand in his purse and offered two small coins. The man recoiled.

"I am not a beggar, sir," he said gathering the shreds of his dignity about him.

"Then how do you live, man?" Otto asked.

"I do what I can; odd jobs, mostly for soldiers, cleaning and polishing kit and the like. I can handle a mule wagon as well. I'm not too good at climbing in or out but I can drive alright; sitting down job you see, this doesn't get in the way," he replied pointing at his left leg.

Otto and Lucius exchanged a sharp look.

"What is your name, decanus?" Lucius asked.

"Felix sir," he said with a wry smile.

"Felix? But that means happy and lucky…." Otto blurted out and then wished he hadn't.

"Former Decanus Felix, I am Tribune Lucius Taurius Longius and this is my oath companion Otto who has also adopted my family name of Longius. There is a tavern not far off where we can get a bowl of soup fortified with wine, that isn't too bad. Would you like to join us? We have a proposition we may wish to put to you."

Felix tried not to wolf his soup down but it was obvious he was immeasurably hungrier than his companions. Another bowl was fetched and he ate that more slowly, finished, he told his tale. It was a familiar story. He had not been in the army long enough to accumulate much in the way of savings and received little other than his back pay when an axe blow to his left leg ended his career. He had arrived yesterday driving a wagon for a trader but it had been a one-way trip. He was standing near the camp gate hoping for work when they met him.

"Why did you not go home to your family when you were injured?" Otto asked.

Felix looked at him with a half-smile.

"Romans despise cripples, sir. My parents are dead. I know my sister would try to hide her shame for my sake but her husband would not. Sitting on their doorstep with a begging bowl is worse than the life I have now."

"What can you do to earn money?" Otto asked.

"As I said, I can drive a cart and I can clean and look after kit and sharpen swords properly. I can bake very good soldiers' bread and make a decent stew. I can keep the billet presentable and tend the horses."

"Would you like to work for us, Felix, doing what you just said? You'd have a room, your meals and a bit of money every month?" Lucius asked.

"What, permanent like?" Felix asked astounded at his good fortune. "Here take my hand on it tribune, before you change your mind."

"What do you say, Otto?" Lucius asked.

"I say this is a good idea and Zeno would be pleased," Otto answered with a chuckle.

Lucius raised his eyebrows at the reference to the Greek philosopher; he recognised the name but knew nothing more of him. Lucius decided he was someone Otto had talked about with Aelia but what he had to do with the arrangement with Felix he could not say.

Titus Attius looked over Felix's discharge papers and confirmed that he could freely come and go in the camp. He also gave him a pass to use the soldiers' baths as a "former comrade" which stretched the rules but no-one objected. Felix lived up to his name. he was cheerful by nature and felt that he had been lucky to find his place with Lucius and Otto. They woke in the morning to the smell of fresh bread baking in the small clay oven and the sound of Felix stumping about the kitchen. They had found him some better clothes but he baulked at accepting them at first, repeating that he was not a beggar.

"Boxer's reputation will be harmed if you go about in worn-out clothes. People will say he is taking advantage of you," Otto told him.

The next day, Felix was dressed in the best tunic and cloak he had put on for years.

When he was not working and the weather was kind, Felix took to sitting on a stool on the veranda letting the warmth of the sun ease his damaged leg. He soon became a well-liked fixture, exchanging greetings with whoever passed by.

Otto watched him one day, ordering Lucius to lift his feet off the floor so he could sweep under his chair and the table. Lucius did as he was told and Felix pushed the dust and dried mud from their boots towards the door, whistling as he always did. It was a scene of almost domestic contentment. Otto thought how much better is was to be served by a free man doing his job than by a fearful or resentful slave. He understood why Aelia had included the quotation from Zeno on the scroll she had given him.

The inward-looking life of the legion went on as spring passed into high summer. They marched, fought and laboured under harsh discipline. Men were killed and injured in combat or accidents. Their food was monotonously plain and their wine not much better than vinegar. But they were compensated by comradeship and pride in themselves. They were a legion of Rome; no-one could stand against them.

Chapter 23

Not all the native inhabitants in their area of operations were hostile. The makeup of the population had changed beyond belief since Caesar's conquest. Whole tribes had been annihilated; either slaughtered or enslaved and their towns razed to the ground. Others had sought terms after realizing that they could never drive out the Roman invaders. Some fled across the Rhine. It had been ethnic cleansing on a grand scale, reducing the total population by more than half. The wars had been over for forty years and more, now people were coming back. The ragged remnants of once numerous tribes were beginning to group together to form new societies, sometimes with peoples their ancestors had fought for generations. The Euberones had been wiped off the face of the earth as far as the Romans knew but some had survived. They and others had joined the Tungri which was a growing force.

And there had been those peoples whose leaders had seen not only the futility of opposing Rome but the advantages to be had from allying themselves with these powerful interlopers from the south. Among them were the Treverii. They had made and broken peace with Rome several times but eventually entered into a treaty that had lasted. In recognition of this, Caesar had presented a gold medallion bearing his bull symbol to the king of the Treverii. On his father's death this treasure had been passed to his son, King Gebhardus,.

On the tenth day of June, three warriors emerged from the eastern forest edge and made their way to the Porta Praetoria. They rode easily, keeping their mounts to a comfortable canter. They were seen when they were well out and by the time they arrived at the gate, a centurion had been summoned and was waiting for them on the walkway. All three were richly dressed and armoured in mail shirts of Roman manufacture. This would have raised the hackles of the legionaries a short time ago. The only way they could have got their shirts was by stripping them off the corpses of Roman soldiers. But the sight of tribesmen wearing them was no longer unusual. Since the army had begun to adopt the lorica segmentata, surplus mail shirts were offered for sale all over the empire. The men carried brightly painted oval shields and each held two lances. They stopped thirty paces from the gate. One of them passed his weapons to one of his companions, hung his shield over his saddle horns and walked his horse forward. When he was within ten paces, he raised his arms and shouted to the centurion in passable Latin.

"King Gebhardus of the Treverii, friends of Rome, has given me a message for the great general Publius Quadratus."

"Give me the message and I'll pass it on," the centurion called down.

The visitor shook his head.

"I am ordered to speak to the general and no other."

A soldier was sent to the Praetorium and returned with Tribune Soranus in tow, helmeted and wearing his decorated breastplate. The tribune climbed the ladder and looked down.

"Give me your message," he said.

This time the messenger smiled broadly.

"You are too young to be the general," he replied.

Soranus took a decision. "We'll let him in but not the other two," he told the centurion. "Send someone over to the legate and tell him what's happening." Then he called to the man below. "You may enter alone. Leave your horse. You must agree to be searched for hidden weapons."

The messenger led his mount back to his comrades and handed the reins to one of them. He removed his cloak and draped it over his saddle. Finally, he took a long knife out of the decorated scabbard at his waist and handed it to the third man. He sauntered back and took up his former position in front of the gate which inched open just wide enough to admit him. With Soranus leading the way, a legionary on either side and the centurion taking up the rear, he was escorted into the Praetorium where Publius Quadratus awaited him in the conference room. The legate was not alone. He sat in a chair with his senior officers, all in their best armour, standing on either side. Aldermar was at his right hand. The escort saluted and left the room. Soranus took his place at the end of one line of officers.

Quadratus saw a lean warrior in his prime. He was unusually dark for a German but his eyes were grey-blue, sharp and intelligent in his tanned face. A green tattooed snake crawled over each of his cheeks with their open mouths meeting in the centre of his forehead, His hair was dressed in two thick plaits falling down to his belt and his beard was drawn through an ornate silver ring. He bowed courteously but without deference.

"I bring you the greetings of King Gebhardus, General Quadratus," he said in his accented Latin.

"You may not call me "general". I am Legate Quadratus. You know my name, what is yours?"

"I am Hulderic…" he replied.

"You are not Treverii," Aldermar broke in.

Hulderic smiled and turned his head towards the big cavalry prefect.

"After the desolation made by Great Caesar, those who were left picked themselves up and forged new kinships. I serve King Gebhardus of the Treverii as you serve Rome although you are not Roman.

"Hulderic, what is your king's message to me?" Quadratus asked.

"General… I apologise… Legate, my king is in a border dispute with the Tungri. The truth of the matter is that they claim cornlands which have always belonged to the Treverii. The harvest is not far off and they are massing forces against my king. If he is forced to fight, the corn may be lost and his subjects will go hungry over the winter. As an ally of Rome, he asks that you will come to his aid with all your men. The sight of your legion will deter the Tungri and the problem may yet be resolved without bloodshed if you will give your judgement on the rights of the matter."

Quadratus looked into the distance as he thought for a moment.

"Whichever side I favour I will make an enemy of the other. There is no advantage to Rome in our intervention."

"No advantage, legate but a peril for you if you do not."

"Explain Hulderic," Quadratus said with an edge in his voice.

Hulderic held up his hands placatingly. "I mean no offense. I simply point out that Rome will be shown to have abandoned one of its allies when they requested aid. What will your other friendly tribes make of that?"

"You dare to stand under my roof threatening me?"

"No threat; if I speak badly remember I am using your tongue not my own. My king needs your help. Will you give it?"

"No, I shall not. It is four days march to the city of King Gebhardus. I am to denude my stronghold of its men to go to his aid because a stranger who claims to be his ambassador rides in out of the wild and spins me a story? This interview is terminated," Quadratus told him flatly.

Hulderic nodded his head and stepped towards the legate. "Here," he said, "thus is the final part of my king's message," he said and drew a soft leather pouch out of his tunic.

The officers stiffened and fists dropped to sword hilts but Quadratus took the pouch and opened it, lifting out a shining ornament on a heavy chain. It was a rectangle of thick gold the size of a man's palm. On one side was a relief of Caesar's bull and on the other the initials "SPQR" symbolizing "on behalf of the senate and people of Rome". The legate looked up at Hulderic sharply.

"Yes, legate, it belonged my king's father, put into his hands by Great Caesar. Now it is the property of King Gebhardus and the sign of his pact with Rome. He charges me to say that he believes the noble Quadratus will come with his men and return it in person. If he does not, it has no value and you are welcome to it."

"Wait outside," the legate told Hulderic and gestured his officers to come closer and look at the medallion. It had the aura of a holy object to them. Caesar was now a god, "The Divine Julius", and here was an object touched by the divinity.

"Does this change anything, gentlemen?" asked Quadratus.

"It adds to the legitimacy of the both the messenger and his message," Tertius said. "But nothing can justify the entire legion marching out other than military necessity or an order from headquarters."

The legate nodded his agreement. "What have you to add, Prefect Aldermar?"

"Putting the famous token into your hands is a powerful argument in favour of going to the rescue of Gebhardus but I remain uneasy, sir."

Various opinions were put forward and suggestions made by the other officers. Quadratus listened to them all then rose to his feet and paced the room looking intently at the golden medallion in his hands.

"Tribune Soranus, get twenty legionaries with shields and lances out the gate and bring in those other two visitors. Kill them if they refuse to come quietly. Lucius, call Hulderic back if you will."

When Hulderic stood in front of the legate once more, Quadratus spoke to him with a smile.

"You have persuaded me. The legion will march to King Gebhardus."

"Thank you, noble legate. My men and I will ride at once to give him the good news."

"No, my friend, you will not. Your king expects me so there is no need. Instead you will be my guests in the stockade until I return. You will be well-treated, have no fear. Tribune Longius, show Hulderic his accommodation."

The stockade was a simple log cage built under the cover of the walkway to protect inmates from the worst of the weather. It was entered through a single gate hung on iron hinges and closed with a chain. Hulderic and his men were bundled inside. Their weapons were taken over to the gate for storage and their horses led into the stables.

Quadratus issued his orders.

"Tertius, I shall be taking the first cohort, three hundred cavalrymen plus half a dozen scouts and seventy of the missile troops. We'll be constructing a full marching camp each night. We need enough supplies for a thousand men in the field for four days but I don't want to be slowed down too much. The Treverii can feed us on the return journey in exchange for our assistance. Sort out the logistics for me, as soon as you like. Titus, I need you, Boxer and Aldermar with me. We'll leave Corvo and Soranus together with the remnants of the cavalry and archers in support of Tertius who commands in my absence. We march at first light. To your tasks, gentlemen."

"That light mule cart of yours might be useful..." Tertius suggested to Lucius.

"Of course, I will make it available, sir. Felix can drive it and Otto will ride with me."

"Is Felix up to it?" Titus demanded.

"Oh yes, he's just not so nimble on his feet that's all but I shall give him the choice."

"Very well, I'll give you a chit so you can get some kit for him. Can't leave the poor sod in just a tunic if it gets interesting...."

At dawn, with three pairs of eyes staring hard at them between the bars of the stockade, the First Cohort of The Second Lucan fell in.

Their cavalry support brought up the rear following four light wagons each drawn by six mules and Felix perched up on the seat of Lucius' cart. Quadratus mounted his horse and walked it to the head his of troops, half-deafened by the thundering of javelin shafts beating on shields in salute. Brass horns blared, the Porta Decumana opened and they marched, heading out to the south and east.

The June weather was what it should be; warm but with enough showers to swell the grass and corn before harvest. The rain was not heavy and prolonged enough to impede the progress of the cohort as it made its steady progress towards the Treverii lands. Tertius had done a good job of organising their transport. The wagons hauled by their teams of six mules easily kept up at the swinging pace of the infantry. Felix was truly happy on his high seat looking along the line of legionaries with their equipment slung on forked sticks over their shoulders. To be on the march under the eagles with the legate's flag proudly carried aloft, the sound and smell of the army all around was a dream made real. For the duration of this expedition he was readmitted into the world he loved above all other; where he belonged.

The days were long in high summer so far north. Quadratus felt secure in continuing on their way for an hour more than usual before sending men out to find a place for their marching camp. A wide glade with a rivulet running through it was discovered and they began construction. Every legionary dug his part of the protective trench three feet wide and three feet deep, throwing the earth up on the inside to form a rampart. Then the sharpened stakes were taken off the carts and placed upright in the ground on top of the soil rampart. Green boughs from the nearby trees were woven between them to make tall hurdles. The archers and slingers stood by on the alert, ignoring the ribald comments of their toiling comrades. The cavalry horses and mules were picketed inside the temporary fortress. Only when the works had been completed and the animals fed and groomed did they light fires and cook their rations. Quadratus had a tent to himself. The officers settled under the wagons. The legionaries and the cavalrymen wrapped themselves in their cloaks and slept on the ground. As the long twilight dwindled into darkness, all was quiet other than for the occasional snorting of the animals and the sound of the sentries calling-in and being rotated. In the morning, they pulled out the stakes, filled in the trench, breakfasted and moved on.

Throughout the second day they had to travel uphill on a long, gradual slope. It did not appear to be noticeably steep but it took its toll of the mules. They were working hard to keep to the pace of the infantry and the column slowed as the morning wore on. By mid-afternoon, groups of legionaries were detailed to lean their shoulders into the back of the wagons to help the struggling animals. Just before they were due to find a place to secure themselves overnight, the ground flattened out again but by the time they were behind their ditch and rampart, they were exhausted. Quadratus was satisfied with their progress. The extra hour they had covered on the first day compensated for the shorter distance they had been able to cover today and they remained on schedule. In a miasma of horse-sweat, man-sweat and woodsmoke, they slept as soon as they lay down under their blankets. The quarter-moon rose and the stars wheeled over them unseen as the night passed.

Back in the permanent legion camp, all was equally peaceful. The sentries paced, the guard was changed and the rest of the legion slept. As the moon began to set, long shadows crept out across the parade ground. In the stockade, Hulderic unplaited his braids and drew out two lengths of finely woven, waxed horsehair with a small loop at each end. On his nod, one of his companions moved forward to the gate and began to make a mewing noise, high-pitched and keening as if he was in pain. The guard pacing his monotonous path up and down in front of the bars stopped and peered into the gloom. He saw a pair of glittering eyes in the gloom and banged on the gate with his shield.

"Get back, there," he ordered but the unblinking eyes stared back at him.

He leaned in closer with his face almost touching the rough logs to see what was going on. He caught a flicker of movement out of the corner of his eye but before he could register that is was a man's hand, he felt something touch the back of his neck under his helmet rim. A second hand appeared and grabbed the other end of the cord that Hulderic had flipped through the gap. The soldier suddenly felt the pain of it cutting into his neck and half-turned as he struggled. It bit in deeper. He bled and choked and died, held upright by the garotte wrapped around the wooden bars of the prison. They pulled his javelin inside and used the shaft as a lever to stretch the locking chain. One link was prised apart. They slipped its neighbour through the gap. The chain was loose and they were free.

They stripped the body of its belt, helmet, cloak and weapons before making their furtive way to the foot of the nearest ladder leading up to the walkway. Hulderic put on the dead man's helmet and flung his cloak over his shoulders. Holding the javelin, he climbed up and stepped out onto the platform. There was one sentry nearby. Hulderic walked confidently up to him. Only when they were face to face did the soldier notice the German's long, unbound hair. Before he could cry out, a pugio hit hm in the base of his throat and ended his life without a sound being made. Hulderic grabbed the body and eased it to the planks. He dragged it into the partial shelter of one of Attius' chests of stones. His two men scuttled up to him at a crouch. They took the belt and weapons off their second victim and pulled his cloak from under him. They bundled up both cloaks and flung them over the wall then buckled the belts together before looping them over one of the sharpened points of the palisade logs. The distance to the ground was fifteen feet but by using the joined belts, it was reduced to a drop of just over ten feet. The first man swung down and let go. He landed safely between the defensive sharpened sticks bristling out of the earth of the rampart. He wrapped the cloaks protectively around two of the nearest just as the next man landed beside him. Hulderic came last. They went down into the ditch and crawled towards the south eastern corner before easing themselves out and making for the forest. When they were beyond arrow-range, they gave up any attempt at concealment. They stood upright and ran, zigzagging around the moonlit tree-stumps as fast as they could go. Lungs labouring and hearts racing, they arrived under the cover of the trees where they were met by a mounted man holding the reins of three spare horses. They flew up into the saddles and were gone.

The sentry stared out into the darkness thinking to himself that half of Germany could be out there for all he could see. He sighed and glanced along the length of the walkway towards his nearest companion but saw no-one. He was not worried at first but he thought it odd. Several minutes ago, he had seen another legionary climb the ladder and walk towards the missing man. He strolled over to where his comrade should be but the stretch of walkway was empty. He called down the ladder but no response came. As he turned to go back to his post, he saw a huddled shape in the shadow of the chest full of stones. He went nearer and leaned over for a closer view. With shock, he realised what he was seeing. He recoiled and his boot skidded in the blood spreading out over the planks.

"Alarm! Alarm!" he shouted through cupped hands.

His shout was taken up and repeated. Whistles blew. The sound of running men floated up to him. The guardroom door was flung open by the duty optio.

"Alarm, sir," he yelled into the darkness of his bedroom.

Before he had even got out of his bed, the senior centurion of the second cohort gave his first order.

"Get the bugler to sound the stand-to," he barked.

Before the last notes had died away, the barrack's doors were all open and men poured out into the night. They ran to their positions, struggling into their armour. It may have looked as disorganized as an overturned anthill but the soldiers knew what they were about. In less than five minutes they were forming their ranks. Torches and braziers were lit to give a wavering yellow light to the parade ground and walkway. The centurion moved among them, dressed only in a tunic but carrying his naked sword in one hand and his vine-staff in the other.

"Explain," he said brusquely to the optio of the night-watch who stood at attention in front of him.

"Two casualties, both dead, prisoners absconded, sir," he said and saluted.

The officer gave a cursory return salute.

"Show me," he demanded.

By the light of a guttering pine-pitch torch he inspected the dead soldier on the walkway and the other slumped against the stockade. His face was a like a mask carved in granite.

"Leave them where they are. Touch nothing," he ordered.

By this time, Tertius had arrived, fully dressed and armoured and looking like he had spent several hours preparing for a parade. He stopped in front of the centurion who had taken control and raised one eyebrow inquisitively.

"It looks like the prisoners have escaped and murdered two of ours in the process, Tribune Fuscus."

"I grieve for our comrades," Tertius said. "The man Hulderic has deceived us once, therefore we must assume nothing. Triple the sentries. Have the entire camp searched for concealed intruders or any other victims of this atrocity." He looked up at the sky. The stars had faded and a green tinge showed dawn was not far off. "Re-assemble the men as soon they've finished. Impress on them they must be thorough. ..." Soranus trotted up looking dishevelled and still a little sleepy. "Tribune Soranus, adjust your uniform and stand by to take roll call as soon the men have fallen in."

Orders were roared out and the legionaries dispersed to perform their search.

Taking the centurion to one side, Tertius told him that they could do little more until they had some daylight and suggested they breakfasted together in the Praetorium while they waited. A good soldier always eats if he can and rests if he can, the centurion agreed but went to his own quarters and put on his armour first. Their conversation was desultory as they ate. Both of them kept glancing at the shutters until enough shafts of light were pouring through to show that full day had dawned. The walked together to the stockade, hearing the chanting of names and the clashing of armour as the roll was taken and each centurion marched up to Soranus and reported his men all accounted for with a salute. The tribune was now wide-awake and fully dressed.

Tertius took a long careful look at the body on the walkway. He noted the linked belts, the foot marks on the earth rampart below and the cloaks bundled around the points of two of the stakes. He examined the other dead soldier, still half-hanging from the stockade. He also inspected the javelin lying beside the corpse with a bruised and dented wooden shaft. When he descended, Soranus had completed the rollcall. No-one was missing.

"Get our murdered comrades down and laid out decently. I am holding a council of officers. Who speaks the best German in the absence of Otto?" Tertius asked.

"Decanus Martellus Flaccus, sir," Soranus responded.

"A decanus? Oh well, I shall need him nevertheless, also Cestus Valens. Off you go tribune; meeting in the Praetorium as soon as possible. In the meantime, send over the sentry who discovered the first body."

The legionary was pale and desperately trying not to shake as he stood in front of his tribune.

"A man was killed within fifty paces of you and yet you saw nothing?"

"Standing orders are to look out over the surroundings sir, not to spend too much time looking along the parapets…. to avoid distractions, sir."

"I understand and yet it happened very close to our position. You are sure you heard or saw nothing?"

"Well there was something. A legionary came up the ladder and went over to Caius, he's the dead man, sir. It was dark so I couldn't make him out properly but I saw his outline. He was wearing an army cloak and helmet and carrying a javelin, sir."

Tertius nodded gravely. "Soldier, you have just confirmed my first impression." He scribbled a note on a wax tablet and handed it to the terrified man. "Take this to your centurion. It says you are to return to normal duty without a black mark on your record."

The Praetorium was packed with the legion's officers. They sat on benches and stools the clerks had borrowed from anywhere they could find them. Behind the seated men, others stood shoulder to shoulder against the walls. Those for whom there was no room crowded into the open doors and spilled out onto the veranda. Martellus sat at attention, acutely aware of his lowly rank in this assembly. Tertius walked around his desk and half-sat leaning on the front, arms folded.

"Gentlemen, it is necessary for me to go back to the beginning for all of us to have a perfect understanding of the position in which we find ourselves. The man calling himself Hulderic with two henchmen alleged he was an ambassador of King Gebhardus of the Treverii and pleaded for our help. He was in fact, a liar, a traitor and a murderer. Legate Quadratus was persuaded in part, as was I, and the first cohort marched to the support of our ally, as you know. Last night, Hulderic and his men fled, killing two of ours. Now, the question I ask myself is why did they not make their escape during the first night of their captivity? The only answer is that they waited until our comrades were so far away that we could not rush to their assistance. Our legate, our first spear centurion and the men with them have fallen into a trap. My instincts are the same as yours; to march at once for rescue or revenge. This we cannot do. Our duty is to hold this camp and await developments. I am putting The Second Lucan on a war footing. Cestus Valens will make the most efficient dispositions of his artillery on the towers, parapets and parade ground to give us the maximum opportunity of both defending ourselves and hitting back if attacked. Stand up Decanus Martellus Flaccus."

Martellus stood up.

"Decanus, I want the men in the fort at the end of the bridge withdrawn and replaced with two cavalrymen. Their orders are to light the signal fire at the first sign of enemy activity on the bridge and then gallop back to the fort. Four others will ride reconnaissance two miles out from the camp throughout the daylight hours. Finally, the three best-mounted of the auxiliary cavalry will follow the second cohort's tracks and report what they find. Now, Martellus, if I give you this as a written order, are you sure you can convey it to the Germans, exactly?"

"I am sir."

"Good, I was told I could rely on you. Tribune Soranus, you will escort the signalling outpost garrison back here leaving two cavalrymen in their place. That is all, gentlemen. Let us prepare and let no-one fail to pray to the Gods for the safe return of our good comrades of the first cohort."

Chapter 24

While Tertius was putting the camp onto a war footing, Quadratus and his troops were making good progress towards their destination.

"If all goes well, we shall arrive at the hall of King Gebhardus by noon tomorrow," Quadratus thought then immediately touched his lucky amulet and made the sign against bad luck. He was an experienced campaigner and knew better than to believe that because there had been no problems so far, that there would be none to come. After only a few minutes, his heart sank a little as he heard hoofbeats approaching at speed. He knew this was not going to be news he wanted to hear. Aldermar pulled up his horse and saluted.

"I am worried, sir," he said.

"Aren't we all?" Quadratus replied then thought he had been flippant. "Apologies, Prefect Aldermar, what is causing your concerns?"

"The men on scouting duty are rotated every three hours to rest their horses. At least two of them should be back by now but none of them has reported in."

The legate pulled his horse to the side and waved the column on. Aldermar joined him. The previous day, they had climbed onto a high heath. The land as far as they could see on every side rolled and dipped into shallow valleys and hillocks. There were some coppices of ash and birch but no densely forested areas. It did not seem likely country for an ambush but still…. Quadratus reviewed his options. He started from the assumption that the scouts were dead and he was now forced to march blind. They were closer to the Treverii than to their permanent camp. If he turned back, a rapid enemy force could bypass him and attack in the forest. He could travel only as fast as his transport would allow. If he went forward, it was possible that they would be in action very soon. If this was to happen, the surrounding terrain was more favourable to the Roman method of manoeuvring than the confined spaces of the forest. He made his decision.

"I grieve for the loss of your good men, Aldermar. Take up a position in the rear and keep your troopers together."

The prefect galloped off and Quadratus signalled for Titus Attius to join him.

"We've lost our scouts, Titus. It seems as if someone plans to dispute our right to march where we will. Shorten the column and double up the ranks, wagons in the centre with my flag and the eagles. I want fifty men designated as reserves under your personal command ready to join the fight, if there is one, where they are needed most. Give Boxer my compliments and tell him to range his men alongside the transport, bows and slings at the ready. Can you think of anything else?"

The first spear centurion thought for a moment and shook his head.

"Nothing. The gods with you, sir"

"And with you. Titus," the legate replied and trotted his horse into the middle of his men.

Helmund, warlord of the Marcomanni, looked at his forces assembled in the valley with bitter disappointment. It was one thing to pledge warriors to destroy the Romans when the ale was flowing and the fires were bright, another to commit to facing them in battle in the cold light of day. He had been promised ten thousand but there were barely three thousand looking up at him and awaiting his words. If Hulderic had cajoled the entire legion to march, Helmund would have been forced to look on while they passed by. His intelligence had reported that a thousand Romans were on the march. He knew the strength of his enemy. He knew the route that they were using. His men outnumbered the Roman force by three to one and had the element of surprise on their side. It should be enough. He stepped forward and began to issue his commands.

The first cohort upped their pace once their new order of march was established. Swords were eased in scabbards, tighter grips taken on javelins and shield handles. Facing forward, their eyes flicked from side to side over the landscape searching for the tell-tale reflection of a spear point or the shape of a warrior accidently revealed in his hiding place. They saw nothing. They went down a shallow incline. When the ground levelled again, they found a hill to their right capped with bracken and a few spindly trees. A narrow stream ran around its base.

The far bank was broad and level, covered in short grass for ten paces back. To their left, a lower hill rose but its side was broken by sharp rocks jutting up between gorse and brambles.

Helmund had chosen this spot with care. He lay in cover near the top of the hill above the stream watching as his oblivious prey walked into the killing ground he had chosen. Then he narrowed his eyes and looked more closely. They were not spread out as he had expected but in a compact, defensive formation. He cursed and gestured to the men beside him ready to launch the assault. There were no large trees nearby so he had ordered four silver birches to be felled. Their trunks had been cut into ten-foot lengths and lashed together in a bundle to give enough combined weight to do serious damage. He raised and dropped his right arm, his men heaved on levers and the logs rolled. They turned slowly at first and for a few moments, Helmund thought they would be stopped by the bracken but they gained speed as gravity took over. Within two breaths, they were hurtling down onto the Roman right flank. They began to bounce and accelerated even faster when they flew through the air. At another signal, Helmund's main force stood up from their cover. The tactic had been that they would begin their charge as soon as the logs were released but they hesitated, waiting to see what effect they would have when they smashed into the enemy below.

The immediate response to the onrushing mass was yelling, whistle blowing and horn calls from the Roman ranks who had halted as one. The logs pinwheeled and jumped the stream but the legionaries standing in their path leaped out of the way, leaving them to smash into the front wheel of the lead wagon. The spokes collapsed and the wagon tottered on its remaining wheels, unable to move. The back legs of the rear mule were broken. It fell in its traces, kicking and thrashing. The driver jumped down and cut its throat. The Romans had been brought to a halt. A fierce cheer rose up from the attackers who resumed their onward rush. As they did, they saw the Roman cavalry cantering away back the way they had come. They checked again, brandishing their spears and yelling their scorn at the cowards fleeing before the battle had even begun.

Quadratus sat calmly on his horse. It was his duty to let the men see him cool and untroubled to give them confidence. The direction of the fight was in the hands of the senior centurion. Titus Attius was already shouting and gesturing to the nearest legionaries to cross the stream and form up, three-deep.

"Never mind getting your fucking feet wet, get over there.

He whacked two or three with his vine-staff to hurry them up, not with any venom, but simply to make his point. A solid arc of Roman shields was almost complete, some of the legionaries standing ankle deep in the water, when the first warriors collided with them. They hit with all the impetus of a downhill charge and their battle-rage but behind each legionary stood two more, bracing him against the impact. The Roman line buckled and reformed as it was heaved back against the pressure. The cacophony of thudding blows, the ringing of metal on metal, war-cries, screams and groans rose and echoed off the hillsides.

The Romans crossing the stream was a major setback to Helmund. He had thought that they would see it as a natural barrier and seek to defend it, leaving his own men more room to manoeuvre on the flat bank. However, their horsemen had left the field and that was a huge advantage both damaging the enemy's morale and encouraging his own warriors. Overall, his plan was working out. He gave another signal and the smaller portion of his force rose up from amongst the scrub on the left bank and began to shower arrows and spears down onto the Romans.

Lucius reacted quickly when arrows began to thud into the ground and wagons around him. Felix knew he was no use in a melee so he had elected to stay on the seat of his cart with a long, broad-bladed siege spear to thrust at any enemy who came within range. Lucius shouted to his men and soon Helmund's archers and spearmen began to fall to sling bullets when they rose up to fire or throw. But several rear-rank legionaries had been hit from behind as they struggled to hold their comrades upright and in position. Titus saw the problem and brought in his reserves to make a shield wall facing the other way to protect them. He looked over the helmets of his front line. He saw a mass of Germans howling and shoving each other aside to get at his own men. A few were armoured in mail or plate, some had leather jerkins but most wore only long tunics, some were naked but they all had spears and axes. Their faces were twisted into grimaces of fury and bloodlust. It was a sight to drain the courage of the bravest but Titus had been there before and survived. He looked around and decided that Lucius' century was responding well to the threat from the rear. It was time for him try to break the grip that the Germans had on his men. Every legionary carried two javelins, over eighteen hundred in all. Titus shouted for them to be passed back.

"Rear rank cast your javelins!" he yelled.,

The was order repeated along the line. He grabbed half a dozen of the weapons and shouted to Otto who was beside Lucius and the transport.

"Here," he said, thrusting them into Otto's hands. "Start chucking these but aim for one of the bastards in armour."

Using them against a dispersed enemy and having to cast uphill, would have been a waste of these effective weapons but now the attackers were packed tightly on the lowest slope of the hill. The legionaries did not have to aim. They lobbed their javelins over the heads of their comrades and let them drop, sure that most of them would hit a target. Within two minutes, they had all been thrown. One third of Helmund's men were out of the fight; dead or wounded. Otto paced behind the ranks like a caged lion. He was tall enough to have a good view over the heads of the legionaries and when he saw the opportunity, he flung a weapon with massive force. He had only one left but knew that his first five had each struck a leading warrior.

Helmund could see his victory becoming less certain as the minutes ticked away and the pile of his own dead rose in front of his enemy. Those wicked short swords stabbed out like striking snakes and his numerical advantage had dwindled sharply after the javelin attack. The Roman officers blew their whistles. Their soldiers rotated, putting fresh men in front of his own. But his warriors were still taking the battle to the enemy whose line could not hold forever; there was still hope. Then he heard a chilling sound.

Hoofbeats shook the ground and the Roman cavalry appeared at the charge. To make it worse, they came from an unexpected direction. They had left the rear of the Roman column but were now at what had been its head. They carved into the flank of his men on the flat ground and lower slopes. Their long swords rose and fell as they chanted their war-songs. Helmund's men were trampled and bitten by the horses as the blades of their riders rose and fell again, now red with blood. A tremor seemed to run through the Germans as the instinct for survival began to take the place of determination. Aldermar's horn call pulled his horsemen back, to re-group as they were irresistible in a charge knee to knee but were vulnerable if isolated. The line formed again, the great war-horses shaking their heads and stamping until the call sounded and their blood-spattered riders gave a roar as they battered the Germans again. Helmund's warriors reeled under this fresh onslaught that they were unable to resist. It looked as if they could not endure for many more minutes. But Fortuna is a fickle goddess.

In the red waters of the stream, a fallen German lashed out with an axe in his death throes. He had not chosen his target; he could no longer see but his blow hit a legionary on the ankle of his leading leg and chopped right through it. The soldier screamed and toppled forward. The second rank man who had been pushing on both of his shoulders with all his strength was caught off balance and he too staggered and tripped over his fallen comrade. In an instant a dozen warriors flooded through, hacking at the breach in the Roman line, causing it to fold back on either side. Titus jumped in, stabbing and thrusting with his sword and laying about him with his vine-staff.

"Reserve on me! Reserve on me!" he yelled.

They responded at the run and soon the intruders were contained and being forced back as the Roman front was re-established. But three had escaped Titus and now dashed towards Quadratus. He drew his sword and defended himself against the leading man who thrust at him with a spear, one of them dodged from foot to foot, unwilling to commit himself but the third had run around to the back of Quadratus' horse. He flung himself under it from the side and sliced its belly open with a long, curved knife. The dying beast screamed as its paunch and entrails slithered out of the gaping wound and it fell forward, flinging Quadratus over its head. He had somersaulted as he was thrown. The wind was knocked out of him when he landed flat on his back. He lay there stunned. The spearman grinned and lifted his face to the sky making an offering of this Roman's life to his gods. He raised his spear to strike. Quadratus was perfectly conscious but unable to move. He looked up at his killer with a composed face, determined to die with calm acceptance as a Roman should.

The German tightened his grip on his spear until his knuckles whitened then fell sideways with a javelin transfixing his neck. Otto had seen his legate fall and had cast the last javelin that Titus had given him. It had found its mark. He ran forward with his long cavalry sword in one hand and his pugio in the other and engaged the two remaining warriors. Otto was big and he was fast but there were two of them and they knew their business. With Quadratus at his feet, he parried and counterattacked. One was trying to get behind him and when he fought to prevent that, he was open to the other one. All the time he knew he could not move freely but had to stand over the legate. In desperation, he dropped to his knees and sent a scything blow with all his force at the legs of the man in front of him. The blade cut him to the bone on his upper thigh. Blooded jetted up and the man fell. Otto felt a hot line of pain on the side of his head. He did not get up but thrust his sword diagonally backwards over his shoulder. He felt the shock as it hit something, stopped and slid on. Suddenly it seemed very heavy. He scrambled to his feet and saw that his blade was embedded in the chest of the horse-killer. Titus ran up shouting for a fresh mount. Lucius dragged his over by the reins.

"Get the legate in the saddle," he commanded.

Quadratus was beginning to come-to and tried to assist them as they hauled him onto the horse's back. He grasped the reins struggling to sit upright.

From his vantage a little way up the hill, Helmund had seen the legate fall.

"Their general is dead! Their general is dead. We have the victory! Press on my warriors and they will break!" He screamed again and again.

They heard him. A triumphant growl rose from their throats and they flung themselves against the Roman shields. But the wordless cry of victory turned to a moan as the legate's plumed helmet rose once more above the heads of the fighting men. Quadratus seized the moment and trotted his horse to-and-fro behind his soldiers.

"We have them now boys, holdfast; holdfast and the day is ours!"

The Germans on the left-hand hill had the best view of the situation. They saw their dead comrades littering the slope with spears sticking out of their bodies. They saw the heap of corpses spread in front of the Roman infantry. They saw the bloody gap Aldermar's cavalry had bitten into the flank of their forces. They decided their fight was over and began to filter away between the gorse bushes and rocks. Soon the men on the other side began to do the same and within ten minutes, they had all melted away over the hill.

"Stand down!" Titus ordered.

The weary legionaries stayed in place but let their aching sword arms fall. They grounded their shields and leaned on them, breathing deeply. Their respite did not last long. A flurry of orders got them scurrying about the battlefield.

Four hours later, they were as secure as they could be in a marching camp one mile upstream. Even though it was only mid-afternoon, cooking fires were lit and most of the men resting. The mule that had been killed was jointed and roasting slowly on makeshift spits. The fifteen Roman dead, including a centurion and an optio were being cremated downwind of the camp. There were thirty-three wounded all of which should recover to march again. Among them was Otto who now had a curved line of black stitches above the ear on the shaven side of his head. The German wounded had been killed with a sword thrust after a good kicking to make them reveal any information they had; it was very little. But at least the Romans knew their attackers had been Marcomanni under Helmund. All the bodies had been looted and their weapons collected. Titus was now in possession of a sack of silver arm rings and scores of spears and axes on behalf of the cohort.

The officers sat on camp stools a little apart around a small fire.

"What I want to know is what they are doing here," Aldermar said. "Marcomanni lands are far to the north and east beyond the Elbe."

"When I make my report to headquarters, they might come back to me with some information on the subject. I shall certainly raise your question," Quadratus told him.

"I would like to ask you something, Prefect Aldermar but I hope you will take no offence," Lucius said.

"Come on then, Boxer cough it up."

"Why were you so late joining the battle and why did you come from the opposite direction?"

"Do you accuse me of anything?" the prefect hissed, turning a frowning face on Lucius.

"No, of course not... But I...." he struggled to respond.

Aldermar laughed. "Sorry Boxer; I couldn't resist it but I'm sure Legate Quadratus will be able to answer you better than I can."

"To maximize their effect on the battlefield, a cavalry unit must engage at speed and in tight formation. When our column was forced to stop so abruptly, the cavalry was at a standstill. They therefore withdrew and circled behind the hill. They let the conflict develop until Prefect Aldermar judged the best moment to charge had arrived. Too early, and his men would have been forced back. Too late, and there would be no point in joining the action. As it was, they came just when our opponents were beginning to lose heart and from an unexpected direction to add to their dismay. Have I explained to your satisfaction, Prefect of Auxiliary Cavalry Aldermar?"

"To perfection, noble Legate Publius Quadratus of The Second Lucan," Aldermar responded with a bow of the head.

Quadratus sighed.

"What exercises me now is what to do about Otto. He saved my life, killed the men who had brought me down and stood over me while he did so. Those, gentlemen, are the conditions to award him a civic crown. But Otto is neither a legionary nor a citizen and therefore does not qualify. I shall give his action prominence in my report and ask for the suggestion of my superiors. In the meantime, I have expressed my undying gratitude."

Chapter 25

Twenty miles away Helmund walked his horse steadily northwards. The half dozen of his lieutenants who had remained with him were downcast but their leader's face was impassive. He was hunched over in the saddle, staring down at his horse's neck, analysing his defeat. He acknowledged that relying on the stream as a barrier had been an error. At a different time of year, the rains would have made it deeper and more difficult for the Romans but that would have applied equally to his men when they were forced to cross it. No, there were other reasons why the battle had been lost. The first was the javelin volleys that had caused such heavy casualties, the second was the way his men had attacked along the whole length of the Roman shield wall. He would have to come up with some way of reducing the devastating losses from the thrown javelins and of putting maximum pressure on one narrow section of the Roman line. He nodded his head and sighed. He promised himself that there would be a next time and then he would triumph.

The first cohort broke camp before the sun rose with Venus setting in an otherwise starless sky. They were continuing their journey to the city of King Gebhardus. By full light they were on the road passing the site of yesterday's battle. Foxes and wolves had mauled some of the German corpses which the legionaries simply spat on or cursed as they tramped along. Hulderic had lied to Quadratus but there was still the matter of the gold medallion. The legate wanted to know what Gebhardus had to tell him. Also, the whole district would have heard the news of the ambush. Rumours would be flying; some of them proclaiming a major defeat for the forces of Rome. Letting it be seen that they had neither been stopped nor turned back would reinforce the belief in Rome's invincible power.

Aldermar found all his missing men before noon. The circling buzzards and ravens had shown him where to seek them. They lay where they had fallen; dead, stripped of their weapons and valuables. One horse still stood by its master, head hanging low. An arrow was embedded deeply in its chest and a fine mist of bright blood escaped its nostrils each time it exhaled. In a demonstration of solidarity, the legionaries dug a common grave for the cavalrymen. Weapons and arm-rings from the battle loot were put in with them so that they should not be impoverished in the afterlife. Aldermar officiated at the sacrifice of the wounded horse to the gods. Everyone took part in re-filling the pit. A cairn of stones was raised over it to keep the scavenging wild animals at bay.

They descended off the heathlands onto lower, more densely wooded ground, travelling without incident until half-way through constructing their marching camp when the riders Tertius had sent out made contact. Otto interpreted as they informed Quadratus of Hulderic's escape and that their orders were to return as soon as possible with any message the legate gave them. The scouts found the first cohort in good spirits; they had survived and gained yet another victory. They did not have to exaggerate the number or ferocity of the enemy they had encountered; Aldermar's men were expert at reading the ground and the whole story was as clear to them as if it they had been there when the fighting was at its height. The brother of one of them was among the dead. His grief was overwhelming but when he was told of the grave-goods and horse sacrifice, he felt the pain of his loss a little less keenly. At least his sibling would have comrades, wealth and weapons when he met him again in the hereafter. The other cavalrymen helped him to get so drunk he could not stand. Aldermar turned a blind eye. They lifted him onto his horse the next day, still half-conscious and he somehow stayed in the saddle as the trio set off for the main camp carrying a message to Tertius.

At ten the following morning, they broke through a screen of trees into the heartland of the Treverii. Homesteads surrounded by fields of corn appeared. The crops were just beginning to turn showing a hint of the yellow ripeness to come among their green stalks but there were no people and no livestock to be seen. Rome may be the ally of their king but the farmers and their families had picked up whatever they could carry and hidden in the woods, driving their animals before them as soon as they saw the glittering armoured column. Quadratus had given strict orders that there must be no harm done to the local inhabitants on pain of death. Even if the peasants had known that, they would not have believed it. Strangers carrying weapons only meant three connected outcomes; fire, rapine and death.

A few miles ahead, they had their first sight of the king's city. A triangular hill stood with its apex in the fork of a river, rising up like the prow of a ship. The two sides nearest to where the waters split reared up in steep, naked rock. But as it widened towards the third, south-western side, the slope grew less steep until it levelled off at its base. The Treverii had dug a deep ditch between the two arms of the river and heaped up the excavated soil to make a rampart, like the Romans did. They had covered it with dressed stone. Above this was a high palisade of upright pointed logs. The defences had been continued at each side until the point at which the almost vertical rock faces offered their natural protection. The front ditch was twenty feet wide and fifteen feet deep; even in high summer there were three feet of water in the bottom. It was crossed by a stone bridge, wide enough for ten men marching abreast, leading to a pair of wide gates which defended the principal entry to the city. The gates were open but the top of the palisade was crowded with armed men, staring down at the approaching Romans. The king's city was a formidable stronghold, big enough to contain his household and garrison in addition to the ten thousand people and their livestock who would head for its protection in the event of an invasion.

Quadratus halted his men just out of bowshot and shouted for Lucius and Otto.

"Carry my flag across to the gate and tell the guards I wish to speak with their king."

The flag snapped and cracked in the breeze as Lucius bore it upright, riding at a canter with Otto at his side. They stopped half-way over.

"The noble legate Publius Quadratus seeks immediate audience with King Gebhardus of the Treverii," Otto shouted up to the warriors crowding the parapet over the gate.

"My king will come out to you. Return to your soldiers," a voice called in reply.

They reported back and in less then two minutes, the king came through the gates.

The sun sparkled off his fish scale armoured shirt, split at front and back so it fell over his legs to the knees when he rode. He was mounted on a huge white horse. It could not have been easy to find one strong enough to carry his weight. He was bigger than Otto and much heavier. His hair had once been golden but now, in his fifties, it was shot through with white. He wore a long sword in a jewelled bronze scabbard by his side and a silver circlet around his brow. He stopped halfway between the end of the bridge and the Roman forces and briefly bowed his head

"Greetings," he called.

Quadratus rode forward alone. "Greetings king, not the friendliest of welcomes," he said, gesturing to the black silhouettes of archers and spearmen framed against the bright sky.

"But you will see that I have not shut my gates against my allies," the king responded. "Forgive my caution but I have heard that a Roman army has come into my land to bring war to me and my people."

"And where did you learn this?"

The king shrugged.

"Brought by birds on the wind; who knows how such tales spread? I also heard that a battle was fought near my borders and that you and all your men were dead; yet here you are."

"Why do you listen to rumours when I am at your gates in response to your urgent request for support against the Tungri who are about to seize your corn-lands?"

Gebhardus looked at Quadratus with complete incomprehension.

"Who told you that?" he asked after a pause to collect his thoughts.

"Your ambassador," the legate replied dryly.

The king shook his head. "I have not sent anyone to you. This is some plot against me...or you. Noble Legate Quadratus, come into my city with some of your officers and we shall discuss this in my hall." He saw the faintest flicker of doubt pass over the Roman's face. "Post fifty of your soldiers at my open gates as proof of my good faith. I will wait for you inside."

Quadratus rode back to his troops.

"I'm going in to speak with the king. Titus, get fifty of your men between the gates, they are to stay on the alert and not to go into the city. Aldermar, I want your cavalry drawn up on this side of the bridge. At the slightest hint of trouble, they are to charge and lay about them. The gates must not be closed at any price. Titus, have everyone ready to follow up the cavalry and get stuck in if there's trouble. Kill anyone who gets in your way. Also, find me the biggest, nastiest-looking centurion in the cohort, other than you, and six matching legionaries to accompany me. Boxer, you'd better come too..." Otto took a step forward alongside Lucius. "... Are you a Roman officer all of a sudden? Infernal Gods! What is the point in arguing? Come along, then. At least you might be useful if they start to talk in German."

Preceded by the King, Quadratus, Lucius and Otto, rode uphill through the city followed by a centurion and two files of legionaries with shields and swords but no javelins. Low, thatched houses with small gardens lined their route with the occasional smithy and other trades carried on under open-sided sheds. There were pigpens and stables, haystacks and middens, hens pecked around on the ground or searched for insects in the thatch. Chained dogs growled, women with babies on their hips or children peeping out from behind their skirts stared at them. Men briefly looked up from their occupations and then took no further notice of the small procession. The king's hall stood halfway up the hill. The walls were built of heavy logs, not the wattle and daub of his subjects' homes but, just like theirs, it carried a straw thatched roof. Inside was a large, dim space illuminated only by the light falling from the smoke-hole in the roof and slanting in through the doors. At the far end was a rostrum on which the royal throne was placed but Gebhardus did not take up his position there. Quadratus, Lucius and Otto were seated on benches on one side of a long, central table with the king and three of his nobles opposite them. The centurion and his six legionaries stood to attention behind their officers. Bread, cheese and mead in horn cups was set down in front of them. Gebhardus tore off a piece of bread and a nugget of cheese which he placed in his mouth and washed down with a little mead. Quadratus did the same. Now that they had broken bread together the sacred duties of friendship and hospitality had been fulfilled and they could get down to business.

"You have no need of a bodyguard in my hall," Gebhardus said.

"Purely ceremonial," the legate told him. "I must have a small number of soldiers about me at all times to uphold my rank. It's a bore, really but there we are. Now to business, do you know a dark-headed chieftain called Hulderic? He has a green snake tattooed on either side of his face."

"I know of no such man," the king replied.

"He came to me asking military assistance on your behalf. He begged me to march with my entire legion but that I cannot do for anyone without the orders of my Emperor or my general. If you know nothing of Hulderic or his embassy, what can you tell me of the Marcomanni?"

The name caused consternation amongst Gebhardus and his advisors. A torrent of German poured out, each of them talking over the other. At last the king spoke directly to the legate.

"They are a fierce and numerous people but their lands are weeks away to the north and east. Why do you ask about them?"

"Because three thousand Marcomanni ambushed me two days ago. Are you telling me that you were unaware of the presence of so many warriors on your borders?

"I swear it. But I have a question. Why did you march your men out on the word of an unknown stranger, is that not unbelievably rash?"

"It would have been if he had not given me this token to prove he was acting on your behalf," Quadratus replied, took the gold medallion from his belt pouch and laid it on the table in front of the king.

Gebhardus paled and his eyes went wide. He looked from the glistening object to the legate and back again without being able to frame a response. The man sitting next to him jumped up and ran into a side room, coming back almost instantly carrying a domed silver box which he reverently placed before his king. Gebhardus lifted back the lid, took out a piece of sable fur and unwrapped it revealing an identical lozenge of gold, marked with the bull emblem of Caesar. A burst of rapid-fire German rattled from the lips of one of his nobles.

"He says that what we have is a forgery made to blacken the reputation of King Gebhardus. The King wears the gift from Caesar to his father on all important occasions, it has been seen by thousands of people. Anyone could have copied it.," Otto translated.

"Let me tell you what I think all this means," said King Gebhardus. "You were lured from your stronghold with a false token. If you had fallen to the Marcomanni, the remaining soldiers in your fortress would have reported what had happened and the Treverii would have been blamed. Rome would have sent an army against me. I would have resisted on behalf of my people but we could not have prevailed. We would have been destroyed. The rest of your friends and client-kings in the Rhineland would see that Rome had made war on an old ally. All trust would have been lost. They would then take up arms themselves or at least make treaties of mutual support with hostile tribes."

Quadratus stood up and held out his right hand. The king rose and took it.

"King Gebhardus, friend and ally, I believe you have spoken the entire truth. I offer you my hand assuring you that no shadow of this incident will weaken the strong bonds between our peoples.

Remember, when we believed you needed us, Rome marched to your side."

With great relief the king asked Quadratus to feast with him that evening.

"I may not, King Gebhardus. I must rush back to my camp as soon as possible as it is undermanned. If you could spare some provisions…"

"We are nearly at the end of last year's harvest, but I shall offer what I can. If we do not have sufficient wheat is barley acceptable?"

"Whatever you can spare; I do not want your people to go without."

The party returned to the cohort and it formed up ready to march. Two wagons came out of the city carrying sacks of grain and leading an ox for slaughter. Quadratus had his soldiers give the looted weapons to the king's men and loaded the provisions into their own transport.

"Farewell, King Gebhardus, it seems we both have a new enemy, the Marcomanni."

"New enemies come along as regularly as the seasons, Legate Quadratus, journey safely," Gebhardus responded.

By eight-thirty, the cohort was twelves miles away in their marching camp with the slaughtered and jointed ox cooking over several fires. The long northern twilight was slowly fading into night and the men were at rest.

"Call an informal assembly, Titus," Quadratus ordered.

"All right you lot, gather round, your legate wants to speak to you. Gods know why 'cos you never understand bugger-all."

The soldiers stood in a relaxed half circle.

"Men of the First Cohort of The Second Lucan, I commend your actions on this expedition and I shall say so in my report to the general at headquarters. Now, politics forced me to give the Treverii the weapons we collected off the corpses of those scum who were so stupid as to launch a cowardly attack on us. Lads, all I can say is they know better now, in whatever hell they find themselves." A burst of laughter made him pause. "We still have the arm-rings to add to the legion treasure but there remains this." He took the medallion off its chain and held it up. "Forgery it may be but it is cast in good, solid gold. Now, I can add it to the other loot or I can have it fixed to our eagle as a trophy of our latest victory. What do you say?"

"Eagle! Eagle!" the men chanted as one.

"Very well, I have heard you. First Spear Centurion Attius, I give this into your safe keeping until it can be added to our battle honours. There remains the gold chain. Who is to have it?"

There was a considerable pause then a voice shouted out, "Felix, the chain for Felix!".

Quadratus raised his hand for silence. "Stand forward the man who named Felix."

A grizzled haired veteran marched over and saluted.

"Why did you choose him? Speak up now, we all want to hear."

"Sir," the legionary bellowed, "Felix is a crippled man with no rightful place on a battlefield yet he sat up straight right through the fight with arrows sticking in his cart and whistling round his head, holding onto his siege spear like a good 'un. He didn't flinch that I saw and he didn't get down behind his seat to hide. That's why, sir."

"Who is in agreement?" Quadratus called out.

"Felix! Felix! Felix" the legionaries chanted.

"I have heard you and agree. Soldier re-join your fellows. Where is Felix?"

He hobbled up and came the nearest he could to standing at attention.

"Former Decanus Felix, I and your comrades in the recent fight honour you."

He placed the gold chain over Felix' head and tried to ignore the tears running down the man's cheeks.

The officers, with Otto at Lucius' side, sat around their fire with watering mouths as the scent of freshly roasted beef wafted over them. It would soon be ready and not a moment too soon.

"The city of the Treverii would be difficult to take," Quadratus said, conversationally to take everyone's minds off their empty bellies.

"Not really," Titus responded. "I had a good look at that stone bridge. Roman engineering that is, must have been some gift from

Caesar. It's impressive but its too wide and too well built to demolish quickly. Capture the bridge and you're in."

"I had thought of damming the ditch and then bringing down part of the palisade with artillery," Lucius suggested.

"Take too long; no, hold the bridge, bring up a ram and smash the gates; quick, straight-forward, job done," Titus insisted.

"But you would lose a lot of men...."

"An officer who is overly-careful with his men's lives risks losing them all," the big centurion told him grimly.

Quadratus and Aldermar nodded their agreement. An orderly arrived with thick slices of smoking beef and platters of army bread which silenced all discussion for several minutes.

Aldermar sat back and wiped his greasy chin with the last of his bread before eating it.

"Now then, Boxer, as a keen student of all things military, you have not yet cross-examined our legate on the doings of the day," the prefect said.

Lucius looked directly at Quadratus.

"There is one thing, sir, if I may?"

"You may."

"Why didn't we camp outside the city? There was plenty of level ground."

"Ah," the legate replied, "a matter of diplomacy; if we had dug a ditch and raised a palisade, King Gebhardus would have been insulted at my lack of faith in his goodwill. On the other hand, I had no wish to leave my men at the mercy of the Treverii without any defences. Let us call it tactical expediency."

Tertius's scouts told him of the imminent return of the first cohort. They were greeted with horn calls from the camp when they came into sight. An honour guard snapped to attention and saluted as the legate rode in at the head of his men. Quadratus noted the number of extra sentries on the parapets and the artillery dispositions. He dismounted and exchanged salutes with Tertius.

"Report, Tribune Tertius Fuscus," he demanded.

"I grieve for our fallen comrades, sir but nevertheless, all is well with your legion and your camp, Legate Publius Quadratus. It is good to have you back."

"It is good to be back but it will be even better once I have bathed. Dine with me tonight, Tertius and we can exchange our gossip." The legate turned to Titus. "First Spear Centurion Attius, dismiss the men, wounded to the infirmary, normal duty roster to be resumed as of first watch tomorrow."

Over dinner, Quadratus listened carefully to Tertius' full account of the measures he had taken and the reasons for them.

"You have made a good beginning with The Second Lucan, Tertius," he told him. "The men have seen you in action and have gained some respect for you and you have taken command of the legion in my absence. I shall make mention of your attention to detail and tactical awareness in my report to headquarters. It will take me the next day or two to write it up so please retain your command unless there is something you must refer to me. I am going to request guidance on a suitable reward for Otto when I submit it."

"Otto," Tertius responded with a sigh. "He is an undoubted asset to the legion but his status…."

"Exactly," Quadratus interrupted. "I cannot now imagine not having him in the camp but there is no official capacity in which we can use him which matches his merits."

On the twenty-second of June, Quadratus received a response from headquarters. It informed him that the Marcomanni were probing in strength all along the border, testing Roman defences and resolve. His ambush experience was not unique. There was no doubt that this tribe was stepping up its aggression week by week and that it would soon launch a major offensive. The legate did not rush to take emergency measures but began to consult his senior officers. Their days of swatting away what amounted to little more than armed bandits were over. He would have to formulate a military response to the menace.

The next day, Tertius received a letter from home. He read it then called Lucius into his quarters.

"Do you remember I told you I had a brother in the courts in Rome? Well, I wrote to him and among other matters, I asked him to find out what he could about your grandfather. His reply will be interesting to you." He folded a scroll so that most of what was written on it was hidden and handed it to Lucius. "The rest of it is not relevant and refers to certain confidential family business. I hope you will not be offended?"

"Not at all; it was very good of you and your brother to take the trouble," Lucius said and began to read.

"The history of the unfortunate Taurius Vitius Longius' dealings with Marcus Antonius are still talked about by greybeards in banking and legal circles. When he held the office of Tribune of The People, Antonius approached Longius and told him that the state needed money, a lot of money and that it would cause a financial panic if he went directly to the bankers for a loan. Longius was a loyal citizen and asked what he could do to help. The upshot was that he borrowed an immense sum against the value of his estates and passed it over to Antonius as a loan at the lowest rate of interest he could manage. Of course, none of it ever went to the treasury. But this is where Antonius was cunning, as usual. He remitted the annual interest on the loan to Longius for a few years so the poor gentleman believed everything was as it should be. However, as soon as he was appointed Joint Consul with the Divine Julius, the interest payments ceased. When Longius approached Antonius, he told him that he could either never speak of the matter again or talk freely about it to his fellow prisoners in jail. The banks foreclosed. Longius was forced to sell his house to pay the lawyers and outstanding mortgage interest. He retired from Rome

almost penniless. I doubt if either he or his family could be numbered among those dedicated to the cause of Marcus Antonius."

Lucius handed the scroll back and tried to think what he could say. His mind was whirling. All he had believed about his family's political history was a lie.

"This is not the story my father told me," he said at last.

"Nor, I suspect, is it what he was told by his father. Put yourself in your grandfather's place for a moment. The head of a wealthy family of senatorial rank is duped out of his fortune by a highly placed rogue. He must have felt humiliated. Imagine looking at the masks of your illustrious ancestors and seeing nothing but scorn in their gaze. Better perhaps, to put it about that he was on the wrong side of politics in a very troubled period than admit he had been defrauded. Lucius, this is very good news for you. The stain of allegiance to the Antonians is washed away from your name. I shall have a scribe make a copy for you with a note from me telling how I came by this information. Send it to your father and between the two of you, make sure the truth has wings and flies. All I ask is that you keep my family name out of the public domain.."

Otto was also reading from his scroll of wisdom. He had made it a habit to read one item each week and then consider what he had read, as Aelia had instructed. He scanned the neat script and settled on a quotation of Lucretius.

"Time changes the nature of the world. Everything passes from one state to another and nothing stays as it is."

He extinguished his lamp and lay back on his cot, feeling the soft air of the summer night on his face. Lucretius' words struck him as obvious and not worth the bother of writing down. Of course, everything changes. Autumn gives way to winter. Rivers form ice, the ice melts and the rivers flow again. Babies are born, they grow into men and women then they die. He began to meditate on the words. The thought grew in him that they were more profound than he had first thought. If Lucretius was correct, there was no present when things were fixed; only a fleeting picture of the constant flux. If there was not really a present, what about the past and the future? Did they truly exist? He gave up and slept.

On the tenth day of July, Lucius and Otto were called to the legate's office. Quadratus was making a bad job of trying to suppress a grin.

"Otto Longius, I wrote to the general telling him of your courage and that I owe you my life. Tribune Lucius Taurius Longius, I also informed him of the unusual bond between you and Otto and how it came about. The general passed my letter to the Emperor and he wants to meet you both, in person."

"Who, the general, sir?" Otto asked.

Quadratus shook his head. "No, Augustus himself. You are summoned to Rome for an audience with the Emperor."

They looked at him in bewilderment, unable to take in the meaning of his words. Quadratus placed a tight role of papers across his desk.

"These are your permissions to use the Imperial Courier Service for horses and inns on both legs of your journey. You are to report initially to Tribune Cassius Plancus at the Praetorian Guards' barracks at the foot of the Palatine. I have added a note granting you ten days leave in Luca on your way back so that you may visit your family, Boxer. Here," he added, putting a bulging purse on the desk, "some money for necessaries or indeed luxuries, there is no need to account for how you spend it. Provided Augustus does not detain you I expect to see you before the end of September. Off you go, then. It really doesn't do to keep an Emperor waiting."

Chapter 26

Lucius and Otto reined in their horses to a walk and took their first look at the beating heart of the empire a few miles away along the Via Aurelia. The imperial seal on their documents had worked the magic that had seen them passed on from waystation to waystation like batons in a relay race. Each morning, a fresh horse was waiting for them and each evening, a bath, a meal and a bed. This was their eighteenth day on the road; they were travel-weary and their backsides protested at every step their mounts took but now the aches were forgotten at the sight of the greatest city in the world; sacred, rich and all-powerful Rome.

They had found the going much faster once they were on the Roman paved roads, as they had done on their previous journey to Luca. But this time they had given themselves no respite in their haste to obey the Emperor's summons; he was a being so close to a living god that his slightest whim demanded maximum effort. There was no real necessity to travel so hard but they were young and believed their strength and energy to be limitless.

The city erupted out of the hilly landscape. The closer they came, the more they appreciated the scale of what they were seeing. It was impossible to comprehend anything so vast had been made by human hands. They began to make out the shapes of walls and towers, roofs and the peristyles of temples. The road was not crowded as they approached in the early afternoon. Later, it would be packed with wagons bringing supplies of every type into the city but their drivers would have to wait until sunset to enter. No wheeled commercial traffic was allowed into the city in the hours of daylight. The ordinance kept the streets clearer for the citizens during the day but the nights of many of them were constantly disturbed by the squealing of ungreased wheels, the cracking of whips and the angry voices of carters disputing the right of way.

About four miles out, row after row of small brick and stone structures lined the road. Some were built like ornate, miniature temples, some like villas but all were practically windowless and secured by metal gates. Lucius had never visited Rome and neither he nor Otto knew what they were. Under the portico of a grand building with marble columns either side of the entry gate, lounged a ragged figure. He wore a nondescript tunic and a wide-brimmed straw hat. His naked feet were blackened with the grime of the gutters. The cloak flung down beside him was such a patchwork of various materials it was impossible to guess its original colour. Lucius pulled up his horse.

"Greetings", he said.

The man looked up. "And greetings to you, prince."

"Can you tell me who lives in these strange houses?"

"I could your excellency if I did not suffer from a serious illness. I can't recall anything unless I have a flask of wine. It's the only thing that lubricates my memory," he said with a toothless grin.

Lucius threw him a coin which he caught adroitly and hid in the folds of his filthy tunic.

"Ah, it's beginning to come back to me. No-one lives in any of 'em."

"Little reward for my offering, friend," Lucius told him.

"It's the truth. They're all empty, unless you count shades, ghosts and spirits. All you will find in 'em is shelves holding the ashes of the dead. They're the family tombs of the rich." He cackled, coughed and hawked up a gob of phlegm which he spat into the dust at the edge of the road. "Rich or poor, we all end the same, lord; a few handfuls of ashes in a jar."

They crossed the Tiber busy with cargo boats bending their oars as they strained upstream to the wharves or flying back down under one small, triangular sail. Their hearts beating with anticipation, they arrived at one of the entry points to Rome itself. They passed under the portico of a gatehouse. Otto nudged Lucius and pointed at one of the heavy gates, half off its hinges and propped against the wall. An unshaven centurion in tarnished armour strolled across to them.

"Papers," he barked, snapping his fingers.

Lucius handed them over. As soon as he saw the imperial seals, he came to attention, saluted and handed them reverently back.

"Pass, sir. Can I offer you any assistance?

"Yes, centurion," Lucius said, "please tell me the way to the Praetorian barracks on the Palatine."

"Strangers to the city, sir?" he asked.

"We are."

"Then I'll do better than that." He gestured to one of his men. "Oi, you lazy fat bastard, see these gentlemen to where they want to go. Then come straight back, no mucking about; I've got my eye on you."

The portly soldier seemed completely unperturbed by his officer's attitude. He smiled up at Lucius and saluted.

"This way, follow me, sir."

He walked beside them as they left the shade of the gateway arch and out into the sunlight slanting down onto the streets. The heat was reflected from wall to wall, contained by the buildings with no breath of a breeze to move the stagnant air. It hit them like a physical blow. The stink of Rome flowed over and around them. A stench composed of the sweat of nearly a million people, animal dung, human faeces, vats of urine on every corner waiting collection by the laundries, rotting refuse and over all the odour of stale food and woodsmoke from the kitchens. Their eyes began to water but their affable guide was oblivious. He began to give them a guided tour.

"That's the Temple of Saturn over there to your left, gents. Straight on for the Forum and the lawcourts…."

All the time, they were wading through a sea of people. Slaves with their owner's brand burned onto their arms or faces dawdled along on errands if they dared or scurried, fearful of a beating if they took too long. Ill-favoured men and slatternly women hung around in wineshop and canteen doors, on the look-out for a careless or feeble-looking citizen to rob or proposition. Boys strolled behind their tutors pulling faces or throwing pebbles at upper windows. Respectable gentlemen wrapped in their heavy wool togas gasped red-faced as they hurried to appointments. Curtained litters carried by six slaves, naked to the waist and glistening with sweat, trotted behind muscular bullyboys shouting for everyone to clear the way and being ignored for the most part.

"On your right is the Aventine and down in the valley is the Circus Maximus. You'll have to have a day at the races, sirs," their guided chattered on. They turned yet another corner. "There's the Palatine dead ahead and there's the barracks."

"Are you a Praetorian Guard?" Otto asked.

The fat soldier laughed. "Gods above and below, what a thought! I'm in the Urban Cohort. We keep the peace and catch the bad boys, sometimes."

Lucius handed him down a few coins to buy some wine. He thanked them profusely and walked away without a backward glance.

The Praetorian Barracks were housed in a rectangular building which possessed neither carved stonework nor external windows. It was entered under an arch beyond which lay a large courtyard. They were stopped by a very different sort of centurion from the first one. His armour and boots were immaculate. He was polite but neutral, neither hostile nor friendly. He examined their papers and handed them back with a salute to Lucius.

"If you would dismount and wait here a few moments tribune, I shall have one of my men request the presence of Tribune Plancus.

It was cooler in the shade of the arch while they waited. The centurion did not speak. Otto looked around with interest. There were four-storey buildings on the three sides of the courtyard he could see from his viewpoint. Each upper floor had a full-length balcony ending in external stone stairs at each end. The ground floors were colonnaded on two sides; the other one appeared to contain storerooms and stables. A figure in a blindingly white toga came towards them, his perfume proceeding him. He wore gilded leather boots and his chestnut brown hair was carefully dressed in ringlets. He was taller than Lucius and in his late twenties.

"Good morning chaps, I take it you are Tribune Longius?" Lucius nodded. "Good-o, well, if you would care to trot along with me...."

"The horses?" Lucius interrupted.

"Imperial courier mounts, sir?" the centurion asked.

"Yes."

"Leave them to us; they will be stabled here during your stay,"

"There, all arranged then. Carry on centurion," their new acquaintance said and stood in between them. "I'm Cassius Plancus by the way but I expect you worked that out for yourselves, ha ha! If you wouldn't be too offended, would you care to take a bath soon as poss? Bit whiffy, old chap, bit horsey. We have excellent accommodation for visiting officers. Your servant can find himself a bed in the storerooms, quite comfy…"

Lucius stopped dead and turned to Plancus.

"You haven't read our summons to Rome, have you?"

Plancus waved him away airily. "Oh, the officer of the watch does all that sort of thing."

"Tribune Plancus, if you had taken the trouble to examine our papers, you would see that my companion is not a servant. He is the German nobleman we call Otto Longius. Our legate was unhorsed during a battle. Otto stood over him to defend him. Single-handed, he killed three attackers bent on murdering our commanding officer while he lay helpless. The Emperor wished to meet him. No servant's quarters, I think."

"I say! Well done you. Three of them? Still he is an extremely large chap, isn't he? How dreadful it must be on the border; all that cold and wet and horrible people with spears and axes," Plancus shuddered, led them over to the left side of the square and opened a door under the ground floor colonnade with a flourish. "There you are, bit Spartan but guaranteed no snow and only the local barbarians. Will you be happy to share, under the circumstances?" Lucius said they would. "Righty-ho, off to the baths then…"

"We have no clean clothes to change into," Otto said. "We were going to buy some…"

"My goodness, you speak our language! Who would have thought it? Don't worry, we'll fit you up and then perhaps we can all go together to find you something better."

Plancus came into the baths with them. Sitting on leather cushions on a marble bench, naked other than for towels around their waists, he and Lucius watched Otto being shaved. His re-grown Suevian Knot was unbound and his blond hair fell across one shoulder almost to his waist.

"May I pose a question, Tribune Longius? Plancus asked.

"Oh course, and please, I'm Lucius…."

"Boxer!" shouted Otto with a hearty laugh."

Lucius blushed. "It's what they call me in the legion; because of my nose... I fell off a horse as a boy…".

"Then I shall call you Boxer too; I'm Cassius by the way. My question is, why doesn't Otto grow his hair long all over or at least on the other side to hide that frightful scar?"

"The half shaven head is a mark of his people and he's only just got the scar. He was wounded saving our legate."

"And what about you," Cassius asked, "who tried to saw you in half?" he asked pointing at the diagonal scar across Lucius' chest and upper belly.

"Attempted robbery at home in Luca; thankfully, Otto was on hand to come to the rescue."

"He makes rather a habit of it, don't he? We must make sure he's with us if we pop out. Well, you've shown me yours so I'll show you mine." He pulled his towel off. A broad white scar ran from the point of his left hip bone up to his navel which had been sliced through on one side. "A Syrian did that to me and I hadn't even been introduced to the chap."

Lucius looked at him straight in the eyes open-mouthed before looking away. Cassius laughed uproariously.

"Ah Boxer, you took me for some spoiled son of a wealthy family whose father had arranged a commission in the Praetorian Guard for him! Nearly right; I am the hope and pride of a noble family but the commission came after a stint in Syria. We were jumped by the appalling locals. What do you call the chap who carries the eagle?"

"The aquilifer," Lucius informed him knowing full-well Cassius was aware of the answer to his own question.

"That'll be him. Anyway, he was dead so I picked it up and shouted for the legion to rally on me and we fought our way out. A pair of very aggressive Syrians wanted my eagle; one of them got his knife up under my armour and tried to open my belly. As you can see, I lived to tell the tale but sadly my legate had no Otto to come to his aid."

"You were transferred to the Praetorians as a reward?"

"Yes, my family are delighted and show me off every time they hold a party. I was given a silver spear as well. You can take a look at it some time."

"If Otto was a citizen and a legionary, he would have been awarded a civic crown for what he did but as he is neither…."

"Oh, don't worry on his account, Boxer. Augustus is a bit on the austere side but he knows when to be generous to someone who is truly deserving, trust me."

He found them white togas matching his own to wear.

"A tunic would have done," Lucius told him but Cassius shook his head.

"The Emperor doesn't want us to appear dressed like soldiers in front of the citizens unless it's absolutely necessary. Anyway, old thing, everyone will think you are a Praetorian as well and give Otto the benefit of the doubt…It has its advantages," he added with a chuckle.

They walked out of the barracks at a leisurely pace towards the forum in the centre of the street to avoid the filth in the gutters. The throng melted away in front of them with wary glances. They entered a dim arcade. There were open booths on both sides, some single, some double-fronted stretching back into interiors filled with fabrics, off-the-peg clothes, boots and belts. Cassius led them to his preferred tailor. They were ushered in by the owner and soon measured for new tunics.

Lucius wanted a blue one with silver embroidery on the neck and cuffs but Cassius warned him off.

"You shouldn't wear something like that when you have your audience with the Emperor. He does not approve of displays of luxury."

The tailor pricked up his ears at the words. He became even more obsequious and practically bent himself double bowing and scraping. Eventually they ordered two each. Lucius kept to his favoured dark blue while Otto preferred green.

"It will take an hour, noble sirs, for hemming and letting the shoulders out for the larger gentleman," the tailor said nervously, hoping that it was not too long to wait.

It was the same at the bootmakers. Servile attention and grovelling apologies for the time it would take to make a pair of boots for Otto, again one hour. Cassius did not approve of their choice of blue and green suede respectively.

"Boring," he told them showing off his own in their golden splendour.

They wandered over to a tavern on the opposite corner. It was quite crowded when they walked in. They sat down in front of a flask of wine and a plate of snacks. Gradually the bar began to empty. There was no rush for the door but men finished their wine, stood up and quietly left the premises. The barman watched the exodus with resignation. Soon Otto, Lucius and Plancus had the place to themselves. After more than an hour of informative conversation with Plancus answering their questions about the city and its inhabitants, Otto and Lucius stood up with him to leave. Lucius went to pay for their wine and food but the barman waived him away.

They were charged a ridiculously small price at the tailor's and nothing at the bootmaker's. In fact, he became anxious when Otto tried to insist and looked like he was about to burst into tears.

All three of them stood in the street outside while Otto complained that he did not understand.

"You are Praetorians today, as far as the citizenry is concerned and Praetorians are never charged the going rate for anything. I told you there were advantages," the laughing Cassius told him.

Otto was outraged. "This is not right. These are poor men working to make their livings. I am not a thief. It is unjust."

"My dear old Otto, please don't upset yourself. They'll make it up by charging their civilian customers a little more."

"Still not right," Otto muttered and sulked all the way back to the barracks.

The bathhouse slave had overheard the conversation between Lucius and Plancus and repeated it to his friend in the cookhouse. He had recounted it to a valet who in turn told the story to his master. The whole barracks knew that Otto was a hero by the time they returned. The stony-faced centurion of the watch smiled and nodded as they went in.

After dinner, Lucius asked Cassius when he and Otto would be seeing the Emperor.

"Tomorrow, next week, next year, who knows? You have been summoned to Rome for an audience with Augustus. Here you will stay until he decides to see you. In the meantime, might as well enjoy yourself, eh? Let's hope he doesn't forget you're here, Boxer old boy," Cassius replied.

Lucius' heart sank.

After breakfast the next morning, Otto disappeared for an hour and refused to tell anyone where he had been. Cassius began to tease him, mentioning girls and brothels but he saw Lucius frantically shaking his head and gesturing for him to stop. He took the hint. They spent the rest of the day taking in the sights. Otto vanished again the following morning but neither Lucius nor Cassius mentioned it. The third morning, he did not reappear until midday. He was covered in a film of white dust and looked very happy. Cassius showed as much anger as his languid manner allowed.

"I say, it's not on, it's really too much. You do realize I am responsible to the Emperor for the pair of you? Anything could have happened. A stroll after breakfast is one thing but you were gone half the day. I must say, it's not on."

Otto smiled contentedly; his eyes were looking on another scene.

"I passed a fence," he said, "and I could hear the clinking of metal behind it so I went around to the gate and looked in. There was a tall block of stone propped up with baulks of timber in the middle of a yard. It was so white it dazzled my eyes to look at it at first. An old man was standing on a scaffold with a hammer and chisel cutting pieces from it; tiny flakes that buzzed through the air like bees. Some fell at my feet. As I looked more closely, I saw he was turning the stone into the form of a man. I walked around to the other side and you could see a shoulder and part of a chest and a hip. It was as if there was someone imprisoned in the ice and he was chipping him free. It was wonderful. The man saw me and told me to go away but I said that I had never seen anyone carve stone before. I told him that my people carved wood but had no knowledge of this art. He came down and explained that like wood, stone also has a grain and will split if struck incorrectly. Then his two servants came back. One had been sent to have some tools sharpened and the other had fetched bread and wine. We ate together and talked and the old man said I could stay and watch if I liked. They had another block of the special stone; it is called marble, on its side waiting for two friends to come and help lift it upright. I said I would do it for them but they laughed and the old man said it was dangerous but then it was my turn to laugh. They levered it up a little so I could get my hands underneath and I heaved it onto its end like they wanted. To thank me, they gave me this." He took a rod of marble two inches long out of his tunic and showed it to them. It had been carved into the shape of a human finger complete with fine lines in the skin and a perfect nail. "Is it not a strange and beautiful thing?

The old man told me it is of no value, just a broken piece but what detail, what skill!"

"Well, anyway, here you are safe and sound. Get yourself off to the baths and have the dust scrubbed off you before we are all covered in it," Cassius scolded him.

"Did you ever hear him talk so much?" he asked Lucius when Otto was halfway over the square.

"Only one or twice in the whole time I've known him. That sculptor must have made a big impression," he replied.

Cassius sighed. "You know, Boxer, I quite envy friend Otto. Everything is so fresh and new to him. It's just service as usual for us, or at least, for me."

That evening, an Imperial freedman arrived with a summons for Otto and Lucius, accompanied by Cassius to attend Augustus one hour before noon on the following day. Cassius had them ready far too early; fussing about their appearance and giving them contradictory advice which they soon began to ignore. He was immaculate. His white toga shone, his boots glimmered and the hairdresser had re-curled his hair. They walked uphill, not a great distance, to a modest house distinguished only by the guards at the door. Cassius announced them, their documents were examined, they were politely but thoroughly searched for weapons and then shown through a pair of painted doors into an anteroom. A clerk sat a desk in the middle of the floor of black and white tiles in a chequer patter; he looked over their papers once more and led them to an inner door which he opened and ushered them past him. They now stood in a small foyer with no furniture. Two more guards entered and searched them again and passed them through yet another door. Finally, they were let into the presence of the Emperor. A civilian official in a pale-yellow tunic smiled and beckoned them forwards to stand in front of Augustus.

Otto looked at him curiously. He saw a handsome middle-aged man with a square face and a nose tending to the aquiline. He had sandy hair and seemed to be of average height. What was most striking about him other than the brilliance of his eyes, was the balanced and graceful way in which he held himself. His expression was one of benevolent tranquillity. He was plainly dressed in a tunic and sandals. His chair was made of delicately carved ivory inlaid with gold; a small, matching table bearing a few scrolls was placed by his right hand. The audience room was of modest dimensions but the walls were exquisitely painted with a scene of woodlands full of birds and deer. An open door led to a garden terrace.

"Praetorian Tribune Cassius Plancus, Tribune Lucius Taurius Longius and Otto called Otto Longius, sir," the official announced and moved around to stand behind Augustus. All three of them bowed.

"Thank you, Menities," Augustus said and then looked at each of them in turn with those bright, liquid eyes before turning his attention to Cassius.

"Do not ask me to send you to a legion again, Cassius Plancus. Won't do it. Promised your mother. Why are you wearing those ridiculous boots?"

"They are the fashion, sir."

"Ghastly," he said with a dismissive wave and looked at Otto. "What do you think of Rome?" the Emperor asked.

Otto took half a step forward with his right foot. He placed his left hand on his midriff. He raised his open right hand upwards and sideways to the full extent of his arm and took a deep breath.

"The inexpressible awe I felt on seeing the marvels of your great city which, from your overflowing benevolence, you are embellishing with architecture to enhance the lives of even the humblest of Rome's citizens, is as a nothing to the intense gratification, nay delight, I feel at beholding you face to face," Otto declaimed in a ringing tone which echoed slightly off the walls.

Cassius sniggered but was silenced by a glare from Lucius. Menities dropped his head to his chest to hide the smirk on his face. Augustus raised his eyebrows almost to his hairline and stared in astonishment at what he had heard. Otto let his arms drop to his sides. A long silence followed.

"What was that?" Augustus asked at last.

Otto looked abashed and then grinned. "I have never seen an Emperor before sir, only kings. There was a sign in the street for a tutor who teaches public speaking for all occasions. He told me what to say and how to stand and speak."

"Get your money back," the Emperor told him.

"I took his word for it when he said it was the right way to address you, sir."

"It isn't."

"No, lord."

Augustus glanced up at the ceiling for a moment and sighed.

"Don't call me lord. Hate it. "Sir" will do. Answer the question, what do you think of Rome?"

"Honestly?"

"Of course."

"Sir, I have never smelled such an awful stink in my life as what hit us when we rode in through the city gates."

The Emperor threw his head back and laughed melodiously.

"Oh, how right you are, Otto. Not so bad up here on the Palatine but down in the streets! Summer, heat, much worse. Make a man gag. Is there anything you specially like?"

"Oh yes lo…sir. I saw a sculptor at work. You wouldn't believe it. He was cutting wonderful likenesses out of marble as easily as slicing bread."

"Glad you like statues. Paid for one each of Concordia, Pax and Salus Publica this year alone."

"Then you do well, sir and I hope people are grateful."

"They aren't. Never are. But thank you for your approval."

He looked at Lucius and consulted a scroll on his table.

"Tribune Longius. Your family were rabid and dedicated Antonians."

Lucius felt his heart race. Now was his opportunity, if he dared to take it. His mouth dried. He swallowed then threw the dice.

"Not so, sir. My family have held Marcus Antonius and his brothers in detestation since the time of my noble grandfather."

"Telling your Emperor that he's wrong?"

"No, sir," Lucius said, swallowing again, he was playing a hand which could result in his death if he played it badly. "Your ministers have misinformed you."

"Explain."

"During the time Marcus Antonius held the sacred office of tribune of the people, he approached my grandfather saying the public finances were dangerously short of funds. My grandfather mortgaged his estates and passed the money he received over to Antonius, allegedly to be used for the good of the state. When Marcus Antonius became consul, my grandfather asked him to repay the loan. He was told that if he ever spoke of the matter again, he would be imprisoned. The lenders foreclosed, my family was bankrupted and my grandfather retired to Luca. Thanks to Marcus Antonius and his deceit, a noble Roman of senatorial rank was ruined and unable to take any further part in the public life of the capital. No, sir. There is no love for that ignoble race in our family."

Augustus made a sign to Menities who produced a wax tablet and a stylus out of a pocket in his tunic. He handed them to the Emperor who scribbled a note, snapped the tablet shut and handed it back. Menities took it to the door and passed it to unknown hands on the other side before returning to his position.

"The Divine Julius," the Emperor said to Otto, "was inclined to offer Roman Citizenship to all and sundry. Dreadful idea. Don't like it. But you have stood over a defenceless legate and protected him, killing three enemies and spilling your own blood. Admirable. As your reward, I confer Roman Citizenship upon you and transfer you to my cavalry."

Otto shook his head and looked at the Emperor with haggard eyes.

"I cannot accept."

"You won't, you mean. You defy your emperor?" Augustus responded, in his unchanging, even tone.

"No, sir; the noble Tribune Lucius Taurius Longius has my oath. I am sworn to him to death. In honour, I cannot leave his service."

"To refuse my gift is to insult me. An insult to the Emperor means public execution."

"No disrespect is intended but if I break my oath, I am shamed in this life and in front of my ancestors who will refuse me their company in the next. I must accept your verdict, sir."

"Honour? Death? This is unexpected," Augustus gently remarked.

"Sir, may I explain?" Lucius asked and went on without waiting for an answer, "Otto values his oath and his honour more than his life. He pledged himself to me. I can formally release him if you will allow it?"

Augustus nodded.

Lucius embraced Otto and then dissolved his oath. "Farewell Otto of the Suevi, my friend and comrade. Otto Longius, I declare your obligation to me is ended. In token of the love and respect in which I hold you, I promise you a warhorse, saddled and bridled and the armour, weapons and equipment fitting for a warrior of your rank."

"Can you afford all that?" Augustus asked.

"I shall borrow the money. I can pay it back out of my army salary in a year or so, sir."

Augustus looked from one to the other in silence for a long while. It was impossible to read the thoughts behind that calm mask of a face.

"Unheard of nowadays. Like a legend of antique heroes," the Emperor said, half to himself and then continued in a louder voice. "You hear this Cassius? Otto accepts death rather than tarnish his reputation. Tribune Longius puts himself into the hands of moneylenders to preserve his friend. Loyalty. Rare. Menities, a scribe and something to eat. I'm peckish. Now, Otto Longius, already said I would confer citizenship. Above that, a gift of one hundred and ten thousand denarii from the Imperial Treasury to maintain yourself as a Knight of Rome. Invest it in land, that's best. None of this speculation. All the rage. Never ends well. Return to your legion as a Decurion of cavalry. You'll be good at that. Tribune Longius, financial dealings are not your family's strength. Avoid them. Donative to you of one hundred, no, fifty gold pieces. Equip Otto and buy him his knight's ring. Don't stand there with your mouths open like fish on a slab. You say, "thank you, sir." Now say it."

"Thank you, sir," they blurted out in unison.

"Should think so too. Where's lunch? Join us, Cassius; we'll eat outside."

Augustus dictated between mouthfuls of the bread, cheese, smoked fish and fruit laid out for them on a table on the terrace. They drank ice-cold spring water. The Emperor teased Cassius.

"No larks' tongues and candied dormice, Cassius. Disappointing for you."

He asked how Otto and Lucius had met and declared the tale worthy of being written down. He took Otto for a tour of his orchard and was astonished that his guest did not know what a fig was and had never seen one. He listened to Lucius talking about artillery.

"Need to understand engineering as well. Easier to knock something over if you know how it was built in the first place."

Documents were placed in front of him by his scribes. He read each one from beginning to end and before applying his seal. He laid them down one by one.

"Confirmation that Otto Longius is henceforth a citizen of Rome. Instruction for Otto Longius to be enrolled in the Order of Knights. Call on the treasury for one hundred and five thousand denarii.," He threw a quick glance at Otto. "Never be extravagant, young man. Call on the treasury for fifty gold pieces for Tribune Longius. Finally, a letter which will be made public, recording that the family of Lucius Taurius Longius residing in Luca are acknowledged as loyal citizens of Rome favoured by Augustus. Your story has been checked, tribune.

"But sir," Lucius said. "it was only an hour or so ago I told it to you."

"Things get done quick as boiled asparagus when you're the Emperor. Pick up your documents and be on your way, gentlemen. Pleasure to meet you. Cassius knows where the treasury secretary's office is. Work calls me. Senators lolling about in the hot springs at Baiae. I have an empire requiring attention

Part I – The End

I hope that you have enjoyed reading this book. Please mention it on social media or leave an Amazon review. "Knight of Rome Part II" is now on sale.

I have also suggested more of my books for you on the following page.

Thank you for your support.

Regards,

Malcolm Davies

You can contact me by e-mail at:-

malcolmdav46@outlook.com.

Best Books by Malcolm Davies on Facebook.

My website is www.malcolm-davies.com.)

Knight of Rome Part II

Now a citizen and enrolled in the Equestrian order – a Knight of Rome – Otto Longius returns to his legion as a cavalry officer. It is a great achievement but comes at great cost. His ties of comradeship with his oldest friend, Tribune Lucius "Boxer" Longius, are beginning to weaken. His rank in the legion allows him to take his full part in councils of war but will anyone listen to him? The question for Otto Longius is, has he become a true Roman and will he be accepted on an equal footing with his brother officers? An uprising by the Marcomanni of eastern Germany sets the Rhine borders alight. A prolonged siege and a mission for the Emperor Augustus test his courage and loyalty to the limit.

The Butterfly Fool Part One

Being an account of the Remarkable Early Life of Mr. Augustus Reynolds of Split Water City, Montana Territory. How he came to leave the Country Of His Birth to travel to the Frontier of the United States of America. His Thrilling Voyages by Steamboat up the great Mississippi and Missouri Rivers. His Dangerous Encounter with a Savage and Fearsome Blackfoot Chief. How he Comported himself in Mortal Combats with Ferocious Wild Beasts and Brigands. And the

Many, Remarkable and Diverse Characters he met on his journeys. Also the History of Miss Charlotte Reynolds, Sister of the Above who Heroically accompanied Her Brother on his Adventure. How an English Gentlewoman fared in the Wilderness with neither Cook nor Maid. Her Primitive Domestic Economy. A Romantic Attachment which would have distressed the Many Friends she had left at Home. In Addition, how the Thriving Metropolis of Split Water City rose from the Plains. Its Rude Beginnings and First Development.

The Butterfly Fool Part Two

The Second and Final Volume Depicting the Exploits and Times of Mr. Augustus Reynolds the Celebrated Frontiersman, his Family and Friends. A Theft and Pursuit across the Vastness of the American Prairies. Retribution upon the Felons. Confrontations with Fierce Natives. A Hunt for the Indigenous Bison. A Violent Death followed by Remorse. The Moral Repugnance of Mrs. Reynolds at developments in Split Water City, Metropolis of the Plains. The Arrival of the Mechanical Wonders of our Age in the Remote Wilderness. Celebration of the American Public Holiday known as "The Fourth of July". Wonder at the Resilience of The Inhabitants of The Far Western Territories. Thrill to the Dangers Faced and Overcome by Them with Undaunted Steadfastness.

Willy Maddox Went To Texas

Coming off a cattle drive from Split Water City to St. Louis, young Willy Maddox has a bitter quarrel with his cousin Ed which changes the course of his life. Willy is in the wrong of it but for all he cares, Ed can go home on his own; he would rather ride off south with his two new friends, heading for Texas. At twenty years old Willy believes he can handle anything that life throws at him. He has already learned the ranching trade up in Montana, endured the rigours of a long cattle-drive and fended off stock-thieves. What could Texas show him he had not seen before? So, what did Texas show Willy Maddox? Only outlaws, deserts, blizzards blowing up out of nowhere, renegade Comanche and worse but also great opportunity, transforming new technologies and finally, his journey's end. (Willy Maddox first appears in "The Butterfly Fool Part Two", the sequel to "The Butterfly Fool Part One".)

Printed in Great Britain
by Amazon